king of darkness

ELISABETH STAAB

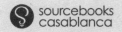

Published by Sourcebooks Casablanca, an imprint of Sourcebooks, Inc.
P.O. Box 4410, Naperville, Illinois 60567-4410
(630) 961-3900
FAX: (630) 961-2168
www.sourcebooks.com

Printed and bound in Canada
WC 10 9 8 7 6 5 4 3 2 1

To Tom. My love, I couldn't have done this without you.

Chapter 1

"JESUS, T. WHAT IS THIS PLACE?"

Thad Morgan scanned the sparse industrial interior of the massive warehouse turned dance club. From just inside the doorway, he passed his preternatural vision over the writhing crowd of humans. Most of the populace bounced in time to bass-heavy techno music, stopping only to grope their nearest neighbor. Some gazed upward in awe at a raised platform of fire-eaters, and still more worshipped at a DJ stand opposite the entrance as if it were an altar. A scrolling sign overhead announced something called the Crystal Method. The humans partied with abandon and apparently little regard for their eardrums.

"I think they call it a rave," Thad murmured to his friend.

And apparently at 3:00 a.m., the night was still young for the party kids in Orlando.

Thad's hands clenched and released. How were they going to do this? The club was friggin' huge and packed to the gills, from the crowded floor full of scantily clad dancers with glow sticks to the teeming balconies where couples and even groups were involved in more intimate acts such as massage and… whatnot. It was hard to fathom how in the hell they were going to find the female they were looking for in this place.

Already overheated, Thad pushed up the sleeves of his leather jacket and fingered the scar on his forearm, tracing slowly over the two intersecting lines that flared into a Y at each end, like a crude Armenian cross. The small patch of skin was even hotter than the rest of him and throbbed in time with the pounding electronic music that was drilling a hole in his skull. He could almost swear the scar was glowing, but the haze of laser lights and cigarette smoke made it tough to be certain.

"She's in here, Lee. I can feel it," he said tightly.

But what would his queen be doing in this... den of iniquity?

They had been traveling for weeks now, searching for the female who would, according to the prophecy, help him lead the vampire race. Finally, his senses told him that they were closing in. They had to be. The whole of their kind *needed* him to find her. He continued to look over the crowd, hoping for a sign to jump out at him from amidst all the sweaty bump-and-grind.

Next to him, Lee Goram also studied the undulating club-goers, not bothering to hide his disgust at the near-orgy playing out in front of him. It didn't seem to make sense: Thad had never been sure where their needle-in-a-haystack quest might lead them, but he hadn't expected a place like this.

Maybe he just didn't get out enough.

"I dunno, man," Lee grumbled. "This doesn't feel right. I smell at least four kinds of drugs. I see sweaty humans all but fucking on the dance floor. Doesn't exactly seem like the kind of place you'd find your destiny in."

Thad's aggravation was piqued, and he turned on Lee so that they were almost nose to nose. "I know, but I'm telling you, Lee, this thing on my arm is like a hot coal. That's gotta mean something."

Lee slowly hiked his shoulders in a vague shrug. "Maybe those Oracles are all just wacko. I mean, who knows what's up with that incense they burn, right? I've heard it's some kind of hallucinogen."

Thad leveled a glare at him. "You know, I realize it's gonna take time to adjust to our roles being reversed, but my nerves are pretty fried and all your negativity is *not* helping. You know as well as I do what's at stake here. So would you kindly stop the bullshit and help me look around?" A deep breath failed to untangle the giant knot in his stomach. The real bitch of it was that his father's advice would have meant the world right about now, but he and Lee might not have even been here if his parents were still alive.

Lee growled and waved away a glassy-eyed, glittery young thing who seemed intent on climbing him to give him a back rub. He clapped Thad on the shoulder. "All right. I've got your back, you cranky bastard. No one in here is wearing much of anything anyway, so it should be easy to look around. Just keep an eye out. I don't sense any danger but it'd be real easy to hide a wizard in here, and finding your queen doesn't mean dick if you get dead."

––––—

Isabel Anthony relaxed in a red velvet armchair in a dark corner of the VIP section of Club Insomniac. Her gaze met the dove-gray eyes of the blonde female who sat astride her lap, looking every bit as lovely as Botticelli's depiction of Venus.

She was the DJ from the last set. DJ... *something*...

Isabel was terrible with names. Great with humans,

though. Cool air from a nearby vent skated over her skin, leaving a trail of tingles in its wake. It nicely accompanied the sensation of the female's deft fingers as they kneaded overwrought muscles in Isabel's shoulders. So relaxing, in fact, that the half-drunk glass of red wine dangling from Isabel's loose fingers nearly slipped to the floor.

The human kids had their party-favor club drugs: their weed and their meth and their little purple pills. For vampires, the sweet essence of red wine produced that lovey-dovey, buzzy high. The wine made it okay to crave connection with others.

She brought one hand to cradle Venus's jaw, swiping a thumb over an errant tear. "What's going on in there, sweetheart?"

The blonde didn't answer, but simply rolled her head back and sighed.

This was usually the best part of Isabel's evening. The one where she took an infinitesimal chip out of her lifetime supply of guilt over all the damage she had done by sharing comfort. By listening to tales of woe and trading back rubs. By being a friend that wouldn't be remembered in the morning. Because more than for the music or the drugs or the wicked-cool performance art, everyone in that club was there because they desperately needed to *belong*.

But she was restless tonight in spite of the mellowing effect of the red wine. Distraction was her middle name, and an odd ache in her lower back intensified with each passing minute despite the soothing shoulder rub from Venus. Isabel blew off the discomfort and returned her full attention to the human in her lap. Certainly the pain would abate soon, whatever it was. She was a fast healer like all of her kind, even if she did feed exclusively from humans.

Until then... Isabel set her wineglass on the floor and gently nudged the DJ off her lap so that they could trade places. "My turn, hon," she said quietly.

The blonde smiled sweetly when Isabel's hands worked their way under all that hair to reach the oft-overlooked muscles under the human's occipital ridge. Within minutes Venus's body went slack, head and neck dropping onto shoulders to fully expose a creamy column of throat. Canines extended, Isabel licked her lips and buried her face in the crook of the female's delicate neck. All the while, her hands never missed a beat.

Lee pushed past a Gordian knot of apparently malnourished and questionably legal females, none of whom seemed to know that they needed to pull their pants up to cover their thong underwear. Damn, he was ready to call it a night. Then again, he'd been ready to call it a night weeks ago.

As Thad's longtime friend and now bodyguard, he would maintain his vow to serve faithfully, but he was beginning to question the sanity of their mission. Even if the mate Thad sought was actually somewhere in this place, there were too many crowds and dark corners, and so far he and Thad had come up with exactly jack.

The risk of danger made him edgy. The telltale aura of malevolent evil given off by their enemy could easily be missed in this sort of environment. Speakers that towered over his six-foot-four frame seemed to be sprinkled about every few feet, and they were cranking out the kind of core-shaking vibrations usually produced by major construction equipment.

In Lee's personal opinion, Thad was putting too much weight on this prophecy business. Thad felt he couldn't rule properly if he didn't find his queen, but they were equally screwed if anyone found out that the newly ascended king was off on a wild-goose chase and technically nobody was at the helm just now.

They had taken all possible precautions to ensure a safe departure. They had even been teleported outside the zone of known wizard and vampire communities to avoid detection. Florida was far from home so the risk was minimal, but still the uncertainty bothered him. As he and Thad moved along a dark and narrow wrought-iron balcony—slowly, so as not to hip-check an unsuspecting party-girl right over the railing, Lee's hands remained poised in case he needed a weapon. The bouncers at the door had been easy to manipulate into letting them pass without being searched.

"Last floor." Thad's words at Lee's ear jarred him out of his thoughts. The balcony dead-ended at a steep roped-off stairway. Thad peered up into the murkiness and then stepped casually over the flimsy velvet-rope barrier. Lee followed suit.

"Good deal. And listen, man, if we turn up dry here, there are some restaurants and hotels on the block we can check out."

Thad nodded solemnly as they tromped up the stairs past the meatheads guarding what looked to be some kind of VIP area. Another brief flex of Lee's mind, and the guards didn't as much as glance in their direction.

Holy… *mother*. This area was a different animal altogether. Softer music and no dance floor to speak of, but lots of dark alcoves, a selection of top-shelf liquors, and a display of human behavior that made the activity on the main floor look practically G-rated. All around them on couches, chairs, and stretches of carpet were humans in different states of depravity. To Lee's left, a Goth girl was being trussed up on a pool table by a guy in shiny, black vinyl pants who obviously knew his way around the business end of a rope.

Sickos.

Only thing missing was a nervous pizza-delivery boy asking what he should do with his extra sausage. The only humans who were fully clothed were the bartender and the bouncers, all of whom seemed oblivious to the porn show going on around them.

Thad had stopped short. He made a slow 360 with his mouth agape. "This can't be right. I don't know, Lee. I'm beginning to wonder about this whole thing. I think I'm about ready to move on. Lee… Lee?"

Lee barely heard him. With his back to Thad, he stood in stunned silence, unable to move. His jaw worked back and forth while he tried to determine whether or not his eyes were playing tricks on him. Or if maybe the place was distributing psychedelics through the air vents. *Holy cow…*

"Lee… you okay, man?"

"I don't think you're going to want to leave just yet, Thad." He gestured to a chair full of girl-on-girl action in a dark corner across the room. No question, the dark-haired female in the driver's seat was into that blonde's neck like it was feeding time and she was starving. Shit, they had finally struck gold. Lee let out a bark of laughter. He couldn't help himself. "Okay, man. I know this isn't supposed to be funny, but dude… of all places…"

Thad flicked his eyes in the direction Lee had indicated, clearly not getting it. "Kind of hot, I guess, but I don't see the funny part."

Lee sobered up and cleared his throat. "No. Seriously, man. *Look*."

———

Thad swept his gaze over the scene that Lee had pointed to. Though he had gotten an instant soft-on from the muscleman by the bar wearing nothing but a leather thong and a dog collar, his dick woke up and took notice when his stare fixed on a pair of long, peaches-and-cream legs that disappeared under a plaid skirt that stopped *just* shy of broadcasting her preferred brand of underwear. Hands roamed, and the red-painted toes of the bottom female's bare feet curled tightly. While the angel-faced blonde arched her back and parted her lips in ecstasy, the pigtailed brunette lapped at her neck. And… ah, he would be damned if she wasn't feeding.

The realization kicked Thad's pulse into high gear. How on earth had he missed that before? Granted, he wouldn't have pegged her for a vampire at first. His own skin was a shade of dark tan, and contrary to the popular movies humans loved to scare themselves with, that pastel skin of hers was something of an anomaly. Thad stood rooted—mesmerized—while the blonde's fingernails dug hard into the naughty schoolgirl's skin, pushing up her cropped top, and suddenly there was no oxygen left in the room.

She bore the mark.

Nestled just above the schoolgirl's waistband in the small of her back, surrounded by a swirl of tattoos, was a scar identical to the one on his forearm. No question—it was the same crudely depicted cross that Thad had been seeing etched on his own skin for nearly a century. The mark that was, at that very moment, throbbing like it had its own pulse.

"Holy *shit*, Lee." Thad tried to lean against the nearest wall and wondered why the fucker was moving. No, wait… the entire room was moving. "Lee… this can't be happening. All the time we've been searching… I've pictured this moment happening a thousand different ways…"

Lee cracked another grin, the bastard. "Not like this?"

"Not. Even. A *little*."

"T, man, I've got to agree she's not what I might've thought you'd find. And this sure as hell isn't where I would have expected you to find her. So your Oracle didn't bother to mention your destiny digs the ladies?"

Jackass. Thad's future was hanging in the balance here, and his friend was cracking jokes. "You know, once I'm done picking my jaw up off the floor, I'm going to kick your ass or die trying for that comment."

"I'm sorry, buddy, but you've got to admit it's pretty surreal. Seriously, though, what's your next move?"

"I… I have no clue." Thad scrubbed his face with his hands and blinked rapidly at the female whose scar was supposed to mark her as his *destined life mate, for God's sake*, but the scene playing out didn't change. None of the ways Thad figured on approaching this seemed to mesh with the scenario he'd been handed. He could only hope that her gate swung both ways. And how the hell should he approach this? "I mean… Shit, Lee… I have no fucking clue."

Chapter 2

Darkness surrounded Anton as he awaited his sentence. His father, the great and fricking mighty Master of wizards, had finally gotten tired of waiting for him to produce the late king's half-human daughter. For that failure, at best, Anton was looking down the barrel at a death sentence. Because nobody failed the Master and lived to tell about it. And death would likely be preceded by torture if the Master suspected Anton to be the traitor that he was.

Suspected? Of course the Master would know.

Thing was, Anton had just plain drawn a shitty lot in life. Born into a clan of men whose only purpose was to wipe out a competing supernatural species, he had been expected to do his father's bidding and be grateful—perhaps even enjoy it—as all the others had. He wasn't like the others, though.

He never would be.

Oh, sure, he had tried. Who wouldn't, in a kill-or-be-killed scenario? But he didn't have the stomach for it. Could barely live with himself. And when he had been sent to capture Tyra Morgan, a creature so lovely and so good that just watching her from a distance made Anton want to be better somehow… well, his way had been clear. As he awaited his fate in his dank little box of a room, he was almost tempted to pray.

Not to save himself, of course. There was no doing

that. The woman he had come to love would be dead, however, if he failed to convince the Master that she was of no use to him.

Anton straightened against the stone wall of his cell when he heard loud footfalls approaching. The door opened with a mighty groan, and light fell across the small space.

To add insult to injury, the Master had sent Anton's own half brother to fetch him. Petros growled in a low voice, "He's ready for you."

Placing a modified report of his last mission in the forefront of his mind, Anton stepped with determination toward his jailer. "You wanna shackle me, Petros?"

The green-eyed wizard sneered. "Master says you're gonna cooperate," he said. "But rest assured, I've got 'em ready if I need 'em, Brother." Funny that Petros referred to Anton as his brother but never referred to the Master as their father.

"I'm sure you do, *Brother*," Anton sneered right back. It was so hard to believe they were of the same blood. Clearly, only one of them took after their father in the personality department. And the animosity radiating from Petros crackled in the air like live electricity. "Ready to go, Petros. Anytime."

Petros stepped behind Anton, shoving him roughly between the shoulder blades. "All right, then. Let's do this."

—⁂—

"Can I, umm, help you two with something?"

Thad's head snapped down to follow the voice that had broken into his cacophonous thoughts. Standing directly in front of him was a diminutive human female, all of five feet tall or so. Wearing angel wings and low-slung party pants, she was like every other girl flitting about the club, save for the look of knowing suspicion that peeked out from underneath her glitter-covered eyelids.

How the hell had she even noticed them? They weren't invisible, technically speaking, but the average human wouldn't spot a vampire hidden in the shadows.

Lee must have been thinking the same thing. He stepped into protector mode between Thad and the young woman, grabbing her wrist a little too roughly. How she could be a threat to either of them was beyond comprehension, but Lee was a machine and the move was automatic.

"Who are you?" Lee demanded in a low voice.

"Easy, big guy." Her free hand came up in a gesture of surrender before dropping to her hip. "Look, I'm not here to give you trouble, but we don't get a lot of your kind around here and you looked a little skeeved out so I thought that maybe I could help you."

"Our kind?"

"Yeah, you know… 'your kind.'" She emphasized the phrase with a pair of air quotes and an eye roll. "You don't have to play dumb. I know what you are." She crooked her fingers in Lee's direction. When he hesitated, she reached up and grabbed the back of his neck, stretching onto her toes until she was able to speak into his ear. Boy, this girl was gutsy.

"See, I've seen this whole cloaked-in-shadows routine before, and if you haven't noticed, this floor is private. The fact that you got past the guards over there and you're clearly packing suggests to me that you probably pulled some kind of mental-manipulation voodoo." She glanced around. "As does the fact that no one else seems to have noticed your presence, even though you guys could have your own ZIP codes."

The girl gave Lee an appreciative once-over. "Plus you're all ripped, and the only *human* guys I've seen who look like you wouldn't be in a place like this cuz they live 24/7 at the gym. Now, I'm just trying to be helpful because you appear to be a little out of your element. You want to go it alone, I sure as hell can't stop ya. Might want to work on your manners, though."

After aiming another pointed look directly at Lee, the female twisted out of his now-slack grip and turned away. It was probably the first time Lee had ever been rendered speechless. Seconds later, she turned back.

"I'm Alexia, by the way. Nice to meet you… gentlemen." A quick heel spin had them looking at the angel wings on her back again as she began to walk away. What *was* the deal with all the angel wings in this place?

"Wait." Thad cleared his throat. Nodded to the opposite corner. "The uh, schoolgirl… I need to speak with her. You know her?"

Alexia took a step back and narrowed her eyes. "What do you want with Isabel?"

Thad blew out a hard breath. *Well gosh, it's simple! I'm here to tell her that the rest of her life was promised to me, an utter stranger, a hundred years ago by some nutty old bat. And oh, by the way, the future of our kind may very well hang on whether or not she chooses to come with me. So no pressure or anything.*

Yeah. Perfect.

Thad cleared his throat. "I, uh, I just need to talk to her. It's personal. Maybe you could tell her for me that I'm here—"

"Hey, mama, you got any Blow Pops in there, baby? I'm grinding the heck outta my fangs." Behind Alexia was a six-foot-tall vampire male with long, dark, kinky-curly hair that cascaded over her shoulder as he bent low to nuzzle beneath her ear and rummage through her pockets. The male reeked of a cheap Cabernet blend, a telltale sign that he had been imbibing red wine. The inebriated male mumbled his thanks, popped a sour apple between his teeth, and flashed a mock salute at Thad and Lee. He walked away shaking his head like he needed to unstick something that was lodged inside. Throughout the entire transaction, the human's only re-action had been to smile sweetly at the male and watch his departure.

What. The. Fuck? It was far from common to meet a human who knew of their kind, period. This one was apparently the patron saint of handing Blow Pops to vampire ravers. Perhaps she and the male were intimate? Sure, occasional trysts were common, but usually the human came away none the wiser as to who or what they had really been involved with. This human... Alexia... she *knew*. Then again, his father had once had a relation-ship with a human. Maybe it wasn't all that crazy.

Thad was busy pondering all the ways that his percep-tion of reality had been shot to shit in the past hour when he realized that Lee was talking. To the human girl.

"Friend of yours or something?" Thad was surprised to see a touch of animosity glittering in Lee's blue-green eyes, but Lee had never been fond of interacting with humans. Certainly he would be bothered by the fact that the male who'd just walked off seemed to have a connection with this one. Or maybe it was the wine. In all the time Thad had known Lee, he'd never seen his friend so much as drink a beer, let alone something stronger.

Alexia hadn't missed Lee's attitude, either. She took a step back, like maybe she had changed her mind about being helpful.

Uh, yeah. Thad cleared his throat. "Look. Just tell Isabel…" The words were thick and awkward and didn't want to come out of his throat. "I'm her king. And I need to speak with her."

The girl's eyes widened, but then she nodded in a manner that was far too perky for the wee hours of the morning and did another 180 to leave.

Alexia headed toward the opposite corner while Thad's previous words to her rattled around in his head. "Fuck! *Seriously?*" he exploded, suddenly irritated by his own sophomoric stupidity. "Maybe you could talk to her for me? Could I *be* a bigger pussy right now?" He scrubbed his hands across his face for what seemed like the tenth time since they'd entered the club. At this rate he'd be fully exfoliated before the night was through.

Lee relaxed against the wall and crossed his arms over his massive chest. "Nah," he said shaking his head slightly. "It was a good move. Less likely that she bolts if it comes at her from someone she knows."

"Maybe I should've passed a note in fucking gym class."

The older male shook his head. "You're being too hard on yourself. It's a tough situation."

"That's touching, man. Thanks."

"Fuck you."

Thad let out a low chuckle. Lee clammed up and continued his vigilant survey of the room. Both watched as Alexia bent slightly at the waist to speak into Isabel's ear. Even for a human the girl was tiny. Tinier seen from across the way.

Isabel's reaction was nearly imperceptible. For a second Thad wondered if perhaps she'd decided to just ignore them. Not that he'd blame her, but his best plan B was to muscle her out of there caveman-style. It wasn't an option he relished, but he hadn't come all this way just to leave without talking to her.

She rose slowly, though, gently sweeping her tongue along the blonde's neck and murmuring some kind of sweet nothings into the human's ear as she vacated her lap. Probably wiped the woman's memory of the whole erotic experience. The blonde rose from the chair without a word and headed toward the stairs.

More words were exchanged across the way. Isabel was the one to stoop down, now that she was out of the chair. Her back was mostly turned to them, giving a fantastic view of her legs and a peek at her curvaceous ass coming from under her skirt. She cast a quick glance in their direction. Furrowed her brow. Another glance. More furrowing. More talking. That brow was beginning to resemble a relief map. Still more talking. Some eyebrow raising. A "what the hell?" gesture.

Abruptly, Isabel turned to face them. Her intense frown shifted to something more thoughtful as she cocked her head to one side and started toward them.

God. Damn. Forgoing the speed with which their kind was able to move, she advanced slowly, purposefully. Thad's cock throbbed and his gut clenched with each fall of her thigh-high boots on the floor. Dark shadows caressed her long legs and shapely body, and as her face came into full view, he noticed a slight smile curling the corners of a very generous mouth. Jesus... so sweet and angelic... but she was wearing such a naughty schoolgirl getup. The combo was as dizzying as the inexplicable realization that had just arrowed straight into his soul: *This was his female.*

He couldn't begin to explain it, but as she drew nearer, Thad was caught in her gravitational pull. That was, until she did a sudden deer-in-headlights and then broke for the bathrooms. "Shit!"

He was on the verge of taking off after her when his guard's paw gripped his shoulder. "Do it, and we'll have to clear the memories of everyone on this floor." Lee jerked his head across the way. "Besides, we've got her. She left the friend."

Thad nodded and started toward Alexia, who had the look of a person who knew she had just been screwed. He had to hand it to the girl: she kept her head held up proudly. But a defensive stance and minute chin tremble gave away her unease. Poor thing. Sometimes it didn't pay to be helpful.

Chapter 3

DESPITE ANTON'S BEST EFFORT, HIS BODY WENT COLD and his blood pressure spiked as he was led into a large, dimly lit room. The walls were bare cinder block, and the ceiling was very low, only clearing his head by a few inches. It was one of the spaces used for sacrificial rituals, and the stale air was thick with the stench of dried blood and fear.

At one end of the room, upon a low, roughly carved throne, sat the Master, his dark robes blending into the shadows, his black eyes glimmering in the darkness. He was the eldest and strongest of the wizards. Their founder, so he claimed.

The man was the greatest evil Anton had ever known, and growing up in his charge had been completely soul rending. It took someone truly fucked in the head to cut open all those vampires day after day, year after year. Anton always half expected to see a gnarled old set of talons peeking out from the arms of the man's robe in place of hands.

Flanking the Master on both sides were two other groups of wizards in dark, hooded robes, a few dozen in all. Their heads were shaven like Anton's and their faces obscured. Only Petros's face was visible, his cruel jade eyes glinting with a spark of satisfaction as he folded his arms in front of his chest and stepped in with the group. Were it not for that evil gleam, he and Anton would look an awful lot alike.

No doubt his half brother had wanted him dead for some time. Perhaps all of them had. For Anton, being the son of the great and powerful Master had held a status akin to that of dog shit on the bottom of a shoe.

"What do you have to say for yourself, son?"

Anton bent low at the waist. It was an act of habit, not reverence. "Master—"

"Think you will save yourself by bowing before me now?"

"No, Master." He straightened. "I have failed you. I am prepared to accept the repercussions."

"And you shall, my son. Most certainly, you shall. First, though, what explanation do you have to offer me?"

Anton cleared his throat and worked to breathe through a windpipe that was trying to close. Willed his heart to calm the hell down. He was going to die. He knew that. But the base instinct of every living thing is to survive, and a sudden panic tried to pull him under. If he had any chance of protecting Tyra, this needed to look good. He would not be weak. He would *not* show fear.

Here goes. "Children, my lord. There were young children around... I could not do violence in their presence. And I believe that we cannot claim Tyra Morgan's power, so the effort would have been wasted. The effort and the collateral damage would not have been worthwhile. She's of no use to you."

The Master's laugh was a deceptively hearty rumble. "You have always been weak, son. Such a bleeding heart. Too much like your mother. Had I known, I would have killed you myself upon your birth. Maybe even before."

Sick bastard.

"I'm sorry, my lord." Anton couldn't begin to understand what else one might say in response to that. There had never been any love between the two men, but the implication that Anton's father would have cut Anton out of the womb? Or what? Killed his mother while she was with child? It made his stomach turn.

The Master was trying to bait him. None of the wizards knew where they came from. The Master made sure of that. It helped him to ensure total control.

As if to prove that dominance, the Master raised a hand. It was a casual gesture. Had the man been standing on a street corner, it might have been mistaken for an attempt to hail a cab or a halfhearted wave to a friend. But with the lift of that hand, Anton's robe came open and was swept off his body. It landed with a whisper somewhere behind him. So it wasn't enough that Anton was going to die; he was going to have to do it naked.

He should have seen this coming.

The coal-black eyes of his father bored into him. There was a dare or a challenge in there, but Anton couldn't really think about that because the Master's hand remained poised aloft, still as death itself. Anton wouldn't have thought it possible, but his heart hammered even faster. Seconds ticked by, echoing loudly in his head as he waited for a hint of movement from the appendage. One twitch could end it all for Anton.

The hand, as they say, was quicker than the eye. By the time Anton had registered the quirk of the Master's lip and the simultaneous flex of fingers, a searing, white-hot pain had streaked across his side and he doubled over. He looked down to find a deep slash crossing his torso and rib cage. Blood welled up from the gash in his skin.

"You're lying to me, son. Perhaps you should like to rethink your response?"

Anton gritted his teeth and straightened. "No. Not lying, Master."

Another flick of his father's hand. Another slash of skin, this from his upper thigh. Some screaming. His own, apparently.

"She was a prostitute, you know. Your mother."

The Master's finger swung through the air like a conductor's baton, and two more searing cuts were made across Anton's chest. Another dangerously close to where Anton thought his jugular might be. Another harsh cry was pulled from his throat. He focused on staying off the floor, but the pain and cold made his body tremble. "I don't… care. About my mother. Master. You raised me sufficiently." He couldn't believe for the life of him that the Master bought that lie, but there was no indication either way.

"So." His father rose and strode toward him. "You did not want to harm the poor little children, and you didn't think there was use in acquiring the female because she's 'too human.' Do I understand that right?"

Anton continued to pant and heave. He swallowed some bile that had shot into his throat and tried not to grimace at the burn. "I admit… has never been in me to kill… my lord… the children… it was too much."

"Ah, but you were not asked to kill. You were asked to bring Tyra Morgan to me. She has unique abilities, and I intend to study them. She is a key to furthering our cause."

And what exactly is our cause, you sick freak? Cutting vampires open just to hear them scream? As far as Anton knew, the Master did not have the power to read his thoughts but the subtle smile on the old man's face almost seemed to answer him.

"I was... only able to find her at the shelter... collateral damage... too likely..." Stupid, stupid. He'd already said that. Anton allowed his body to sag just a little. The slick of blood and sweat made it difficult to keep his hands braced on his thighs. "Besides, we don't even know for certain that she has multiple powers. I didn't witness any when I was tracking her."

His father took a step closer, and Anton was struck by how much smaller than himself the man was. Maybe it was the way he wielded his powers, but Anton had always seen his father as larger than life. But now? The Master stood a good few inches shorter than Anton's six feet, and he was much thinner. Almost scrawny. Didn't the guy ever eat?

"Surely you must have. How else did she manage to slip into and out of the shelter without you being able to track her?"

Anton managed to stand a little straighter. For the briefest second he wondered if perhaps he could overpower his father physically. A glance over the man's shoulder at the restless huddle of underlings put the kibosh on that idea fairly quickly. "One power, my lord. We have established that she is able to transport herself in some way without being detected. A single power is nothing unusual."

"But her father had the power of fire."

Yeah, he had hoped that the Master didn't know

about that. If she hadn't inherited the power to teleport from her father and her mother had been human, that certainly left a gaping hole in his argument. But what if... "It could be from her mother."

"You must think me a fool, son."

"I d—"

"Silence." The command came out in a quiet growl.

"No. Wait." The Master drew up to his full height, nearly vibrating with anger. "Fath—Master. Are you really so sure that there are no other supernatural beings on the planet besides us and the vampires? Much of our intelligence about Tyra Morgan is unverified rumor."

He stepped forward, holding his head high despite the fact that he was naked and blood ran down his body. He gave a pointed look at Petros, who had put them on Tyra's trail to begin with.

"Master, you have lived a long life. You are well traveled. Surely you have encountered other species of powerful beings. We have—" *Oh, Jesus.* "We have performed the ritual on half-breeds before. Most of them are weaker than their full-blooded counterparts. They don't have even one power. How can we discount the idea of the king's daughter being something more? Something different?"

There was loud whispering and rumbling at the far end of the room. Anton lifted his chin as high as he was able. He tried to be as imposing as he could under the circumstances and to make his father work to meet his stare. The Master clucked his tongue and circled Anton... very... slowly. His skull throbbed. When the Master faced him again, there was the briefest flash of— not fear exactly, but something. Doubt?

Yes. Anton had him. This time, hope fueled the heavy thump in his chest. He pressed the point home. "In the interest of your safety, Lord, I would suggest that you be very sure that Tyra Morgan truly *is* only half human before trying to capture her."

His father was silent. Thoughtful. His cruel lips pressed together in a thin line. "Tell me, if I offered you an opportunity to redeem yourself, do you think you would stand a better chance of acquiring the late king's daughter?"

"I would welcome the chance to prove myself, Master."

The Master began to circle again. A cold hand landed on Anton's shoulder. A whisper fluttered in his ear. "You will understand if I doubt your sincerity."

The blistering heat of his father's other hand was astonishing, and an impossibly small shove sent Anton up and back, landing him against the stone wall with a dull smack. Pain exploded through his skull and radiated everywhere as his body dropped unceremoniously to the floor. Dampness and warmth spread out beneath his skull.

Heavy footsteps headed away from Anton. "Petros. Take him to the woods and dispose of him."

Peace filled Anton from the inside out. It wasn't much, but he had the small hope that he'd planted a seed of uncertainty in his father's mind. Maybe that would buy Tyra a little time, enough to realize that she was being hunted. To get herself to safety. A new set of boot steps came closer… and then blackness settled over him.

—◦◦◦—

WTF?? Where R U?!?!!?

Isabel was painfully aware of the cold, wet bathroom counter against her skin. She hated the chilly marble under her ass. She was fond of self-flagellation though, so the discomfort was welcome. She drew her knees to her chest, dropped her head into her hands, and listened for a few beats to the aural torture that was an incessant *drip, drip, drip* from the sink's leaky faucet. What in the hell was wrong with her?

The phone beeped again. You didn't seriously think they were going to just leave, did you?

"Shit." Her hands shook with each button press as she tapped out: R U OK?

Isabel stared at the phone. Why wasn't Lexi responding? Oh, God, she was going to kill herself if they hurt Lexi. She couldn't *believe* she had been so stupid. At first it had sounded like some weird joke that Lexi was playing. Isabel's eyesight hadn't been good since the accident, and it was hard to see in the club with all the flashing lights.

By the time she had gotten a good look at the two huge males, she just... well, she didn't really remember exactly, but next thing she knew, she had been huddled in the corner of the bathroom counter like some kind of refugee. Why the hell hadn't she stayed to help Lexi? God, she didn't even know where they might have taken her friend and—The phone beeped. M fine but these guys R on me like cougars on Adam Lambert. U need 2 talk 2 them!! Come out or I will send them in after you.

Isabel didn't know whether to laugh or cry, so she went for both. Then she sent a mental command to lock the dead bolt on the bathroom door.

The slick bottoms of Isabel's stiletto boots lost

traction and her feet clattered into the sink. Her head rested on the yellow ceramic-tiled wall and she let it loll to the side, catching sight of herself in the large mirror over the counter. Staring back at her from behind the lipstick smears and numbers to call for a good time was a disappointing, sad loser. A failure. A total fricking mess.

Someone who dressed like a cheap stripper and whose body was weary from decades of partying and drinking nothing but human blood. Someone whose makeup was starting to sweat off, revealing the ugly spider web of angry scars over her neck and jaw. Someone who had amassed enough street smarts to survive for forty-three years on her own, but when push came to shove, she ran off in a blind panic like she was a young girl again.

And she had left Lexi holding the bag. I'm sorry, Lex.

Screw sorry. Just get ur ass out here.

She licked an errant tear from the corner of her mouth. OK if I change?

Lexi's response came more quickly this time: Fine. Starving. Taking em 2 el churro. Be fast!

Isabel's exhale was shaky. The rest of her wasn't too steady, either.

Another beep: Bring my hoodie. S colder than a witchs tit outside.

Total relief flooded through Isabel, leaving her limp. Lexi was pissed, but she didn't feel threatened. They hadn't hurt her. Thank God.

Okay. Lexi was okay. That was the important part. Isabel breathed deeply. The adrenaline from before had left her weak in the knees. Another deep breath. Okay.

Good. She made a sour face at the disheveled party-girl in the mirror. "This is why we had a rule about not getting attached. You survived for decades just fine, and as soon as you drop your guard and make friends, you bring trouble for them." For good measure, she wagged an accusatory finger.

Both Isabel and her reflection, ungrateful for the sage I-told-you-so, hissed and gave each other the finger. She sighed and jumped down from the counter. A bank of metal lockers lined the back wall of the VIP bathroom. They were a little dented and dingy. For high-class, the place had seen better days. She passed the bathroom entrance as she headed toward them, glanced at the door, and then yanked the padlocks off each of the two rightmost lockers.

She didn't know the combination for either one, but even without her parents around to teach her, Isabel had managed to learn a few vampire parlor tricks over the years. The smell of Lexi's hoodie when she pulled it from the locker suggested that her friend's latest efforts to quit smoking were not going so well.

Isabel swapped her plaid skirt and cropped button-down for jeans and a fuzzy brown turtleneck. She shimmied into her favorite pair of Luckys while she dug at the deepest recesses of her mind. Why on earth would a vampire show up claiming to be king and ask to talk to her? Had her parents done something back in the day? But if that were it, they wouldn't have just tracked her down now.

Was she going to get in trouble for drinking human blood? Even if that was against the law, who the hell would have reported her for it? And would they really send the king himself? Nothing could be that bad. Could the two large males have been lying about their identities? And if so, who were they really?

Oh God. Unless... could they have somehow found out about that human she—

"Fuck it," she said to no one in particular. They hadn't hurt Lexi. They hadn't come after her and dragged her back out of the bathroom. They probably weren't evil. And if they were? Once she figured out how to get Lexi away from them, there wouldn't be a thing they could do to scare her. She'd seen plenty in her lifetime that would make even a couple of large males like them squirm.

"You can do this... You can do this..."

Isabel slid her phone open again for one last text: On my way.

Her feet were still bare, and her gaze ping-ponged back and forth between the stripper boots and the pink Ryka running shoes that she usually wore for the walk back to Lexi's place. After a few beats, she grabbed the boots and tugged them back on. They always made her walk taller.

Chapter 4

Two crunchy beef tacos later, Thad sat in the early-morning chill on the patio of a place called El Churro. It was an interesting little garden-esque oasis, fenced in and planted with palm trees, as if that would block the harsh neon glare of the surrounding shops selling tourist T-shirts, lewd shot glasses, and salt water taffy. The restaurant itself was little more than a tiny clapboard shack, with barely enough room to stand and order. Obviously, Orlando was not used to cold the way Thad would have defined it.

A few humans lingered, but the majority of the customers had already spilled out of the clubs and then taken their orders to go. The whole affair had been amazing to watch, like a swarm of locusts descending to devour the fatty meat and cheese that was necessary for their survival.

Throughout the whole "Let's have a polite meal" thing, Isabel had been avoiding eye contact with Thad like it was her job. He cleared his throat to get her attention. The second her eyes met his, the grease-laden mass in his stomach began to churn, cement-mixer style. He needed a force of will almost greater than himself to keep his legs from bouncing off an abundance of nervous energy. It wouldn't do to appear unsure of himself with this female.

Every muscle was strung tight, and he could barely

breathe through the tight ball clogging his throat. This would be his first significant task as king, and he'd had the conversation with a faceless female in his head dozens of times, if not hundreds. Now that she was there in the flesh, he wasn't quite sure how to begin.

Thad drew himself up and sucked a bunch of winter air into his lungs. It smelled of spicy sauces and cooking grease. He was gonna have to get used to the problem-of-mammoth-proportions-that-I-don't-have-clue-how-to-handle-and-I'm-scared-shitless BS, because this was only the beginning. His father would have weighed the options thoughtfully and then acted with ninja-like speed and precision. Thad felt less like a ninja and more like the proverbial bull in a china shop.

"Can we talk privately?" They might as well get this over with; it couldn't get much worse. He glanced at Alexia. The little human was a very uncomfortable question mark.

Isabel waved a hand dismissively. "I don't hide anything from her." Awesome. Just awesome.

Behind him, Lee shifted and grumbled his reservations but was wise enough not to butt in. Thad often chose to defer to his friend's advanced years and experience, but this particular minefield was one he needed to navigate on his own. Even if his ass got blown up in the process. And the outlook for that was currently quite good.

"Fair enough," Thad said finally. He leaned back in his seat, opened his leather jacket, and slowly began to unbutton his shirt. The chilly December air skated over his skin and his nipples hardened instantly, apparently in cahoots with his still semi-erect cock. Cuz after all, in the face of crushing life-or-death responsibility and a hot female who might have no interest in him whatsoever, it was important to have priorities.

"Just so there are no questions, I want to offer you proof that I am who I say I am." His fingers were unexpectedly steady as they slipped over each button. He stopped just above his navel and slid his gaze around carefully before pulling the shirt aside. The glint of gold in the moonlight elicited a gasp from both Isabel and Alexia.

The medallion was impressive—Thad had been in awe himself when he'd seen it on his father as a boy. Embedded in his sternum was a thick, gold disk that was roughly the size of a half-dollar and bore the royal emblem and the old family name: "Yavn."

"Let me see." Isabel leaned closer and pushed his shirt farther out of the way. Her fingers were warm and firm against his skin.

"Holy crap," the human gasped as she, too, leaned forward. "Is that like... *in* your skin?"

Thad nodded soberly but kept his stare trained on Isabel, who leaned in and touched her finger gently to the piece of gold, tapping it with only the slightest pressure. Her full lips parted a little and a nervous laugh escaped. Well, she hadn't yet left a trail of dust as she ran away again. That was a start.

"That's the king's medallion?" Isabel's eyes widened further, giving her an almost childlike countenance. Decorative Christmas lights festooned the perimeter of the outdoor eating space, adding a pleasant shimmer to her emerald-green eyes. Something was odd about the left one. It was darker, and... a little cloudy, maybe? It added a sexy sort of otherworldliness to her stare.

"It is." Acid and salsa swirled in his gut as if on a personal mission to make him hurl. How could he be turned on and nauseated at the same time?

"So." She cleared her throat. "Do I call you... your highness?"

He almost collapsed as relief flooded his insides. She believed him, or at least she was willing to humor him, and thank goodness. There was so much he needed to say. First though... "My name is Thad. Call me Thad."

Isabel pressed her lips together, chewing them nervously while she studied him, eyes narrowed in apparent concentration. "Okay, Thad." Her sigh was thoughtful and breathy, and she rubbed at a deep wrinkle in her forehead. She didn't seem to hide her worry well. "So what's going on here, exactly? What do you want with me?"

Here we go. Thad cleared his throat and leaned toward her. "In the royal family, at each birth, an Oracle is brought in to bless the baby and, I dunno, predict its future or some such shit. When I was born, the Oracle predicted that I was destined to meet a mate who would lead with me a century later. And until then, I would not come into my power. The Oracle marked me so I would know how to find my mate." He brought his arm forward, sliding his sleeve up to reveal the unique scar. "It's the same scar you have on your back. I believe that..." He swallowed. "You are my destined mate."

Alexia chuckled. Isabel, whose lips were parted in an understandable show of incredulity, flashed a dirty look in her friend's direction. "You can't be serious."

You have no idea how serious I am, and how badly I wish I wasn't. "Look, I know this kind of a big bomb to drop—"

"Wait. No. This is not just 'kind of a bomb.'" Isabel lowered her voice slightly, despite the fact that the after-hours crowd had all but cleared the street. "First of all, I'm nearly half your age, so I didn't even exist when your supposed destiny thing happened. That mark on my back is a cattle brand. I got it on a dare, like, forever ago. It's probably just a coincidence.

"How do you know that you simply never will come into your power? Some of us don't get one. Just because you're royalty doesn't make you immune to drawing the short straw." Alexia's continued tittering capped off Isabel's tirade.

Thad turned to Lee and then Alexia. "I'm sorry, but could you guys give us a minute? This would be easier without an audience." And without Lee's thinly veiled coughs of displeasure and Alexia's schoolgirl giggles.

"Sure, buddy." Lee turned to Alexia. "C'mon, I'll buy you a drink or something."

"Sweet!" Alexia jumped from her seat and grabbed Lee's arm, pulling him along. Lee looked like he was being marched off to the gallows.

"Just be right over there if you need anything, T."

In spite of himself, Thad chuckled at their retreat. "I don't think Lee's ever been dragged off by a female like that before."

"Yeah, Lexi's really something else."

"So what's the deal with you and her? How'd you wind up being so tight with a human?"

Isabel smiled. "Just did. Kind of getting off topic, don't you think?"

They were. Thad leaned in more, legs apart, elbows on his thighs. "Look," he said. "I get that this sounds pretty insane, but believe me when I say I've got better things to do with my time than make up stuff like this. If I didn't think there was something to it, I wouldn't have been combing half the country looking for you.

"I thought it was all a crock of shit too, ya know?" He sat back up and studied her face for a second. Her expression was blank and her mouth was slack again, like she couldn't quite process what he was saying. But his jaw was tight and his blood pounded in his ears with the urgency of what still remained to be said. So he kept going.

"The Oracle you asked about is long dead. My parents—both of them—are also dead. I am close to a century old, and I have no power whatsoever. When word gets out about that factoid, it's gonna put a crack in the ice. My experience and training up to this point have been completely theoretical. I'm running out of time to officially announce my ascension, and our race *needs* to have faith in its leader.

"We are down to tens of thousands, Isabel. *Thousands*. On a planet of billions of humans. We work damn hard to keep the communities protected from wizard attacks, but if the folks get scared, they might scatter. And if they scatter…" He closed his eyes and shook his head slowly. Jammed his fingers into his hair. The cement mixer in his stomach started up again.

"If they scatter, the wizards are gonna be able to pick them off easier than a shotgun-toting psycho at the top of a clock tower. We won't be able to protect them." By the time he came up for air, his face was burning hot and his head threatened to split wide open.

Isabel remained silent, her expression unchanged.

Had none of that gotten through to her? Thad pressed his lips together for a moment, then pulled his chair closer and got right in her face so that she would have no choice but to hear him. Really hear him.

"I'm not asking you to believe, Isabel. I'm just asking you not to dismiss me yet. Just give me a shot. Are you willing to do that much, Isabel?"

—◦◦◦—

"Selena! What were you doing out of the room?"

Tyra gave her most reassuring smile to the petite Hispanic woman who had spoken. The woman now stood before Tyra, hand over her heart and sleep-mussed hair shooting in all directions like a mad scientist, in the doorway of the tiny room that was her temporary residence at the Ash Falls Interfaith Shelter.

Tyra released the small hand of the woman's daughter, whom she'd found wandering the halls. Again. The girl stepped forward reluctantly with the guilty smile of a second grader who knew she had been caught doing wrong but had no appreciation of how dangerous her actions had been.

Selena was suddenly very interested in the worn, rust-colored carpet that lined the otherwise bare hallway of the women's wing. "Felt funny. Couldn't sleep."

"You have to stay with me, Selena. I was freaking out when I found you were gone!" Mom's eyes swung over to Tyra. Relief shone brightly in them, despite the weak lighting. "Thank you so much for bringing her back."

"No problem, Lisa. I was just heading out when I found her." Tyra squatted down to meet the eight-year-old's gaze head-on. "Listen to your mother, Selena. It's very dangerous to be out by yourself. You never know who you might run into."

Or what. She'd been a bit terrified herself to discover the child loitering outside her office. For weeks now, Tyra had felt an uneasy prickle at the base of her skull. Someone or something was watching the shelter. She wasn't feeling the distinct sock-you-in-the-gut terror and nausea usually caused by wizard vibes, but still the feeling was concerning. Anything from a wizard to an angry ex or a dealer looking to get paid could be out there, and Selena had been just wandering around, barefoot, unguarded, and completely oblivious.

"You were up all by yourself too, Miss Tyra."

Tyra stood and smiled. "But I have magic powers to protect me from bad things that go bump in the night, Selena." She winked at the girl.

The girl grinned. "Will I have magic powers someday, Miss Tyra?"

Tyra lifted her shoulders in an exaggerated shrug. "Maybe someday. Who knows?" The girl's mother laughed and herded her nightgown-clad daughter inside their room.

"Thank you, Miss Tyra. You should get some sleep yourself, huh? It's almost morning already."

Tyra gave a tiny good-bye wave and headed back to her office, doing a quick check to ensure that the grimy hallway was otherwise empty. They ran on a skeleton staff at night, but the relative safety didn't slow her heart rate. It was always good to be sure. She stretched her senses, feeling around for bad mojo, but oddly enough, everything seemed quiet tonight.

She opened the door to her office, which was dark

except for the warm, amber glow of her cell phone display. As she grabbed the phone off the clunky, old schoolteacher desk, it buzzed joyfully in her hand to indicate a new text message: Think we found her. Will let U know asap.

Lee.

"Oh, thank you, thank you, thank you." Tyra hugged the phone to her chest. Already there were rumblings in the community. Folks wanted to know why Thad hadn't officially announced his ascension.

Due to a recent uptick in wizard sightings, many of the elder conservatives were pushing for a ban on inter-acting with humans or breaking up the vampire com-munities and moving out of the area in smaller groups. Some civilians were even talking about taking up arms against the wizards themselves, Michigan Militia-style. The whole situation had "impending shit storm" written all over it.

A drop of moisture escaped from Tyra's eye. Her half brother might be inexperienced, but if he didn't rise to the challenge of being king, the vampire race was in trouble. If he had managed to track down the mate that had supposedly been prophesied for him, then he could finally come the hell back from wherever he was and get down to business. There was still hope. She sniffed and swiped hastily at her wet cheek, turned the lock on her office door, and sent herself home in a scatter of tiny molecules.

Chapter 5

THAD PACED ISABEL'S BEDROOM. THE SPARSE furnishings—from the functional Ikea desk and the explosion of party flyers on the walls to the bed decked out in spaceship-themed sheets—all screamed college-kid chic. He compared it to his own home. His life.

Nothing about the two of them was similar.

Easing onto the bed, Thad ran his hands over a soft pillow that could have been made from the hide of that Wookie character in *Star Wars*. He could just picture Isabel's face resting upon its furry surface in the daytime. His chest tightened at the thought. There were stickers on the walls and ceiling, too. Little white glow-in-the-dark stars and planets that scattered all over like their own special solar system.

A bulletin board over the desk was packed full of pictures of Isabel and her human friend, Alexia, with their tongues out and their arms slung around each other. Most were taken in club settings like the one where he'd found her. She had a life here, and while not exactly prosperous by Thad's standards, she seemed happy. How was he going to make this work?

Thad's thoughts vanished into the ether as soon as Isabel stepped from the bathroom, having changed again into black yoga pants and a plain, white form-fitting T-shirt. Her skin was paler than his, peachy and freshly scrubbed of her heavy club makeup. A faint network of scars, which hadn't been visible before, traversed her neck and cheek. While he ached to know more about them, his gut told him not to ask. Not yet. Vampires didn't scar easily, so whatever had caused them... well, he and Isabel probably weren't "there" yet.

That she had allowed him to come back to her apartment was a huge victory, even if he might have elicited the invitation by insinuating that he and Lee would be stuck without a place to hide from the sun.

A hint of lemon wafted in her wake, and Thad couldn't help but suck it into his nostrils with gusto. His chest squeezed again, even as his dick swelled in appreciation. Whether because of lust or the prophecy or just an intense longing to do right by his kind, damned if he didn't already want to fall on Isabel and wrap around her until there was no way to tell where she ended and he began.

Damn. He had planned and he had strategized, but every time he looked at her, his mind went completely blank. He simply hadn't expected this. How could he have? He'd expected his destined mate to be like the other females he'd known: desperate for the status of becoming queen. And yes, admittedly, someone well bred. Not that he was pretentious; he just hadn't counted on a potential mate who looked at him as if he had sprouted horns when he suggested the idea of them being together.

"Do you mind if I put some music on?" She headed toward the desk.

He shook his head. "Not at all."

As she leaned forward to pull up an MP3 player on her computer, Thad got a really good look at how well the yoga pants hugged her rear view. Her ass was practically begging for his attention while she bent at the waist to scroll through her playlist. After a few clicks, something he assumed to be techno started to come out of the computer speakers, but it was altogether different from what had been playing at the club. He cleared his throat and did his best to act casual as she straightened up and sat herself in a desk chair with one leg tucked beneath her.

"So what are we listening to?"

"It's a set by Anthony Pappa. He's, uh, he's one of my favorite techno DJs. This is an old recording of a live show that he played in Mexico, I want to say..." Her eyes locked on Thad's. He had no clue what she was talking about, and that must have showed. "I get the feeling this isn't really your thing. I could put on something else—"

"No, no. It sounds good. I've just never really listened to this stuff. I'm more of a jazz man."

"Ah." She bit her lip and looked at her lap, picking invisible lint from her pant leg. An uncomfortable silence lingered, because yeah... it was a damn awkward situation. Thad didn't figure it was the right time to blurt out how sexy he thought she was, or how he was terrified he'd be a shitty king if she didn't save his ass.

"You know, I feel like I owe you an apology," Isabel blurted out.

Thad frowned. If anything, he owed *her* one. "I'm not sure I understand."

"Earlier, I was kind of rude to you. I just wanted to apologize for that. I was still kind of feeling the wine I drank, and I was in a weird place. And frankly, you freaked me out with that whole…" She leaned back on an exhale.

Yeah. "I get it. And you don't have to apologize. I mean, I'm still sufficiently baffled over this whole thing myself, and I've known about it for a long time. If someone had approached me the way I did you, I'd have thought they were crazy too."

Isabel smiled and leaned her head to the side. "The thing is, I don't see how I can be who you think I'm supposed to be. I… I don't even know how to imagine that." She shifted uncomfortably in her seat. "I mean, you've probably figured out by now that I'm not exactly royalty material. Not by a long shot."

He tapped his thumb against his chin. "I'll be honest with you. I'm not sure what I expected, but you weren't it. You know, when my parents first told about the prophecy, I just kind of nodded and smiled. And then I blew it off." He rubbed again at his arm, where the scar continued to pulse insistently. "Wasn't till after my parents died that I finally decided maybe I needed to figure out what was going on."

He was quiet for a second, but Isabel still said nothing. No questions, no comments. She continued to stare. Her green eyes were wide and fixed on him, but she made no move to reply. It was like at the taco stand all over again.

Drawing in a deep breath, Thad continued. "See, about a year ago, I started feeling things where this scar is here. Throbbing, tingly, buzzy sensations. They've started to get stronger, more intense. Right now, it's really sore. Pulsing. Feels like my arm has a headache. Nothing like that's happened to you?"

Her answering shrug was fairly noncommittal, but her hand went to her lower back, almost unconsciously. He took that as an affirmative.

"See, all I've got to go on is what's right in front of both of us. The fact that I found you where we were tonight. Then there's the matching scar on your back. I don't know any better than you do where we go from here.

"What I do know is that more and more vampires are getting hit by the wizards. Folks are getting nervous. *I'm* getting nervous. I've stepped up as my father's successor, but if it comes out that I've got no power, they'll see me as weak. So I feel like I have to try whatever I can, even if it seems completely crazy. And it does. I know that. At the risk of sounding dramatic: for the sake of our entire race, I need you to keep an open mind."

She blinked. "But you're the king whether you have a power or not. Being able to hurl lightning bolts or whatever doesn't make you a smarter ruler."

In a perfect world. He smiled slightly. "You'd think that, but you'd be wrong."

Isabel groaned softly and rubbed her temples. She thought about her parents and the reasons why they had moved to Florida decades earlier. "Actually, no. I wouldn't. I know our kind can be stuck-up about abilities."

He raised his eyebrows. "Oh?"

"It's why I've always lived in the human world." She gestured vaguely. "Neither of my parents ever came into their power. They kept me away from the rest of our kind so I wouldn't face the same kind of discrimination they had."

"Ah... I was wondering." He blinked, which seemed to highlight how incredibly blue his eyes were. He didn't look the way she would have expected a king to look. She had seen plenty of the human royal families on TV, and he didn't look a thing like any of them. Honestly, he was more like a cross between a bodybuilder and a frat boy. Lord knew Lexi had brought enough of both specimens home for Isabel to know what she was talking about. He was dressed in denim and leather, and she was fairly sure he carried a gun. He wasn't scary, but he radiated strength and a touch of danger.

Very sexy.

"You know," she said softly. "Even if I'm not on board with this, you are the king. You can do whatever you want, right?" A tremor went through her body at the mere thought of it. He was handsome, yes. But... well, there were an awful lot of buts.

"I won't club you over the head and drag you out of here." He smiled, warming his somber expression. "I guess I'm hoping maybe my wit and charm will be convincing enough."

It was going to be hard not to like him if he kept saying things like that. Against all logic, she found herself wanting to touch him. Or lick him all over. But she'd had her fun at the club already, and she was pretty much sober now, so she didn't really know what to do. This was the king. The *king*. The enormity of it practically made her brain shut down.

He cleared his throat. "I've been wondering something, so I'm just going to go ahead and put it out there. Are you attracted to males?"

What? "Of course." Oh. Right. The female she'd

fed from. She could see how that might have looked to a passerby. She laughed again. Inexplicably, a tight squeeze in her chest loosened a little. "I guess you're asking because of the human at the club?"

"You seemed pretty into her."

Isabel squirmed in her seat again. "I'd had some red, and I needed to feed." Heat crept over her face. "And besides, she was in a bad place. I could tell. Sometimes when I find a host, I try to make up for taking their blood by offering solace." She drew a deep breath. That last part, well, she hadn't even said that to Lexi. Why she so did now was a mystery even to her.

Thad frowned. "How do you know? About the female being in a bad spot?"

Isabel resisted the intense urge to squirm some more. It was a long story, and one she didn't want to tell. "I've been through some rough stuff myself, and I've just figured it out over the years. Body language, stuff like that. Sometimes you just know. I figure if I'm going to drink their blood, I should provide a little comfort first, right? Lend an ear, rub their shoulders… that kind of thing."

Now he was looking at her like she was a Rubik's cube. "And you drank from her?"

Hadn't they established that? "Yeah, well, I've never had a mate in my life or anyone else consistent to drink from. Being in the party scene makes it easy because there are huge crowds, a cornucopia of hosts, and usually lots of dark corners where I can do what I need to without being noticed." She was startled by her compulsion to be so open, but she kept going. Lying to the king seemed wrong.

"Drinking wine started out as a way to meet people

and lower inhibitions, but I guess I started really getting into the scene and everything it had to offer. I love the music. The fact that things don't get started until late at night is a huge bonus."

"So that's what red wine does? Lowers your inhibitions? I've only tasted a tiny amount, and you never know for sure about the stories everyone tells." His eyes widened with apparent interest.

She nodded slowly, choosing her words. "It does a lot of things, but that's one of the biggies. It, uh, it feels really amazing, actually. I mean, individual mileage varies but in general you feel kind of euphoric and buzzy; your senses are heightened. It enhances physical and emotional intimacy. Even if you're talking to a total stranger, it's like you're connected to them. Which is why it's so easy for me to cozy up to a strange human and drink from them. It always feels really natural in the moment, you know? It's not just your garden-variety, alcohol-induced mellow, but also a rather sensual experience." She narrowed her eyes at Thad, who had his eyebrows drawn downward, deep in thought. "I'm weirding you out, aren't I?"

His face relaxed, and he chuckled. "A little. I mean, that sort of thing was discouraged when I was younger, and it's not like I've gotten a lot of time off to party. It's all a little foreign to me."

Her face burned hotter. "Yeah, sorry I—"

He held a large hand up. His fingers were thick and strong. Calloused. He might be royalty, but he wasn't afraid of a little hard work. "No, wait. Don't apologize."

Isabel bit back the growl that had bubbled in her throat. She couldn't stand being cut off. By anyone.

Thad rolled his shoulders a few times and cleared his throat again. Goodness, he did that a lot, didn't he? "What about negative side effects?"

Isabel's arms crossed in front of her chest. Where was this going? Did he think that because of this supposed destiny thing, he could grill her about a little recreational drinking? King or not, where did he get off judging her? It wasn't like she was the first vampire to ever drink blood from an unsuspecting human who was otherwise intoxicated, and she *never* hurt them or anything.

Thad's eyebrows remained elevated. Fine, he wanted an answer, so she'd give him one. "For humans, too much wine can make them sick or give them headaches. For us, not really. Sometimes you grind your teeth, so it can be rough on the fangs, especially if they're extended for feeding. I've always been extra careful about that one since I can't just go to any random dentist if I crack one. I've heard that on rare occasions males have trouble getting hard for awhile, but like I said, usually it's a major aphrodisiac."

Thad cringed. "There's a thought to make me feel cold and clammy all over. How rare is the, uh, performance issue?"

She shook her head. "I don't think it happens often. This area isn't teeming with vampires, and I haven't exactly taken a poll."

"Huh."

Thad's far-off gaze gave her pause. She wrinkled her nose and studied him hard. "Thad, why are you asking me about all this?"

Thad rubbed his eyes and forehead, and took a couple of deep breaths through his nose. Myriad thoughtful expressions seemed to flash across his face, but then he met her gaze head-on. Goodness, those eyes were blue.

He coughed nervously. "Yeah, well, I've been thinking about it as you've been talking just now. And I think I'd like to try some. With you."

Chapter 6

ISABEL LOOKED AT THAD LIKE HE HAD JUST SUGGESTED they go streaking. Through a gang of wizards. At sunrise. "You can't be serious."

Yes, absolutely, 100 percent seriously crazy. "Do you have more available?" Suddenly he realized that red wine might not be the kind of staple one kept around the house like toothpaste or flour.

"Sure, I do. But I'm surprised you would want to try it. You just said it was discouraged."

He scooted closer to the edge of the bed so that their knees were barely touching. It was the slightest of brushes but enough to evoke a nice zingy sensation all over that got him slightly more aroused. The thought of consuming the slightly illicit beverage was nuts, but a sense of excitement was overriding that. The idea of getting intimate with her the way she described... his pulse raced with anticipation.

Thad clasped his hands together and leaned to rest his elbows on his parted thighs, just as he had during their conversation outside the taco stand. "You said, did you not, that this stuff lowers inhibitions? Fosters intimacy?"

She nodded without comment, still staring him down like he belonged in a zoo.

"So it would seem to me that for the two of us and this unique situation, it could be a useful tool in getting to know each other better. Maybe even for getting more intimate… seeing as how I've been given the message that we are destined to be mated." He flashed a smile. Females usually loved his smile.

The corners of Isabel's mouth lifted just slightly. Bingo. "It amazes me that you seem to have a sense of humor about this."

Yeah, that was one way of putting it. Thad leaned against the headboard and stretched his legs across Isabel's rocket-ship-themed duvet. To buy himself some time to respond, he loosened the laces on his heavy boots and kicked them off. Might as well get comfortable.

"See, it's like this. The more I think about it, the more I figure there must be something to this whole prophecy thing. I've spent the last few weeks and God knows how many miles playing some wacky version of hot and cold, and somehow that led me to where I found you. Now here we are. It's just past dawn so we're not going anywhere anytime soon. Why not make the most of it and see where things go?

"Unless you plan to shoot me down, in which case we're stuck playing twenty questions, or maybe go fish. And as for my sense of humor, I've run the gamut of emotions tonight, from pissed off to freaked out and everything in between, so for right now, focusing on what's funny about this whole thing seems like the best way to keep from blowing my brains out."

She grinned. She wasn't fully fanged the way he was, but still her smile was amazing. Sexy. Her entire face lit up, even when she narrowed her eyes at him. "Don't you think it would look really bad to the society if word got out that the king was hitting the Merlot?"

Thad crossed his arms over his chest and swept his

gaze pointedly around the small space. "Just you and me in this room." He smiled back at her. "Come on, you don't want to say no to this. I can see it on your face."

She studied him, hard. "You're really sure about this?"

Hell, no. "Absolutely."

Isabel continued to give him a dubious raised eyebrow, but after what seemed like forever, she rose from her chair and disappeared from the room. When she returned just moments later, she was carrying a large glass of water and two squat tumblers. A bottle of dark-colored liquid was wedged under her arm. After placing the water and smaller glasses on the desk, she conjured up a corkscrew as if from nowhere. A sommelier couldn't have opened the bottle so fast. Strangely, her experience was almost comforting.

"Mmm." She leaned close to the glasses as the velvety liquid flowed, drawing the scent into her lungs. "Beaujolais. One of my favorites. Low in tannins, too. It'll be a good one for your first time." A hint of impishness lingered in her smile.

Okay, he hated to look stupid, but... "I have no idea what that means."

After Isabel took a small sip from one of the cups, a girlish giggle lilted from her lovely throat. "It's thought that the tannins and anthocyanins in red wine, along with the age of the bottle itself, are what cause the drug-like effects that occur in vampires. So I thought I'd go with a lower tannin red for this—What?"

Not a single taste of the vino, but already Isabel's words had him half hard and leering inappropriately. Damn. *Damn.* She was smart, too. Nothing turned him on like an intelligent female.

He shook his head. "Just enjoying the lesson."

A flush crept across her face. "Okay. Well. Here we go." She proffered a full glass, keeping one only half filled for herself. "I'm sorry we don't have real wineglasses."

He raised an eyebrow. "More for me?"

"I already had some at the club. I wouldn't want to overdo it, or I'm liable to forget myself and try to take advantage of you." Isabel's eyes crinkled at the corners. "Now who's got a sense of humor?"

She smiled again, not as broadly, but it was amazing how his chest swelled at her change in expression. "Here. I'm gonna go put the rest away. Gimme a sec."

Thad watched her go and then turned his attention to what he held in his hand. Before he could second-guess himself, he all but guzzled the fruity, plumlike drink.

As the red made an effortless descent into his stomach, a cold wave of panic swept through his bloodstream. *What the fuck am I doing?*

Isabel reappeared just in time to see Thad bolt upright on the bed, sucking wind as if he'd just run a marathon. "Whoa, whoa, easy… easy." She rushed over and put her hand on his back, rubbing in lazy circles. Her hand was solid and satisfying against the fabric of his shirt. "You freaking out a little?"

His eyes met hers, but he didn't respond. Didn't need to.

"Okay, no problem. Totally normal. Everything's fine. Breathe deeply for me."

Thad dropped his head slightly and complied, noting that his heart rate stepped down a notch on her command. A few more breaths. Even better. He smiled his gratitude. "Thanks."

"No problem." She removed her hand from his back. He hadn't realized how warm it was until it was gone. "Listen, nothing bad is going to happen, okay? I drink this kind all the time." One elegant finger ran around the rim of Thad's now-empty glass. "Besides, you're only having one glass. It can't do too much damage. You already drank it, so you might as well sit back and enjoy the ride. It'll be over before you want it to be, I guarantee it."

Thad nodded. Right. She was right. He was such a flaming idiot. He had asked for this, after all.

At some point, Isabel must have swallowed hers as well, because the other tumbler had gone from half full to completely empty. He didn't notice precisely when, because despite Isabel's reassurance, his heart was still pounding out what-the-fuck-are-you-doing-how-could-you-think-this-is-a-good-idea-you-are-the-king-for-God's-sake-do-you-really-think-a-stupid-glass-of-wine-will-put-you-on-the-path-to-your-destiny-your-father-would-be-so-ashamed, and no amount of deep breathing would make his heart shut up.

Thank goodness, Isabel rescued him from his internal monologue. "All set, Your Highness. I hope you enjoy your trip to Wonderland." Thad couldn't help but chuckle. Wonderland. Boy, didn't that sound fun? When her tongue caught an errant drop of the Beaujolais and licked over the fullness of her lips, he managed to forget his fear altogether.

He leaned back against the headboard, stretching his legs out as he had previously. "So now what?"

Isabel reclined on the bed and aimed another angelic smile at Thad. "Now we wait."

Chapter 7

SIX FREAKING A.M. AFTER A FITFUL HOUR OR SO OF sleep, Tyra was in the gym working out her frustrations and amping up her adrenaline. She'd woken up before the alarm, as predicted, and would be back at the shelter before too long. But she needed the exercise for her sanity, since she hadn't been going out to hunt wizards. Wouldn't be until Thad returned. It was imperative that she be able to reach him if he needed her.

Warm air stirred, and she stiffened in the middle of a squat before standing to rack the barbell. Her eyes rolled as she blew out a heavy sigh. "What the hell are you doing here, Siddoh?"

The reflection of a hulking male appeared behind her. His short brown hair was mussed in that I'm-too-sexy-to-use-a-comb way, and his hazel eyes burned with desire. "Oh, come on, Tyra. Is that any way to greet a friend?"

She glanced around the room, her gaze bouncing from the door to the mirrored walls to the bench that Siddoh stood beside. "I didn't hear the door open. Don't tell me you've been lurking in here since I showed up." She gave a little tsk-tsk. "That seems pretty lame."

He arched an eyebrow and threw a wicked smile her way while he stroked his chin. God, what a sexy smile. No matter how he'd pissed her off, that smile had always gotten to me. It was probably why this whole thing between them had gone on so long past its expiration date. The tips of his pearly white fangs peeked flirtatiously from behind his full upper lip. "Maybe I just wanted to see how much weight you could squat." He eyed the barbell she had racked. "Five hundred, not bad."

"It's five twenty-five, asshole." She smirked at his reflection in the mirror. "I keep the weight light so I can maintain my girlish figure. Now what's up with you sitting around all invisible while I do my workout?"

He took a few slow, predatory steps toward her. At five foot eleven she was tall and strong, as most of her kind were, particularly the females. Yet as he drew closer, her knees wobbled little, and she was reminded of how immense and well-muscled he was. How his suggestive gaze could make her want him even when she was angry. How he could occupy so much space with his dark, moody, yet playful personality.

"I think you know what I'm here for, Tyra."

"Siddoh, my father is dead. You don't have to sleep with me to get back at him anymore." She walked over to a weight bench and sat down, cracking open a bottle of water. They had become lovers long ago. The relationship had been born of Tyra's need to rebel and Siddoh's desire to stick it to the king's daughter as a way to express his feelings about being passed over as second in command.

Somehow, what had started as a one-night stand had become a years-long relationship of convenience. Something like friends with benefits, but contrary to Siddoh's earlier assertion, they had never exactly been friends. They were dynamite in the sack, but otherwise they couldn't stand each other. More like antagonistic combatants with benefits?

His face contorted in a mock scowl and he walked in a semicircle to face her, still advancing, still prowling toward her with lustful purpose in his gaze. "You think my little annoyance with your father is the only reason I like fucking you?" Closer. Hoo, baby. "I like fucking you because you blow my mind, female. And it's been awhile."

Tyra rolled her eyes. "It's been awhile because you only want me on your terms, Siddoh, and I'm awfully tired of that."

Still he continued, closing the space between them. Kneeling at her feet, he slowly pulled off her shoes and started to massage her tired arches. The pleasant kneading made her groan. His strong hands rubbed her ankles and her calves, and had just begun to creep farther when she placed a firm hand over his.

Siddoh was a crutch. One she really needed to stop using… starting now. Tyra heaved another exasperated sigh. "Siddoh. Stop."

His hand stilled and he remained crouched so that they were eye to eye, but he rocked back on his heels. Full, dark brows drew together in a deep frown. "You're serious?"

She needed to take a slow breath in and back out before she could find her voice and respond. "Yeah. Yeah, I am." A little tremor of weakness went through her. Why was this so hard to say? It wasn't as if they were in love, or anythi—

Oh.

Tyra's eyes widened. "You need to feed, though, don't you?"

Siddoh's answering smile was almost cruel. Angry. But underneath the tremors of hunger that flowed not just from the bare touch of his hand on her foot, but also through traces of his blood in her own veins, was a pang of something unexpected.

Hurt?

A subtle shake of his head, a gentle pat on her foot, and he was on his feet. "Thanks, sweetheart, but no thanks."

Habit had her reaching toward him, but she stopped just short of contact. No way could he go out into the field this way. "Siddoh, I can feel your hunger. We can still feed from each other, you know, even if we're not lovers." She smiled. "I think we're both adult enough for that."

Siddoh grinned again as he backed toward the door, all trace of sadness gone. "Generous offer, babe, but I think I'll just call Blood Service."

She grimaced and rubbed her hand over her forehead. It hardly made sense for him to pay somebody to come from Blood Service when she was already right there, but then again maybe it would be better for them to make a clean—

The gym door slammed shut, and with it, her train of thought came to a screeching halt. Well. That was that, then, wasn't it?

———

Thad Morgan was completely overcome. He drifted and floated through the man-made glow-in-the-dark galaxy on Isabel's walls and ceiling, completely relaxed yet humming with energy. With need. His skin buzzed with heightened sensation; his fingertips ached with the desire to touch and explore. Something. Anything. Even Isabel's furry pillows seemed to beckon, tempting Thad to run his fingers through the silky hair.

Isabel was right. This was beyond amazing. She had sought to ease his anxiety by rubbing the back of his neck, and all of a sudden he'd gone from wondering when the wine was going to kick in to wondering if it would be bad manners to curl into her lap and purr.

Fuck me, what the hell happened? Not that he didn't know the answer, but he couldn't quite shake the sense of bewilderment.

Isabel was now leaning against the headboard, legs akimbo. Thad sat between her perfect thighs, head bowed, letting her work the muscles in his shoulders with adept fingers. Some last shred of logic shouted in Thad's head about how he was stupid, stupid, stupid to be sitting in such a vulnerable position with a near stranger, but he couldn't bring himself to care.

Wine or no wine, his gut told him that he was safe with her, and he'd always had damn good instincts. And holy mother, did Isabel have good hands. He sighed deeply as his body liquefied under her touch.

"So." Isabel's hot breath fanned his ear. "Are we feeling more relaxed?"

A low groan rumbled in Thad's throat, and he leaned a little more into her hands. If she were to let go, Lord knew where he'd land.

"I'll take that as a yes." She chuckled, a quiet breathy laugh that made him fly even higher than before.

"Yes."

Her hands moved to his shoulders, leaving warm tingles in their wake. They worked their way slowly down his spine to the small of his back, where she paused and drew in a slight gasp.

Thad stiffened when Isabel pulled the Kahr P9 out of his waist holster. It wasn't his usual piece, but holy hell, that was a fuckup for the record books. Thank God they were alone. Lee would never let him hear the end of something like that. Her discomfort with the find was obvious. She handled the gun like it was a sweaty gym sock.

"I'm just going to put this over here." She eased from behind him and laid the pistol carefully on the desk. "Any others I should know about?"

Thad pulled up his pant leg quietly and withdrew a knife from an ankle holster and handed it to her, handle first. "The rest are in my jacket," he said, nodding to where he had left it, in easy reach by the bed. He was sure this time. God *damn* it. At least he knew for certain that she wasn't going to kill him.

"Okay, then." She smiled and crawled back onto the bed, slinking toward him with a lazy catlike grace. "Now. Where were we?"

Thad sat forward. He could not ignore the sudden compulsion to touch her. Caress her. He couldn't deny it; the urge for intimacy was there just like Isabel had said it would be. His left hand crept across the bed to touch hers. "You are... *so* fucking sexy," he breathed.

Isabel leaned toward Thad and smiled at him. An unexpected growl rumbled in the back of his throat. That smile of hers was like a prize to be won, and he was caught unaware by an overwhelming desire to lie down and pledge his undying loyalty to her right then and there. He clamped his jaws so tightly that his molars ached. He wasn't too far gone to know that saying so could be a real buzz kill.

"You're not so bad yourself, you know." She moved closer, rubbing her nose against his like an Eskimo kiss. And boy, would you look at that! Turned out he definitely had no trouble getting hard. "Are you going to kiss me now, Thad?"

He snarled quietly, an oddly playful sound that he couldn't recall making before. He tilted his head ever so slightly and leaned his mouth into hers. He'd intended to go the slow and gentle route, but his tongue decided to barge right in to that lush mouth of hers, stroking... probing. He groaned and pulled her body against his, taking the kiss harder and deeper.

Her mouth was so sweet that it was like kissing a piece of candy. More of those exquisite tingles popped up all over his skin, concentrating where their bodies met. Every frenzied breath seemed to bring more of the same delicious feeling, intensifying exponentially with each gasp until Thad was enveloped in a mind-blowing full-body vibration.

Something in the back of his head warned him to pull back, maybe slow this down a little so they could actually talk, but before he had a chance to think about it any further, he felt Isabel's teeth and—oh God, her fangs—scrape over his tongue, drawing just the tiniest bit of blood.

Her loud moan of satisfaction reverberated inside his mouth, and she pushed against him as she crawled forward to straddle his lap. *Oh, man*. Her tongue danced and stroked against his, as if trying to taste the blood she'd drawn.

Thad tightened his grip on her hair, and the pull only spurred her to press harder, grinding against the erection that was screaming to be freed from his pants. She sucked his tongue and nibbled his lower lip, making his breath and her heart speed up in unison. He could feel her heartbeat tap-dancing against his own.

"See?" Her voice was low and sensual. "No trouble at all getting hard." And wasn't it good to know that they were on the same page? Her hand traced a path down the front of his shirt, reached his pants, and started searching for a way to undo them.

"Isabel—"

"Shh." She continued to kiss him but backed the lower half of her body away. Then the kissing stopped, too.

Why was she stopping? And why did he suddenly feel like he was standing in the noonday sun?

"Isabel, I'm burning up." And thirsty. His tongue had stopped bleeding, but now it was very, very dry.

"Probably just the red. It can jack up your body temperature. Here, let me help." After passing a glass of water, Isabel reached forward and began to undo his shirt. Lithe fingers caressed his skin where she pushed the fabric apart. Firmly, but sensually, she ran her hand along his stomach, his pecs… he shivered as her fingers brushed once, then twice over his nipples. Pinched at them gently, and then not so gently. *Oh, God.* Her touch then drifted to the medallion that was fused into his sternum and she hesitated, uncertain.

"It's okay. You can touch it." Yeah, she definitely could. He moaned and dropped his head back, wanting those fingers to continue to stroke him any way they could. Most of his skin was completely numb around that disk, but somehow he felt every brush of Isabel's fingertips. He nearly dropped the water glass as he passed it back. "Please... take it."

She placed it on the floor gently and then circled a finger around the flesh that surrounded his medallion. More delightful shivers pricked Thad's skin in the wake of her hand. "Did it hurt?"

He breathed out a low chuckle. No one had asked him that. "I think so. I passed out."

Isabel seemed to consider this for a second and then swept her hand lower, spanning her fingers over his abs again. They seemed to bunch and flex all by themselves, as if each fiber was trying to clamor for the attention of her fingers. *Finally* she arrived back at the fly of his jeans. The buzzing all over his body grew, impossibly, more intense.

His whole body thrummed in time with the quiet techno music that whispered in his ear. Shit, he was going to embarrass himself at this rate. A few firm tugs and Thad was free of his jeans. He gasped as the cool air of the room blew seductively over the tip of his erection. Following close behind was the sensation of those lovely, lovely fingers again. If he didn't know better, he'd have thought she had, like, twenty of them. First circling the tip, then brushing downward in long, too-gentle strokes.

"Isabel... fuck..."

Her free hand came up to his shoulder, gently pushing him back onto the bed. "Relax, Thad. Let me drive."

Unable to put words together in his head, he lay back as she commanded. For a moment—or maybe many moments—his eyes drifted shut. He usually took control in bed, but now he was inundated by sensation. Her fingers continued their gentle up and down, sending glorious shivers through him. The heat inside him that had begun to feel all-consuming faded only slightly, but God, it was good. So good.

The dark wrapped around Thad, and for the first time in a long time, he allowed himself to just… be. Funny how even with his eyelids closed, the stars in Isabel's sky shimmered and danced in his field of vision. Every touch of Isabel's hands, every breath of air heightened his euphoria until he was almost ready to swear that he truly was hurtling through space, completely out of control.

Or rather, under Isabel's control.

But suddenly, he was hit by an almost painful chill. His eyes opened. "Isabel what—" Oh. *Oh*. Not a sound was made when her clothing hit the floor. His pulse pounded double-time when those green eyes met his, moving closer and closer.

"Oh, yes." Creamy flesh slid over his own. Soft, voluptuous breasts and peaked nipples pressed against his chest, sensuously abrading his skin. Their gazes held and locked. Her eyes were captivating, one dark and glittery like the stars on the ceiling, one intensely stormy and sultry. He was feeling like he could be lost forever in those eyes, when… "Oh, *hell* yes."

Moist heat gripped his shaft. Isabel flowed around him like water. Each of her legs entwined with each of his, and her arms slid between his back and the mattress while her hips undulated and sweat slicked their bodies.

As if it had been written to score their lovemaking, the music in the room began to build and intensify. Drums thumped harder, and some sort of ethereal chanting mixed in just as his hands gripped two fist-fuls of Isabel's *perfect* ass. On her exhaled "Thad!" he growled and thrust hard, meeting every slide of her sex with the pump of his own. No longer content to leave the driving up to her, he grasped around her waist and lifted, shifting until she sat straight up astride his cock.

"Holy hell." A feminine stomach led up to that lush chest he was already so fond of, a chest that heaved in and out with every ragged breath. A strand or two of Isabel's hair clung to her cheek possessively. The rest cascaded down her back in dark waves. Her eyes were sensuous and wild. Hands down, she was the most amazing female he had ever seen.

Intense tribal beats sucked Thad back in time about a thousand years to the most feral part of his inner nature, spurring him to fuck her harder. Isabel's head dropped onto her shoulders, hands planted on his upper thighs. Nails dug into his skin, and he hissed at the pain and the pleasure of it. Hopefully they would leave a mark, at least for a little while.

She rode him faster, rising and falling in time with a primitive rhythm that seemed to take them on a journey, to lift them higher and higher, both panting and gasping as the sounds of skin against skin joined the claps and thumps and crashes that filled the air around them.

A bead of sweat made its way down her face from her temple... racing in fits and starts over her neck and chest. Thad's hands skimmed her stomach and rib cage, and he caught the errant drop with his thumb just as it entered the valley between her two luscious breasts. It eased the way for his thumb to sweep across the tight bud of one nipple, eliciting a heavenly gasp and shiver.

Isabel moaned and her core squeezed, milking him. A playful hand crept along his leg to gently massage his balls. Suddenly, Thad's orgasm bore down like a runaway tractor trailer with no brakes. "Isabel... I can't hold back." The music crescendoed, and thank the moon and stars above, throaty cries and spasms of muscle announced her release.

Knotting his hands in the sheets, he grabbed with all his strength to keep from launching off the mattress as he exploded into her. A white-hot wave of pleasure and pain swept through him, concentrating at the scar on his forearm. There was no controlling his body as it trembled and jerked with each climactic aftershock.

Fate help him, it had never been like *that* with anyone before.

When at last Thad floated down from Isabel's ceiling-sky, she had crawled up to meet him. Her hair was damp on his shoulder as she laid her head on it. So was his skin. Their sweat practically hung in the air, there was so much of it.

Isabel traced her finger along the side of Thad's jaw. "So, let's get to know each other, shall we?" Her green eyes twinkled at the joke. "Tell me about your family or something."

Thad was still working to catch his breath. Turning onto his side so he faced her, he finally found his voice. "I know... this is gonna sound nuts... but—"

Her lips found his, and they were sweet and soft, but why the hell had she stopped him from talking? "Hon, I feel really good right now, too," she said. "But trust me, I do this all the time. It's the wine that's making you feel all warm and fuzzy, and it's going to wear off."

She eased onto her back and stared up at the ceiling, entwining her fingers with his. "Now," she said, giving him a nudge with her shoulder. "Seriously. Let's do some more of that getting to know each other."

Thad stared at the ceiling. The glow of the stars seemed to have disappeared with his good mood. Sleepy and sated segued rather quickly into hot, angry embarrassment. His unfettered hand balled up in frustration.

Just the fucking wine. Seriously?

Chapter 8

JUST AFTER NOON, LEE FOUND HIMSELF STARING DOWN Alexia from across the room.

"Well, good morning, sunshine," she drawled as Lee removed a hand from his MK23. "That's an impressive piece of equipment you've got there."

"You're up early." He studied her from behind while she walked into the small kitchen area and stretched to retrieve a water bottle from a rickety cabinet with obnoxiously squeaky hinges. She was wearing running shorts and a tank top, and he couldn't help but note the muscle definition in her legs and arms that hadn't been apparent with the baggy pants she'd been wearing on the walk home from the club.

A tribal tattoo of some sort covered her left bicep and extended up over her shoulder, disappearing underneath the back of her shirt. Her hair had been washed with something that smelled of green tea, and the remains of her makeup had been scrubbed off, revealing soft, olive skin. He had to admit that she was rather attractive for a human.

She glanced at a clock above the stove. "Actually, I'm up late. Most of the human world has been out and about for hours. I'm off to the gym, and after that, I'll stop and pick up something to eat. You want anything in particular?"

The corner of his mouth quirked. "You provide delivery service?"

She hiked one lean shoulder up to her ear. "You guys can't go out and we're low on food. So yeah, I'm delivering."

"Thanks, but no need to worry about anything special for us." He wouldn't be beholden to a human for special favors.

"Suit yourself." She busied herself gathering her gym bag, filling her water bottle, tying her sneakers. She seemed to check and recheck her bag for something—a lot of bending over was involved. Eventually, the satisfaction in her face and the jingle of keys announced that she had found what she was looking for.

Lee cleared his throat. "So how is it you're so tight with Isabel?"

She leaned forward on the counter that separated the kitchen from the living room. "You mean how am I close friends with Isabel, or how am I close friends with a vampire?"

"It's a valid question. In our world, contact with humans is usually on a very limited basis. Long-term relationships, romantic or otherwise, aren't done all that often."

"Why not?"

"Just doesn't work out well, generally speaking. It risks exposure, and it's not really safe for either side. We have enemies who would delight in hearing you scream while they cut your heart out, if you were known to associate with us."

Actually, he didn't think wizards would bother to cut out a human heart, but he could see them engaging in a little recreational torture for the sake of information gathering. And sick bastard that he was, he derived a certain sense of satisfaction from Alexia's subtle gag.

He leaned back against the dilapidated, puke-green couch and looked at her thoughtfully. "Besides, human blood doesn't have the same properties, so feeding can be a problem."

"How so?" Her face held a frown of confusion. "Isabel drinks from humans all the time."

"It's just not the same. Not as good. For someone like me who needs strength for battle, it would never work. Vampire blood is richer. Stronger. It's best that we stick with our own species."

"Hmm." She bit her lip as she seemed to consider his words. "Not as good... gotcha." She sighed, flipped the top on her water bottle, and grabbed her keys. "Well, I guess I'm off."

"You never answered me."

"About what?"

"How did you and Isabel get so tight?"

"Why do you care?"

His raised his eyebrows at her. If only to himself, he admitted that he didn't want to think too hard about the answer. "I'm curious. I've been around a long while, and this is the first time I've seen a human kicking it in her living room with one of my kind as if it happened every day."

"It does happen every day. I live here, remember?"

Yeah. "That's kind of my point," he said. This female was infuriating. "You going to answer me?"

"Eh." She gave a halfhearted head tilt on her way toward the door. "Long story." She paused just as she stepped into the building's outer hallway. The leanness of her back and the revealing nature of her clothes gave a near-perfect picture of her spine when she turned slowly to make eye contact. It spiraled gracefully like an elegant staircase. "Actually, it's not that long. I just don't feel like telling you."

She turned and closed the door behind herself before he thought of a good response.

Bitch.

Having lived in the days when humans tended to chase after his kind with pitchforks and flaming torches, Lee was justified in his opinion of them. Where the hell did she get off acting so superior?

That his body responded to her as it would to any other attractive female just made his blood boil more. Taking humans as lovers on occasion was fairly common among his kind, but he had chosen never to do so. Certainly he had never wanted to feed from one. Not that he wanted to now.

It was curiosity. Novelty. He'd never wanted for willing partners of his own species, but he and Thad had been on the road for some time. The mission had him thinking with his dick.

He indulged for a second in the fantasy of what the rest of Alexia's petite body looked like without clothes on and how or even *if* their bodies would fit together, given their size difference. She'd have to be on top. She was so tiny that it was hard to imagine not crushing her otherwise. His mind's eye conjured up a picture of her riding him, hands stroking his chest, and breathing heavily like she would be after her workout. A pleasured snarl escaped from his lips.

He couldn't deny that it was tempting; she didn't seem to be the clingy type, and maybe he could engage in a noncommittal experiment to see if fucking a human was all the boys in the locker room had cracked it up to be before he and Thad blew town.

The erection raging between his legs was all for that ill-advised plan. It was still back on the part about what Alexia would look like in bed. Naked. Those skimpy gym clothes forgotten on the floor. *Christ*. He growled again and slid a hand over the hard length straining his fatigues, and then pulled it away with a groan.

No. He and Thad would be headed home soon enough, with or without Isabel. He could wait to find a hookup when they returned or at least get some sparring in with Tyra or Siddoh to take the edge off. He trained his stare on Isabel's bedroom door. Even without strings, sex with the human was a distraction he didn't need.

Chapter 9

HE'S MAD AT ME.

Blowing off Thad's declaration of burgeoning love was inevitably going to sting a little. This wasn't the first time Isabel had needed to let someone down gently. Maybe he was a little disappointed, but what he'd felt wasn't real. It was the drink. Wasn't he smart enough to understand that? He was trying to hide it, but the flush of his neck and the tight ball of his fist spoke of a male who was grappling with aggression. And that bothered Isabel a lot more than it should have.

The passage of time was hard to grasp in her current state, but they seemed to have stayed there a long time—him staring silently at the ceiling with jaw set and eyes narrowed, and her grasping his hand and waiting. She didn't know what to do with the insecurity that filled her and made her jittery.

She rarely got depressed when she'd been drinking. That was a big part of the draw. If she spent her nights buzzed on red wine, she didn't ever need to be alone with all of her morose thoughts. All of a sudden, though, a well of hidden emotion sprang up in the center of this awkward silence they were sharing. She cursed the burn of tears in her eyes and blinked rapidly to clear them away before they fell. That she had upset him made her stomach knot up and her chest get tight, and she didn't understand why.

Fuck him if he couldn't handle it. Right?

She had untangled her fingers from his and started to pull away when he stretched his hand and began to rub her arm in long, slow strokes. Her skin buzzed and hummed at his touch. "Is it all right if I do this?"

She moaned quietly through her closed lips and nodded slowly. "Mmm. Feels good," she murmured. Too good, in fact. She wasn't used to being on the receiving end of such a basic but decadent pleasure.

He got bolder, tracing the veins over her wrist with his fingers, then traveling with the flat of his hand up her arm again and finally across her collarbone. His fingertips brushed over the raised network of scars, lingering longest at the big one on her neck. A deep, drawn-out inhale made her wonder if perhaps he was trying to tease out the scent of her blood, as her mother had once spoken about. Or if maybe the fact that two of the marks intersected just at her pulse point turned him off.

And why the hell did she care? She was fooling herself if she thought for one single minute that this idea of being the king's destiny was even a remote possibility. Things like that didn't happen to her. It wasn't safe for her or anybody else if she got too close. That she had put Lexi in danger earlier that night was a painful reminder.

The moist heat of Thad's tongue traveled over her throat. "I've never let anyone touch me there," Isabel whispered. Oh, God. What was she saying? How many times had her blood hosts poured their souls out to her? They didn't call red wine the "vampire hug drug" for nothing. That was twice in one night she had acted without thinking.

"I'm glad you let me." A zingy kind of tingle spread

throughout her jaw when Thad rubbed the largest of the scars again. The thickest, ugliest one that ran from behind her earlobe to the base of her neck. "I want you to tell me about them," he murmured as he gently traced the small one on her cheek with a fingernail. It seemed impossible, but the feathery brushes of his skin against hers weren't bothersome. They were… nice. Pleasurable.

And out of the blue, she wanted to tell Thad everything. Not wanted. She *had* to.

"That one…" Isabel swallowed against the gentle pressure of his hand. "A piece of glass got stuck in it."

He nodded and continued a gentle one-handed massage over her jaw, neck, and shoulder. It made her whole body melt. "Was it some kind of accident?"

Isabel turned onto her back and stared at the ceiling, picking out the Big Dipper. It was the only constellation she knew, and she had made a point of putting it over the bed when she and Alexia had covered the ceiling with stars. Isabel's version had a greenish-glowing likeness of Han Solo perched on the handle. Ready for battle.

It was pleasant but mystifying that, for the moment, she was more or less at peace. "My parents and I were driving across this bridge." She took a very slow, very deep breath. As she let it out, a gentle shiver spread over her body, both energizing and relaxing her. "Traffic stopped. It was foggy… there was a pileup. This whole cluster of cars and trucks went off the bridge, and we were right in the middle of it."

Thad's fingers tightened around hers.

She kept going. "The windows all shattered and I was hit by a lot of flying glass. I…" *Just breathe*. "I could tell my parents were dead. I got out through the back window, but I don't remember anything else after I surfaced from the water. At the hospital I guess they thought I was dead, too. There were shards stuck in my neck and in my eye. Somebody was picking broken pieces out of my hair when I woke up."

"I'm so sorry, Isabel."

Isabel's head rocked side to side in a lazy shake. "Don't be. It is what it is; it's part of who I am. Can't change it now." Not that she hadn't tried. The past decades had been a ticker tape of bargaining and blame. Aimed at herself for arguing with her parents from the backseat, at her dad for hitting the car in front of them, at the truck behind them for not stopping soon enough, and so on. All in the not-so-subconscious hope that pointing enough fingers could somehow change the outcome of the past.

"It's hard not to be," he said.

Yeah, she guessed it probably was. She wasn't ready to tell him about the human.

Most days, the emotions were suffocating if she allowed herself to think about that, and she spent a lot of effort on keeping the memories at bay. She could still see the orderly's pale body on a stark white floor when she closed her eyes. The bright red trickle of blood that dripped from his neck. Could still feel the wax of a crayon-and-construction-paper drawing that had been folded up in the pocket of his lab coat. For once, she allowed the sorrow to wash over her and it wasn't completely paralyzing. Isabel sighed. She'd done what she'd had to for survival. Why hadn't knowing that ever helped?

Thad propped his head on one hand. "How old were you?"

"I don't remember exactly. I want to say it was 1966. Maybe 1967. I guess I was thirteen. I remember that the Monkees were on the radio. I haven't liked listening to them since then." Their songs had always brought back unpleasant memories.

Thad smiled slightly, just enough to show the tip of a fang. "I never liked listening to the Monkees very much anyway."

Isabel wasn't sure she had ever laughed the way she laughed right then. Not because it was the biggest or the loudest laugh—really, it was barely a chuckle. But it was pure, something she had managed because she felt comfortable and safe like she never had before.

"So, listen. My father began his rule in the Middle Ages. Near the end of them, I guess." He blew out a puff of air. "Anyway, I don't know much about his life before he mated my mother, aside from the fact that he fell in love with a human and she gave birth to my sister, Tyra. That was a big scandal."

Isabel wrinkled her forehead. "Did she become queen?" *Could* a human be queen? Not that she knew much about it, but that seemed unlikely.

"I don't know the whole story." He shook his head and licked his lips thoughtfully. It brought back a memory of what his tongue had been like sliding against hers. She took his hand in both of hers and began a little pressing and kneading action on his palm.

"Apparently she disappeared and then showed back up with Tyra, then disappeared again. No one really knew what happened to her after that. Dad loved Ty, but he was pretty tight-lipped about her mom. Like I said. Scandal. What you're doing to my hand feels reeeally good, by the way."

"Gives a whole new meaning to the phrase 'hand job,' doesn't it?" Isabel smiled and met his gaze for only a second. She did love to make others feel good.

His answering laugh was husky and sensual. "Right."

"Your sister."

"Yeah. So... my sister was born about twenty years before I was. Somewhere in that time, I guess my father and mother were mated, and then there was me." For a short while, neither of them spoke. His chest rose and fell with his breath. "And then my father left the family estate alone one night and was killed. My mother felt his life force die out so she cut her own wrists as well."

Isabel gasped. "Oh shit, Thad. I'm so sorry."

"No, it's okay. Really," he added. Her doubt must have been obvious. "My parents loved each other so much that my mother couldn't live without him. I miss them both, but it's an amazing example of the kind of love I hope to have."

"Talk about putting a positive spin," she mumbled.

He smiled a little wider at that. "I try."

Thad closed his eyes and seemed to revel in the motion of her fingers against his hand, or maybe he was trying to hang on to the wispy tendrils of a high that she knew was fading for both of them. In the silence, a significant question popped into her head.

"Thad?"

"Hmm?"

"You said your father became king in the Middle Ages? How did he go so long without a mate?"

He swore under his breath. "Technically speaking," he said slowly, "our law does not require the king to be mated."

"Technically?"

"Technically."

"But *you* need a mate to be king?" Thad opened his eyes to look at her again. They really were quite lovely. Lexi had a poster in her room of a sunset off the coast of Fiji. It was the same kind of blue as his eyes. Rich and deep, with a glow that seemed to come from Heaven itself.

He turned to his side, facing her again. "I don't need *a* mate. I need one very specific mate." Slow and precise speech, it would seem, was his way of making sure she took him seriously. Or maybe he thought she was slow, but she preferred to think the former.

"Me," she said, finally.

His response was to reach out with his free hand, brushing fingertips lightly across her lower back and tracing the stretch of skin that bore her matching scar. Each bump and pucker of her skin rose up to greet him as he stroked gently over the too-familiar shape. A hot throbbing sensation spread from its epicenter throughout the rest of her body. "It would seem so, yes. And I would bet that patch of skin where you're branded is aching and pulsing just like mine."

Isabel opened her mouth but couldn't manage to say anything.

"Can I ask you something?" he murmured.

"Sure."

"About Alexia. You never really answered me."

"We, uh, met in the party scene."

"Care to elaborate on that?"

She smiled. Her buzz was fading and the impish side of her was coming out to play. "I can, but I'm not sure you're going to like it."

"You drank from her, didn't you?"

She nodded.

"Do you still—"

"No," she said quickly. "Not for a long time now."

"So why didn't you wipe her memory?"

That was an excellent question. "I tried. It didn't work. We ended up becoming friends."

His mouth formed a silent "oh." It wasn't clear whether he had more to say, but a hearty knock on the door effectively ended the conversation. Truth be told, Isabel welcomed the intrusion. The weight of their conversation was making her twitchy now that she was sobering up. "Yo, Izzy, I've got doughnuts! The 'Hot' sign was on!"

Mmm. A rumble of anticipation came out of Isabel's stomach. Nothing she loved like a fresh glazed doughnut.

She bounded off the bed to open the door. According to the clock, they'd been together in the dimly lit room for many hours. Somehow, it barely seemed like minutes had passed. Time really did fly sometimes.

"Hey, Lex, did you get coffee too?" It was midafternoon, and Isabel hadn't slept yet. Something told her she wouldn't get the chance until Thad and his bodyguard left town.

"You bet," Lexi called as she headed back toward the kitchen.

"Oh, I could kiss you. We'll be out in a sec!"

"What's the hot sign?"

What? Isabel spun around. "Hello, the 'Hot' sign at Krispy Kreme? Don't tell me you've never had a Krispy Kreme."

He held his palms up. "Sorry. Not a big staple of my diet."

Okay. All heavy stuff aside, she had to introduce this male to the pleasures of a nice warm doughnut. "Well, you've gotta get out here and try one then. They totally melt in your mouth when they're warm."

Reaching back toward where he now sat on the bed, she tugged his arm and led him out the door.

Anton surfaced to consciousness, aware of little more than the impossible combination of searing agony and bone-numbing chill that engulfed his body. The sounds around him indicated that he was in the woods. Wasn't that where the Master had told them to leave him? He wondered why he'd been allowed to live, or if perhaps they had assumed he wouldn't. Why hadn't they bled him out to ensure that his body turned to dust? Maybe they wanted him to suffer before he kicked it.

Through the fog of pain he attempted to take stock of his injuries. His skull throbbed, his skin had been stripped off his body in many places, and for some reason he was unable to open his eyes. And that was just the good stuff. The fact that he was bruised and probably sporting a few broken bones was the least of his problems. His stomach was full of acid, and he wasn't sure he could move. Dampness on his skin indicated that it was slicked with a whole lot of fresh blood, and if his former comrades didn't return to kill him, it was only a matter of time before some predatory animal would.

He pictured Tyra's face in his head, and hot tears began to stream down his temples. The woman he'd been sent to capture for his father's use and had fallen in love with instead. The ache of humiliation over failing to warn her in time was more excruciating than any physical pain he could bear. He could only hope that he'd bought her some time.

Without a doubt, if Petros got his hands on her, she would be captured. At best, she would be killed. At worst... he couldn't bear to think about that. He had to get the fuck out of here. Had to find her. Somehow, he had to warn her. Providing he could get her to listen. Providing he could even get himself off the ground. That last bit was looking very iffy.

He shifted his right arm slightly and groaned at the pain. Broken wrist, he would wager. And—*gaaah*—ribs, too. He was still naked. Patches of skin were stiff and sticky. The coating of blood would soon dry or freeze all over. Hypothermia was a distinct possibility. It was winter, after all.

As much as Anton despised himself for it, now was the time when he needed to use the only power he had ever acquired. If he even could. Agony shot through him as he willed his arm off his body to lie palm up by his side. The left one was already there. Excellent. Things were looking up already.

A wave of nausea rolled from Anton's gut to his throat. The stars behind his eyelids suggested that he might black out again, and then he would be 100 percent screwed. He willed himself to focus, to perk the fuck up just a little so he could perhaps save himself from bleeding out or leaking gray matter onto the forest floor.

He saw Tyra's face in his mind's eye, protecting and caring for the homeless souls in that shelter he'd tracked her to. She was everything he wasn't: beautiful, pure... *good*. Even if he made it out of here in one piece, even if he saved her, there was no chance she would ever return his affection.

Even if they weren't supposed to be sworn mortal enemies, she would probably take him for some kind of psycho. That falling-in-love-from-afar shit was the stuff of Hallmark movies, not for the son of evil incarnate looking to reform himself and a half-human vampire who could probably use him as a shot put. If he hadn't known she was still in extreme danger, he would have been inclined to just give it up and let himself die here in... wherever he was.

Focus, asshole. Panic caused Anton's heart rate to surge. He had to get out of here. He had to get the fuck out of here. Tyra was still in danger, and pain or no pain, he needed to get his act together if he had so much as a snowball's chance of saving her.

A deep breath set off a coughing fit, and white-hot agony shot through his chest and arm. A punctured lung, maybe? He focused all the brain power he could muster, until... Hallelujah... he felt the sensation of static electricity at his fingertips. His body began to get warm. It was working.

"Thank God," Anton murmured. Never mind that God was probably waiting to smite him. God was gonna have to get in line.

An arc of energy sparked from one palm to another,

but it was as weak as the rest of him. Thankfully, the excruciating pounding in his skull seemed to be dialing itself down to a mere agonizing throb. Some sort of pulse began to flow between his hands, but after a few seconds the energy faded again. God *fucking* dammit!

Through his mental fog, he registered a distinct shuffle of footsteps. Leaves rustled and twigs cracked, and Anton knew it was too much to hope that some friendly woodland creature had come bearing painkillers and a change of clothes for him.

"No." A bone-deep understanding sank in. They had not, in fact, decided to leave him alive. His father's last kiss-off to the son he'd so despised had been to give the illusion of a reprieve when there was none. They were coming back to finish him off. With what he knew to be one of his last remaining breaths, he prayed that perhaps his beloved Tyra still might be saved. Sure, God was probably pissed, but praying was all Anton had left.

Heavy boot steps halted just short of stepping on Anton's head, and a handful of blurry figures gathered around him. Then, there was nothing but darkness again.

Chapter 10

Movement stopped Thad short just as he was buttoning his pants. Isabel was behind him. Her citrusy scent filled his nostrils, and just by remembering what had transpired after he'd smelled it the first time, he could practically feel the heat of her mouth on him. Lemons would never be the same again.

She didn't seem to know that he was aware of her presence, so he took advantage of the opportunity to do what males of every species have done in the presence of a desired mate since the beginning of time: he showed off his assets.

He left the button undone and pushed his Sliders jeans down discreetly under the guise of resting his hands on his hips while he studied her collage of party flyers. Most of them seemed to be from Insomniac, the club where they had "met."

Then he squeezed his shoulder blades a bit and stretched as one would upon waking, complete with a low groan, before flexing and reaching in an exaggerated arc to grab his shirt from her bed. It all felt incredibly silly, but when his sensitive ears picked up the slight hitch in her breath, he smiled with satisfaction.

"Hey there," he said, turning to her as he shrugged into a denim button-down shirt.

She ran her gaze back over Thad and licked her lips a little. Once or twice she returned to the medallion on his chest before she spoke. "I didn't mean to barge in. I kind of thought you'd be dressed already."

Since Alexia had first returned with the doughnuts, things had taken a decidedly uncomfortable turn. The open, impassioned, connected energy that had flowed between them a few hours earlier in this very room seemed to have evaporated with the last sizzle of effect from the wine they had consumed together.

Talk of her returning home with him had been met with a very bleak "I can't," and despite the small size of the apartment, she and Alexia had both managed to avoid him successfully for a good while as he and Lee discussed strategies for after they returned home.

She was nervous and fidgety now. Distant. Still, he said, "Nothing you haven't already seen. Thanks for letting me use your shower, by the way." The suggestive smile he gave her only made her step back a little.

Damn.

"I see you left your number," she said quietly. "So. I'll call you."

He nodded. "Good. I hope you do." A small smile came to her lips as he drew close and tucked a silky strand of auburn hair behind her ears. Her eyes, however, remained strangely vacant. Like in her mind she had already said good-bye.

Still, he refused to let her off the hook too easily. He maintained eye contact as he fastened his fly and buttoned his shirt. This, too, he did more slowly than needed. Isabel might be trying to pull away, but clearly the desire was still there for both of them. Her eyes flicked repeatedly to follow his fingers, telling him he was right about that. He didn't intend to let her forget it.

His leather jacket went on and they stood staring at each other, an awkward silence stretching between them.

Gently, Thad reached forward and threaded his fingers through hers. Just as she had done with him earlier while they were lying together on the bed. There was a low rumble in his voice. "Thank you for today. I truly enjoyed it." He winked suggestively. "In more ways than one. I do hope you'll give some thought to what we discussed. Maybe just come visit. Stay a few days. No pressure."

"I definitely will."

They were lying to each other. The nervous dart of her eyes, the sudden flush of her neck... she had no intention of calling. Was she hoping he'd simply forget that the safety of their race was on the line? That a well-placed meteor would strike earth and wipe out all of their wizard enemies in one fell swoop?

For his part, Thad had assured her that she could take all the time she needed to think things over, but that wasn't true, either. Time was running short. His earlier conversation with Tyra had revealed that a conservative member of the Elders' Council was pushing for the society to be run by committee only, effectively rendering Thad's position obsolete. Having that gang of old bastards at the helm would send their society back into the Dark Ages.

And all of the political stuff aside, there was a pull between Isabel and himself that he could not ignore. She didn't seem able to ignore it either, but she was really fighting hard. He suspected that she had not opened up to many about the gruesome death of her parents. Subsequent questions had led to her hesitant admission that she had drifted for some time, feeding from humans and hiding from the sun in abandoned buildings and the like before stumbling onto the rave scene.

It was heart-wrenching to know that she had been on her own from such a young age. He wasn't the sharpest knife in the drawer when it came to the emotions of females, but he would wager that opening up had left her feeling quite vulnerable.

So yeah, he'd give her a little space. Enough to regroup and to come up with a plan for convincing her to be by his side. And if he couldn't convince her? Well, he was the king, for crying out loud. He'd make it happen one way or another. After all, he knew where she lived now. Even if she went elsewhere to hide, he could find her as he had before. She had to know that.

This was only the beginning.

The moment was broken when Lee banged loudly on the door. "Yo, T, your sister's here."

Thad smiled, squeezed Isabel's hand again, and turned to go. "Coming."

Lee was on high alert. Thad's sister was pacing the tiny living room with a black duffel bag slung over one shoulder. It was one of the two she'd retrieved from Thad's rental SUV a short while before. Lee had taken his and changed into a clean T-shirt. He was now checking and rechecking the clock, feeling as antsy as she looked.

"Something's coming, Lee," Tyra said.

He'd already begun to screw the silencer onto his H&K MK23.

"Yep."

The inky black yuck that wizards went around cloaked in was permeating his senses. For most vampires, that was a clear sign to run the hell away. The closer the wizards got, the stronger the urge was to turn tail. Lee had spent a lot of centuries conditioning himself to run toward it instead.

"Better get ready," he told Tyra. "Thad, stay with Isabel," he called over his shoulder.

Tyra shook her head but drew her gun anyway, keeping it cocked and locked. "I don't understand. How could they find us here?"

"Doesn't matter how; just matters that we have to get everyone out of here." He held up a hand for quiet as he cast his senses about to ascertain what they were up against. Despite his centuries of experience, that was always hard to determine. A wizard's malevolent aura varied in strength depending on how many there were, how powerful they were, and how close by. With sickening clarity, he realized that there was a good chance he couldn't get a direction because the bastards were right the hell on top of them.

The door of one of the bedrooms opened quietly, and Thad stepped out with a large knife in his grip, one arm back to keep Isabel herded behind him. He'd felt it, too.

"I don't get it. Everything was quiet. How'd they show up so suddenly?"

"I think I brought them," Tyra said. "But I don't know how. I didn't sense anything until just after I got here."

Lee started toward Alexia's door, "Tyra, cover Thad and Isabel. I'm gonna grab the human."

Tyra's eyebrows shot up. "There's a human he—"

A strangled cry and a loud thud cut her off.

Lee shoved into Alexia's room just in time to see her body crumple onto a flowery area rug. A mangled chocolate doughnut with incongruously festive colored sprinkles remained clutched in her hand. His extra-sensory hearing picked up her breathing, but she sure didn't look good. Her skin was pale, her forehead was bruised—and he was gonna kick some fucking wizard ass for the split in her lip.

There was just the one, but it was bigger than most. Soldiers like Lee were bred for their power and size, but wizards generally used their theft of vampire powers to compensate for their lack of physical prowess.

"Not so fast there, vampire. I can end her in a second." The wizard pointed a long finger. Poised on the tip was a small marble of light. "Nice human you have here." The smug bastard smiled and waggled his eyebrows, and Lee cursed. "Well, not that nice, actually. The bitch tried to attack me. Quite a little firecracker. Now, I suggest you stay right there. She's still alive, but just barely."

Lee set his jaw. "She's nothing to us." His attention stayed focused on the magic projectile at the end of the wizard's finger. He couldn't tell what kind of firepower that orb was packing, but he wasn't taking chances. He extended his free arm downward, palm out. An invisible aura of hot energy radiated first from his hand and then outward from his entire body, even as he kept his gun trained on the enemy in front of him.

The wizard let out a dark chuckle. "I imagine she's something, or else she wouldn't be here in your midst. Now is that the lovely Tyra I see over your shoulder?" Lee didn't move. It would take a hell of a lot more than that to distract him.

The cords in Lee's neck pulled tight as he focused on the shield radiating around him until it filled the doorway. "Ty," he growled under his breath. "Get 'em out of here."

There was a rustle of movement. Thad murmured reassurances to his female. "It's going to be okay, Isabel. Just close your eyes." No doubt that female had gotten a whole lot more than she'd bargained for tonight.

The wizard took the opportunity to strike, hurling a stream of concentrated light just over Lee's shoulder in an attempt to hit Ty or Thad before they vanished. The bright projectiles hit Lee's energetic aura and exploded on impact. The force knocked Lee to the side and jarred his shoulder something crazy but otherwise did little harm. The superior gleam in the wizard's eyes disappeared.

The air at Lee's back stirred as Tyra disappeared with the other two, and the wizard bellowed his anger: "That's an interesting power you have there, vampire." He took a run at Lee, but Lee launched forward, snarling and palming a dagger just before their two bodies crashed in midair. Faster than the inferior wizard could blink, Lee thrust his arm up and sideways, slicing cleanly across the throat. It was a low cut, close to the collarbone, and Lee barely flinched when a warm, acrid spurt of the wizard's blood hit him front and center.

The wizard's actions were classic: Hands groped desperately to stop the bleeding, but it continued to flow steadily through cracks between the male's fingers. His effort was no more effective than stopping the great floods with a cocktail napkin. But they always tried. Every living thing tried.

There was a gasp and a gurgle as the dude tried to draw breath. A leg sweep from Lee laid him out on the floor, a few feet from Alexia's body. The wizard clawed and shook, but he was fading fast. Anger was all over his face. More gurgling and sputtering, more clawing, and finally the robed figure went still.

"Jeez, Lee. You killed him." Lee turned to see Tyra standing in the doorway.

He grunted. "Works every time. They're paying attention to the gun so they don't think about the other hand. Stupid motherfuckers." He shook his head and toed at the body, looking it over for any possible signs of life. It never hurt to double check.

"K, but you killed our only shot at knowing how they found me." She said it patiently, like he was simple. "No wizard has ever managed to follow me before, and we're like a thousand miles from home."

Closer to eight hundred, but he was smart enough not to correct her hyperbole.

"Kinda doesn't matter now. Killing that thing was too damn easy, which means either he was a stupid cowboy or there are more on the way, and it's better if we don't stick around to find out. Besides, we'll get another shot. If it was you they tracked, they'll find you again." He jerked his head toward Alexia, ignoring Tyra's answering eye roll. "She's hurt pretty bad."

Tyra nodded. "Grab her."

First, Lee got down on his haunches and looked over the dead wizard. Typically, vampires would slice and dice vanquished wizards a little, and then relieve the bastards of their stupid robe getup. Once the body drained, it would crumble to dust like a vampire left out in the day. Short on time, Lee settled for a quick vertical slice on each wrist and hoped for the best.

A tug on the wizard's finger netted one fugly signet ring, embossed with a small heart. Lee stowed it in his pocket before turning to Alexia. She was definitely still breathing, and he detected a pulse, but it was very faint. Shock, maybe.

Even as deadweight the girl couldn't have been more than a buck ten, and lifting her was child's play. "Wait." He yanked a fleece throw from a nearby futon and tossed it over her before propping her face-forward against his shoulder. Not a chance in hell he was gonna get wizard blood on her.

Tyra gasped. Unseen while Alexia had been lying like a rag doll on the carpet, a deep, inflamed wound crossed her back and shoulder blade. Whatever the wizard had hit her with seemed to have cauterized on impact, so at least she hadn't lost a ton of blood. But that didn't explain why she was unconscious, and that was a bigger worry.

"All right," Lee growled. "Let's just get home." He wanted to put Alexia down as soon as possible. That disgusting, fetid wizard blood was seeping into the blanket.

Tyra gripped Lee's shoulder gently, wrapping her opposite arm around Alexia's body. He glanced around at the sparse furnishings. White walls, red futon. Small cheapo desk with one of those tiny netbook things on it. The only other furniture was a giant industrial shelving-unit packed full of books that the girl would never read again.

Lee braced for the inevitable loss of control as Tyra turned all of their bodies into nothing more than vapor.

Damn, but he hated to travel this way. Tyra closed her eyes and drew a deep breath, gathering the power and strength she would need to move so much weight a second time. Alexia's blonde hair faded before his eyes.

Then they were gone.

Chapter 11

THAD SAT NEXT TO ISABEL ON A PRISTINE WHITE PADDED bench in the pristine front hall of what was now his pristine home, wondering how things had gotten so messy so fast. The foyer's large, glittery chandelier cast the kind of elegant glow one would expect to see at a dinner party, and Thad couldn't figure out how the light could be so bright when their moods were so dark.

It probably had been Isabel's first time seeing a wizard. That alone would be a shock, even without the added head fuck of seeing her roommate in a heap on the carpet and then teleporting across the East Coast. She was wide eyed and slack jawed, with a healthy dose of this-is-not-happening all over her face.

Thad grasped her palm and gently interlaced his fingers with hers. Her hands were the softest things he'd ever touched, and they shook like crazy. He struggled with how best to care for her. How could he reassure her when he wasn't entirely sure how it would all turn out? When they'd left, they hadn't even been sure whether Alexia was alive or dead.

"Listen, I know you're probably shaken up right now. I just want you to know I'm going to do whatever I can for you, okay?" She nodded slightly. "Okay." He took a deep breath. "Now, maybe you should lie down. I can get a room prep—"

"No." She squeezed his hand. A good sign. "No. I

don't—I don't want to go anywhere until I know Lexi's all right." Her emerald eyes widened and focused on Thad. "She will be, right?"

He had, of course, no freaking clue. "We'll do our best. Lee and Tyra wouldn't leave her. They'll be back any minute now."

Thad looked up and, as if on cue, the three materialized in the foyer. "Brayden! Ivy!" Lee called. As if she'd been waiting for Lee's command, Thad's house manager came running in at breakneck speed with her long, black hair flapping behind her.

"Sorry, Thad. I was in my office dealing with development requests and I didn't know you were ba—Oh, my God," Ivy said. She stopped short, eyeing Alexia's body as Lee laid her down gently on the deep-blue-and-green diamond-patterned carpet.

Relief pushed the breath out of Thad's lungs. Lee had called for the doctor, so Alexia was still alive. Thad waved his hand, dismissing the apology. "Ivy, I want you to grab Brayden, pronto. Then I want you to find a couple of guest rooms for Isabel here…" His head tilted sideways. "And her friend, for *when* she's feeling better." He put stress on the "when."

Ivy disappeared down the hall, her hair flowing in the breeze once more.

Isabel stood, still clutching Thad's hand. He hated the circumstances but loved that she clung to him for support. Stopping about a foot from Alexia's small form, she leaned forward. "She's going to be okay," she said again. "Right?"

Thad squeezed her hand again. "They'll take great care of her."

"Thad. Hey." Greg Brayden approached briskly, and from the look of his flannel pants and rumpled T-shirt, he was straight out of bed. "Sorry. Ivy woke me; I overslept this evening."

Why was everyone apologizing to him? Cripes. When his father was alive, no one had apologized to Thad for shit. Getting apologies now made him squirmy.

"Just take care of her," he muttered, gesturing toward Alexia's body. He tugged Isabel's arm gently, urging her away so Brayden could get a look at her friend.

Thad resisted the urge to rub at the pain in his chest. He ached to make this better for Isabel, and he was completely, totally, utterly helpless to do anything but wait for Brayden's assessment.

Kneeling by the body, the doctor did his thing. Checked her over, took her pulse, flashed a penlight in the eyes, and whatnot. Thad wondered if Brayden slept with the penlight in his jammies, given the way he'd conjured it up so fast. Isabel cringed beside him when Alexia's body was rolled forward, exposing the nasty wound under her shoulder blade. Brayden prodded at it gently and then rocked back onto his heels.

"Well, the good news is, it doesn't actually look that bad," he said, running his hand through his bedhead. "She's unresponsive, but shock and trauma could cause that. She's got some bruising around her temple. The wound on her back is deep, but it didn't hit anything major. Might have effed-up her tennis game a little."

Lee scowled. "What caused the wound?"

"Hard to say, but the skin around it is pink and inflamed, almost like a sunburn. Could have been some sort of concentrated UV thing. Lucky she's human, I guess."

There was something you didn't hear every day.

Isabel stepped forward, still gripping Thad's hand. "What can you do for her?"

Brayden's brow furrowed. "We can give her blood to speed the healing. Other than that, just wait and see, I suppose. I'd X-ray the head, but we don't have equipment here and I hate to transport her across town just now. We'll need to get an X-ray, though, if we can't wake her soon."

"I'll do it." Isabel said immediately. "She can have my blood."

Thad squeezed her hand again. "It's better if someone else does it," he said gently.

"She's my friend." Isabel twisted free of Thad's grasp, and her eyes glittered with unshed tears. "I want to do it."

"The older the vampire, the stronger the blood. You must know that." His shoulders pulled back, and he looked over at the doctor. "It's better if Brayden does it himself. Or Lee."

Brayden nodded quickly. "I'd be happy to provide for her if you like."

"I'll do it," Lee said abruptly. "Just tell me how you wanna play it, doc. Should we move her first?"

"Better we give her the blood first. We'll get her settled when we're done with that." He paused to look up at Lee. "You want a scalpel?"

Thad noticed Brayden reaching for the medical bag sitting between his feet. So much for the theory of him sleeping with a penlight.

Lee pulled an unnecessarily large knife from his boot. "Got it covered, doc."

Lee held his wrist above Alexia's mouth and drew the tip down as Brayden tipped her head back and gently pulled her chin down. After a bit of blood had drizzled in, Brayden massaged her throat to force a swallow and then held up his hand.

"I think that's enough for now."

Lee drew his brows together. "It wasn't much at all."

"You're one of our oldest, Lee. Your blood is so strong that we don't need a lot, and she's not conscious so I don't want to risk aspiration. Let's go ahead and move her. If she comes to soon, you can give her more. If not, I can try to transfuse her."

Lee licked the score on his arm and stepped back, turning to Thad. "I'm going to go clean up and then check in with Siddoh. See how things have been going since we left."

"Sounds good, man. Just follow up with me before dawn, if you would."

Lee nodded again curtly and stalked down the west hallway toward his room.

Thad looked up at Tyra, who had been a silent observer on the periphery. "You've been awfully quiet."

"I guess I'm trying to analyze the whole thing, you know?" Tyra cocked her head to the side. "Just doesn't make sense... I don't know." She waved her hand. "No matter. Maybe I'll pop in later when you have your pow-wow with Lee. We can talk about it then." She smiled kindly at Isabel. "I'm sorry we had to meet on such difficult terms, sweetie. I'm sure we'll talk more later."

Turning back to Brayden, Tyra rubbed her hands together. "All right, doc, let me help you get her down the hall before I go."

Brayden gestured toward the east hall, from where he'd originally come. "I think Ivy usually puts guests in the rooms next door to hers. We can put her in one of those."

Watching them go, Thad reached again for Isabel's hand. He so wanted to help her make sense of things, to sort out the confusion for her. That said, he had a lot of unanswered questions himself. "Come on, let's get you settled. We can talk more if you want, or you can just get some rest. I'll put you right next door to Alexia."

She bit her lip and nodded. Her face bore the vacant expression of someone who was too shaken up to process anything. "Yeah, sure… that would be… good."

Isabel floated down the long hallway, aimless and clumsy but for Thad's grip on her hand, like one of those giant parade balloons they always showed on television. She was so shaky, and her head swam with confusion.

Who would have thought that things could get worse *after* being told that she was destined to be queen of a race she'd never known?

Inviting Thad and Lee back to their place had been such a mistake. Alexia might never have been harmed, and both she and Isabel would have gone back to their boring but safe little lives by now.

They stopped at an open doorway, as the female named Ivy stepped out of the room. With her gorgeous mane of black hair and tan skin, *she* looked like the type who could be queen. Not Isabel, with her Halloween mask of a face.

"There are fresh towels and a robe, and if you leave

your clothes out here by the door, someone will come by to wash them for you." The female reached out and touched Isabel's arm gently. "Brayden is still with her, and her color looks better already."

Isabel barely managed to command her tongue. "Thank you."

Ivy turned to Thad. "What else can I do for you, sir?" *Sir*. It was so surreal. Thad wasn't a "sir." He was some guy Isabel had met at a party.

He shook his head. "You go do whatever you need to do, Ivy. I'll handle it from here."

"Brayden asked me to help keep an eye on the human, so I'll be right next door if you need anything."

"Great. Thanks."

She bobbed her head and left.

Thad pushed the open door a bit to widen the view into the room. It was much bigger than Isabel's own, but somehow not austere or cold. Cute little tables flanked the queen-sized bed, and the walls were an unassuming eggshell color, accented by an attractive border of brown and teal that matched the duvet. A comfortable reading chair sat in the corner to her left, and one of those elegant but clunky tall dressers dominated the corner to her right. Dim lights glowed, and the bed was turned down. Isabel had to admit that it was awfully inviting.

Thad's hand was on her arm. "I know it's still early in the evening, but you and I didn't sleep at all during the day, and I know that this has all been a lot to handle. I figure maybe you want to just get some rest."

Isabel worked her lip between her teeth. Glancing back and forth between the two rooms, she was plagued by indecision. Leaving Alexia alone didn't feel right, but damned if her adrenaline hadn't just crashed and left her running on fumes. She wasn't sure how much longer she could remain upright.

Thad squeezed her hand, like maybe he got it. "I promise you, she's in great hands."

Isabel bit her lip again. "I am really tired." As if on cue, her eyelids drooped to half-mast.

"Go ahead and rest. I'll make sure you know as soon as anything changes with her."

Leading Isabel into the room, Thad grabbed a plush terry robe from the bathroom and laid it on the bed. "In case you want to shower or change clothes."

She nodded but remained rooted to the spot where she had stopped, just inside the room. It was funny how times of stress could either spur you to action or leave you frozen in place. When her parents died, she had had no choice but to run. To survive. Now, she was sort of adrift and unsure. Empty. Something as simple as whether she should go put on the robe or get straight into bed was a monumental decision that she just couldn't manage to make.

Thad decided for her. His large, reassuring hands pulled aside the covers and guided Isabel gently by the shoulders over to the bed. She started to get in and then hesitated once more. "Thad?"

"Yeah, is there something else you need?" He snapped his fingers and pointed at her. "I should get you something to eat. All you had today was doughnuts and coffee." He started toward the door. "I'll run to the kitchen myself."

"No." Isabel hesitated, shaking her head slowly. She hated herself a little for what she was about to ask. Just then, she was numb and freaked out enough to admit the reality that she needed comfort. That she couldn't be alone.

"No, Thad. I just—I was wondering if maybe you could stay with me for a while?" When he stopped and turned toward her, she went cold. She shouldn't have asked. "Or not. I mean, I know you have... stuff to do probably. So listen, just never mind." She sat on the bed and noticed ten toenails polished in the color of "Grand Canyon Sunset" peeking up at her from the floor. God, she had never even put on shoes.

The lights in the room dimmed. Thad removed his jacket and came toward her. He nudged the door closed with his boot. "I'd be happy to stay with you."

Isabel's relief was immense, and it pushed her over the edge of exhaustion. She quietly swung her legs onto the mattress and curled onto her side. Thad's boots hit the floor and the mattress shifted as he lay beside her and pulled the covers over both of them.

And then... there it was. Easing into the warmth of his sturdy body against hers was even better than she'd remembered. Comforting. Safe. A muscular arm came around to tuck her against him. Isabel sighed deeply, weak but appreciative.

As she placed a tentative hand over Thad's, Isabel tried to get a handle on the wild leap her knowledge of the universe had made. Somehow she had gone from just another night at the club to hearing that she was the king's destined mate and being invited to move in with him, and then to being attacked in her apartment by something that she'd only heard of in childhood stories. All of that before teleporting to some big-ass mansion she didn't even know the location of with her sister-in-law. No, no. Thad's sister. God, she was even more fried than she thought.

Worry about Lex was really cooking her noodle. On top of everything that had come before, the idea that she could lose her best friend to an attack that had been her fault… she just couldn't live with that. She stroked her thumb over Thad's but if he was awake, he didn't move. Didn't speak.

She had so much more to think about, but ultimately the only thing she could do was go back to basics and wait until Lexi was better. The rest could wait. Allowing herself to bask a bit more in the peace of Thad's touch, she closed her fingers around his and let her weariness pull her into sleep.

Chapter 12

A LONG, HOT SHOWER WAS SUPPOSED TO BE RELAXING. Nevertheless, Lee found himself leaving his bathroom even more tightly wound than when he had entered. He made a half-assed effort to ignore the cold weight in his chest while he pulled a fresh pair of fatigues and a clean T-shirt from his dresser drawer.

He was bugged about giving Alexia his blood. Minor physical attraction aside, she was human, and he didn't like humans. The disturbing truth he'd run up against while rinsing dried wizard gore from his skin was that he *had* wanted to, and for reasons that went beyond his duty to Thad. He needed to nip that shit in the bud. A quarter-century since his split from Agnessa, and he still wasn't right in the head. He didn't go out of his way for any female. Not anymore.

He yanked his clothes on without finesse and was donning his boots when a knock on the door interrupted his contemplation. "Lee?" Tyra.

The door swung open, and she marched into the room without waiting for an invitation. "I need to talk to you," she muttered, settling herself in the large leather armchair by his dresser.

"How's it going, Tyra? Would you like to come in? Please, have a seat," he said flatly. He ignored her eye roll; she doled them out like treats on Halloween. After closing the door, he sat on the side of the queen-sized bed, facing her. "What's up?"

"I need to talk to you about that wizard thing. It's been bothering the hell out of me." She paused awkwardly and rubbed her temples a little. "And I, uh, was hoping to catch you before you went to talk with Siddoh."

Frustration made Lee drop his chin to his chest. "Christ, Tyra. What the hell is wrong with you?" He was getting the urge to roll his own eyes, juvenile though the gesture was. "I gotta be honest. I don't see how the two of you can fuck like bunnies and yet be unable to tolerate each other's presence otherwise. You work together, for goodness sake. You've gotta be able to deal with him."

"I actually prefer the bonobo ape as an analogy."

Lee sat straighter on the bed. "What the hell are you talking about?"

She smiled. "They're one of the only animal species to have sex for reasons other than procreation. Including conflict resolution, I might add. And I'm pretty sure they have sex even more than rabbits."

Oh, for the love of—"Ty, I don't want to know how you know that, and I definitely don't want to hear any more about it."

"What? I like trivia. Anyway, I don't know that it's so far-fetched." She tilted her head sideways and gave him a smug smile. "You've never been physically attracted to someone you didn't particularly like? Not even, say, very recently?"

He stood up, fists clenched. "Stop reading me, Tyra. You know that pisses me off."

She shifted positions in the chair and met his stare. Amusement made her brown eyes sparkle. "I wasn't trying to pry, but all sorts of inner conflict were pouring out of you when we were bringing that human back earlier. I'm sorry. I won't bring it up again."

"Good."

She chuckled. "All I'm saying is that it's not as cut and dried as you might think. Anyway, I told him it's over."

Again? "How many times would that make it?"

Ah, yes. Now her amusement was fading. "I know, I know. I tell myself all the time I should be smarter than this. Thing is, you know I'm not much for relationships. It started out to piss off Dad. Then it became a convenience, and eventually it was just kind of a bad habit that I had trouble breaking. I've finally gotten sick of it, though."

"I just hate to see you get dicked around, sweetheart." Tyra was the closest thing he had to a sister. She was a fully grown and capable female, but Lee was still oddly protective. And he had never liked Siddoh much.

Tyra straightened in the chair and threw her shoulders back as if she had a point to prove. She lifted her chin. "You don't need to worry about me. I can handle myself. Tell you what: you don't ride me about Siddoh, and I won't bug you anymore about that tiny human girl down the east hall."

"You already said you wouldn't."

"Yeah, well, now I'm attaching strings. You mind your own business and let me take care of mine."

"Fine, but if Siddoh pulls some kind of dumb shit, I reserve the right to rip him a new one."

"Not if I do it first."

"Fair enough." He nodded. "Now. The wizard thing."

He sat on the bed again and steepled his fingers. "Here's the problem. I've been killing those idiots for the better part of a millennium, and I'm good at what I do, but I gotta tell you, that guy didn't seem to put up much of a fight. I mean, he did, but it seemed like kind of a tired effort, you know?"

"Maybe he was just a newbie."

"Maybe. Except that he had a pretty strong aura. And there's the question of how the hell he found us. We've never known of any ability to trace a teleport, and you can bet his finding us wasn't random."

Tyra's face scrunched up in frustration. "I know. That's been bugging me too. 'Specially since if it's legit, one of my best evasion tactics just got thrown in the toilet."

He nodded grimly. "No shit. You're gonna have to be a hell of a lot more careful. You might need to lie low on your volunteer stuff for awhile."

"Ugh. Yeah." She slapped her hands down on the arms of the chair and vaulted up. "Well, I will. After tonight, anyway."

Lee raised an eyebrow.

"They're short-staffed tonight. I got a call on my way down about one of our counselors having a seizure or something, and we've got a new guy checking in. I'm actually headed over in a few minutes."

He glanced at the clock, frowning. "You've got a new guy checking in, in the middle of the night?"

"It happens more often than you might think. Local ER can't turn away a patient with no insurance, but once the patient's stable they want 'em out ASAP. As I understand it, administratively their day ends at midnight, so they try to street them before the clock chimes." She sighed. "It's not the best system. Humans don't always take such great care of their own when there's money on the line."

"Yet another mark in the pro column for your mother's race, eh?" he said wryly.

Her eyes narrowed, and a little pang of guilt squeezed Lee's chest. Tyra's mother was a sore subject, and he was a thoughtless bastard sometimes. More than sometimes. "Anyway, I'm outta here. Hit me up if you need anything. Otherwise, I'll try to meet with you and Thad at the end of the night." She gave him a cutesy little finger wave and faded out of sight.

Hands on his hips, Lee lifted his face to the ceiling and blew out a puff of air. On the bright side, he didn't see how the night could get much worse. He grabbed his gear from the bed and headed out the door.

Chapter 13

A STRANGE SENSATION PULLED THAD FROM SLEEP. Trembling. Isabel. Immediately, fear for her well-being made his gut clench, and breathing was a struggle. Disturbingly enough, he had also woken up painfully hard, and being turned on under such circumstances made him feel like a real asshole. It was just that Isabel's gorgeous backside tucked up against his pelvis that way was so very... *right*. He struggled to reconcile the two base emotions.

"Isabel." Her fingers were still curled around his. He unclasped his hand and reached to jiggle her shoulder. "Isabel. Are you okay?" Jesus, how was that for a stupid question? She was fine; she was just practicing interpretive dance.

She mewled discontentedly in her sleep and wiggled closer to him, pressing her soft curves more tightly against him. He groaned his frustration a little louder. "Isabel... wake up..." He started to shake her again, but before his hand could move, she came awake with a loud intake of breath and turned toward him.

"Oh, God. Thad?" Her breathing was labored, and her heart pounded against his chest. She still shook like a leaf. "What's going on?" She started to look around, even as her slender fingers gripped at his arms to pull closer. "What time is it?"

"I don't know," he said, his voice hoarse. Her

breathing grew even heavier, and it puffed gently against his neck.

Thad's cock twitched, and he sighed. Here was Isabel, confused and probably out of her mind with fear, and yet he was primed and ready to do the horizontal mambo again. He really didn't want to be *that* male. Aware that she could most likely feel his erection, he started to pull away from her.

Isabel's hand went to his back. "No... please... don't go anywhere." She kept pressing, urging him toward her, wiggling and scooting until their bodies were flush again. "I'm really cold, Thad. Please let me be close to you."

Well, how could he say no when she asked that way? But something was very wrong. He was burning up. How could she be cold and shivering? He wracked his brain, wondering if he should go for more blankets, get a hot shower going. Maybe get the doctor. Yeah. He should get Bray—

The sudden press of Isabel's lips against Thad's popped his eyes wide open. The lower half of her body rolled away slightly, and then her hand was pulling at his shoulder. She was trying to get him on top of her.

Oh, this was such a bad idea. It had been a terrifying and emotional night for Isabel. She was worried about her friend. She was... *think, Thad, think!* She might need medical attention. That was important. The truest reason was that this was already about more than just a prophecy for Thad. If he wanted it to be the same for Isabel, they needed time to get to know each other before they made love again. Time for it to grow into something real.

He needed to be more than just another one of her club hookups.

But when he resisted, she tugged harder, parting her lips to slide her tongue inside his mouth and digging her fingers into his back. Her leg hooked around the back of his, and her pelvis got into the mix by bridging upward to grind against his hard-on some more.

"Isabel," he murmured against her mouth, "we really shouldn't... not like this." But even as he said it, his hips pressed harder toward hers, his dick throbbing and straining as if it were loudly urging him to shut the hell up and get with the program. Damn, he had about ten seconds to get himself under control before he lost all of his resolve.

No good is going to come from this.

But there was more pulling, and Thad shifted so that he was more or less lying on top of Isabel. He hadn't meant to do that, had he? Hell, maybe he'd already lost his resolve, after all. "Thad," she whispered against him. God, he loved to hear her say his name. "Please..."

A few quick tugs and his shirt was untucked. Simultaneously, her nibbling teeth and fangs began an erotic assault on his earlobe that sent a shiver straight down his spine Thad knew that it was Game Over. He wanted to be a gentleman, but he was no fucking saint.

A switch flipped, and Thad's feral nature came roaring back to life in a way he had never experienced with another female. He growled and groaned, nipping at her neck. One hand roughly caressed her jaw while the other moved south to the curve of her waist and then around the back to dip inside the waistband of those *amazing* stretchy pants of hers.

His tongue traced Isabel's bottom lip before it plunged inside her mouth. His hips began to move of their own accord, his hard length pressing insistently against her core. Isabel, too, moaned deep in her throat as her pelvis started to undulate, the rise and fall of her hips making music with his just like before.

Deliciously cool fingers brushed against his rib cage and his pec, then crept to pinch his nipple. "Oh, yeah... *shit*..." he breathed, trailing hot kisses down Isabel's throat. Unable to stop himself, Thad swept his tongue across the skin covering her carotid artery, loving the frenetic beat of her pulse beneath it. Jesus... he would just bet her blood tasted *so* sweet. His fangs thrust long into his mouth.

"Thad," she said urgently. "Thad. Please..."

He couldn't take it anymore. Thad sucked in a breath and pushed himself off the bed.

~~~

Isabel's nipples tightened from the chill in the air. The tremors were so strong that even a gun to her head wouldn't have made her able to hold still. She fought the urge to scramble off the bed and go after him, to pull his warm skin against hers, to wrap around him so completely that there was no way he could let go.

They really shouldn't. He was right about that. Not when mere hours earlier she had decided she couldn't do what he asked of her, prophecy or no. After their brief hookup in her bedroom, it had become clear this male wanted something from her that she wouldn't be able to give. But God, her body hummed with *need*.

Alexia could have died tonight. Any of them could

have. Life may be too uncertain for forever, but cling-ing to Thad—allowing herself to feel alive for a little while—she needed that. What the hell was he doing off the bed, anyway?

Thad… please don't go…

Isabel could only watch from under half-closed lids as he unbuttoned his shirt and roughly shucked his pants and boxers. Her head sank into the pillow with a small sigh of relief. As he stood before her, the shadows in the dimly lit room played seductively over all that hard mus-cle. He was absolutely the most beautiful male specimen she had ever seen. Even the royal medallion embedded in his chest looked erotic, the way it played to the scant light and threw warm flecks of gold into his blue eyes.

God, she ached for him. She needed more of the heat, the chemistry that flowed between them with such strength that her body and the air around her seemed to pulse with it.

His erection jutted proudly from between his legs, ruddy and already weeping as he prowled toward her. By the time Thad's knee once again dented the mattress, Isabel had pulled her T-shirt off and started to caress her breasts. Though her hands were cool, delicious warmth wound through her at the self-touch, more so when the heave of Thad's chest gave away his need.

He liked watching her, and he was on the verge of losing control. How magnificent.

The bed shifted as his weight came down fully. Her thighs parted to accommodate his immense presence. Slow and gentle segued to a wilder urgency, and she was more than ready for him by the time strong fingers gripped her hips and ripped her leggings off in one fluid motion.

When Thad surged forward to kiss her, Isabel was prepared for wild. Frenzied. Hard and fast and now, now, now, just like it had been the last time. But the kiss was sweet and gentle. Tentative, teasing probes of tongue were accompanied by whisper-light caresses as his fingers traveled over her face, her shoulders... her neck. Her entire body sighed into his touch.

In a gesture that was almost unconscious, Isabel's chin lifted to bare her throat. The anticipation lit a fire in her core. She'd never offered her blood to anybody and, until that moment, had no idea that she would ever want to. Every lick, every nibble, every puff of breath over the vulnerable column of her flesh ratchetted the wonderful tension in her body and the already too-rapid thrum of her pulse until she thought she might literally explode from it.

But he moved on, trailing more kisses over her collarbone and chest. "Thad." His lips enveloped first one nipple and then the other, delicately, but the sharp tip of a fang just barely scraped her. The pinch gave way to pleasure almost immediately as his saliva closed the cut, leaving a sizzle of want behind.

He growled, and one large hand splayed its fingers out wide before it began a smooth slide over her stomach. *Oh, yes.* One and then two fingers slipped inside her, pulling a loud moan from her throat.

"Like that?" His voice was a soothing growl in her ear.

Isabel may have responded; she may not have. It was hard to say because the circular motion of Thad's thumb on her clit while his fingers plunged in and out of her lit up her nerves and veins like a Christmas tree. A thousand questions and problems banged on the door of her brain, but they faded into white noise as Thad picked up the pace with his fingers and murmured filthy things in her ear. All the while, her body rushed toward what promised to be the most perfect of free falls.

"Oh, God... Thad." A wholly undignified whine came out when he backed off, slowing the pace just enough to keep her riding the edge without going over. Isabel's fingers combed through the short brush of his dirty blond military haircut and then marched down the back of his neck to grab his arm so she could urge him to pick up the pace. The muscles of his arm bulged and flexed delightfully beneath her fingers.

Firm, velvet lips nuzzled at her cheek. The heat of Thad's tongue seemed to trace over each and every scar on her neck and face, giving them the sort of loving kindness not even she had ever graced them with. Heat and cold shimmied through her.

The cap of one muscular shoulder hovered near enough for her to do a little tasting of her own. Thad's skin was musky and salty and all male, and as the pace of his fingers sped up once again, Isabel's gums throbbed with the lengthening of her fangs. When he paused from his ministrations and his blue-eyed gaze met hers, the swallow and bob of his Adam's apple pulled her gaze to the frenetic ticking of his pulse like a heat-seeking missile.

Before she realized what she'd done, Isabel had already struck.

She broke apart the second the flavor of his sweet, spicy blood burst on her tongue. Just like before, a blast of searing pain spread across her lower back, although that quickly dissipated and left her with a pleasurable vibration at the apex of her thighs. Thad uttered a sibilant "yes" and twitched against her lips, but somehow he continued to fuck her with his fingers as she rode wave after wave of the most intense orgasm of her life. She clung for dear life while she sucked, raking her nails over his back.

He seemed to rather like that.

Just barely, she managed to sweep her tongue across the punctures in his skin before her head dropped to the pillow. His forehead pressed against hers. One hand rested lightly on her hip, so warm against her chilly skin. Just as she had started to float on a blissful cloud of sleepiness, a harsh shiver shocked her back to reality.

She had just drunk Thad's blood. The *king's* blood. What on earth was she thinking? Only hours before, she'd been intent on putting distance between them, and now she had helped to bind them together.

Nice one, Isabel.

And the kicker, if she were being totally honest with herself, was that she had never been more content. No matter how they moved, their bodies fused together seamlessly like an ocean against the shore. His golden skin heated hers and chased away the chill. His breath fell in a warm, sweet mist on her mouth. If she allowed herself to, she could almost see staying forever this way.

Until he spoke again.

"I'm sorry," he whispered.

Chapter 14

OKAY, THAD, LET'S REVIEW THE PLAN. THE PLAN WAS TO GIVE her a little space and then to find a way to convince her to be at your side. To talk. To encourage. Not… not to jump right into sex again, fresh on the heels of her friend getting hurt, and risk that she would treat this like some random hookup. Not doing so well with the plan, are you, Thad?

Clearly, he needed a new plan. At least she couldn't blow it all off as the effects of the wine this time, right?

Her forehead shook back and forth against his. "Don't be sorry," she said. "Don't you dare be sorry."

Thad propped himself on his elbows so his eyes could meet Isabel's. She was so lovely with her skin flushed and her auburn hair damp against the pillow. Her lids were heavy, but her eyes were sharp and assessing. Fierce. In another life, she could have been a warrior. She reached to caress his jaw. He closed his eyes and leaned into the touch.

"Isabel, we shouldn't—"

The sharp smack that landed across Thad's mouth nearly made his head spin. *WTF?* Blood welled on his stinging lower lip, courtesy of a large mood-ring on her right hand. How had he not noticed *that* little accessory before now? Fucking hell, no one had ever slapped him before. Ever.

Isabel pointed an accusatory finger in his face, and

her stare held his, narrow and unyielding. The emerald sparkle he'd noticed before now took on a darker cast, especially in her scarred eye. Her nostrils flared, and her chest rose and fell visibly with each deep, hard breath she took. She sure as hell didn't look like she was about to apologize.

"Screw *shouldn't*, Thad. It's too late for that."

Thad's jaw hardened, but he wasn't sure how to respond. He was a little pissed off. And, according to the lower half of him, still more than a little turned on. This fiery, passionate side of her was exciting. As he considered her, his tongue peeked out to lick off the small smear of blood on his lip.

It was that same glimpse of that fire he'd seen in her from across the VIP room, just before they had met. He loved this take-no-shit willingness to stand up to him, even in the face of everything they were dealing with. His queen would need that.

The offending hand rubbed his jaw, the thumb gently sliding over his split lip. "Did I give you some indication that I was an unwilling participant in what we just did?"

"No." Suddenly his throat was raw, and his voice was raspy.

"Good."

The corners of Isabel's full mouth turned up slightly. Her eyes seemed to soften. Thad was struck again by how impossibly beautiful she was when she smiled. If he could, he would make her smile every day for eternity.

"Ill advised or not, it was what it was. And I, for one, was very willing. As far as I could tell, so were you."

He nodded. "Willing" was an understatement.

"So let's not screw it up with a bunch of awkwardness

and regret. See…" Her head came up, and the hand still grasping his jaw pulled downward until their lips were separated by only a few molecules of air. "I was so cold, but I feel much better now." She captured his lower lip between hers, suckling gently at the already healing cut. "Much." She licked inside his mouth, going harder and deeper. "Better."

Oh, *hell* yeah. Thad buried his confusion and guilt, and just gave in. Let his tongue play and dance with Isabel's. His skin was slicked with sweat from their first go-round, making easy work of sliding down the length of her body. He stopped to kiss and nuzzle the creamy skin around her perfect little navel, trailing downward to her hipbone, her thigh, her knee, and then her calf.

Curling upon himself, he moved down just a little farther to kiss the top of her foot. Isabel had such sexy feet, her toenails polished beautifully with a sensuous mauve that seemed very "her." After taking a few moments to kiss and revere her toes, he lifted each leg onto his shoulders and slid back up between her legs.

His tongue flicked a couple of times over her clit in a playful gesture before deepening into longer strokes with the flat of it. Licking. Worshiping. Her thighs tightened around the sides of his head, but even though his ears were partly covered, Thad could hear her whimpers of pleasure loud and clear. A rumble of accomplishment came from his throat when her hands grasped the back of his head, pressing and guiding him until her whimpers turned into moans and groans, and eventually the throaty cry of another orgasm.

They were both sweating profusely now, as wet as if they'd both just stepped out of the shower. He stroked an idle finger over the sheen of moisture on her abdomen. They'd been going at it pretty hard, but still. Wow.

Isabel shifted beneath him, bringing her legs down off his shoulders and onto the bed. Thad slid toward her lips, but before he finished the journey, she had shimmied from underneath him. Kissing against his chest, pressing until he was flat on the bed. Her tongue twirled around his nipple. Playful bites made a trail down to his groin. A gentle nuzzle warmed the thatch of hair at the base of his still hard penis before more nips and—*oh, yeah*—her mouth engulfed one testicle at a time, followed by more little bites on his inner thigh.

"My turn," she murmured.

Motherfucker!

Thad moaned when Isabel's mouth closed around his shaft. She took him to the back of her throat and up again, sliding her tongue along the length while she made the slow, steady glide. The hot suction of her mouth was gentle but firm, and fucked if he didn't seem to have a hair trigger where this female was concerned because he was already on the verge again and fighting to hold back.

"Damn," he breathed.

She swirled her tongue around the head of his cock and scraped a fang along the length. Had she drawn blood? Was she sipping it from there? The thought of it only got him hotter. Harder. And how had he never known about *that* kink before?

"Isabel." The vibrations of her mumbled "mm-hmm" around his dick went straight to his balls. So, so close. "Isabel, you might wanna stop."

She pulled off just long enough to ask, "Do you want me to stop?"

Holy shit, there was an option? Most females he'd been with didn't—

Oh, hell yes. Isabel seemed to have taken his lack of response as an invitation to continue. As well she should have. Thad's fists squeezed shut and punched into the bed. His balls drew up in anticipation of his coming orgasm. He thrust his hands into her hair, massaging and guiding her head as she had done with him moments ago. His spine tingled. "Oh, damn." His fingers brushed over more scar tissue at the base of her skull, and for the briefest second he lost his focus.

Getting it back wasn't hard.

Seconds later, she took him deep into her throat and swallowed. His hoarse shout bounced around the room as the head of his cock blew and his upper body came off the bed almost of its own accord. His fangs crowded his mouth, and at the sight of her delectable arm across his hip, he couldn't stop himself. Before his cock had stopped twitching, Thad had her hand in both of his, and his fangs buried deep in her wrist. Something hot and sharp burned in his forearm just like the last time they'd fucked, but the first taste of her blood washed away any questions he might have had about it.

Her blood was even better than he'd imagined. Rich and flowery and sweet. Like dark cherries and honeysuckle. It was so intense that his mind's eye could practically see a kaleidoscope of colors flowing down the back of his throat. With the first swallow, a warm glow filled his body and spread throughout his limbs. A hundred years and who knew how many hosts, and he suddenly couldn't recall a single one that had come before.

But he would never forget the taste of Isabel.

Though it seemed he could drink forever, Thad forced himself to cease. After he licked and dropped to the bed, his breathing started to even out again. He closed his eyes and relaxed into the pillow, stroking his fingers through Isabel's damp hair. He couldn't remember a time when he'd felt more satiated, more satisfied, or more totally wrung out. Couldn't think of much of anything, really, at the moment.

"God, Isabel, I think you literally blew my mind."

———

Isabel closed her eyes and sighed, resting her head on the top of Thad's thick thigh. For all of her resolve to distance herself from Thad, she was going in exactly the wrong direction. But she was content and she had bigger issues for the moment, starting with making sure Alexia was all right. She'd worry about the rest later.

"Isabel."

"Hmm?"

"Isabel," he said again, more insistently. "Open your eyes."

"What's wrong?" She blinked and focused her good eye. "Holy cow… Thad?"

A fine mist hung in the room, almost like a fog. A strange tingle in Isabel's fingers prompted her to look down. Some sort of glow illuminated where her hand rested on Thad's leg, and—whoa, was that *steam* coming from between them? She jerked back to look at Thad, whose blue eyes met hers.

"Yeah, this is pretty fucked up," he breathed.

"What the hell is going on, Thad?" Everything was suddenly very surreal and floaty.

He ran his hand over his hair, which now stood up in wet spikes. Turning his hand palm up, he focused quietly until a tiny fuzzy, warm orange ball formed in his palm. "I think," he said with a slow chuckle, "I have a power. Some kind of fire. Like my dad." Pride shone brightly all over his face.

Isabel sat back on her heels, staring at that little glow with deep concentration. "Wow... that's..." She forced a smile. Because holy, holy freaking cow. This scored a solid ten on her no-damn-way-o-meter.

"God, that's amazing, Thad." Suddenly her skin prickled all over. She couldn't sit still. "You know, I'm going to go take a shower. We'll talk later?" Heart slamming into her ribs, she speed-walked into the bathroom and closed the door without waiting for him to answer.

Chapter 15

THE NIGHT WAS BITTERLY COLD, AND LEE'S BREATH puffed out ahead of him as he quickly traversed the grounds on foot. The estate was divided roughly into four quadrants: the working farm on one, Thad's home on another, the training center and barracks on a third. The last held homes for other residents of the estate, and that was where he was headed.

As Thad's primary guard, Lee was the only member of the military branch not allowed a home of his own.

Siddoh lived in a cushy but oddly banal redbrick colonial with white shutters, a stone's throw from the training area. Lee found the scruffy male in his bookshelf-lined office with a pair of granny glasses perched on his nose, bent studiously over a mass of papers spread out over what was probably an overpriced mahogany desk. He looked up at Lee with a cocky smile and threw his feet up on the desk, then leaned back in his leather swivel chair with his hands clasped behind his head.

Siddoh had the same arrogance that Lee's father had once had, and Lee couldn't stand the son of a bitch.

"Hey, man, welcome back. How was the big adventure?" Siddoh had been among the many who had thought the trip was a total waste and didn't mind sharing his opinion. There was never any filter between the younger male's brain and his mouth.

"Actually..." Lee stopped with his arms crossed,

looking down on Siddoh from across the large desk. "We got a match." He couldn't hold back his satisfaction when Siddoh's eyebrows shot up.

"No shit? Huh." Siddoh straightened in his chair. "Well, that certainly is interesting." He stroked his chin thoughtfully.

"Indeed. So you want to give me a status update?" He nodded to the papers on Siddoh's desk. "What's all this? And what the fuck is the deal with the glasses?"

Siddoh shot a glare, removed the glasses, and rubbed a red spot on the bridge of his nose. "Status? Everything has been quiet. Too quiet. No missing reports in the past two weeks, and our boys haven't run into much. Except Xander, who's convalescing in the barracks after his shoulder had a nasty run-in with a very large wizard knife. The knife was large. Not the wizard. The wizard was fairly average, actually. Anyway..."

He paused to study Lee, who held his stance and said nothing. Then Siddoh gestured to the papers on the desk. "This? Demographic research. I've been thinking we could start branching out to patrolling not just the residential areas of our kind but also some of the high-crime human areas where the wizards are likely to pick up their incubators. Not only might we be able to take down more of them that way, but if we keep 'em from reproducing, we keep their numbers down. The glasses? I like 'em. They make me look smart, so fuck you."

"Gonna take a lot more than glasses for that, bro," Lee grumbled.

Siddoh jabbed the glasses in Lee's general direction. "You need to lighten up, my man. Now listen. I'm thinking we can use Tyra's social-service connections to get a better handle on young women coming up miss-ing and young boys disappearing that might actually be wizard offspr—"

"We're keeping Tyra out of this. I already told her that after tonight I want her out of rotation for awhile. We had a wizard hit when she was picking us up in Orlando. It's not safe for her to be outside the estate until we know how they tracked her."

Siddoh held up a hand. "Cut the bullshit, Lee. She's a good fighter. She can handle herself." He tossed the glasses onto the desk and leaned back. "That female's got more power in her little finger than you and I have combined."

"I'd think you would care more about making sure she stays safe."

"I do care. I'm just not concerned."

Lee growled again. "She's not invincible, Siddoh. You're telling me things have been too quiet. Maybe that means they're planning something. They tracked her to Orlando, which most likely means they traced her teleport. They might even be gunning for her specifi-cally. You can't sit there and tell me that's safe."

Siddoh gave him a mock grimace that smacked of you-must-be-joking. "What I'm telling you is that she knows the risks and she wants to take down these bas-tards just as much as the rest of us, so why not use her? This is a good idea, and you know it."

Lee did know it; he hated it just the same. If wizards had gotten wind of Tyra's multiple powers and were after her, it would be bad news. The smug SOB was right, though. She was a good fighter. She could handle herself. "Fine," he grumbled on a heavy exhale. "Show me what you've got."

"Great. So here we go." Siddoh replaced the ridiculous glasses on his face and pulled a large map of the area from below the heap of papers in front of him. He gestured, using a pen as a pointer. "We know they tend to reproduce by jacking druggies, runaways, hookers, and the like, and the resulting offspring usually wind up going into the foster system and eventually disappear.

"So in the past we've figured, 'Well, no one gives a damn about them, and that's why they're difficult to trace,' but what if..." He stabbed the pen into the air towards Lee. "*If* they have someone in place in the child welfare system, or worse, multiple someones, maybe even in the police force or whatever. Maybe that's how they're slipping under the radar."

Lee weighed Siddoh's words. "I'm not sure I'm buying it. We've considered similar theories in the past but they've never panned out."

"*But*," Siddoh said, stabbing his pen into the air again, "I think things are different now. Check this out." He circled an area on the map. "Over here is where Xander had a run-in with a group of newbies. No big deal, except that these guys actually knew how to fight. We're talking serious hand-to-hand skills. That's unusual."

Lee nodded. It was more common for the wizards to rely on whatever straws they'd drawn in the vampire lottery, a plan with varying degrees of effectiveness. The wizards depended on stealth to avoid security patrols, and they were strictly cash and carry when it came to the civilians. Fighting skills had never seemed as high on their to-do list as their ability to grab and go. "Our guys have martial-arts training; Xander still should have been able to take 'em."

"Well, he did, but not easily. I'm guessing our guys have gotten a little lazy and the wizards are stepping up their efforts so they managed to catch us with our pants down, so to speak. And Xander's been distracted for months now. Since the funeral. I've had a few talks with him about it."

"Gotcha. What else?"

Siddoh circled another area on the map. "So over here is where the folks get their drugs and where we've seen a lot of human women disappear from in the past, and over this way," he said circling a third spot, "is a low-income neighborhood where we've seen a lot of adolescent boys disappear from, presumably from families who take on foster children. Some of the families may do so for the sole purpose of gathering more income, or they might even be in cahoots with the wizards in some way." He sat back and allowed Lee to survey the map. "So. You see what we have in the middle of that triangle?"

Well, shit. "Tyra's shelter."

Siddoh nodded, grimmer this time. "So she's already perfectly positioned. I want us to see if she can do some daytime recon, maybe even look into child welfare—"

Daytime. "No fucking way. Let's say your theory is right and they've got some wizard masquerading as a social worker out there, and they're better organized with better skills. You wanna send Tyra out there during the day with no backup? You're out of your mind."

"We've been over this. She can handle it."

"Worst case happens and she can't, *no one* will be able to get to her. Everyone needs backup once in awhile."

"Even you, Lee?"

Lee didn't dignify the question with a response.

Siddoh's pen jabbed toward him again. This time Lee's hand shot out and grabbed the younger male's in a crushing grip. "That's getting real irritating."

Siddoh's eyebrow quirked at him. "What crawled up your ass and died?"

He'd be damned before he gave Siddoh a straight answer to that one. Instead, he just shrugged. "This wizard thing. The attack we had earlier tonight wasn't anything like you're describing. It was one of my easiest kills. Something doesn't fit."

Siddoh pulled his hand away, shaking it a little to get the feeling back. "How's this? We'll keep Tyra's recon activities limited to late afternoon or early evening. That way, if something goes down, we can be out the door soon after. Night falls early this time of year."

"I want to be sure she's cool with it."

Siddoh lifted his palms. "Absolutely."

"Deal," Lee ground out. He rolled his shoulders a couple of times. His muscles should have been looser after having just had a shower. Palming his chin, he twisted his head fiercely over his left shoulder and then his right until there was a satisfying pop at the base of his skull. "I'll talk to Tyra later on. Anything else I need to know?"

Siddoh shrugged. "Had a couple dead humans show up over the weekend in that part of town we were just looking at. They appeared to have been electrocuted but the 'how' part was unclear. We're thinking there's a chance of nonhuman involvement, but it wasn't obvious enough so we left it for the human cops. Be good to keep an eye out, though.

"Other than that... C and D teams are out on patrol

doing their thing. No one's checked in yet. Usually no news is good news. Team A has the night off, and I'm headed to the training center shortly to put B through their paces after they finish sparring. You want to come with?"

"Thanks, but I want to see how Xander's holding up. After that, I'll be back at the main house if you need me for any reason. We've got an unconscious human and a freaked-out queen to deal with over there." He threw up his hand in a half-assed wave and headed for the door.

"Damn, buddy. You get all the fun."

Yeah.

Tyra grimaced. Her boots echoed down the hallway of the shelter's men's wing, a loud reminder that in her haste she'd left Lee's room without bothering to go and change into normal street clothes. Good thing she could make it a short night. Get the new resident checked in and then head right back.

She wanted a chance to talk with Thad's female. She had gleaned a lot of conflicting emotions from her, and she was itching with the urge to help play matchmaker. After spending the last several decades sowing his wild oats, Thad deserved to settle down with a good female. Tyra couldn't see him ruling alone as their father had for so long.

She punched a code into the security keypad that guarded the shelter's main lobby. For security's sake, all the sleeping areas were under electronic lock as well during the night. Tyra nodded to the police officer and "Anton Smith," who were standing by the front desk waiting for her.

"Mr. Smith, I'm Tyra Morgan." She extended her hand, which he shook awkwardly. Like he wasn't sure what to do with it. The man radiated an overwhelming sense of loss and confusion. "I've got a room ready for you. I'll show you to it as soon as we get you all checked in."

The officer handed her a file containing information she already knew. White male, midthirties, treated for multiple lacerations and head trauma. Memory loss, which certainly explained the confusion. No ID or personal effects were on the body, which had been brought into the ER by a couple of hunters who had found him in the woods naked and bloodied to within an inch of his life. The man remembered his first name but not his last. "Smith" had been added by the hospital for administrative purposes.

She shook her head, giving him as much of a subtle once-over as possible. His jeans and flannel shirt were baggy—obviously donations, as were the ratty sneakers on his feet. While his wardrobe screamed "homeless," his body did not. He was fairly well built, and his hands were calloused like they were used to hard work. His head was neatly shaved and still bandaged.

Perhaps he'd been law enforcement or military? She could see an undercover agent of some sort getting beaten and left for dead like he had been. Or a drug dealer who'd screwed the wrong supplier, maybe. And then there was the way he was looking at her. He had yet to speak but he seemed to be sizing her up in the same way she was assessing him, his shrewd, hooded eyes regarding her with cautious interest.

She finished the intake, bid good-bye to the officer,

and gestured for Mr. Smith to walk ahead of her to the door of the men's wing. Standard procedure in such circumstances was for the officer to accompany the new resident to his or her room, but Tyra never saw the need, given that she was stronger and faster than even the toughest human male. Besides, the average resident just wanted a warm bed.

Mr. Smith walked ahead of her and she was able to evaluate his broad shoulders, his confident gait, and the fact that his arms appeared to swing freely but his hands were still ready for action. She'd seen that walk on every soldier she'd ever trained with. *Ex-military, then.*

Tyra stopped and swung open the door to the room that had been set aside for him. "Here you go. It has all the spaciousness and comfort of a shoe box, but I hope you'll manage to make yourself at home."

The bare eight-by-twelve room held a bed, a chair, and a small table, all metal and hard to break. There had been a lamp, but anything not bolted down disappeared eventually. A clock on the wall was covered by chicken wire so the face couldn't be damaged, and it clicked and buzzed incessantly in a way that would have driven her absolutely bat-shit crazy if she'd ever had to sleep in the same room with it. She always gave this room away last because of the thing.

She tilted her head slightly, taking a closer look at Mr. Smith's face. He had kind eyes. Soft and gray. Not a word yet, though, had come out of that firm, full mouth of his.

"Thank you," he said finally, as he sat tentatively on the edge of the bed. His voice was low and rich. Soothing.

"Is there anything I can get for you, Mr. Smith?"

"Please, call me… Anton… I guess." He frowned. "I wish I could at least remember my last name."

"I know it's easier said than done, but try not to let it get to you," she said warmly. "According to your file, there's a very good chance this is only short term. Once your injuries heal more, you could very well find it all coming back to you. The room is yours for the next six weeks, so you've got some time to figure things out.

"If it helps, I've read that often memory loss is psychosomatic. You'll probably remember when you're ready to." She was getting a stare from him that was part confusion and part rapt fascination. Like the way a cat would stare at a fish tank. "So, are you all right, Mr. Smith?"

He shook his head as if to clear it. "Sorry. I guess I was thinking that something about you seemed familiar." He chuckled sadly. "Maybe I'm just so desperate to remember something that everything seems familiar."

She stepped forward and gave his shoulder a quick, reassuring squeeze. A follow-up scan of his emotions revealed anxiety, confusion, sadness, and *who-ho-hoa*… lust? Tyra shivered.

No deception, though. No guile. She stepped away quickly, turning toward the door to hide the blush creeping up her cheeks. She cleared her throat to cover the sudden discomfort. "Uh, breakfast is at seven. It's already late; you should probably try to get some rest."

He nodded and swallowed, still looking at her a little too intently. Her hand was on the doorknob when he spoke again. "Are you—have you maybe been to the hospital recently for some reason?"

Tyra's responding head shake was probably a little more emphatic than necessary. "Nope. Sorry. I really don't think we know each other."

"I'm sure you're right." His deep scowl showed that he didn't feel as sure as he claimed, but he seemed satisfied enough to let the subject go for the time being. Thank goodness. "Well, thank you for your help. I guess I'll see you around soon?"

Tyra nodded a good-bye, twisted the knob, and inched her way out of the small room. The desire to be polite was warring with her need to speed-walk the hell away from the ambiguously homeless hunk who was apparently lusting after her. Perhaps telling him she wasn't going to be around might help cool his jets.

"Actually, I'm planning to take a little vacation after tonight. As soon as I'm sure you're all squared away, I'm heading out, in fact."

She hadn't expected him to jump up from the bed like his ass was on fire. "I could walk you to your car, if you like. It's late, and this isn't a good neighborhood." Bless him, he seemed genuinely worried about her safety. Little did he know.

"I'll be fine, but thank you so much for your concern. You get some rest, K?" A final quick step back had her out in the hall, pulling the door shut behind her. She indulged in a self-directed eye roll and a slap of her palm against her forehead before turning on her heel and high-tailing it back toward her office. Anton Doe—or Anton Smith, or whatever the hell his real name was—made her extremely uncomfortable.

He was out of her head by the time she had sped back to her office and pushed the door shut behind her so she could teleport home to where they had real problems: wizards and humans and prophecies.

Oh, my.

Chapter 16

SHIT, SHIT, SHIT, SHIT, SHIT, SHIT SHIT SHIT SHIT SHIT SHIT SHIT shitshitshitshit… shit! Isabel's wet palm smacked against the tile.

While the steamy hot water sluiced over her body, she tried to put recent events into perspective and only succeeded in scrambling her brain. When the knocking in her knees got to be too much, she decided to sit down but wound up bonking her head against the bath spout. Good grief, she was clumsy. Then the water was too cold so she had to turn it up. Damn, she couldn't even collapse gracefully. At last, she eased back against the tile.

The cold ceramic at her back brought a new awareness: that patch of skin near her tailbone didn't hurt anymore. Yeah. Huh. The niggling ache she'd felt for days was totally absent. Had that happened sometime while they were making love, just like Thad's power? No, no. No. Not making love. The sex had already thrown a big, giant monkey wrench into things without adding *feelings* to the whole mess.

Man, Alexia would totally bitch her out over this. Poor Isabel had a hunky, rich king come track her down and fuck her into next Tuesday, and waaaah, she was supposedly destined to be his mate.

"Aaargh!" Maybe there were worse predicaments to be in, but damn. She was just plain not queen material. That she was sure of. And it sure as hell hadn't occurred to her that sex with Thad would be the thing to kick this whole prophecy business into high gear. But it must have, right? Somehow the sex had unlocked Thad's power. Or the feeding. Or both?

Now that she thought about it, though, maybe this had been a good thing. Since Thad now had his power, maybe the whole joining-for-eternity part didn't have to happen. Her longest romantic relationship had been for like two hours, for crying out loud. She did not do long term; she wouldn't begin to know how. Even if she tried, someone was bound to get hurt. This way, Thad could find himself a more suitable mate and she could go home.

As soon as she turned the steaming water off, her shivers began again with renewed vigor. Isabel felt both physically weak and totally psychotic at the same time. She still couldn't believe she had smacked Thad while they were making lov—fucking.

Shit. The robe was out in the room with Thad. And she was freezing. Isabel grabbed a towel and wrapped it around herself, still shaking despite the warmth and softness of the luxurious bamboo fibers. Wow, she really loved these towels. Too bad that alone wasn't the basis for a relationship.

She grabbed a glass from the counter and filled it, looking around the elegant bathroom with its gold-accented etched mirrors and marble countertops. She couldn't see herself living in a place like this.

Isabel tipped the glass to sip her water, but nothing came out. She must have been further out in orbit than she'd realized. She could have sworn she had filled it. Isabel reached for the tap again—and dropped the glass.

The expensive-looking tumbler shattered into a million pieces when it hit the sink, along with the frozen chunk of ice the glass contained. A sudden light-headed feeling swooped down over her like a swarm of those freaky winged-monkeys from *The Wizard of Oz*, and she backed toward the door.

She needed to find Thad.

Isabel stumbled bleary-eyed into the room, and her heart sank. The rumpled bed was empty. His clothes were gone. Making her way to the bed in a somewhat herky-jerky fashion, she fell onto the sheets and flopped over, curling into a ball. She couldn't deal with this now.

She needed to get more sleep. As soon as Alexia was better, they needed to find a way to leave. She couldn't handle any of this, and she damned sure couldn't handle the fact that her only connection to the outside world had left her here alone.

Thad stormed down the hallway. His footsteps pounded heavily against the diamond-patterned carpet runner. A deluge of emotion poured over him, but rage prevailed. At the moment he was so livid that his vision was blurry and he was ready to jump the hell out a window. His fists clenched and unclenched by his sides, desperate to grab something long enough to hurl it across the room.

So, okay. He had upended Isabel's world with the whole destiny business, but he had thought that the passion between them had meant something. It had to him. Shit, even if it didn't mean anything more to Isabel than what she'd done with the humans at the club, she could at least have had the balls to stay, not skitter off to the bathroom like a frightened bunny. The fact that he had developed a power while they were together meant something, dammit. Meant *everything*. Didn't she see? It was proof they belonged together.

Thad stopped near the main foyer to collect himself, but frustration swamped his senses until suddenly his fist hit the wall and sank deep into the plaster. *Fuck*. A rumble of laughter from the doorway made his head spin, and he pinned Lee with his best don't-say-anything-if-you-know-what's-good-for-you stare. Turned out Lee didn't know shit about what was good for himself. Or if he did, he sure didn't care.

"Jeez, buddy, what'd that wall ever to do you?" Lee's laughing eyes regarded Thad, clearly unaffected by the waves of nastiness Thad was trying to project at the older male.

Thad exhaled heavily, shaking dust off his hand and forearm. Huh. The scar on his arm didn't hurt anymore. Didn't feel like much of anything now, as a matter of fact. Perhaps that was fitting.

"Ivy!" Thad bellowed toward the west hall, expecting that she'd be in her office. He was surprised when the answering jog of her footsteps came from the direction he'd just traveled, but then he remembered that Brayden had tasked her with keeping tabs on Alexia.

"What's up, Thad?"

"How's the human?" Ivy seemed to flinch. The staff wasn't used to seeing him in fuck-off mode. Frankly, he was a little put off by it himself.

"Actually, she's good. She's conscious but really confused. Brayden gave her a sedative, and she's gonna need a little more blood soon probably. Well, that and someone to explain to her what's going on. She kind of panicked when she came to." Ivy swallowed.

"I'll take care of it," Lee broke in. "Let me know when she's awake again. I'll talk to her." Ivy's nod reminded Thad just a little of a bobblehead doll. She had been raised old-school and was a little too agreeable for her own good.

Thad gave his fist a final shake. "You sure you're the one to play welcome wagon, Lee? You're not exactly known for the warm and fuzzy."

"Fuck you."

"Again with the fuck you," Thad muttered. He gestured to the wall. "Get someone to fix that," he said to Ivy. "And find some clean clothes for our guests. Shoes, too." He remembered that Isabel had still been barefoot when they made the trip from Florida.

Ivy remained, staring at him like a puppy waiting for the tennis ball to get thrown. "That's all," he said tersely. She nodded once more and scampered off.

Thad didn't bother to apologize. He was king now. He needed to grow a set and get used to handing out orders.

God, he was so freaking tired of himself.

He wiped drywall dust from his hand onto his pants and walked past Lee. "Come with me," he growled and headed toward the elevator at the rear of the mansion. They made the descent to his father's old study in silence. When he closed the mahogany-and-glass double doors behind both of them, Thad noticed that the humor hadn't left Lee's face.

"What?"

"Nothing," Lee said as he dropped into a large wing-back chair by the empty fireplace. His conversational tone feigned casual innocence. "It's just that usually when I smell blood and sex rolling towards me, the individual on the other end is in a much better mood."

Thad pointed a finger at him. "Don't start with me."

"O-kay. So what's up, my man?"

Thad gestured around at the walls of bookcases and file drawers. The flowery photographs on pastel-colored backdrops. "I want to go ahead and clear my father's stuff out. Make it my own space." With his hands on his hips he surveyed the room. The decor was far too dainty. He'd never given it much thought before, but his mother must have done this. "Maybe get some new furniture in here."

"So you're finally moving in?"

Thad stared at the fluffy beige carpet for awhile before nodding an affirmation. With or without Isabel, it was time to figure out how to move forward. "It's about time I get my ass in gear. I'm still acting like a guest in this house, even though my dad's been dead for months."

Leaning back in the chair, Lee crossed his left ankle over his right knee. "Letting go is hard, buddy."

"Yeah, well…" Thad swept his arm out dismissively. "It's necessary."

Lee sighed and uncrossed his legs, ready to stand. "Just lemme know what you need." He rolled his neck around on his shoulders a few times before he stood up. "So. You wanna talk about it?"

Thad scowled. "About what?" Well, that was the no-shit question of the year, wasn't it?

"Come on," Lee scoffed. "You think I want to know your feelings on pink being the new gray? What's going on with you and your female that's got you throwing out pissed-off like beads at Mardi Gras?"

"I don't think pink is the new gray, and I don't want to talk about it."

"Sure?"

"Very."

Lee shrugged. "Fine." He stood and crossed his arms over his chest. "So this all you wanted then, to announce you're branching out as an interior decorator?"

Thad made his way to his father's Victorian-style desk, easing one hip to sit on top of it. The groan of protest from under his ass confirmed that he needed sturdier furniture. "You talked to Siddoh, right? Give me a status report."

Lee grumbled and seated himself in the chair again. "No news is good news, apparently. He said it's been pretty quiet the past few weeks, aside from a couple of suspicious human deaths. No conclusion on those, though. Thing is, he also thinks maybe the wizards have some new moves, and he thinks they're reorganizing—maybe even using some undercover tactics. He wants to get Tyra to nose around during the daytime."

Thad's head snapped up and his eyes narrowed to scrutinize his best friend's face. "You told him no, right?"

Lee grimaced. "Initially. Thing is, she might really be able to help. His theory involves stemming their supply of new blood by hitting them where they grab their women and their offspring. It's…" He sighed, running his hands over his almost military buzz cut.

"I hate to say it but it's a reasonably good idea, if we can work it carefully. We've never known for certain how they reproduce, but putting a little time and recon into it could be a good thing. I told him I'd talk to Ty about it. We agreed to stick with early evening so she's not out there without backup for long."

Thad's lips pressed together. "An hour. She goes out an hour before dusk, tops. No earlier. She can change her volunteer schedule accordingly. Lately, she's there nights mostly anyway. Have her stay off patrol duty for awhile. If she does run into a wizard out there during the day, we don't want her to be recognized as one of us."

"I'm actually a little concerned that they already know who she is, based on our encounter with that wizard in Florida."

"Be that as it may, I'd rather not take chances. We don't know if it was just the one guy you dusted, or if the whole clan knows. They're selfish and secretive enough even with their own, so either is possible."

"True. Anyway, I'll talk to her when she gets in." A small vibration on his hip had Lee tapping out a text and holstering his phone within a few seconds. "Speak of the devil; she's on her way over."

Thad cracked a smile, coming down a little from his angry hard-boil. "You know, you're fast with that phone. I never would have pegged you as a gadget guy."

Lee threw his head back in a rare moment of true laughter. "When you remember days of bathing in a frigid lake and reading by candlelight, you learn to embrace technology."

Thad smiled. "Okay," he said, clapping his hands together. "Anything else we need to cover on patrols? Or is it basically just the all-quiet?"

"One other issue. Xander got into a major disagreement with the business end of a wizard blade, couple days ago. Doesn't seem to be doing too well. I just got back from seeing him."

"Do we have enough guys for him to be out?"

"That's not the issue."

Thad frowned. "So what's the issue?"

"He refuses to feed."

"Ah. Shit…" Thad let out a long slow breath.

This was tough. Alexander—Xander as he was known to the team—had recently lost the love of his life. For many, feeding was a personal and private thing, particularly between mated couples. Thad could sympathize, but Xander was a soldier and he couldn't afford not to feed.

"What about that new doc over in the barracks. Abel. Or Brayden? Doctors do that sort of thing sometimes, right? Or maybe it's better if we get a female. What about Ivy? Can we get a transfusion, maybe?"

"Dunno. To my understanding, alternate delivery methods only work for small amounts. He's gonna need a lot. Both Ivy and Brayden are tied up with your human now. I'm sure Abel would do it, but we can't force Xander to feed, no matter who's doing the offering."

"Maybe we need to call Blood Service." Blood Service existed for vampires without a mate to drink from, but many looked down on it as little more than glorified prostitution. As far as Thad was concerned, it helped to keep their population going, and that was fine with him.

"Still need Xander's agreement."

"Well, find a way. For his own sake, we can't have him down and out. I don't want to force anything, but I don't want him fighting till he's back to a hundred percent. So it's up to him."

"Understood." Lee stood again and ambled slowly toward the office doors. "Anything else you need from me tonight? Not sure why Tyra isn't down here yet, but I wanna have a quick confab with her and then see about the human before I call it a night."

"I think I'm good. Let me know how she's doing. The human, I mean." Tyra was never one to hide how she was doing. She was terrible at the stoic thing but no one had the stones to tell her.

"Good deal," Lee replied as he moseyed out.

A lick of pain against Thad's palm, and the scent of charred wood startled him. When he looked down, he noticed ash from a newly burnt piece of paper and marks where the fingers of his right hand had scorched the wood on the top of the desk. He'd almost forgotten about his newfound power in the wake of his conversation with Lee.

"Shit!" A squeak of rubber in the hall announced that Lee had changed direction. Thad looked up to see the dude's head poking back in through the door.

"Something wrong, buddy?"

"Turns out I do need something else from you after all." He held up his hand. His palm and fingertips glowed a little. "I need you to help me get this under control."

"Huh." Lee rested his bulk against the door frame and smiled. "Well, all right then. We'll get together on that later. Try not to touch anything important." The larger male's eyes sparkled with humor as he righted himself and walked out again.

―――

"Thank you so much, Ivy."

Alexia handed the raven-haired vampire an empty teacup and winced as she settled against the headboard of the bed. His shoulder ached like crazy. Then again, that wasn't the half of the unpleasant sensations she was experiencing. Her head ached, her lip was swollen, and she was totally and completely disoriented.

Ivy accepted the cup and settled her hip onto the bed. "You're sure I can't get anything else for you?"

"You've done plenty. I really appreciate the tea and the clean clothes. I don't think I'm up for handling anything that resembles real food just yet." She took a deep breath and smiled at the kind face that had been hovering over her when she woke up. "I appreciate you explaining what happened. Sorry I went ape-shit on you and that doctor guy before."

Ivy put her hand on Alexia's forearm, squeezing gently with long, elegant fingers. She had very nice hands. Golden. Smooth. Well-manicured. Alexia's own nails were bitten to the quick so she was always envious of pretty hands.

"You had a scary and confusing experience. Anybody would have freaked out."

"I still feel bad."

"Don't mention it, really." Ivy leaned forward, long dark strands of hair cascading gently over her right shoulder. Her golden eyes were wide and innocent. Childlike. "Can I ask you what it was like? I hear the soldiers talk about the wizards all the time, but I've never seen one up close."

That probably was a damn good thing. Alexia was getting the strong sense that she had lucked out, since she was not actually dead. "I don't remember much.

He was definitely intimidating. Tall, probably as tall as Thad or Lee, but I'm not a very good judge of height. His head was shaved, like, totally bald..."

She searched her foggy memory for more. "Oh, and he had this stupid-looking robe on. And being around him felt... I don't know... gross, I guess. Nauseating. Does that make sense?" In fact, the mere mention had her stomach doing the kind of unpleasant drop that it did on the rare occasions that she rode a roller coaster.

Ivy nodded with an energy that made Alexia look catatonic on even her perkiest of days. "It does. I've heard that because they're so evil they have this, like, disgusting black aura around them. You can feel it a mile away."

Alexia nodded along, taking a look at her surroundings. The room was gorgeous. Like the pricey hotel room she'd stayed in once on her way to a massive party, only she'd been sharing it with ten people at the time. The memory still made her smile: The guy she'd hooked up with had wound up going home with the other guy who'd shared the king-sized bed with them.

She'd gotten a ride home with a hottie named Darren who drove an Audi TT. He'd said he was in the Marines, which at the time had turned her off because she wasn't into military guys. A picture of Thad's bodyguard, all leather-clad and menacing, popped into her head. *Funny how things change.*

Alexia shook off the mental tangent and focused on Ivy. "So we're safe from the wizards here?"

"Oh, gosh. Definitely." *Gosh?* "I mean, the estate's pretty well camouflaged. They've never been able to find us. Even if they did, it's wired with all kinds of crazy high-tech security. I had it installed myself." She beamed proudly at that but then faded a bit. "Well, I mean I hired someone for the king... well, for Thad's father. There's magic security, too." The pretty vampire smiled again, but the smile didn't reach her eyes this time.

Wow. Self-esteem issues, anyone?

Still, Alexia was grateful to have someone so friendly for company. She'd already known that vampires existed but the whole shebang that Thad had brought to their door was some kind of crazy nightmare, and she was still reeling from it. She'd gotten the impression, though, that Ivy had led a very sheltered life. That was a bizarre departure from what Alexia was used to. She didn't quite know how to act around the beautiful female. The awkwardness made her a little tense.

And what had been a dull roar in her head upon waking was now a sensation much akin to tiny miners drilling out the inside of her brain. Alexia rubbed her temples. There was just too much to figure out.

"Actually, Ivy, would it be too much trouble to get some Tylenol or something?" She'd kill for a Percocet or two, but she didn't dare ask.

"No trouble, of course not. I texted Lee to let him know you're up, by the way. He's going to come to give you more blood. That will make you feel a ton better."

Alexia blinked rapidly and shook her head. "I'm sorry... more blood?"

Ivy froze. "I'm sorry. I think maybe I was supposed to let him explain that all to you."

Alexia's brow furrowed. No. She wanted an explanation now. "Please. By all means."

"It's kind of a standard triage measure for us, to help speed the healing. They gave you a little of Lee's blood when you first got here, but they thought you'd need more." She eyed Alexia with uncertainty.

So, that was weird. She and Isabel had been roommates for two years, but Alexia had never partaken of the stuff. "I think I get it. It was a surprise, that's all."

Ivy patted Alexia's knee through the blanket. "Let me go ahead and grab you that Tylenol."

A quiet tap and the snick of a lock drew their attention. Lee's imposing form filled the doorway. Funny, she had expected Lee to have a powerful, booming, heavy-fisted knock, if knocks had personalities.

"Ivy, would you excuse us please?" Lee's voice was low and calm, but the commanding undertones made Alexia shiver. In both good and bad ways.

Ivy patted Alexia's leg one last time. "No worries, you're in good hands. I'll be back with that Tylenol." Ivy rose from the bed, turned to smile at Lee, and then sidled out of the room. As Ivy disappeared, Lee closed the door behind her with a very significant-sounding click.

Chapter 17

"TYRA, TYRA, TYRA... MORGAN... TYRA MORGAN... Tyra Morgan... shit!"

Nothing. All but the past few days of Anton Smith's life lay just out of reach, cocooned in a big fuzzy ball of darkness. Unable to be still, he paced the tiny room that was now his temporary residence. He had spent too much time in bed, too much time wondering. Worrying.

What had he done in his life that had resulted in being beaten and left for dead? The questions weighed heavily like a stone in the center of his chest, and lying down to sleep in a new place without the benefit of a morphine drip was just not something he could manage.

He'd thought that having a soft place to land and get his head straight would make a difference, but so far he was only more anxious. For some reason, thoughts of that olive-skinned social worker were running through his brain on a continuous loop and he couldn't make them stop. Some gut-deep instinct told him that she was somebody he knew. Somebody special. But no matter how many times he said her name or pictured her face, it didn't ring any bells or evoke any memories.

"Dammit." Anton Smith sat on the thin, hard, lumpy mattress that made his former hospital bed seem like luxury accommodations. He hunched his shoulders and tapped the knuckles of his clasped hands against his chin. Tyra... Tyra... if he didn't know her, then what was the deal? She certainly hadn't shown any spark of recognition. In fact, she had been adamant that they had never met.

She was a beautiful woman, well put-together with dark curls, warm eyes, and a firm but sensual body. Maybe he was mistaking lust for something more? Or maybe this was one of those signs from God that the hospital chaplain had talked about.

He had a very fierce and yet totally inexplicable urge to protect the shit out of her. As in walk her home and stand beside her bed to keep watch while she dreamed. Could that just be his nature? Perhaps he'd been a cop or something in his "old" life, but the police officers who'd met him at the hospital hadn't seemed to recognize him, either. Anyway, he seemed to have a strong resistance to authority. Firefighter, maybe? Firefighters were protectors.

"Uuuggh!" He dropped his hands and slumped farther on the bed until his head hung between his knees. Who the hell knew? He kept telling himself to put the matter aside and get some sleep, but he found himself coming back to the whole thing like a junkie with a bad habit. Did he have a little sister somewhere who resembled the pretty social worker and the sense of familiarity was just transference? The hospital psychiatrist had taught him that one.

He was desperately hollow inside. He had no idea who he was, and only a handful of weeks to figure that out before the shelter kicked him out. Who even knew if the life he'd had before was worth going back to?

He jerked his leg and struck a rickety chair nearby. It danced across the floor with a satisfying clatter before falling to the side and resting on the floor. An unexpected *bang, bang, bang* sounded from the left wall. "Hey, man, tryin' to sleep over here!"

"Sorry," he muttered. Sighing, Anton switched off the light and stretched out on the small bed. He tried some deep breathing they'd taught him in the hospital. Supposedly strong emotions like stress and anxiety could affect his memories, so they'd taught him meditation. But how did anyone expect him to relax with no clue about where he belonged in the universe? Being told that it would all come back "eventually" wasn't helping his perspective.

Anton's head throbbed like a bitch. Migraines had plagued him since he woke up in the hospital. Common with head injuries, they had told him. He supposed he was lucky. The guy in the bed next to him had a head way more messed up than Anton's. He might have no long-term memory, but at least he didn't slur his words or have trouble picking stuff up.

As Anton tapped his fingers against his chest, his brain churned hard enough to make smoke. He grudgingly stretched out into the "corpse" pose he'd learned from the hospital OT. He lay with his arms palm up by his sides, and soon his breathing slowed and his body got heavy. He jerked a little when his hands and feet began to tingle. The occupational therapist had explained that it was a normal response to the deep breathing that was carrying extra oxygen to his extremities, but damn, it felt weird.

Stupid biology. It was screwing with him at every turn.

As his breath moved slowly in and out, the headache diminished and he finally got sleepy. With no warning, his eyes burned and a wet trickle slid down the side of his face to land in his left ear. "Not again," he mumbled to absolutely no one.

Emotions kept popping up with no experiential reference to tie them to. Just… feelings. This time, sadness, but over what? Maybe memories would start to follow the emotions. Maybe he was just lost forever. Or maybe, just maybe, he would find out that he had been somebody great who could be worthy of a woman like Tyra Morgan.

Chapter 18

"WHAT ARE YOU DOING HERE?"

Isabel's body went still, halfway in and halfway out of the massive stainless-steel fridge. Or as still as she could make it, considering that rummaging in the thing had given her another case of the shakes. Foraging without permission was seriously rude, but Thad's sister had stopped by for a chat, after which Isabel had slept longer, and now she was ready to gnaw her own arm off. She straightened slowly, turned to face Thad, and pressed the refrigerator door closed with her back. "I'm looking for something to eat. What are you doing here?"

His stormy blue eyes seemed to assess her as he leaned against a stretch of granite counter with his arms folded and his ankles crossed. The stance was somehow both casual and defensive. "*I*... live here. I can do anything I want." He raised his eyebrows. "Or at least I'll be living here soon."

Isabel's chest heaved and she felt a friendly *zing!* shoot through the center of her body at the mere sound of his voice. Her brain might have been trying to forget about their earlier interlude, but her body sure wasn't. She swallowed hard. "I thought you lived here already."

"It's my house now that my parents are gone. Moving is on my to-do list. It's important that I get down to business, don't you think?" Was that some kind of innuendo? Thad stepped toward her as he spoke. The fall of his boot seemed to echo loudly on the white tile beneath his feet. Something she couldn't place flashed in his eyes. He was different, somehow.

Harder.

"Is—are you okay, Thad? You don't exactly seem like yourself." She pressed herself a little harder against the refrigerator door as he continued to advance on her. As if that would matter.

"I'm just fine, Isabel." His smile was sensual and wicked, showing a hint of fang. Mercy, those lips of his were soft and full. "Besides, how can you tell? We barely know each other, right?"

Ouch. "I guess you just don't seem like you did before." He just kept prowling toward her like a lion stalking a gazelle, and damned if her feet weren't glued to the floor. The full-body tremble gained intensity.

"Do you mean before when we were fucking?" Closer. "Or when you were going down on me?" Closer still. "Or waaay back to last night when you were waltzing around in that schoolgirl outfit?" Thad stopped dead in front of her. "Cuz I've gotta tell you, Isabel. You seem different now, too." Holy Christmas, could blue eyes really smolder like that?

"Umm…" She hugged her arms around herself. She told herself to move away, but the not-so-gentle throbbing between her legs strongly disagreed. Just reaching and touching him would be so easy… She clenched her fists to avoid temptation.

And then Thad leaned, effectively caging her in with an arm on either side of her. So much for avoiding temptation. His chest pressed so hard against hers that she wasn't sure whose heartbeat she could feel. "You're cold again." It wasn't a question.

There was no denying it. Shivers continued to wrack her body despite her layers of clothing. Ivy had brought a bag of clothing, and Isabel had put on damn near every piece of it. And she was supposed to be able to control this somehow? "Thad, I just don't think—"

"See, that's your problem, Isabel. You're thinking way too much," he said darkly. He reached around and grabbed the handle for the refrigerator door. "You're hungry?"

"A little."

"No, you must be very hungry," he corrected. Well, hell. "You haven't had anything but doughnuts recently." Thad leaned down, his breath deliciously hot on her neck. He tapped playfully at his own pulsing artery. Quirked his eyebrow. "Besides, I can feel it."

Isabel closed her eyes. She didn't have a snappy comeback. No doubt he could sense her desire, too. This whole situation was a mess. Being near Thad was like having committed to a diet and then stumbling into one of those all-you-can-eat buffet places. There was just something about him, especially when he was so warm and she was so cold. Her body, her libido, her whole being sought him out. God, she wanted to just curl up in the crook of his arm for about a century, and how was *that* for being an independent female?

"Here," he said softly. "Let me help you find something." He pulled the handle of the refrigerator door behind her. Isabel couldn't help but gasp when the movement brought her forward and Thad's hips ground into hers. His erection was obvious. Heat seeped into her as she stood there, deliciously sandwiched between Thad and the door.

Reaching into its depths, he pulled out a carton of milk, then leaned to the side and pulled a glass from the nearest cabinet. All the while his body rubbed against hers and his eyes held a certain suggestive smokiness. He wanted her again, and he knew damn well she wanted him, too. Again. Still.

Shit!

For an interminable stretch of time he reached, nudged, and brushed against her until he had conjured up a burrito along with the milk and guided her into the nearby chair of a cute little glass-topped bistro table. He leaned down to whisper in her ear. "Are you going to eat? Or do you want me to feed you?"

"Thad, don't you think we should talk—"

"Shh." Ooh, she couldn't *stand* being shushed. Her jaw clamped hard, preparing to spit out a nasty comeback, but Thad's hand smoothed over her arm from behind and pushed her plate and glass toward her. His fingers lingered over hers as he guided her hand to wrap around the glass. "I can feed myself, Thad."

"By all means, then. I know it's not a gourmet meal, but the chef is in bed for the day, and it's good protein. You can't live on doughnuts and coffee, and it's not right for my queen to be hungry."

His queen. Good, freaking Lord, what were they going to do about that? Her stomach clenched and growled again, as if to remind her that now was not the time to be petulant and stubborn. She picked up the milk, took a big swallow, and put the glass down again. She didn't want a repeat of the frozen-water incident from before. Her throat hurt to gulp down the milk, but she refused to let that show. "There. Happy?"

"Happy." From the corner of her eye, Isabel caught Thad's frown. "I wouldn't say happy, exactly. But it's good to see you eating."

"Are you going to stand behind me the entire time?" Her nerves couldn't take much more of his close proximity. She wasn't certain they could handle him leaving, either.

He rubbed the back of her neck, massaging the base of her skull gently while she chewed. She shivered a little as the pads of his fingers brushed over the scar tissue under her hair.

"Just keeping you company." Lord, she couldn't stand it. The husky growl of his voice was enough to undo her completely. "Besides." His massive chest pressed against her shoulders as he leaned into her a little more. "You're cold. I'm here to keep you warm." His arms enveloped the tops of her shoulders.

Thad's warmth was nice; she couldn't argue that. Better than nice. Comforting. Luxurious. She wasn't shaking anymore. And the whole food thing was sweet, if she were being honest with herself.

Isabel chewed uncomfortably through the burrito and washed it down with the milk. The whole mess settled like lead in her stomach. She turned her head to look at him, her pulse racing as her cheek brushed against his. "Good?"

She knew the kiss was coming but was unable, or perhaps just unwilling, to resist. His voice was raspy as his mouth claimed hers. "Good."

Lee stifled a string of his favorite expletives. What the hell was he doing here? Alexia looked small and pale sitting in the middle of the large queen bed, propped against an excessive hotel-style formation of pillows. Shit, he'd never gotten that. Only reason he had two of 'em on his bed was to keep the maid from getting antsy about where to put the other pillowcase.

The human's legs were drawn up to her chest, hands clasped in a nervous gesture atop the peak of her knees. Her anxiousness vibrated in the air around her. She drew back a little when he approached the bed and sat down beside her on the mattress. Like she was afraid of him. What if she was? It didn't matter. Just... didn't.

But then a transformation occurred. Her shoulders rolled back and she smiled slightly with one quizzical eyebrow raised. She was no longer glammed up with several pounds of spackle and fairy dust, but the sassy party-girl who had waltzed up to him and Thad at that club in Orlando was back.

"So. You're here to give me blood?"

Lee chuckled. And to think, he'd been working up a way to break it to her gently. It was probably better this way, since "gently" wasn't really his cup of tea. "Yeah."

"Why?" She frowned and shook her head a little. "I mean, I know it's supposed to help me heal or whatever, but I... kind of got the impression you didn't like me very much."

Yeah. That's the problem. Lee gave his best casual shrug. "You're important to Isabel. Isabel's important to Thad. My job is to take care of Thad, which by extension means taking care of you."

"I see."

Her face fell a little, but Lee proceeded as if he hadn't noticed. Getting involved with this girl was bad eight ways from Sunday, and he would do well not to lose sight of that. He reached into his jacket to pull out a blade similar to the one he'd used before.

"It's cleaner." He met her curious stare. "To cut myself with this. Rather than using my fangs. Not that it can hurt you either way…" Shit, this was awkward. He leaned a little farther onto his hip. Alexia kept staring. The truth of it was that he wouldn't bite his own vein for her. It was too intimate. "You lived with Isabel. You've never done this before?"

"No. Never." The expression on her face and the vigorous shake of her head drove home the truth of her response. Not only hadn't she, but he may as well have asked if she'd ever mud-wrestled the Tooth Fairy.

"Thad mentioned that Isabel drank from you—"

"That was strictly a one-way street. And in my defense, the first time she didn't exactly ask my permission."

Lee gritted his teeth. "Do you mean to tell me that you take offense somehow to the whole thing?"

"No!" She put her hands over her face. "Listen, I'm… I'm still really out of it. It's just… I didn't mind Isabel drinking from me. It was actually kind of… nice." The mention of it made Alexia's face take on a far-off, wistful expression. A muscle jumped in Lee's jaw. "It's just—" She sighed and relaxed her arms. "I wasn't sure what it would do to me. That's all."

She seemed to search his face, but for what, Lee wasn't sure. Huh. Her eyes were brown, as it turned out. And comparing her golden blonde hair to the darkness of her eyebrows told him that the drapes definitely did not match the carpet. All the more reason to steer clear. He didn't go for females with high-maintenance beauty; not anymore.

"You think that's lame, don't you?"

He shook his head. "Nah."

She didn't believe him. The confident mask she'd thrown up when he entered the room slipped just a little before she slid her gaze away.

He reached gently to grasp her chin, using the barest pressure he could manage to turn her face back toward him. "Look," he said quietly. "You don't need to worry about my opinion of you." He laid the dagger carefully on the bedside table. "You don't need to drink from me if you don't want to. Here's the thing: our blood speeds healing and cellular regeneration even in humans, so it will help you bounce back from your injury.

"It would be complicated to take you to a human doctor because your wound was made by something supernatural. Some kind of mutated, hijacked power. Now, Brayden can probably get you antibiotics or whatever you might need, so if you don't want the blood, we have other options. This is supposed to help you, not frighten you."

His little speech had come out with a larger helping of impatient and annoyed than he'd intended, but that couldn't be helped. Too much else was going on for him to coddle and handhold her through the whole thing.

Her eyes closed for a beat. They were wider than before when she opened them again and studied him. Jesus, he felt like a bug under glass, the way she kept doing that.

"Okay," she said finally.

He placed his hand on the blade's handle once again. "You're sure?" He searched her face, eyebrows raised.

She nodded. "I'm as sure as I'm going to be."

Before Alexia could change her mind, Lee quickly scored his wrist and held it to her. A line of crimson rushed to the surface and ran down his arm. The sight seemed to stun her.

"Alexia," he said in a low voice. "Don't make me bleed out all over the bed. If you've changed your mind, tell me now."

Quickly, she grabbed Lee's forearm and placed the flat of her tongue beneath the flowing rivulet, tracing upward to the source of the bleeding, like she was licking the drip from an ice-cream cone.

That really wasn't necessary, but... oh, *hell*... The warm trail of her tongue turned into a gentle lapping and suckling at his wrist and then very quickly to more urgent pulls. The suction of Alexia's mouth pulled Lee's skin between her teeth, which made him immediately, achingly, unbelievably hard.

Nothing hotter than being bitten by a female.

Some of his kind were able to separate the blood exchange from sexual urges, but he wasn't one of them. Given his unwanted attraction to Alexia, he probably should have recused himself from this duty, but he'd always been a masochist. And truthfully, he hadn't expected to react quite like this.

Alexia began to writhe a little as well. The pads of her fingers turned white as they dug more urgently into the flesh on his arm. A tiny little moan sounded from the back of her throat as she continued to suck harder at his arm. The pale olive of her skin flushed pink across the chest, and the stain spread up her neck to her cheeks. It wasn't too difficult to imagine what she would be like on her back in all those pillows, minus the clothes.

Lee's breathing quickened and his heart tried its damnedest to escape the walls of his chest. Already his fangs crowded his mouth, and the biological urge to push Alexia onto her back and have his way with her before biting into that delicate-looking vein was gripping tenaciously at the base of his skull. The whole situation was on the verge of going straight from zero to FUBAR.

On the verge of snapping completely, Lee placed a hand over one of hers. "Easy, there." Her eyes lifted to his, a desperate plea shining in them. Her face was flush with desire. She wanted more, and damn him straight to Hell, he wanted to give it to her.

Instead, he said, "Time to take a break. You've had plenty. Trust me."

Alexia pulled back but maintained possession of Lee's arm. Her breath hit his skin in warm puffs. "Oh, man. I feel like I had too many martinis." She paused, her mouth hanging slack. Her tongue explored her lower lip tentatively, sliding out to taste the traces of blood that lingered there. Lee very nearly helped her lick the remnants away.

God, he despised how badly he wanted her.

Determined not to let on about what was happening in his pants, Lee shifted subtly on the bed. He nodded his understanding as he licked the cut on his wrist. Her saliva tasted of chocolate and Earl Grey tea. Knowing that only made his cock throb harder.

"Even for us, it gets a good buzz going."

"Holy mother of—I had no idea it would be like that."

The implied "or else I would have done it before" was left hanging in the air. Dumb son of a bitch that he was, Lee couldn't deny a perverse pleasure in giving her that first experience. And then he shut himself down before he dared think of her having a second.

"Yeah, well, brace yourself. You just put high-grade synthetic in an engine that's used to running on the stuff they make for lawn mowers. You should be feeling better in no time." The analogy was insulting, but pissing her off was for the better right now. Seriously. He started to rise from the bed.

Her hand shot out to grab his before he made it all the way to standing. "Wait."

Chapter 19

"I HAVE SOME QUESTIONS," ALEXIA SAID SOFTLY. BOY, that was one bulldozer of a cocktail. Her lids were heavy, and she was afraid to close them. When she'd had too much to drink, that was usually when the room started spinning. She forced herself to focus on Lee's face. That kept her grounded, while looking at any other part of him only spurred her desire to crawl over and give him a lap dance.

She always had been an affectionate drunk.

Lee returned to his seat on the bed, rubbing his hands over his face. "Right. Questions. I just thought, you know, maybe you'd want to rest first. Let yourself level out. Your body's gonna need some time to adjust to the blood."

"I'd rather do it now." She paused, giggled a little at the absurdity of the moment, and then tried her damnedest to put a serious expression back on her face. "Man, it really is like I'm drunk."

"Uh, yeah." He cleared his throat. "Anyway… what do you want to know?"

"Let's start with where am I? Ivy said I'm at the king's estate, which doesn't tell me much. So far I've got a weird guy—with robes, for God's sake—coming up behind me in my own bedroom, waking up in a strange place, you feeding me blood, and Mrs. Peacock in the library with a candlestick." She rolled her eyes at his questioning look and continued. She should have guessed he wasn't into pop culture. "Anyway, all of it adds up to a whole lot of 'holy shit' in my book."

"Okay." Leaning forward he rubbed his hand across his face and chin stubble. Some guys looked sloppy when they hadn't shaved. Lee didn't. Of course he didn't. He clasped his hands together. "So. The wizard—that was the weird dude in the robes that attacked you." He paused, tapping his index finger thoughtfully against the bottom of his lip for a moment. "You said he came up behind you?"

"Yeah, I was standing in front of my closet, and all of a sudden, *blammo!*" She clapped her hands together for illustration. "He was just there. Like, out of nowhere." She sat up straighter in bed, her mental fog was already beginning to clear. Thank God.

"You tried to attack him?"

How did he—"Yeah, well. Tried is the operative word." Embarrassment washed over her. She'd taken self-defense classes, dammit; she should've been able to do some damage to the bastard.

The corner of Lee's mouth quirked. "That was brave... but stupid."

"Well, I didn't manage to get any hits in, so I guess you're right about the stupid part."

In what Alexia must have guessed was a very rare gesture, Lee put his hand over hers. It was nice. Big, warm, and reassuring.

"Hey, listen up for a minute. These guys aren't really any more human than I am. We're talking evil men who deal in black magic and steal supernatural powers for kicks and giggles. I don't mean this as an affront of any kind, but you didn't stand a chance."

Alexia tried to make sense of that. "So that's the deal with these guys—they steal powers from you?"

He seemed amused. "Well, not from me personally, but yeah. That's pretty much what they do."

"You have a sick sense of humor."

"Thank you." He smiled. God, he was wicked hot. The smile showed off his fangs, which seemed surprisingly long and prominent. Much more than Isabel's or even Ivy's had been.

Enough already, Lex.

"So why do they do it?" She couldn't believe what an effed-up concept this was. Why hadn't Isabel ever told her anything about it?

"I'm pretty sure power for the sake of power has generally been a good enough reason."

"So how—" Oh, sweet merciful God, his hand hadn't left hers. Lord, she was such a loser. One tiny crumb of affection and she would all but run off to Vegas if he asked.

Act casual, dammit!

"How do they steal your powers?"

Lee's head gave a side-to-side waggle, like he was waffling a bit on his answer. "Well, we don't know all the details. There's some kind of black magic involved. What we do know at least is that it involves eating the heart."

Oh. *Nasty.*

Alexia gagged. "You're not serious about that."

Oh, but he was. She didn't know much about Lee, but as sure as she lived and breathed, she was sure he would not joke about that sort of thing. Still, she searched his face desperately for a sign that he was just messing with her. In keeping with her feelings of inebriation, her gut churned with the intense urge to hurl. She tamped it down, unwilling to ruin the whole Lee's-hand-on-hers moment by getting sick in his lap.

"I wish I were joking," he said grimly. "If what they did was as simple as jacking an old lady's handbag, my job would be a lot easier."

"Shit, that's... oh, my God... that's just so disgusting." Alexia gave a little cough, trying to head another gag off at the pass. She'd always been squeamish about blood-and-guts stuff. As a child she'd wanted to go to veterinary school until she found out the job often entailed much ickier responsibilities than just petting puppies and kittens all day.

"Yeah, well..." He shrugged a little. A chill traveled up Alexia's arm when his hand lifted from hers and landed again on his inner thigh. A shadow of emotion flashed briefly across his face but she couldn't quite name it.

"Yeah. It is. Anyway," he continued. The tiny hint of whatever it was disappeared as quickly as it had come.

"As far as the where part, we're in Ash Falls, Virginia. About an hour outside Washington D.C., in horse country more or less."

"Horse country."

"Yep."

"I can't believe there's horse country outside Washington. I always thought it was, you know, like a big city." She wanted to smack herself for the number of times she'd heard herself use "like" in the course of this conversation. She must sound like a freaking idiot.

"There's actually lots of land around here if you know where to look."

Farm country. Yikes. She swallowed. "Swell." Then again, they probably wouldn't be here long, right? That begged the question she really wanted to ask: "So when do I get to get to go home?"

Lee's responding throat clear did not fill her with warm fuzzies, nor did the way he crossed his arms and leaned away from her. It was a defensive posture. But hey! Here she was, finally using that psychology degree she'd worked so hard for. "Yeah. I have to talk to Thad about how we're gonna handle that."

"How you're going to handle what, me?" He was talking about handling her like she was some kind of golden retriever. And it hadn't escaped her notice that he'd compared her to a lawn mower earlier in the conversation. What the hell was up with this guy? And why the hell did she want to jump him so badly despite what a total *dick* he was?

Another throat clear. "Here's the thing: you were attacked by a very dangerous enemy, and we don't know how he found us or you. We don't know exactly what his intentions were, or whether or not one of his cronies might try to return to where I killed him. We're in a war with these wizards, and we're not used to having humans in the mix this way."

"You killed him. Right." The quiet voice she managed to push past her lips was little more than a whisper. Her head began to swim again. Killed him. Lee... *killed* the man who attacked her.

Duh. It made sense. Of course it did. Big-ass vampire, built like a brick shithouse and packing all kinds of heat versus some kind of black-magic junkie who was out to get the vampire's race. Of course he'd... kill...

him. She had assumed that was the outcome, but the reality hadn't hit her until he'd just said it.

Talk about going for the bad boy.

Holy shit.

Lee shrugged. "It's kind of an 'us or them' thing."

"I guess so," she said, nodding like an idiot.

"Anyway," he continued, and this time his voice had a softer edge to it. "Even if we knew you were safe from future wizard attacks—and that's a big if, given that you've been seen associating with us by our enemy—going back there could get you into any number of problems. It's a security risk for you and for us.

"So. I'm not just trying to be an ass here, but there's no way we can let you go home at this point."

Alexia blinked. "Didn't you say before that it was a bad idea for me to be here?"

"I did."

"So what's changed?"

Lee rubbed his hand over the back of his neck like he was tense. Good. Because the news flash that she was not allowed to go home had sucked her out of her drunken warm fuzzies fast enough to make her head spin, and now she was tense, too. May as well share the love.

"Nothing changed, really. It's still a bad idea for you to be here. However, it's an equally bad idea, possibly a worse idea, to let you go. It's a lesser-of-two-evils decision, and I will not make that call without going over the options with Thad first."

Suddenly Alexia's body was hot. Her blood was on a hard boil. She was getting damn tired of Lee's game of insult the human. "What the hell? First you compare my blood to freaking two-stroke engine oil, and now I'm a problem you have to handle? *A lesser of two evils?* Look, I get it that you aren't very fond of humans, but I didn't do a damn thing to deserve your ire so you need to back the fuck off. You can't make me a prisoner here!"

Her breath sawed in and out. She was fairly sure her nostrils were flaring. Lee did nothing, said nothing, but continued to regard her with the same cool, impassive demeanor. All at once she wanted to shove his cocky, well-toned ass off the bed.

The heady buzz in her veins after drinking his blood made her wonder if she might really be strong enough to do it. Not that she'd actually try. Her famous temper had caused enough embarrassment. But for Pete's sake, she did not do helpless and powerless. She did not wait and see at the mercy of others.

Finally he said, "I didn't say that you—" He broke off and his irritation was clear. His jaw was set. He stood, looming large as if to intimidate Alexia with his gargantuan size. She was forced to crane her neck to see his face now, and she couldn't say she appreciated that, either. How was it that only minutes earlier she had been ready to get naked for him? "Look, think what you want, but this is for everybody's safety. I'll tell Isabel you're feeling better."

It was gonna take more than that to intimidate her, and she was used to going through life with a stiff neck. "So… I'm near Washington, and I got here from Florida how? How long was I out?"

"Not long. A few hours." He shrugged. "Tyra brought you here. By teleport."

"Tele… port…" Sure, that would have been her first guess. "How—"

"She disappears and reappears someplace else. *Star Trek* style. Sometimes she can take stuff with her. Like small human females." The smile was back. God, he was hot with that smile. Shit. *Shit! Stop that!*

"Oy." Her head flopped back against the bevy of pillows behind her. In the past hour she'd woken up, drunk blood, then been told she couldn't go home again, and she was lusting after a giant killer vampire. Oh, and she'd been brought to a huge mansion in Virginia by way of freaking teleport.

Happened every day.

"So… if I can't go home, what am I going to do?"

"Just hang tight. We'll figure it all out. For now, you're our guest here." He turned to go.

Guest. "That's reassuring."

He seemed to ponder something for a moment, then nodded curtly. The room temperature seemed to have dropped by about twenty degrees. Alexia propped her elbows on her still-bent knees, rubbing her eyes good and hard as she did so. It was all too fucking much. "Great, and…" She trailed off as her eyes opened again.

She hadn't heard the door, but he was already gone.

Chapter 20

"THAD." THE MOVEMENT OF ISABEL'S LIPS AGAINST HIS and the vibrations as she murmured his name only spurred him to kiss her harder. Hands down, these were the most amazing lips he had kissed. Ever. "Thad!"

Her hand pushed insistently against his pecs. "Hmm?" He kept kissing. Couldn't stop. Couldn't stop massaging her arms and shoulders as he went. Or trailing his fingers along her spine. He would almost swear the taste of his blood lingered in her mouth, and damned if that wasn't kind of sexy in a weird, kinky sort of way.

"Thad, stop. Please." She wedged her arms between his, breaking their embrace. "We need to talk." Those were words to pound a spike of cold, splintering fear into the center of any male's chest, even on a good day.

Thad growled as he stepped back—but only a scant few inches. He could still smell the clean, damp scent of Isabel's hair when he dipped his head to her ear.

"I've been doing a whole lot of talking," he whispered. "You're the one who's not saying much."

The need to touch her bordered on compulsive. Painful, almost. He leaned his weight against the table and crossed his arms over his chest, locking them firmly to protect against the urge to reach for a silky strand of hair or to brush against her cheek. How could she deny the connection between them? They had shared something special when they'd made love. Something meaningful. Rage mixed with agony mixed with confusion, and his face hurt from the effort of keeping it from contorting so the emotions were obvious.

"So go ahead, Isabel. Talk."

The strong breath she blew out ruffled her hair a bit. Long fingers rubbed at her tired eyes. He could hazard a guess as to what she was working up to, and he didn't want to hear it.

"Thad, I can't do this." She gestured back and forth between them. "Whatever it is that's going on here."

There it was. His insides boiled. He couldn't bite back what flew from his mouth next. His fangs crowded the inside of his mouth, and he just had to open the damn thing.

"And what exactly is going on here, Isabel? I'm still trying to figure that one out myself." His fists clenched and released. "Aside from you running hot and cold on me."

Isabel's raised her hands in front of her chest, palms forward. It was hard to tell whether it was a gesture of surrender or if she was warding off an attack.

"Look, I'm sorry. I really am. But to be honest with you, things are getting way too weird for me here. In the last few days I've had my life turned upside-down. My best friend has been attacked by something I've only heard about in stories, and I somehow get hurtled through space by your sister. Then we *fuck* and suddenly I've got a power? How do you expect me to handle all of that? I'd be a candidate for the loony bin if I wasn't freaking out right now."

What the—"Wait." He straightened. "You have a power?"

She nodded, wrapping her arms around herself. "I froze a glass of water into ice. Your sister said it probably happened after we fed from each other or after we were intimate, or maybe both. And probably that's why I've been so cold."

"You talked to Tyra about this?" Yuck. He and Tyra had always been close, but discussing their sex lives was something Thad would have never done with Ty, not even under duress. As far as he was concerned, his sister didn't have sex at all, and the whole business about her and Siddoh was just rumor and conjecture.

"She stopped by my room. Brought me some clothes. She seems nice."

"Yeah, Tyra's awesome." He cleared his throat. "Anyway. You want to tell me what? That even though the whole thing about you and me being destined for each other seems to be totally on par here, you're going to chicken out and bail on me?"

"Not exactly. I just... well, you don't need me anymore, right? We had sex, and you have a power now so you can do the whole, uh, kingship thing. If you've got your power, there isn't really any reason that I need to stay, right?"

Thad glanced around the kitchen as if someone else were present to see his expression of abject incredulity.

"You can't go home, Isabel. Too dangerous. And besides, what of your power?" Thad stepped closer again. No way was he going to let her bail this easily. He *did* need her, for fuck's sake, even if she didn't want to see it that way. And he wanted her. From the beginning, he had been drawn to her with a passion that defied all logic.

She shrugged away, clearly looking uncomfortable. "I don't know. I'm sure I'll get a handle on it somehow. Your sister could help me, or maybe Lucas."

"Lucas."

"Our friend back in Orlando. He came into his power a long time ago, and he seems to have a pretty good handle on—"

"Wait a minute, you mean hair guy? The wino vampire who was feeling up Alexia for lollipops? You expect him to help you master your power?"

Her eyes narrowed. "Listen, most of us are not soldiers or royalty. Some of us just want to be left alone."

"Is that what you want? To be left alone?" His jaw and neck were strung tight. The discomfort started to creep down his back. Why was she fighting this so hard?

"What the hell are you mad at me for?" Now she was the one leaning in, exasperation all over her face. "We had a good time together, and you got your power. You can't possibly think I'm supposed to be your queen. I wouldn't know what to do. I'm a professional party-girl, for crying out loud. Besides, how can you honestly think I can stand up as a figurehead for a race that rejected my family?"

Thad grabbed Isabel's wrist and pulled her against him. Maybe a little harder than intended, but he was too far into pissed-off for apologies. "Boo-fucking-hoo, honey. You can't base your entire outlook on the fact that your parents felt rejected by society."

"I don't even know how to live among our kind, Thad. I've never done it."

"So you're not even willing to try?"

Air rushed out of Isabel. Her entire body seemed to droop. "This is going nowhere, so can we just drop it?

It's just too overwhelming." She yanked her arm backward. "And you're hurting my wrist."

"Fine," he growled. "But this is not over."

Not by a fucking long shot.

"Why do you even care about this? You got your power." Vexation was edging into her voice. *Join the club, babe*.

"Gah!" His hand slammed down on the table, rattling the cup and plate left from her meal hard enough that they both paused for a beat to see if the heavy tumbler would fall over. "You keep saying that. Is that really all you think I care about? You think I was just using you to come into my power?"

She blinked. "Well, actually, no. At first I thought you were just using me for sex." *Jeez*. "Which I didn't mind because you know full well that you're an extremely desirable male. The power thing freaked me out, though. I won't lie. I mean, come on, Thad. Even if I thought the prophecy was true, there was no telling it would happen like *that*."

"And the part about being my queen?" Thad's voice got soft. Too soft. He hadn't wanted to ask it again, because the tone and the question itself held more vulnerability than he cared to show. He didn't expect a different answer. He just hoped.

"Thad, I'm no kind of royalty. You deserve someone much better. Someone upper class who comes from an old family, who knows the ways and traditions better than I do. Someone good for your image. I can see that you have a steep learning curve ahead of you, but I don't doubt for a second that you'll handle it just fine without me dragging you down."

Dragging him down? Good for his image?

Oh, for Pete's sake!

"Isabel, I care for you. I don't give a shit about my image. Nor should you. I can see us having a future together, don't you get that? I don't want someone else."

"Thad, we barely know each other."

He grasped her hair in his fist, pulled gently to the side, and leaned down to nuzzle her neck. Ah, she was so soft and smooth. "I know all I need to, Isabel. We already have amazing chemistry, and you've helped me gain my power. That means you're destined to be my mate. The rest…"

He kissed her jaw, then her neck. He wanted to go further but her sweatshirt was in the way. He settled for moving one hand between her shoulder blades and pressing forward so that her breasts heaved against him as she breathed. He lifted his chin to kiss her lips again. "The rest we'll figure out as we go," he murmured.

"Thad," she gasped, "I've never been in a long-term relationship. I've never had any kind of responsibility. I've never so much as returned a library book on time. You want a mate? A queen? You need to find someone who's worthy of you. Of what you're asking. I'm not that girl."

He stepped back and stroked her cheek gently. "You can," he growled. "And you will." His gaze lingered on hers, and he knew his desire was projecting loud and clear from every pore on his body. The thickness of his arousal was apparent even behind his heavy jeans, and she was taking it all in with wide eyes.

He took another step back. She wanted to pull away? Two could play at that game. "Get comfortable, Isabel.

You're gonna be here awhile." Without waiting for a response he turned and headed out the door.

———∾∾∾———

Freaking males with their macho bullshit.

Isabel stared down Thad's retreating form until he rounded the corner. She seethed from anger and cold and from anger at being cold and a ton of other confusing emotions. This experience was messing with her head. Not to mention, she did *not* take kindly to being told what to do or how to feel.

Couldn't he see how scary this was for her?

She took a deep breath. The thing was... the thing that she could only admit to herself was that when Thad was around, there was more to it than just the fact that he chased away the cold. He was right. They connected. That seemed like such a positive thing, but the ramifications and the baggage that came along with that admission were far too much to handle.

Another full-body shiver hit, causing her teeth to clatter loudly. What she needed was a way to gain some perspective. No easy task since being in this place meant being surrounded by everything that was Thad.

What she needed was reality television.

Lexi had gotten her into it, starting with all those awful dating shows and eventually things like *Hoarders* and *Project Runway*. Whenever she felt overwhelmed, an episode or two of *Survivor* never failed to remind her that life could be much, much worse. Heaven knew she wouldn't last two minutes on a sun-drenched desert island with nothing but a chicken and a loincloth.

Hard to say if the sun or the boredom would kill her first.

Isabel headed out through the kitchen doorway in search of a room with a television. The sound of angry muttering caught her attention. She looked up from the repetitive pattern of the floor runner to see Lee farther down the hall, hustling away from Lexi's room and around the corner. She was struck by how gracefully he moved, for such a large male. Years of being a fighter, probably. Lexi always did go for the bad boys.

For a moment she compared him to Thad, who was much younger and certainly less mature... rougher, even. They were similar in a lot of ways, though. Thad had the same resolute square to his shoulders and kept his head held just as high. Both radiated power. Both were huge, muscular, and totally hot.

Thad had such a shiny innocence, though. Lee had the hard, impassive edge of a guy who'd seen too much and probably kept everyone at arm's length. It was sad, really, and yet another good reason for concern. Isabel's heart broke when she thought of what that poor girl had been through in her short life. Going after Lee would only get Alexia's heart stepped on. Hopefully, she wouldn't try.

When Isabel had first arrived at the mansion, she hadn't looked closely at her surroundings. Her focus had been fairly narrow. Now, she was in awe. The walls were an elegant, creamy white, adorned with equally elegant art... Impressionist, maybe? Lexi would know. Fancy molding ran the perimeter of all the walls, and the mini-chandeliers hanging in the hallway were like what might be hung in a pricey hotel.

Near the main hall was an open set of double doors that she hadn't seen before. The sounds of a sports game and voices came from within. Well, human sports were sort of like reality TV, weren't they? And sometimes the players were quite nice to look at.

It took a great deal of self-control for Isabel not to stop dead in her tracks when she entered the room. She hadn't counted on running into a dozen vampires, a few of whom looked rather angry. There wasn't much room to sit, so she made her way to a bar area at the far end of the space.

A casual lean against the bar… that she could totally do. She kept her shoulders back and head held high—just like at the club—though she would have been far more comfortable in boots and party clothes than in the jeans and sweatshirt that Tyra had brought by. No one seemed to take much notice of her, at least.

Ivy, that beautiful raven-haired female, bustled in with a plate of fruit and cheese. Isabel caught her arm. "Ivy, is there some sort of… party or something going on in here?"

The female's long hair shimmered when she shook her head. "This is the multipurpose room. We use it for parties and receptions sometimes. Mostly, though, it's just where everybody waits."

"Waits for what?"

"For Thad. When his father was alive, this was where he received visitors. Now that Thad's returned, they're waiting to see him. I was just bringing in some snacks for everyone. Please." She gestured with the fruit tray at what appeared to be the only available seat. It was a somewhat ornately carved armchair, upholstered with burgundy velvet and conspicuous in that it didn't really match the other furniture in the room. "Have a seat. Can I get you some coffee?"

The strange mood in the room nagged at Isabel, but she hadn't slept much, and coffee sounded fantastic. Besides, she refused to act as if a bunch of strangers had run her off. "That would be great. Thanks, Ivy."

No sooner had Isabel lowered herself into the chair, then a female who'd been stationed just inside the door came forward. She was... well, her skin was oddly pale. Not like Isabel's, which was peachier and less golden than a lot of their kind, but *way* pale. Given the female's platinum hair and her all-white clothing, Isabel might have mistaken her for some sort of ghostly apparition, except for the diamond choker and red-bottomed Louboutin stilettos. Isabel wasn't sure ghosts existed, but if they did, they probably didn't wear shoes that cost a grand per pair.

The inviting scent of gardenias enveloped Isabel when the female clasped her hand warmly, just like they were old friends. "Welcome. I'm Agnessa."

Umm. "Thanks. Isabel. Hi."

Agnessa smiled. She did, it seemed, have fangs. So she must be a vampire. Maybe there was more variety in the species than Isabel had realized. "Yes, and it's wonderful to finally meet you." The snowy female did a small, elegant curtsey. "I won't keep you; I just wanted to introduce myself to the new queen and to offer my services as a spiritual advisor, should you need any assistance."

Oh. Shit. As soon as Agnessa busted out the *Q* word, a flurry of murmurs and movement sounded among the other visitors. In the blink of an eye, a line had formed behind Agnessa, as if Isabel was a newly opened amusement-park ride and they were all waiting to get on it.

This was so, *so* not good…

Chapter 21

"You're juiced something awful, Brother."

Thad paused in the middle of a lat pull-down to give Tyra a scathing look before he continued with his reps. "What the hell are you doing here?"

She raised her eyebrows. "Well, someone is testy this morning, eh?" She stepped from the doorway into the gym, closing the door behind her. "I was looking for you. Wanted to make sure you were all right."

"Oh, hell yeah, I'm just dandy." He gritted his teeth and yanked the pull-down bar a little harder.

"Your form is all wrong."

"Do me a favor and shut it, will ya?"

"Whatever you say, but you're not doing it correctly. You're gonna be sorry."

He ignored her. He had come here to work off his barely tenable aggression, and Tyra was here to push his buttons again.

Siblings were such a pain in the ass.

On the next rep Thad yanked the bar with enough force that his grip slipped, causing him to bash the bar painfully into his collarbone. "Shit!" The sharp curse bounced around the mirrored room.

"I toldja you were gonna be sorry." The smugness in her tone made him shiver. Not the oh-goody kind of shiver, but the kind where he needed what little self-control he possessed not to succumb to the temptation of petty insults, hair pulling, and name-calling.

"Yeah, whatever." He released the bar slowly, and then grabbed a towel to wipe his face. He'd been lifting rather furiously. His lats and pecs ached from it. Still, the balls of his feet bounced hummingbird-fast on the padded floor and his fists emanated heat that could only be quenched by making contact with something.

Maybe it was time to jump on the treadmill.

"Careful, baby brother." He aimed another nasty glance her way.

Thad blasted himself in the face with a water bottle, grateful for the cool sensation it brought to his over-heated skin. As soon as the night was over, he was rousing Lee's ass out of bed so the older male could help Thad learn control of his power.

"I'm the fucking king now, Ty. Don't 'baby brother' me. Seriously, did you come here just to piss me off?"

"Seriously bad mood," she amended. "You wanna talk about what's going on with you and your 'lady friend'?"

He hopped on the treadmill, punched it up to ten miles per hour, and jacked the incline until his hamstrings screamed for mercy that he wouldn't grant them. "Nothing to talk about," he breathed. "She wants to go home; I'm not gonna let her."

Tyra's answering laugh was rich. Damn her. "That simple, huh?"

He sped the treadmill up a little more, somewhat mesmerized by the movement of the belt under his feet. "Why the hell not? She can't go anywhere anyway. Eventually she's going to have to admit that we're good together."

Strained by the combination of exercise and conversation, he exhaled in labored pants. It was hotter than hell inside his skin. "And you know… the whole prophecy thing… I'm convinced now more than ever. She's meant to be with me. She just needs time to realize it."

Tyra's amusement faded. She cocked her head to the side and regarded him seriously. "I went to see her earlier, you know. She's all kinds of confused. I'm not so sure that strong-arming her is the best way to go."

"I'm not… strong-arming. She just has no other choice. Period… and stop… rolling… your eyes… at me." He had no need to look. The eye roll was her signature move when she was annoyed, and she was definitely doing it.

"You know, Thad, this isn't like you. I'm thinking you might be overdoing it there. Maybe you could slow down or, uh, take a break?"

"I'm fine." He should be capable of working himself much harder without being so exhausted, but he dismissed the thought. Sure, he was a little queasy and his heart was beating like someone had set it on "random," but that was no big deal, right?

The thing was that Isabel wasn't the only one who was overwhelmed. Thad was freaking the hell out ten ways to Tuesday. But he was going to quit being a coward and just power through—as soon as he ran off some excess energy. He kept his head down, and Tyra's boot steps got louder as she approached him.

"Are you sure you're all right, Thad? I mean it. You really don't look good. You're all flushed, and uh… hey, sweetie? Thad?"

The room started to blur and spin around him, and Thad finally had to admit defeat. Bile rose in his throat at the same time that his body started to slow down. He reached for the treadmill's "Stop" button with a clumsy swipe but missed by a mile. White-hot pain shot through every conceivable nerve ending. The last thing he saw was the back end of the treadmill heading in the opposite direction from him as a whole lot of nothingness came into view.

———⁓———

When Thad came to, Brayden was standing over him. And Tyra. And Lee. For pity's sake, had the whole household come to hover over him for falling off the treadmill? Brayden leaned down and flashed a light in his eyes. "Hey, Thad. Glad to have you back."

Thad groaned and tried to speak, but his tongue didn't work and nothing came out except more groaning.

"Man, you are one stupid son of a bitch." Tyra. He tried to turn his face toward her but winced at the ache of his brain trying to comprehend its own foolishness. "I tried to tell you to slow down."

Thad blinked, breathing slowly as he searched inside for his voice. When he finally coaxed it out, the sounds from his throat were barely more than a strained croak. "In my defense... I didn't agree with you."

She gave him her "Lord help me" look and crossed her arms defensively. "As soon as you're not flat on your ass any longer, we're gonna have a real talk. Straight up, you're being a dumb ass." She jerked her head to the side. "Lee agrees with me."

Lee appeared in Thad's field of vision again, nodding curtly. "Dumb ass, son of a bitch. You bet."

"What the hell are you doing here?"

Lee shrugged. "Ran into the doc and Tyra in the hall

upstairs. Thought I'd come take a gander at you while you were flat on your back." He cracked a smile.

"Fuck you. Help me up," Thad grunted. Apparently, while he was out, someone had driven a pike through his skull and used it to pin him to the floor mats.

"Not so fast." Brayden held Thad's wrist to get a pulse. "You've got hyperthermia, your blood pressure is still too high for my comfort, and you're damn lucky you didn't have a seizure, so I'm gonna ask you to stay the hell put for a moment."

Whoa. Either this was seriously serious, or Brayden had suddenly grown a pair.

While Thad balked at being told what to do, he could only argue so much when the ability to make an indignant and punctuated exit still eluded him. "Hyperthermia?"

"Heat stroke. Body's temp-control mechanism goes wacky, can't cool down." He looked down the bridge of his nose at Thad while he placed a wet rag on Thad's forehead. "If you were human, you coulda killed yourself. As it is, you could have induced a coma, you dumb bastard."

"What the fuck? Yesterday everyone was kissing my ass, and now you're calling me a dumb bastard? You guys are supposed to be kissing my ass even more now."

"Sorry," Brayden muttered. "Just… jumping on the bandwagon."

Well, anyway, I'm not human so I don't care. That seemed too childish to say out loud, but he did allow his lower lip to jut out just a little.

"May I ask what the hell you were doing?" Lee had assumed a stance similar to Tyra's: legs wide, arms folded, forehead creased, lips pressed sternly. Fucker.

"Just trying to work out my frustrations, man."

"Dude, you've got heat running unchecked through your body, and you decide to hop on the treadmill for a jog? Are you fucking out of your mind?"

"Ugh." Thad finally pushed himself up through the pain to a sitting position, resting an elbow on each knee. "You said it's important to have a clear head, so I was trying to clear my fucking head. Shit." He ran his hand through hair. "My head is fucking killing me, doc."

Brayden nodded his agreement. "Yeah, that'll happen. You need to get some rest, sir. And you need to get hydrated. Wouldn't be a bad idea for you to feed, while you're at it."

"I, uh…" He coughed. He didn't particularly want to say it out loud, here on his ass surrounded by his sister and close staff. That somehow made the whole thing with Isabel less sacred. "I just did… a few hours ago."

"Fair enough. Let's get you to bed then." The doctor held out a hand to help him up.

Thad waved it off.

"Actually I'm feeling much better already. My head still hurts but I'm not hot all over anymore." He'd managed to get himself off the floor, but making it all the way to standing was going to be an effort. This must be what others of his kind talked about. A power drain. Vampires who did not use their powers judiciously risked putting too great a strain on themselves.

"Probably your power surged right before you passed out. Blew your wad, so until you recharge, you'll be cooled down for awhile." Lee also offered Thad a helping hand.

While Lee and Brayden each heaved an arm, Thad

gave a final push to get himself vertical. Tyra continued to stare him down with disapproval all over her face. "Tyra, come on. Don't look at me like that."

Yet another fucking eye roll. "I'm sorry, little brother, but somehow you've gone from nice guy to asshole and straight on toward stupid in record time."

He might have pulled off a snappy retort if he hadn't still had two males holding him up like he was a sloppy drunk being escorted out of a bar. He threw his arms up. "I will get myself to bed, thank you." He pointed a finger at Tyra. "You and I will talk later."

With what energy he could muster, he attempted a confident swagger and pushed open the gym door, leaving them all to give his back the hairy eyeball. He had been a dick and a jackass, and he knew it, but he'd have to deal with the peanut gallery later.

As Thad slowly made his way back upstairs, he weighed his options of where to crash. Technically, he didn't live in this house yet. Since his parents' passing, he had continued to live in his own house on the property, not ready to officially move into the mansion that had been their home. Truth be told, he still wasn't ready. But he was running out of reasons to put off the move.

There were several guest rooms. While he hated the fact, he had to acknowledge that he wanted to find Isabel and beg for her to soothe his aches as she had asked him to do before.

He finally stopped in front of her door, but his confidence waned. Perhaps Tyra had been right. Maybe instead of using the hard sell, he should back off a little. Give her some space. Handle things with more finesse.

Oh, who the fuck was he kidding? He didn't know

jack shit about finesse. He was used to females lying at his feet if he so much as snapped his fingers, women interested in nothing more than his title. He'd sure as hell never had one bolt from the room after sleeping with him. Then again, he couldn't say for certain that he would have cared before if one had.

With one hand on the doorknob, he leaned his head against the door as another wave of nausea assailed him. He might as well face the fact head on: prophecy or no freaking prophecy, he was drawn to her in a way he couldn't even put words to. She was unlike anyone male or female he had known before—gorgeous, independent... amazing.

Being with her had awakened feelings he hadn't thought possible. She had argued that he didn't know her well enough; he knew all he needed from the way holding her in his arms was so amazingly, achingly, perfectly right.

And the sex... heaven above, he'd never had that kind of chemistry with any female. He smiled slightly, thinking of how she'd slapped him. No one in the history of his kind would have had the guts to smack the king across the mouth like a disrespectful school kid. Thad wasn't into the kinky shit, but he had to admit he'd loved that she had the balls to stand up to him that way.

He had already admitted that he was falling for Isabel. In a big way. That seemed like a misnomer, really. Not that he had much experience with this sort of thing, but once you realized you were falling in love with someone, wasn't it already too late? He shook his head slowly against the door. Yeah, might as well admit it.

Thad Morgan really was in love.

To truly claim it, even if only to himself, lifted him up. It loosened the hard squeeze around his heart that had nagged him quietly since he'd first met Isabel and made him stronger. Somehow, he would find a way to work this out with her. Get her to hold on until he could court her properly. Show her how good it could be with him and how he could take care of her. Clearly, her life had been rather solitary, except for her friendship with Alexia, and he wanted so much to take care of her.

It was something he had desperately needed. He just hadn't known that before now.

"Damn," he whispered to the air molecules in the silent hallway. "Now what?"

From the moment he was born, Thad had been groomed for the position he was now to fill, yet he had always been too overwhelmed by the enormity of the role to take it seriously. He was ashamed to admit that he'd stuck his head in the sand and naively assumed that his father would continue to rule until he retired to the Council of Elders on his one thousandth birthday. In theory, Thad should have had another century to get accustomed to all of the responsibility that now sat squarely on his shoulders.

Part of him still secretly felt like the ten-year-old boy who had gleefully tromped up and down the hallways of this house, swimming in his father's boots. It was time now to put on the big-boy pants and grow a pair. If he didn't, Isabel would never trust him to take care of her. Nor would the rest of their kind. Then it would only be a matter of time before the race fell to its enemies.

He straightened from his pansy-ass lean against the door. Isabel was probably talking to Alexia. He would wait, but he still felt light-headed, and unmacho though it was, he wasn't going to stay standing much longer. Had someone opened Isabel's door while he was leaning there, Thad would have eaten the carpet.

He twisted the doorknob. He'd go in and wait, and maybe catch a few z's while he was at it. Yeah, that'd be good.

Chapter 22

ISABEL SMILED HER BEST SMILE AT THE TWO SEETHING males looming over her, even though she desperately wanted to flee for the nearest bathroom. Again. Because when in doubt, fake it.

The larger one was almost as big as Thad, but with beefier muscles and the face of a bulldog. He clutched a medium-sized cardboard box to his chest. The other male was smaller, with the handsome look of a vampire Ken doll and a wobbly smile. She hoped like crazy that she was doing a better job than this guy at hiding her nerves.

Ken Doll stepped forward. "Your Majesty—"

Isabel held up a hand. "Whoa, there. I'm not—" Okay, probably best not to correct everyone just this second, especially not with the angry bulldog-man right in front of her. "Isabel is fine. Please."

Ken Doll nodded eagerly. "Yes, ma'am, thank you."

Ma'am. She supposed she could live with that.

"We sincerely apologize for taking your time, ma'am. Really, this is all just a misunderstanding," Ken Doll continued.

"Misunderstanding?" Dog Man stepped forward, casting a heavy shadow over Isabel. "It's *his* fault that my Lucy got pregnant!"

"Accident then," Ken Doll said.

Isabel swallowed. "And Lucy is your..." *Don't say mate. Please don't say she's your mate...*

Dog Man straightened. "I raise and sell beagle puppies." A shaking finger pointed at Ken Doll. "His brute Rottweiler got my Lucy pregnant, and now I've got these mixed-breed puppies I can't do a thing with."

Isabel placed a hand over her mouth. That poor beagle.

Dog Man placed the box in her lap. Inside was a pile of velvety, black-and-brown sleeping cuteness. Ken Doll was fidgety, and the reason was clear: Isabel could squeeze all of her dog knowledge into the tip of her nose, but even she could see from the markings that the puppies were part Rottweiler.

But really, this was what they were waiting to see the king about? She frowned. "And you needed to see Tha—the king about this?"

Dog Man sputtered. "My puppies sell for four hundred dollars apiece. I'll be lucky if I can get a hundred each for these things. All because he can't keep his dog inside during the day!"

Ken Doll hung his head with a sigh. "I've apologized. Rufus has a doggie door in case he needs to go out during the day. There was a weak spot in the fence…"

Isabel couldn't keep the frown off her face. This seemed so trivial in the grand scheme of things. It would almost have been funny, had it not been for the two males looking like they might lock proverbial horns at any moment.

Isabel turned to Ken Doll. "Can you not afford to pay him the difference?"

Everything went quiet. Dog Man's angry shifting from foot to foot ceased, and he turned to Ken Doll hopefully. "Could you?"

He hadn't *asked*?

Ken Doll's head bobbled. "I—sure, yeah. I could do that."

"And," Isabel prompted. "I assume you've fixed the fence?"

"Of course, ma'am. It's just that, well, I didn't know for sure that my Rufus was to blame until just the other day."

Isabel swung her gaze back to Dog Man. "So if he pays you what you would've earned if they were pure-bred puppies, will that work?"

Dog Man nodded. "I suppose it would, yes."

"So then what's the problem?" The males had the decency, at least, to look properly chagrined. She handed back the box of puppies. "Listen, guys. I don't really understand why you needed to see the king for something like this. You both seem like intelligent males. Surely you could have worked it out on your own."

Dog Man shrugged. "The king always handles disputes."

Good grief. Isabel sighed. Visions of Thad's blue eyes, wide with worry that first time they spoke, danced in her head. *We are down to thousands, Isabel.* "No offense, guys, but I think the king's energy would best be spent keeping our race alive, not dealing with petty stuff like this. All you had to do," she gestured from Dog Man to Ken Doll, "was ask him for the money."

"Yes, ma'am," they both mumbled.

Ma'am. Forty-eight hours earlier, Isabel might have laughed in the face of someone who dared to call her that. The two left amid a flurry of apologies and more "Yes, ma'ams," and with each *ma'am* Isabel winced a little less. A few individuals in the line whispered, grumbled, and left, as well. Her spine straightened and her shoulders lifted. Was this what being queen was about? It didn't seem so hard.

A petite female approached tentatively. She was lovely, with delicate features and sandy-colored shoulder-length hair, but she had the saddest face Isabel had ever seen. And considering the number of lost souls Isabel had met on the party scene, that was saying something.

The female extended a hand. "I'm Diana. I am so sorry to be taking up your time, ma'am. I just wasn't sure who to go to with a problem like this. You see, I want to have a baby."

Isabel's head swam. Clearly, she had been a little too quick on the trigger with that whole "easy" business. "I'm not sure…" Seriously, what could she *say* to something like that?

Diana clasped her hand. "My mate is one of your soldiers."

One of *her* soldiers? Yeesh.

The female continued. "I know our numbers are low because he's out there fighting and training six nights a week. I want to be a mother, and I want to help carry on our race. Birad is too exhausted to try, even on his night off. He just sleeps. I know the ongoing battle is depressing him, but he won't admit it. I was hoping maybe Thad could talk to him, soldier to soldier. Male to male. Maybe he'd be able to get through."

Okay. Isabel worried her lower lip between her teeth. She didn't even know where Thad was at the moment. Not to mention that things were still a little awkward, and seeking him out didn't seem like a good ide—

Just then, Ivy breezed back in. "Here's your coffee,

Isabel. I'll just put it over here on the bar until you're ready to drink it."

The bar. Isabel squeezed Diana's hand. "Ivy, you don't happen to have any red wine back there, do you?"

Ivy disappeared behind the marble-topped counter and, after a few clinking and sliding noises, reemerged holding what was probably a very pricey bottle of Robert Mondavi Reserve Cabernet Sauvignon. "Will this work?"

Would it ever. It was an intense red. "Perfect." Isabel grabbed the bottle from Ivy's outstretched hand and put it into Diana's. "One glass. One, okay?" The female nodded slowly and eyed the bottle like Isabel had just handed over a bomb.

"Trust me, this'll work. Wait until the next full moon and give him a glass with his meal. Have one yourself, while you're at it. Maybe you even serve it to him wearing nothing but your best pearls and some strappy stilettos. After dinner, put on some sexy music, shove him down on the bed, and spank him like the bad, bad boy that he is." Diana recoiled a bit. "Or, you know, whatever you feel moved to do."

The poor female's eyes were wide as saucers. "Are you sure about that?"

Isabel smiled. She might not be sure about much, but *this* she had experience with. "Seriously. It'll feel great. And if it doesn't work, I'll send Thad over there myself to talk to him." Diana thanked her profusely and left. Isabel pushed aside the fact that she had, more or less, just committed to following up with the female at a later date.

Things got a little blurry after that. Most of the issues,

though, seemed mundane and frivolous to Isabel's way
of thinking. Property-line disagreements were easily re-
solved by just telling them to split the damn difference,
and a young female who'd been disowned by her parents
for refusing an arranged mating was sent to Ivy to see
about a job and a place to stay. When Ivy returned, Isabel
was flipping channels and sipping her coffee, which was
thankfully still a little warm. "Everyone's gone?"

Isabel glanced around the room and shrugged. "It
seems so. Were you able to help the female I sent you?"

Ivy nodded. "She cooks and cleans. We can always
use help with that stuff around here. It was very gracious
of you to help her like that."

"You're the one who helped her, Ivy. Not me." She
honestly hadn't done much at all, had she?

<center>~~~</center>

Isabel found Alexia lying back in bed, hands over her
face. "You want me to turn the lights off, Lex?"

Alexia peeked at Isabel through her fingers before
moving her hands to her sides. The poor girl had that
groggy, glassy-eyed look of exhausted confusion that
so often graced the faces of partied-out club kids in
the early predawn hours when things were coming to
a close.

"Izzy, hey. Thank God it's you. This room has
been like Grand Central. Everyone's all 'Hey, come
check out the human!'" This said as Alexia waved her
hands comically.

Isabel chuckled. "I'm sure it's not really like that."

"No, I'm mostly joking. It's just been a lot, you
know? Waking up in a strange place, then having the

doctor stop by, then that Ivy chick, then Lee…" A strange, awkward, pensive look came over Alexia's face for a moment before she snapped back to attention. "Anyway, I'm so glad you're here."

"You sure?" Isabel eyed her curiously. "You still look tired and kind of… oh… right… Lee was here…" Understanding dawned, and the reason for Alexia's hazy appearance suddenly became clear. Isabel leaned forward, eager to dish. "So, what was it like? I mean, I know what it's like for me, but I don't know what it's like for a human."

Alexia shifted and fidgeted, biting at her lower lip as she did when she was thinking hard. "It was… weird. Interesting. A little like that time I had ten shots of tequila at Breakstone's and ended up climbing the DJ in the bathroom. You know, except without as much nudity."

"No nudity, huh?" Isabel teased, but honestly two seconds with Lee had told her that he would have been completely aboveboard and businesslike.

"Are you kidding me? Of course not."

Oh, poor Lex.

"You want him bad, don't you?"

"What's not to want?" Alexia held up a fist, ticking off on her fingers. "He's built, gorgeous, there's that whole ancient and mysterious thing, he like… exudes power, he—"

"Is completely inaccessible," Isabel admonished.

Alexia sighed and smooshed her hand against her cheek. "Yeah, that's probably the most attractive part."

Isabel winked. "Yeah, well. It's kind of your thing. In all the time I've known you, I've never seen you go after anyone you could have something meaningful and long term with."

Lexi responded with a mature jab of her tongue. "You're one to talk."

"Yeah, well…" Isabel shrugged. "What can I say? I'm a hypocrite." She smirked a little. "If it helps, he wants you, too."

Alexia scoffed. "Whatever."

"I'm not kidding, Lex. I saw him leaving, and he was frustrated as hell."

"Probably just cuz I talked his ear off asking a bunch of lame questions," Alexia muttered.

"Nah. He wants you. Drinking can be very erotic, and that one's about as male as they come. Unfortunately, he's also about as old-school as they come. Ain't no way he's going to own up to being hot for a human."

"Yeah," Alexia grumbled. "I gathered that much. He made it about as clear as he could that he was only letting me drink from him because of your being important to Thad." She waved her hand dismissively at Isabel's concern. "Whatever, don't worry about me. Tell me about you and the royal hottie."

Isabel laughed. "Hmm. Well, I guess you could say it's a long story."

Alexia sucked back a dramatic gasp. "Oh, man! How was it?"

"Bizarre," Isabel said, wrinkling her nose a little.

Alexia frowned. "Is he into something really kinky?"

Leave it to Lex to go there. "Not that way. The sex itself was great, actually. I've never experienced anything like it."

"So what is it, then?"

"My power developed. Apparently I can freeze things now. It happened during, I think. Or after, when we drank from each other. I'm still not sure."

"What the hell?" Alexia sat up and leaned far enough forward that her bangs brushed Isabel's forehead. "How does that work?"

"Beats me. It was either from sleeping with him or feeding from him, or maybe both. Apparently I can freeze things. I'm really cold all the time." The mere mention of it sent an intense shudder through her.

Alexia looked down to where Isabel's hand had been resting on her leg through the sheets. She flinched and quickly swatted the hand off herself. "Sorry, but you said you could freeze stuff and I'd rather not take chances."

"Please," Isabel scoffed. "That wouldn't happen... probably." She still didn't have a clue how to control or wield her power, so she couldn't exactly make that promise, could she?

"So what's the deal with this stuff? I mean, so you have a power... now what?"

Isabel thought for a second. "You know, I'm not sure it means anything." Confusion pressed a crease in the center of Lexi's forehead. "Honestly, I guess I don't know a lot about it since I've been so far removed from our race, but what I know from my parents is that the special abilities evolved along with our kind. You know, a few had 'em, then they started breeding specifically for them, and now most all of our kind have powers. I always got the impression from my parents that having a power was more of a status symbol than anything else."

Feeling a chill, she rubbed her arms a little through her sweatshirt. "I mean, you've got Lee, who uses what he can do to protect Thad, but I wonder whether the rest of the general population really even use theirs. But the mere fact that we have these powers makes us a target for these wizard guys, I guess."

"So what kind of power does Lee have?" Clearly, greater effort would be needed to divert Lexi's attention from Lee. Isabel smiled.

"I dunno, some kind of force-field thingie. I only know because I saw him use it when that wizard attacked back at our place."

Lexi cocked her head to the side and opened her mouth as if she might ask another question, then stopped. The open, close, open routine happened a couple more times before she sighed, relaxing back on the bed again. "Ugh, just shoot me. I don't know what I'm even thinking, mooning over him like some fucking schoolgirl. This is depressing. And lame. And depressing.

"Anyway, what's the plan from here? Has a decision been made about how to 'handle' me yet? Because as much as I enjoy this gilded-cage business, I can't stay stuck in a fancy bedroom forever."

Isabel sighed again, toying with the comforter on the bed. Lexi was trustworthy; Isabel had never doubted that. For Thad, the perceived risk was greater. The best thing, most likely, would be to send Lexi home or to some equally faraway locale. Isabel's heart sank. If she chose to stay with Thad, she would lose her best friend.

"I don't know. Thad hasn't said anything to me about it. I assume you want to get back to the sand and sun as soon as you can, right?"

Alexia bit her lip, hard enough to nearly draw blood. Funny how that didn't spark Isabel's interest like it had before. "I dunno. I guess I probably would, but you know me. Home is where you hang your toothbrush." Her friend scowled. "I'd miss you if you stayed here, you know, but you deserve to be happy."

Isabel's eyes burned suddenly. *Aw, Lex...* "I'd miss you too, sweetie."

"So, are you going to? Stay, I mean?"

A little throb took up residence in Isabel's right temple. Everything that had gone on lately was way too much to make sense of. "Thad wants me to, I think. Which is nice."

"Are you kidding me? That's awesome."

"It is, I guess," Isabel said slowly. "I like the way I feel with him, you know? I just... I'm not queen material, Lex."

"What constitutes 'queen material'?" Lexi asked. "What would you even have to do?"

Isabel had wondered that herself. The answer couldn't possibly be doing nothing but sitting around sipping coffee while folks unloaded about their problems. "I have no idea, to be honest with you. I just know whatever it is, I'm not it. I mean, that human queen they're always showing on television? All the dressing up, and the pomp and circumstance? No freaking way."

"You might be wrong," Alexia murmured. "You never know."

"Maybe." Everything had been turned so irrevocably upside-down and backwards that Isabel didn't know much of anything anymore. "I need to get some fresh air. You mind if I go take a walk around? Maybe it'll help me get my head on straight."

"You get down with your bad self, girlie." Alexia

stifled a yawn. "Somehow I'm still ridiculously tired."
As if to prove the point, the blonde's eyelids started to
drift shut.

Isabel patted her friend's leg gently and left the room.

Chapter 23

THAD POUNDED THE HUMAN'S GUEST-ROOM DOOR HARD and fast enough to leave scorch marks. No, really, he'd left scorch marks. If he didn't get his shit together fast, he was going to have to replace a whole lot of furniture.

When he had woken from his post-meltdown nap to find that Isabel had not returned, he'd immediately ordered a full security check of the estate. The results had shown that a very blurry likeness of Isabel had left the grounds on foot, headed in the direction of Route 9. What the hell she had been thinking he could only guess, but he was going to strangle her as soon as they found her.

If they found her.

Alexia jerked the door open, sporting a face flushed with sleep and confusion, and a major case of bedhead.

"Where the fuck is she?"

"What?" Alexia blinked. "Who?"

Thad pushed past her and marched into the room. He didn't have time for this playing-dumb bullshit. "Isabel. Where is she?"

"I don't know… she's gone?" Alexia shook her head slowly.

Thad's fists clenched as he crossed his arms tightly over his chest. "Don't give me that bullshit. You two are thick as fucking thieves. She wouldn't have left without telling you where she was going."

Alexia gave him the same suspicious, flinty gaze as on the night he'd met Isabel, assessing him for a minute before finally giving in. Her small body deflated like an untied balloon, and she dropped onto the edge of the bed with her head in her hands.

She shook her head again, more emphatically this time. "She told me she needed to take a walk to clear her head, but I really have no idea where she went. Or when, exactly. What time is it?"

Thad checked his watch. "Almost midnight. It's been dark for hours. I fell asleep waiting in her room to talk to her. When I woke up, I realized she'd never showed." He took a deep breath and blew it out. Heat continued to simmer just below the surface of his skin, but the strong exhales seemed to be pushing it off a little. "Seriously, if you know anything at all, now's the time to tell me, Lex. She has no idea how dangerous it is out there."

Alexia slid her hands over her short hair and looked up at him. He dropped into the green wingback chair in the corner so she wouldn't have to pull something up just to make eye contact, but he couldn't stop the nervous bounce of his legs. Every minute they didn't have Isabel, her chances of survival grew worse out there. She wasn't used to the protective measures a vampire had to take in this part of the world.

"If you don't mind me asking, Thad, do you really have feelings for her?"

How could Alexia sit there and act like she couldn't hear the way Thad's heart was pounding? In his own head, it sounded like one of those big fucking kettle-drums they used to have on Viking ships. Rubbing his forehead, Thad cursed and looked up at her solemnly.

"Yeah. I do. We—" He shifted positions abruptly, leaning back in the chair and taking a wide stance with his legs. Perhaps if he looked more casual, she would open up and talk. "Screw the whole prophecy thing, you know? I just want to be with her. We just seem to fit, you know? But listen, Lex, we really don't have time to discuss this. I've got guys out looking for her, but I want to go and join them."

Alexia's lips pressed together in a thin line. Her face showed a mix of apology and worry, and there was still a hint of the protective urge that she clearly had for her friend. Good for her, but they were on the same side here.

"I'm so sorry. I wish there was more I could tell you. We talked a little about staying versus going, and she said she needed to think things over. I fell asleep after that."

Thad nodded slowly. A modicum of tension eased out of his face. "She's supposed to come back, I assume?" Isabel wouldn't leave without her friend. Then again, she'd pulled that disappearing stunt back at the club, so one couldn't assume. Maybe she had decided to just go.

Alexia nodded. "I think so, but I didn't think to ask when or anything. Sorry."

"You're still busy trying to heal. No one expects you to be back to full strength yet." Thad stood, bracing his hands on his upper thighs. "Plan A, we'll keep an eye out for her to reappear on the property. And patrol the surrounding area for signs of her."

"What's plan B?"

"I'm going out to look. I fed from her so I should be able to sense if she's nearby." He stood and prepared to leave. Alexia's mounting anxiety was apparent, and he made a note to see if Ivy could bring her some food. Maybe keep the girl company. "I'm sorry for barging in on you."

"It's cool." Alexia bit her lip. "Um, so how does that work? You drank her blood, so you can find her?"

Thad gave a palms-up gesture. "That's it in a nutshell. Feeding creates a tie, of sorts. Just one time isn't much, but if I'm close enough I should be able to sense her."

Alexia nodded silently. "I really hope you find her. I had no idea it was dangerous for her to leave, or I would have asked her to stay."

"Yeah, the problem is that she's got no idea, either. It's not the same as where you guys came from."

"I know you're mad and everything, but try not to read her the riot act when you find her, okay? She's really misguided sometimes, but she has a big heart. Her parents' death really messed her up."

"Yeah, she told me." He started for the door.

Clearing her throat, Alexia continued. "She, umm, killed somebody that night. Did you know that?" Thad's eyes popped wide at *that* awful tidbit. "Yeah, she came to in the hospital when some orderly or something was picking glass from her hair in the morgue. She, uh, drank too much. Of his blood. She had to leave him and sneak out of the hospital in stolen scrubs. I don't think she even meant to tell me. It kind of slipped out one night when she'd had too much wine."

Thad nodded grimly. He was, he hoped, projecting calm understanding. Because inside, his heart was both breaking and overflowing. He was awed and humbled by the strength Isabel must have had to survive that on her own. Tears that he refused to shed pricked at his eyes, and he pretended to inspect something on the ceiling until his blurry vision cleared.

"It's why she's afraid, you know?"

He looked back at Alexia. "I'm sorry. What?"

"Hard to believe in happily ever after when you've had to struggle to survive all alone for so long. And when you're afraid you'll hurt anyone who gets too close."

Alexia spoke in a very authoritative way that suggested her knowledge was more firsthand than whatever Isabel might have told her. Not that it was Thad's business to ask.

"Sorry again for waking you. Hope you can rest some more. Don't worry, I'll find her." He didn't know what to say about the rest of it. There was no good response, except maybe some variation on the words "holy" and "shit."

Alexia wrapped her arms around herself as if she was chilly. "Thad," she said cautiously, "she's really in danger?"

Tons. And I'm scared shitless that I'm going to lose her before we've even had a chance to get started. She has no idea what it's like around here, how dangerous it is to be out by herself. She'll be lucky if she's not dead by morning.

They weren't going there, either. No good would come from scaring the girl even more than she already was. So he prevaricated. "Let's hope not."

Tears sprung to Alexia's eyes. As they pooled and ran down her face, Thad pretended not to notice and turned, closing the door behind him.

Chapter 24

NOW WHAT?

Another knock at the door, and Alexia paused in the middle of splashing water on her face. Her stomach rumbled and she hoped that perhaps Ivy had arrived with more food, rather than Thad with more bad news. A damp hand through her hair did a little to tame it. She turned away from the mirror before she could get distracted by messing with something that would never look perfect. No matter what she did.

"Come in."

The door opened to reveal what could only be described as a bigger, buffer vampire rendition of Hugh Jackman. But closer to the scruffy Wolverine version of Hugh Jackman, minus the mutton-chop sideburns. Not like the *Kate and Leopold* one who was less buff and more clean-cut.

"Delivery service," he said, carrying a tray. His smile was full and broad, and displayed an intriguing mix of dark mystery and boyish charm when he flashed those lethal choppers. "I ran into Ivy in the hall and figured I'd bring you this stuff myself. Mind if I come in?" He stepped through the doorway, not really bothering to wait for a response.

Damn it all, she'd been doing that jaw-on-the-floor, deer-in-headlights routine, hadn't she? "I'm sorry. I thought you were Thad or Ivy. Uh, who are you?"

He stuck out his hand. "Siddoh. I work for Thad. One of his generals, I guess you could say." Alexia shook his hand tentatively. Lord help her, he was shorter but a little broader than Lee. She wondered if she could even lift his massive arm, but she still gave it the old college try and was surprised to find it easier than she'd anticipated. And her shoulder was barely sore. The big male gestured to a chair in the corner. "Mind if I sit?"

She nodded her acquiescence. "Go right ahead. That chair has seen more tail than a rock star lately." She plopped onto the bed across from him, hesitant to ask why he'd come. Any more bad news and she might just hang herself.

He placed the sandwich tray on a dresser and lowered himself into the seat quickly, landing in a somewhat lazy sprawl. His grin widened, so the news couldn't be that bad. Right?

"I'm very sorry if I'm being intrusive. I'm sure this has been a lot for you to handle." He smiled again, more subdued this time. "I was hoping I could ask you some questions about the wizard who attacked you."

"Yeah, sure. I'm not sure I can tell you anything I didn't already tell Lee, though. It all happened really quickly."

He frowned for a moment. "Of course," he said gently. "Just try your best. That's all I ask. Can you describe him?"

"Ugh," she rubbed her eyes, hard. Granules of sleep crud seemed to be all over the place. "Not really. I mean, he was taller than me, but so is everyone else in the world." The corner of Siddoh's mouth curled up just a bit.

"I guess he was about six feet, but I'm so bad at judging that I can't be sure. His head was shaved, but it looked like his hair was probably dark. He had a long-ass brown robe, like a monk or something." She stared into space while a fuzzy image formed in her head. "Brown eyes. Oh, and he talked funny. Kind of like a cartoon character with a British accent."

"That's new." Siddoh shifted, as if to get more comfortable in the chair. "I don't think I've heard of one having a British accent, but there's a first time for everything. I wonder if they could be recruiting," he murmured. "The implications of that could be catastrophic if they were able to launch a successful campaign. Especially if knowledge of their existence leaked out into the human world."

Umm. "Recruiting?"

Siddoh's head snapped up. He swept his hand dismissively. "Oh, sorry. Sometimes I think out loud. Don't you worry about that. It just seems odd, this thing about the accent. Most wizards are born and bred locally, so a European accent would be hard to come by. No worries, just something I need to check out." He smiled at her again. "Anything else you can think of?"

Alexia shook her head quickly. Frankly, she'd prefer not to think about it. "I don't think so." She leaned forward on the bed, propping her chin up with the palm of her hand. "He didn't seem to mind pain. I used all my best self-defense moves on him but he barely budged."

He barked a hearty laugh. "You attacked him? That's fantastic."

"You mean stupid." Lee's pithy comments from

before came back to smack her across the back of the head. "Right?"

"Eh." He launched himself out of the chair and grabbed the tray of sandwiches. "If you're gonna go down, go down swinging, I always say. Here." He brought the tray to the foot of the bed and sat next to her, holding out a turkey on rye. "Eat. You need to keep your strength up."

"Will you eat with me?" She smiled slightly. "I hate to eat alone."

"Sure." He grabbed the other sandwich. Pastrami on pumpernickel. "Cheers," he said lightly, pretending to clink his sandwich against hers.

Like Ivy, this vampire put her at ease. Come to think of it, the only one who hadn't was Lee. "Thanks." She took a small bite. "Mmm. So good." She took a bigger bite, this time chewing thoroughly before swallowing and speaking again. "You were right. I didn't realize I was so hungry."

"Stress," he said sympathetically. He gestured to her arm. "That's a fantastic tattoo. Does it signify anything?"

She laughed. "Not really, no. People, um…" She cleared her throat. "I get asked that a lot." She wasn't sure if referring to a vampire as a person was a major faux pas. They weren't people, really. Were they? "It's just something I drew. I doodle a lot when I get nervous, little random patterns. I thought it looked cool."

"It does." He nodded. "Goes all the way down your back?"

"Yep." She turned away, lifting her shirt to reveal the remainder of the design on her back. Swirls of black ink streamed from her shoulder down to her lower back, ending just above the waistband of her shorts. Splashes of color accented the design here and there. The piece had taken hours, and it was the one she was most proud of. She loved to show it off.

"That's lovely," he murmured. He stooped to look closely but was respectful enough not to touch. She turned back around, leaving the back of her shirt untucked while she returned to her sandwich. "I have a couple myself." He unbuttoned his shirt to the navel, pulling the top half to the sides to reveal his ink: a roaring lion head on the left pec, a cuddly little cub on the right.

"That's awesome. May I touch it?" She leaned forward as he gave a slight nod, running her fingers along the shadows of the lion's head. The details were gorgeous. Done with a single needle, maybe. "The shading is really fantastic. Who did the work?"

He closed his eyes and sighed deeply. "An old friend. He died not too long ago, rather tragically. Wizard attack."

"I'm so sorry." Her hand dropped awkwardly. Such a lame and pointless condolence, but what else could she say to something like that? "So why lions?"

"Hmm." He chuckled. "I like to be fierce… and I also like to be playful." His smile turned coy.

"I'll bet you do." He was flirting with her, and while she couldn't exactly say she was interested, it was a nice break from all the heavy freaky-scary that had been going on since Thad and Lee had showed up at Insomniac looking for Isabel.

"Yeah, well…" He stuffed the rest of his sandwich into his mouth and chewed steadily until he was able to swallow. "What can I say? I'm a male who likes to do everything big." Alexia had no doubt about that. Siddoh stood, and she had to stifle a sudden yawn. "Tired?"

She rolled her eyes. "You know, I actually am. It doesn't make any sense. I feel like I've done nothing but sleep since I got here."

"Hey, don't sweat it. You've been through a lot." He strode slowly toward the door. "I noticed that wound back there on your shoulder. It's healing well, but you need more time before you'll be a hundred percent again. You're just lucky it didn't damage your tattoo," he said with a wink. "I'm gonna get out of your hair so you can rest."

She nodded, following him to the door. "Thanks, Siddoh, for stopping by. It was very nice to meet you."

He smiled again. It was a brilliant, charming smile. She had no doubt it opened a lot of doors for him. And legs. "No sweat." He pointed to a shopping bag by the door. "By the way, Ivy sent those. Clean clothes, in case you want to change into something warmer."

She blushed, looking down at the shorts and tank top she had on. "Yeah, good idea. Thanks. Again."

Siddoh's hand reached behind to twist the doorknob. Footsteps caught her attention, and she saw the back of what must have been an absolutely gorgeous vampire retreating down the hallway. Alexia would have killed for a silky mane of platinum blonde hair like this female had. Not to mention the couture clothes and designer shoes. Alexia sighed wistfully. She would have easily blown her last dime on a pair of Manolos if she had any place to wear them.

Siddoh's eyes narrowed in the female's direction, but his jovial smile returned in a second. "Well, thank Ivy. She handles everything around here. Without her, we'd all be clueless," he said with a twinkle in his eye. "And listen," he said, getting serious. "I want you to rest assured that we'll find your friend. Our guys on patrol are all over it, and Lee, Thad, and I are going to go out too. Thad used to fight for me before his father passed. He's top notch, and he's dead set on bringing her back safe. And Lee and I have been doing this since practically before God." He puffed his chest out proudly.

Alexia leaned against the door frame, studying him. "You don't have a self-esteem problem, do you, Siddoh?"

"That I do not. Seriously, though. Get some rest. We'll find her."

She nodded slowly. "K. Umm..." She pointed uncomfortably. "Not sure if you care, but your shirt's still undone and it looks like you've got some Thousand Island on the corner of your mouth there."

He laughed heartily as he started to button his shirt. "See what I mean," he said with a wink. "Clueless." He wiped at his mouth with the back of his hand and then resumed buttoning his shirt. He reached out, giving her shoulder a gentle squeeze. "Now, you get some sleep. Don't worry about a thing."

"Thanks again, Siddoh. Really." Alexia smiled sadly. He nodded to her once more as she eased the door closed. From the corner of her eye, she had spotted Lee stalking toward them but pretended she hadn't.

"Hey, buddy," Siddoh's voice came to her through the door. "Thad ready to roll out?"

It was almost Christmas, not that that meant a whole hell of a lot.

For some shelter residents, it was clearly a time of near-suicidal depression. Anton found that concerning, but mostly he was concerned that he wasn't as concerned as he probably ought to be. Others still found joy, albeit muted by their meager existence. What Anton experienced, as far as he could tell, was something akin to murderous rage. But damned if he knew who or what all that hot-blooded desire to kick ass was directed at, which pissed him off even more.

"Fuck." He seemed to have a habit of punching his fist into his hand when he was frustrated. Unfortunately, his wrist, which they'd informed him at the hospital had been broken in three places, did not appreciate the gesture. He did it anyway, pounding away and muttering to himself like a crazy person as his overlarge, worn-out sneakers squeaked down the hall of the men's wing.

It helped to take his mind off the swirling blackness in his gut. Something small and out of reach had been growing steadily and was now so prevalent within him that even the saliva in his mouth was bitter and vile. It was the worst kind of displacement: no home, no money, no identity, and Anton Smith was even a stranger to himself. He was afraid, he could admit, to be inside his own body.

But Tyra Morgan somehow blew it all away. She had said she would be on vacation but instead had been there serving dinner tonight, an unexpected beacon. Just standing near her sent the light of a thousand candles blasting through the dark to make him almost human again. If only for a little while.

Returning to his room, Anton Smith promptly got horizontal and sagged gratefully into the mattress of his bed, which was barely better than the floor. That dinner had sucked, but he wasn't complaining. Any food was better than no food, for sure. Even if it was all tainted by the caustic flavor in his mouth.

Flipping off the light, he shifted uncomfortably, then tugged up his shirt, undid his jeans, and felt for the hard-on that was straining to defy the bounds of his zipper. God damn, that woman lit him up from the inside out. And dwelling on her was undeniably better for his meager sanity than anything else he could possibly choose to put his gray matter toward.

Anton Smith closed his eyes. In his mind's eye, Tyra's statuesque figure stretched up, head back, lips parted... *her* slender fingers were stroking him off, while his own hands slid over her naked stomach... all the way up to envelop one perfect breast and then the other with his hands.

Anton Smith's breathing picked up even as the awful blackness inside began to recede...

Chapter 25

ISABEL THANKED THE OVERALL-CLAD GAS-STATION clerk and stepped out the door into the late-night chill. She opened the bag in her hand and greedily inhaled the mouthwatering aromas of cinnamon and pecans that she'd charmed her new buddy, Joe the clerk, into giving her.

Her acute sense of smell had picked up the scent of these bad boys while she was out walking the grounds of Thad's estate, and she had never been able to say no to the delectable salty-sweetness of spiced nuts. Even though she had eaten not that long ago, her tummy rumbled as soon as she put the first one to her lips.

"Oh, man, that's good," she mumbled to herself as she chewed.

Cold air stung her nose while she made short work of the bag of pecans. Shivering, Isabel cursed herself for not thinking to grab a coat from somewhere before she left. Damn, she couldn't wait to get another hot shower. Not that she'd had any major epiphanies while out communing with nature, but it was time to get back to the estate. Gun to her head, it would be a comfort to get back to Thad, as well.

Isabel kept to the shadows while she sidled around the convenience store, and once she was out of view of the main road, she took off at what she liked to call "warp speed."

This wasn't the bustling part of town, that was for sure. The massive bale of hay she'd just sped past told her that much. She wasn't the world's best judge of direction, but she'd passed a sign for Route 9 on her way to the convenience store, so if she kept along that road, everything should be fine.

Nearby, a rustle of grass and leaves got the hairs on the back of her neck standing at full attention. A full-on heart-stopping, breath-stealing, deer-in-the-headlights panic hit her like a ton of bricks.

God, she was *so* stupid. This wasn't home. Here she was out traipsing around in a strange place where enemies could actually be lurking around any corner. She just hadn't fucking thought about it. Back home in Orlando, the vampire population was small; everyone kept to themselves; and wizards were nowhere to be found. *Shit*.

Back home, she was the toughest thing roaming the streets at night. Not so, anymore. And how had it taken all this time for *that* little nugget to dawn on her? God, stupid didn't even begin to cover it.

A blanket-covered horse whiffled and snorted from just beyond a nearby fence. It seemed to be asking her what she was up to, and at that very moment she wasn't sure what her response would be. The frantic bang of Isabel's heart slowed just barely. It was the horse she had heard. Had to be. Her body deflated like someone had removed a stopper from her chest, tension flowing out of her like water. Man, she really needed to get a grip. She had survived on her own for a lot of years before Thad had walked into her life, after all.

Isabel gave herself a somewhat comedic clunk on her

head and leaned against another bale of hay. She and the horse sized each other up while the hay pricked at her through her clothing. Maybe this was further proof that she and Thad weren't really meant for each other. She'd waltzed out into the night because she wasn't used to considering that she couldn't. And she would never be able stay sequestered in the mansion. That would make her loopy.

Clearly.

Right now, she had no idea where wizards might be or how to sense them. She'd heard tales of feeling an evil presence, but before at her apartment she hadn't known anything was going on until it was too late. Better to just get out of Dodge while the getting was good.

She did miss Thad quite a bit. If she really thought she could trust herself with him, his warmth and strength—the utter comfort and safety that had come just from being near him—would be heaven to lean on. He wanted to take care of her, and a part of her really wanted to let him.

But when was the last time anyone had taken care of her? She had been alone since her parents died when she was fifteen.

Cripes. She was all over the place, and she hated it. For damn sure, she needed to get a move on, but her previous jolt of alarm hadn't totally faded and her feet were inexplicably rooted to the spot.

Maybe it would be safer to borrow a vehicle so she could make it back to the mansion faster. Clandestine feeding from unsuspecting humans and recreational wine-drinking aside, she'd tried to lead a reasonably moral life. Her parents had taught her the importance of karma, and while her own personal moral code didn't always necessarily follow the straight and narrow, she generally worked toward doing more good stuff than bad stuff.

She'd atone for what she was about to do later. Right now, as she listened to the nature sounds around her and watched large masses of clouds slink around the crescent moon overheard, Isabel's desire to be honest was totally getting spanked by her desire not to get dead.

Every crackle, every scrape, every engine noise in the distance pulled her attention in a different direction. Every snort and snuffle of that damned horse. Didn't those things sleep at night?

Isabel scanned the landscape in the darkness. She was shivering harder with each passing minute. Not to mention that her new realization about the potential danger of wizards going bump in the night had her quite squeamish about continuing to commune with nature.

Finally, her acute vision spotted the answer she'd been looking for. A large house not even half a mile away, with a bright and shiny silver SUV parked in the driveway.

"Bingo," she whispered. It was so perfect that she could envision the giant red bow on top, just like in those rich-people car commercials.

Her heart racing with anticipation, Isabel took off again. To the casual bystander, if there was such a thing in a place like this, she was nothing more than a blur in the darkness as she sped toward the house.

Isabel clapped her hands silently at her good fortune when she crept up on the Lexus hybrid. Though she hadn't done such a thing in some time, it wasn't hard to use her mind to unlock the door and slide inside.

With the vehicle in neutral, Isabel released the brake and backed silently down the drive, checking the time as she went. She got as far as starting the ignition and pulling around the bend of what looked to be a service road when the damn thing died.

"Fuck," Isabel muttered. Not that she knew anything about cars, but perhaps the whole hybrid thing meant having to do something wacky to keep it running. Stupid modern technology.

A quick look back toward the house didn't reveal any noise or movement, so probably the residents were still none the wiser. She proceeded to chew her lip raw while she reviewed her options, studying the lights on the dash for clues to the problem. She flexed her mind to try and start the car again. Not a damn thing. It was like the power had died entirely.

She tapped her fingers nervously on the steering wheel. Made sure the doors were locked. More tapping, more lip chewing. Still more tapping. Shit, shit, shit. Okay. She made yet another attempt to start the stupid luxury paperweight before she was forced to acknowledge that she would have to ditch the thing and try something different.

The prime directive was to keep moving.

Resigned, Isabel opened the door and stepped out, inching around to the hood of the car, as if looking at that would tell her anything. A mechanic she most definitely was not. She groaned and leaned her hands on the vehicle for a moment before giving the tire a juvenile kick and turning away to look for another option. The breeze kicked up again as she stood there, and suddenly she was possessed by an inexplicable but overwhelming urge to get away immediately.

A twig snapped behind her and spurred Isabel like a cattle prod, but before she had made it even a few steps, a flare of bright light erupted from behind her. She knew with total certainty that whatever was happening was terribly bad and that she could do nothing to stop it. She had recognized the warning bell but too goddamn late.

Her body seized and pain flashed through her like a lighting strike. If she didn't know better, Isabel would have thought she'd tripped over a live power line. She was falling but couldn't move, couldn't catch herself. Her brain and her limbs refused to get on the same damn page.

As her vision dimmed, she saw a dark figure looking down at her, laughing. The air around him crackled like it was heavy with static electricity. She could have sworn she saw the gleam of fangs in the moonlight, but that wouldn't have made sense. After that, she didn't know much of anything because the world went dark, her brain powering down like someone had clicked the shutdown sequence for a computer.

Just before Isabel lost consciousness completely, it occurred to her somehow that her heart had stopped beating.

Chapter 26

THAD WAS BEGINNING TO BELIEVE THAT THIS WOULD be the longest damn night of his life, and that included the one where his father had disappeared and his mother had killed herself. Christ.

"So what were you doing in Alexia's room, man?" Lee and Siddoh were flanking Thad as they patrolled through the dismal countryside.

"What?" Siddoh turned his head, eyebrows raised. "Oh, yeah. Just interviewing her on the wizard thing, man."

Lee bristled on Thad's right. "Should've talked to me. If you had asked, you would have known that I already did that."

Siddoh shrugged. "Well, no harm done. We can compare notes later. No big."

"So what were you doing buttoning your shirt on the way out if it was just an interview, huh?"

Uh-oh. Thad didn't know what this was about, didn't wanna know, didn't give a shit if it wasn't about finding Isabel. But damn it all to hell and back, they did not have time for some kind of "interrogate the human" pissing contest.

Siddoh waved his hand dismissively. "That was nothing pertinent. What do you care, anyway?"

Lee clenched his fists. "You have a history of inappropriate behavior is why I care, Sid. That human—"

"Don't call me Sid, motherfucker, you know that

pisses me off—" Thad stopped short and threw both arms out wide, nearly clotheslining the two other males. Enough was enough.

This was where those new big-boy pants would come in handy.

Thad pivoted to face Siddoh and Lee with extreme impatience and a tiny desire to commit murder. That depended on how the evening unfolded.

"Okay, ladies." He pegged each of them in the chest with a pointed middle finger. "You, and you"—he swept his gaze from Siddoh to Lee and then back again—"shut the fuck up right now. If it's not about finding Isabel, I don't want to hear about it. Save your little bitch fight for later." He turned away and started walking again.

If he hadn't know better, he would have sworn that he heard a low whistle from Siddoh immediately after, but no, that couldn't have been what he'd heard. Definitely not, because Siddoh was smart enough to know not to work a dude's nerves at a time like this. Not when Thad was edgy enough to go ahead and pop the smarmy bastard. Especially since while he was at it, he might be obligated to get in a few extra hits for Siddoh getting it on with Thad's sister.

Lee cleared his throat. "Yeah, all right. We've worked up a search area based on the speed we think she'd have been able to travel on foot, as well as in a vehicle. I've diverted the guys on patrol to search within that area, and with the exception of Xander and a couple of others who weren't quite at a hundred percent, I've pulled in all of the reserves as well. I've focused them primarily within the area we think she could've covered on foot, since that seems the most likely scenario.

"We don't think she picked up anything on the estate grounds but she could've jacked a car at some later point. I'm thinking that if her plan was to try to get back home, we want to focus on gas stations, rental cars, hotels, airports—"

"She wouldn't have gone to the airport." Thad stopped, shaking his head vehemently. "No way. She wouldn't leave Alexia behind."

"She did leave her at the mansion by herself," Lee said. Damn him for even suggesting Isabel would do such a thing. Okay, so Thad had considered it at first. She was afraid and most definitely not thinking clearly, but she would not have skipped town and left her best friend behind.

"No. No. Isabel told Alexia she would come back for her. I believe she'd do that."

Lee nodded. If the older male still disagreed, he was at least wise enough to keep his trap shut about it. "All right, then."

The three started walking again. "I've got the patrols searching from the outside in. I think we have a better chance of intersecting with her that way. Also, Tyra's going to meet up with us later if you haven't caught a whiff of her by then. I'll ask her to bring a vehicle so we can kick it into high gear."

Thad's head dipped slightly in agreement. He was walking slowly, purposefully, pausing every few steps to take a deep breath and get quiet. The hope that he'd catch her scent or feel a stirring in his veins kept him moving along steadily, even though impatience and frustration were working him like an itchy rash.

Unable to contain himself any longer, Thad stopped

short and whipped around to plant the sole of his boot into a tree. As bark flew and his head kicked back to release a primal roar, his bare palms both smacked the tree bark, stinging at the contact. The heat of his power rose in him, boiling out through his hands to leave black marks on the trunk he'd assaulted. A waning moon mocked him from overhead.

"Yo, easy." Siddoh's hand landed firmly on Thad's shoulder and helped bring him back to reality. What the hell was he doing? They'd never find her if he ran off half-cocked into the forest. So far, getting his shit together was not going so well.

A quiet buzz behind him barely registered. Lee spoke briefly to someone on his phone and hung up quickly with a look on his face that told Thad his buddy had info.

"Clerk at a Shell station about a half mile over that way gave a free bag of roasted pecans to a female matching Isabel's description." Lee gestured toward Route 9.

Thad nodded and clapped both males on the shoulder. "Let's go then."

Their boots crunched on frozen grass as they chewed up the countryside, moving past the pungent vegetable and horse farms. Nothing like sucking wind when the air was thick with manure. As they neared the Shell station, Thad slowed down, confused.

"I don't see the guys. Aren't we supposed to rendezvous here?"

Siddoh wandered around to the side of the building while Lee pulled out his cell phone to check in. Pacing impatiently, Lee cursed and pocketed the phone again. "No answer."

Thad stood in a shadowy portion of the parking lot

next to an ancient and questionably functional air machine. Arms akimbo, he muttered a string of expletives under his breath as he pondered their next move. "Lee, who talked to the store clerk?"

"Gary."

"Call him again." Thad's nostrils flared. He was getting a hint of Isabel's scent. He followed along the side of the building until he traced the scent toward a neighboring field. With not a small amount of irritation, he glanced at his arm, rubbing the scar that had been nagging at him for so long. Nothing now. Not a tingle, not a prickle, not jack shit.

What the hell good was that thing now?

A rush of air swirled around him. Siddoh had caught up. "Yo, buddy, you want to wait up?"

Thad sniffed the air again, drawing a lungful of country air. Filtering out Isabel's faint scent once more, he turned toward the field, following along the road. "Yo, buddy, you wanna turn off the cloaking device for now?"

Siddoh laughed. His form rippled into view. "Hang on. Lee's bringing up the rear. You got a bead on her?"

"Her scent's weak, but I'm getting it." His brow furrowed. An uncomfortable realization had begun to dawn on him. "But... I'm not feeling anything, you know?"

"You fed from her?" Lee's right eyebrow hiked itself up a little as he fell in line beside Thad again. "If you can smell her from here, you should be able to sense her."

"Not necessarily. If she was by here but then left, her scent could still linger." Thad understood Lee's implication. If her scent lingered but he could not sense her in his blood, then there was the possibility that she was no longer alive. Thad may have been holding on to his optimism by a thin thread, but he still fought to stay positive.

He'd just found her, for God's sake; he couldn't lose her.

"Right." Lee seemed to catch Thad's underlying message in the dismissive reply: *Shut it down.*

The wind kicked up and Thad paused again, breathing deeply. The crisp night air zinged up his nostrils. He was being overly cautious, but it was too important not to lose her trail. "She headed that way." He gestured confidently with his hand, a feat of great proportion given how much he was shaking on the inside.

Between the literal boiling rage and the concern he had for Isabel's safety, he was a veritable powder keg. He'd told Alexia that he'd get Isabel back, and he meant it. He wasn't going to consider any other possibilities. Just wasn't.

"I'm gonna go ahead of you. Hang back a little, yeah?" Siddoh's form faded into the darkness again as Thad nodded. The cold grass crushed softly under Siddoh's boots.

"Dude's power would be cooler if he could make his footprints disappear, too," Lee said wryly.

Despite his tension, Thad chuckled for a moment. "You two ever going to get along?"

"It's a possibility. Frankly I don't get how you're so sanguine about the fact that he's been doing your sister for like the last twenty-five years with no promise of mating her."

Thad's jaw tightened. He didn't need to think about this now. "My sister does not have sex. That's how I deal with it."

"Whatever works for you." Lee smiled, but he turned tense just seconds later. "Shit. Heads up, Thad."

"Yeah, I feel it." A vague tremor of unease had settled in Thad's gut. Wizards, one at least, somewhere nearby. "Must be why Siddoh went up ahead. He always seems to have good radar for these guys."

Suddenly the night exploded in a torrent of bright light and smoke. Squealing brakes and urgent shouts could be heard in the distance, just beyond the road. "Fuck. Let's go." Thad tapped Lee's arm but he was already in motion, shields charged, hands poised.

Their boots tore up the grass beneath them as they raced along the fence line of the field they'd been traversing, closing in on the stretch of barren country road up ahead. Thad's chest burned with a mix of fear and bad wizard vibe. He blinked quickly, closing out everything but his focus on the battle that waited up ahead.

He'd trained for years under Lee before his father's demise, but he'd never fought with a power before. He would need his focus now more than he ever had.

An SUV sped toward them. It had a cracked windshield and a blown-out headlight, and judging from the smell of burnt rubber, its tires were not long for the world. Tearing up the road behind it was Gareth. Gary, as he was known to most. The dude showed severe signs of strain, like he was about to drop from exhaustion. Gary had the power to move things with his mind, and Thad presumed he'd been trying to hold back the vehicle, which was a nearly impossible feat.

No matter how powerful you were, you just couldn't hold a five-thousand-pound vehicle when it was heading in the opposite direction. Thad was utterly amazed that

Gary had tried. Even more amazing, it appeared to have worked, at least a little.

Thad's arm shot out to aim at the runaway vehicle. In an astonishing instant, the heat that had raged throughout his body coiled in his gut and then shot out of him, leaving his palm in a fiery orb the size of a watermelon.

Well, how about *that*?

A cluster of holes shattered the back window, courtesy of Lee's silenced MK23, and at the same time, a series of daggers shot toward the moving target from the blank space in the darkness where Siddoh was located. Two knives hit a back tire of the vehicle, puncturing the sidewall as Thad's fireball struck the undercarriage and rocked the vehicle sideways. Sparks flew. The thing was down to its alloy wheel, but the driver kept going and even managed to gain speed as Gareth dropped to the pavement, utterly spent.

For a moment, Siddoh came into view, whistling and jutting his chin toward the car. "Yo, Thad! Call Tyra." The big male pulled out all the stops then, running at top speed toward the busted-up car, and evanesced once again. A distinctive thud could be heard in the distance. Siddoh must have caught up.

"Crazy fucker." Lee whistled quietly. "Guess he grabbed the roof rack."

Thad shook his head. "I don't know, but I hope he hangs on. I'd bet every cent I have that Isabel was riding shotgun in that thing. And from the quick glimpse I got, she wasn't conscious."

Lee's face was grim as he pulled out his cell and hit a speed-dial number. "Ty," he said quietly, "we need you."

Chapter 27

"THAT STUPID SON OF A BITCH! I'M GOING TO KILL HIM after I find him." Tyra's heart thudded in her chest, and a cold, panicky sweat had broken out on the back of her neck. One of these days, Siddoh's cocky ass was going to get him killed.

"I'm beginning to see why Lee handed me the phone," Thad said dryly. "Look, you can bitch him out all you want later, Ty, but for now let's just get him and Isabel back."

"Jesus Christ, Thad," she hissed into the phone, closing her office door behind her so she could talk privately. "What was he thinking?"

"Are you kidding me? It's brilliant! We might not only get Isabel back but maybe also finally find out where their fucking bat cave is. All you've gotta do is track him. It's perfect!" Thad's exasperation was apparent.

Tyra pressed her back against the door, breathing deeply. "Look, I'm just worried about him."

"Ty, he knows what he's doing. As long as he stays cloaked, the chances are slim that they'll catch him." Thad's voice hitched just barely on the other end of the phone before he continued. "It's our best chance of finding Isabel."

Tyra sighed. "Of course I'll help, Thad. I just freaked, you know?"

"I know."

"Do you have an idea of where they were headed?" She rubbed her forehead. Suddenly the days and weeks of exhaustion were settling into her body. Now, when going home to get some rest was not an option in any way, shape, or form. Not unless she was dead.

Thad's voice broke into her thoughts. "Looked like they were going down Route 9, toward downtown."

"Well, there's a chance they're headed my way then. Don't worry, Thad. I'll track him down."

"Thanks, Ty. Love you."

"I love you, too, baby brother. I'll call you soon." She started to pull the phone from her ear.

"Wait. You'll need backup. We should come and meet you."

"No way. You'll slow me down. Besides, it sounds to me like you've got things to clean up over there."

"Yeah," he said on a loud exhale. "It's pretty fucked up. We're not sure exactly what went down yet. Gary's completely maxed out, and we can't find the rest of his patrol."

"K, well you take care of that. I'll drop you a line soon as I can." She started to hang up again.

"Hey, Ty?"

"Thad?"

"You, uh, you love him?"

She smiled slightly into the phone. Of all the things—

"Thad?"

"Yeah, Ty."

"I'm going to hang up now." This was *so* not a subject to delve into with her brother. Definitely not right now.

He cleared his throat. "Yeah, okay. Be careful."

She smiled again. "Of course. You too. Bye." She flipped the phone shut before Thad could ask any more questions.

Tyra took a moment to get still and quiet, focusing her mind on where to begin searching for Siddoh. If they came anywhere nearby, she'd sense him, after feeding from him for such a long time. Hooray for long-term dead-end relationships.

No chance in hell was she gonna sit by and wait to see if they came near her. Dead-end or not, infuriating cocky asshole or not, Siddoh was precious to her and she was gonna get his ass back. And Thad's mate, too. She'd head outside and start in the direction Thad said the car had come from. If she was lucky, she'd meet up with it head on, and boy what fun that would be.

But first... she had nothing with her other than her phone. She'd left her coat in the kitchen off the cafeteria, and it was cold as the proverbial witch's tit outside. And why a witch's tit? Was there anything said about the temperature of, say, a warlock's testicle? What about a wizard's? Tyra was willing to bet any part of their bodies would be plenty frigid.

God, but did she ever have a gift for thinking of the stupidest things at the most ridiculous possible times. She cursed and muttered to herself while she locked up her office and hurried down the hall to the kitchen. The dingy linoleum tiles disappeared underneath her feet as she cursed more, realizing she also didn't have any weapons aside from a small dagger in an ankle holster.

Good thing she usually didn't need them.

Tyra attuned herself to the rush of her blood as she hurried along. Her footsteps echoed in a hall that was blessedly devoid of humans at the late hour. Inattention could cost her precious seconds. She was so preoccupied that she didn't see Anton Smith, or whatever the hell his name was, standing in the hall until she was about to plow right into him.

"Holy cow!" She pulled back soon enough to avoid knocking him down but not before she found herself pressed against him like they were two halves of a grilled cheese sandwich.

"I'm sorry," he said in that rumbly, soothing voice of his. "I didn't mean to run into you."

"No, don't be." She put her hands on his shoulders with the intention of pushing him away, but she found it taking more self-control than she'd anticipated. What on earth? "I was the one not paying attention."

She frowned then. It was getting late. He shouldn't be out of his room so close to quiet hours. "What are you doing out here this late? You should probably get back to the men's hall before you get locked out for the evening." She backed only a step away, dropping her hands at her sides awkwardly.

"Actually, I was looking for you," he said quietly. She didn't even try to hide what must have been a very puzzled expression.

"I'm sorry. I know I shouldn't be. I just—I feel drawn to you. I can't explain it." A blush hit his cheeks, and in a different set of circumstances, it would have been the sweetest damn thing. "I can't seem to stop thinking about you. I feel this overwhelming need to protect you…" As his voice trailed off, his intensely dark gaze met hers and the stain on his cheeks deepened. "I'm sorry. It's stupid…"

Oh, she so did not have time for this.

"Mr. Smith... uh, whatever... look. You barely know me, and as sweet as it is, I don't need you to protect me." Hell, he didn't know the half of it.

"I know. I'm sorry." He shifted to lean against the wall but left the distance between them the same. He absently scratched at his arm and rubbed the back of his neck. The gestures were nervous ones, but he maintained eye contact.

"Thing is, I've been trying to remember something about what happened to me. Or my past in general. All I get is this vague impression of darkness. Of things around me being evil and scary and... feeling really alone, you know? When I try to follow those impressions to see where they lead, I just get more of the same. Or worse, the urge to throw up."

Ew.

"But when I see you, I light up. I feel so good in a way I can't really even describe." He coughed. "I'm sorry. That probably sounds really creepy and I know it's inappropriate, but the honest truth is that if this were another time and place, I'd ask you out to dinner or... or wherever, in a heartbeat." He stopped to catch his breath, his steel-gray eyes still staring her down.

Daring her to answer.

Despite the enormity of what she was on her way to do, Tyra couldn't help but give him props for having the balls to come up to her like this. And she was truly flattered. Really. It wasn't as if she got approached like this every day. Or even every decade.

Tyra gave him a slight smile. She needed to shut him down fast but gently. "I'm honestly flattered, thank you.

But you're right, it's inappropriate. I can't be involved with a client. Besides, you said it yourself: you still don't have your memory back. How can you move on with your life when you don't know where you came from? You should focus on yourself first and find the missing pieces before you try to bring a relationship into the picture."

His face fell, but he recovered fast and nodded quietly. "You're right. Again... I'm sorry."

She touched his arm gently, in that same comforting gesture she used with all residents. Immediately his feelings of sadness, disappointment, and even desire washed over her. Poor thing, how could he want her that badly? The despair was something greater. Something bitter. Angry. His missing past, perhaps.

"It'll come back. Don't worry. Now, let's get you back to the men's wing before they lock the doors for the night and you're stuck sleeping in a cafeteria chair."

He nodded again but didn't move. "It's just frustrating, you know, like I can see these shadows in my head, and I want to reach in and pull them out so I can look closer and figure out what they are. But I can't." He took a few steps while he dug in his pocket, his face lined with frustration.

"Take this thing, for example. They said at the hospital that significant items could help jog my memory, but all I had on me when I came in was this, and so far it doesn't jog anything. I keep thinking maybe it's too big to have belonged to a sister or a girlfriend or something, but I really have no idea. It seems to evoke some really unpleasant emotions, but I just can't pin it down."

When she looked down at his open hand, Tyra went

cold. Lips parted, heart racing, she stood frozen in place like some dumb ass in headlights. Nothing could have prepared her for this, not in a million years.

Sitting squarely in the middle of Anton Smith's palm was a gold signet ring with a heart embossed on it.

A wizard ring.

Anton Smith... or whatever his name was... was a freaking wizard. And he had no idea.

He curled his hand around the ring and stuffed it back into his pocket. "I'm sorry. You're right. I should really go. This is not your problem."

Jesus Lord, if that wasn't the misstatement of the year...

Before she could do much more than stand there gaping like a hooked bass, adrenaline arrowed through her, so intense that it lit up every vein in her body.

Siddoh.

Her eyes met Anton, uh, Whoever's. "I have go. I'm sorry." This whole other can of worms was going to have to wait. Without waiting for an answer, she pivoted on the ball of her foot and booked back to the cafeteria to grab her coat.

Inside the kitchen pantry, Tyra clutched her jacket to her chest and pulled the door shut. Her eyes squeezed shut. It was a struggle to get control of herself so she could get a bead on Siddoh when her heart rate and breathing were set on overdrive, and the stench of corned beef and cabbage lingered in the air like toxic waste.

A thought blinked into her mind about how she'd raced away from Anton Smith without bothering to hide her preternatural speed, and damn, but that was stupid. Still, she had bigger and nastier problems. Anyhow, if his memory returned, that little tidbit would be the least of her issues.

Sucking air like it was an Olympic event, Tyra fought to calm her nerves. She had to find Siddoh, and doing so was going to require all her focus. Teleporting to him was no biggie by itself but she needed to go in cloaked. Trying to exercise two powers at once caused an exponential drain on her physical and mental energy.

The hum of Siddoh's life force in her blood was like rushing river rapids beneath her skin. He was anxious but energized. Alert. He was priming for a fight. All in all, that was good news.

When Tyra had a lock on him, she concealed herself, blending in with the massive cans of tomato sauce and pumpkin puree. After a few more deep breaths, she said a quiet prayer and sent herself into a scatter of molecules.

Chapter 28

"CHRIST, HE'S HEAVY." THAD STOOD BY TO LET LEE hoist Gareth's deadweight over his shoulder. The monumental effort that Gary had exerted trying to stop the car from getting away had left him effectively worthless. Poor bastard couldn't pick up his own pinkie at the moment. Meanwhile, they all continued to trudge in the direction the runaway SUV had come from.

"I can help carry him if you want." Lee would decline, but Thad offered anyway. The older male's face was grim but his eyes were sharp as he continued to face forward, constantly scanning the road and the field in front of them.

Finally, Lee shook his head slightly. "It's cool. I can handle it." Sure, he could handle it, but a two-hundred-plus-pound sack of lean muscle was no picnic when it was effectively deadweight. Then again, Lee would sooner kiss Siddoh full on the lips than cop to needing relief.

Thad inclined his chin. "Let's keep to the shadows here but stay along the road. They came from up here so I wanna check out that access road coming off Route 9."

Lee nodded and forged ahead. He didn't need the instruction, but Thad needed to give it. For much of the time before his father's death, Thad had been a soldier like any other, and while they were indeed friends, Lee had been his superior in command. For Thad, having their roles reversed was still very foreign.

Both males swore in disgust when they crested a small hill heading toward a community of luxury homes and were met with a horrific sight: they had found the rest of Gary's patrol.

In the ditch flanking either side of the access road leading from the gated luxury community lay the bodies of Levon and Eamon. "Lee, get on the phone and get Brayden the fuck over here, and call the other patrols and have whoever's closest bring a car," Thad barked. "And check out Eamon."

Levon lay in a pool of his own blood, leaking from a large gash in his neck. The slick expanse of it coated the grass, shining in the moonlight like a puddle of motor oil. Thad dropped down beside him in the grass while Lee hurried past, having laid Gary on a patch of grass with a hasty, "Sorry, man."

Lee was already on the phone. "Yeah, we need pickup at the Fox Hill Estate community, pronto. Gary's spent, and Levon and Eamon are both down. Get a doctor, and if you can, get their mates. Hurry." He flipped the phone shut and knelt by Eamon.

Thad ripped off the bottom of Levon's shirt, using it to stanch the bleeding. Lee had already begun CPR on Eamon. All the while, Thad and Lee kept vigilant watch for more enemies, even though the night air was crisp and peaceful. Whoever had taken Isabel was gone and would have their hands full with Siddoh's shenanigans for awhile.

"Fuck!" After a few minutes of compressions, Lee snarled, "Can't get a heartbeat."

The sound of vehicles rolling up came just as Lee was baring his fangs, poised to open his own vein.

Doc Abel had arrived and was continuing CPR while Eamon's mate, Theresa, had scored her wrist to give him blood. Her blonde hair fell in front of her face as she leaned down, cascading onto the shoulder of a blue flowered nightgown that covered a very large, very pregnant belly.

A guilty pang hit Thad. Jesus, he was such an ass. He'd forgotten Theresa was so close to her due date. It explained why she was dressed for sleep in the middle of the night. She shouldn't have come out here; the stress was no good. In the moment, he hadn't thought to say anything about her pregnancy to Lee. He was screwing up right and left at this gig.

Thad clenched his fists so hard that his knuckles screamed for mercy and his short fingernails bit into his palms. Fuck mercy. Not for himself, not now. The murmur of "I'm sorry" from Abel and then Theresa's plaintive sobs floated to him on the cold breeze. Damn. Just... damn.

Thad's gut clenched at the realization that he had just lost a fighter and a friend. Casualties were an inevitable part of their jobs, but he had never handled them well. Not with the kind of stoicism the others did. He managed, at least, not to puke right there in front of everyone.

Boy, that would be stellar. *You know the new king? He gives the old Technicolor heave-ho in the presence of death. What a leader.*

He glanced up to see Levon's wide-eyed mate, eyes full of tears and questions. Waiting for him to give instructions. Quickly, he guided Ani through getting blood into her mate's slack mouth. Even though he was weak, Levon began to drink, and there was a collective sigh of relief. He would probably be just fine. Thad looked over to where Eamon was being loaded into the back of a Land Rover.

Eamon would not be.

Thad stayed still, even though anxiety filled him with the almost unbearable need to pace like a caged lion. Having civilian females out in the field like this was no good. Having them come made more sense than losing precious minutes getting the injured males home, but it was dangerous as hell. He prayed that Lee's instincts were solid on this one.

Once Levon finished his feed, Thad walked over to guide Ani into the back of one of the SUVs. She sobbed quietly but uncontrollably as she climbed in, tears streaking her pale cheeks like rain on a window. And he was asking Isabel to sign on for this? Thad's position prevented him from sobbing and openly broadcasting his fear for her, as Eamon and Levon's mates had done. He was forced to admit that he didn't know how the mate of a soldier survived this uncertainty night after night.

Like so many things, he had never thought of it before.

"Come on, Theresa, let's get you guys home." Eamon's mate looked on helplessly as his body was secured in the backseat of the other vehicle. Thad urged her around to the front door and motioned for Lee to get Gary—who was shaky but mobile again, thank Heaven—into the other Land Rover that had pulled up.

"No, I want to stay with him!" The petite female dug in firmly and lunged, large belly first, toward the backseat where her mate's body lay. It was not the time to argue, so Thad helped Theresa climb in. As he started to close the car door, there was an urgent gasp. "Oh, my God, he's breathing!"

Abel came around the door with his stethoscope to check things out. "It may just be trapped air in his lungs leaving his body," he said carefully. The stethoscope moved slowly under Eamon's shirt, and then Abel pulled aside the ear buds and gave another once-over. "I guess I was wrong. It looks like he's back!"

Immediately, he grabbed Theresa, who had let out a sob of gratitude and was trying to hug the large body of her male. "Easy, let's get the two of you home to bed." He gently eased the doors shut and went around front to drive the pair back to the estate.

Thad surveyed the area once more before heading to the remaining SUV. He turned to the three males who had ridden in the second vehicle. Again, someone was waiting for him to lead.

"I'll ride with these guys back to the estate. You three backtrack and make sure there aren't any more wizards around the property, then grab another car and head back out. Siddoh's offline for the moment and so is Tyra, so you need to keep alert in case they call for backup."

The three nodded and turned to head out in the direction from which Lee and Thad had come on foot.

Lee hopped into the driver's seat and hit the ignition before turning to check the situation in the backseat. Gary was slumped over up front, so Thad had crammed himself into the cargo area. "How we doing back there?"

Thad glanced over. Levon appeared to be stable but not out of the woods. Levon's mate, Ani, was stroking her male's face as it lay in her lap. She had stopped crying. Her breathing was even and deep, her eyes unfocused. Shock would do that.

"I think we're good," Thad said. "Let's just get out of here."

"All right," Lee concurred as he closed the car door. "Let's rock and roll."

There were times in life when you just had to acknowledge the ridiculousness of a situation. Tyra took form in a dark room, still reeling from the night's events. Thad's female and Tyra's just-barely former lover were in danger. The man who had said the sweetest words any male had ever spoken to her was apparently her sworn enemy; her body was shot to shit from trying to teleport while she was invisible; and she was catching her breath while leaning up against a rack of... waterproof vibrators?

"Remind you of the good times we had?"

"Christ almighty!" Tyra's head whipped around in the direction of the voice. As Siddoh materialized, his cocky grin seemed to lead the way like the Cheshire cat. She'd been so busy ruminating that she hadn't felt his presence.

"Siddoh, what the hell is going on?" she hissed.

His eyebrows wiggled playfully while he lifted one of the packages to take a look. It was almost like he hadn't heard her.

Almost.

"Hardly seems fair, though. There you are leaning up against the dildos, and here *I* am standing by a box of anal plugs."

"Maybe you should put one in your mouth," she said wryly.

Siddoh scoffed and then gave her an aggravating little pout. It was that same pout that had gotten her into bed so many times. Strangely, it didn't affect her now. "All right," he said, clapping his hands together. "Let's talk strategy."

A weight lifted that Tyra hadn't even realized was sitting on her chest. She had made the right decision in breaking it off with him. Siddoh had opened up to her more than to anyone else, but that would never be enough to sustain anything real. She needed the kind of connection that he could never provide. If only it hadn't taken her a quarter century to figure that out.

"Great," she said, clearing her throat softly. "I would love to hear why I'm cooling my heels in a room full of sex toys."

"Well…" His arm gestured around the cramped space. "In case you haven't guessed it, we're in the old adult toy store on Eighth Street."

"We couldn't have done this in the tattoo parlor next door?"

"Too much activity. This place appears to be closed down, finally. Although they still have inventory." Siddoh slid his gaze around the tiny room. "I'll have to remember that for later," he said with a chuckle.

"*Anyway*," Tyra said with aggravation.

"Anyway," he said. "Isabel is being kept upstairs in one of the 'abandoned' shithole apartments." His hands rose into the air to perform a dramatic set of finger quotes. "There appear to be two others held in the room with her. All three are hog tied and apparently sedated.

Also at least three wizards, including the fucker that brought her. Some sort of dusty, oblong circle out in the main room suggests that they've been using the place for ceremonial purposes, and the toilet doesn't work."

What? "You tried to use the bathroom?"

He laughed. "Nah, I shadowed one of them so I could get out of the place undetected. On his way out he stopped to take a piss in the bathtub. It was funny, that's all."

Leave it to Siddoh to find humor in a situation like this.

Suddenly a thought occurred to her. "Wait. They're using an abandoned apartment in the middle of downtown to hold their ceremonies? This can't be their base of operations, can it?"

"Dunno. I mean, we've theorized that they move around, so maybe they keep to disposable locations, as it were. It fits, if you ask me."

"I guess so," she said crossing her hands over her chest. "So can we move now?"

"Oh!" Siddoh snapped his fingers. "I almost forgot. One of the dudes up in that apartment looks like one of us."

"What?" Tyra blinked her confusion. "What the hell does that mean?"

"He's got fangs."

"Are you serious? How?"

Siddoh did a palms-up shoulder shrug. "Search me. It's weird, though."

"Not weird enough for that to be the first thing you tell me?"

He shrugged again. "I got distracted when I saw you cozied up next to all the personal massagers."

"You're such a pig," Tyra sighed.

"Part of my charm, right?"

"No." She narrowed her eyes at him. "Now, why do you say we can't move yet? Seems to me we ought to get up there and do a smash-and-grab before anyone's the wiser, yeah?"

He shook his head. "No way. First off, Thad wants a piece of the action. He's in charge now so that's non-negotiable. 'Sides, one or two of those dudes are really strong, Ty. We're talking those evil vibes and whatnot that make you wanna throw up if you stand too close. I'm not kidding. We don't know what they're working with or how many more might be coming. Now I know you and I are good," he said with another suggestive twinkle in his eye, "but Thad will have my ass if we don't wait for backup."

Tyra was back on the wizard with fangs. Had they recruited a vampire somehow? If so, were their homes in danger? Suddenly an alarming thought stopped her cold. "Oh, God. Siddoh, wait! You said they have a ceremonial circle up there. So they're probably holding Isabel and those others to do surgery on them. Shit, we can't wait. We have to get up there!"

His strong hand shot out to grab her wrist. "Not so fast, sweetheart. I get what you're thinking, but we have to hang back. No one was being prepped while I was up there. We have some time."

Her head shook fervently. "No, no. Bad idea. We can't risk it."

"*Good* idea, Tyra," Siddoh said through clenched teeth. "Do not challenge me on this! This is a dangerous situation. We can't afford mistakes. We need to wait for backup."

"Uh-uh," she said quietly, twisting her wrist out of his grasp. She may be tired, but she was still stronger than Siddoh. And she wasn't willing to risk the wait. "Screw. That."

"Tyra," he said with warning in his voice, "don't do it."

"Go ahead and stop me, Siddoh." His face contorted in a mask of rage as she faded into the background. Yeah, she was gonna hear about this later.

"Tyra, goddammit!" Siddoh's hand swept to grab where she had been standing, but she was too fast for him. She would bet he was wicked pissed that she'd been able to absorb his power of invisibility now. He sure looked it. Smiling to herself, she teleported to the apartments upstairs.

Chapter 29

"FUCK ME RUNNING!" THAD SMACKED THE DOOR FRAME in the mansion foyer, where he'd come to grab more gear before heading back out. He rubbed his throbbing temples and thrust his cell phone into the pocket of his jacket.

"'Sup?" Lee had just walked up to the door, looking grim.

"We have to get out of here. Siddoh called, and apparently Tyra's gone in ahead of us, lone-fucking-cowboy style."

"Shit," Lee muttered. "Well, I have more bad news. Eamon didn't make it."

"What?" Thad's jaw fell open. "What happened?"

"Heart stopped again. Abel's checking it out."

"Fuck!" As Thad stood hands on hips, his chin dropped to his chest in frustration and defeat. He wanted to go comfort Theresa but they didn't have time now. They needed to help Tyra and Siddoh before shit got crucial. They needed to get Isabel. The only good news in Thad's call from Siddoh had been word that Isabel was, indeed, alive. Sedated, but alive.

"Jesus. All right. I'll go see Theresa as soon as we get back. Send Ivy over to see if she needs anything in the meantime."

"Already done." Of course it was. "Gary's resting up. Rena's taking care of him. You know how Levon's doing. I've got a vehicle ready to go."

Thad nodded curtly. "Then let's get the hell out of here before my sister does something stupid."

"Thad!" Ivy was jogging toward him. He most definitely could not handle her bright and sunny disposition right now.

"Ivy, not now."

Her head bobbled. "I'm sorry, I know you're leaving." She held up a stack of Post-it notes. "It's just… I'm getting a lot of calls from folks trying to book appointments to see Isabel. I wasn't sure what to tell them."

Isabel? "Ivy, we're not mated yet." Damn, he hoped it was still just *not yet*. "Her presence here wasn't even announced."

Ivy nodded and gestured down the hall. "She handled your office hours for you earlier. Cleared the room in no time flat. Everyone seemed to really like her. I guess word travels fast."

Thad cursed. In all the confusion, he had forgotten that he was supposed to be receiving subjects earlier in the night. Isabel had handled the appointments? It was hard not to be impressed; he'd been dreading that part of taking the throne almost as much as he'd dreaded dealing with the Elders' Council.

He shook his head. "Sorry, Ivy, but you're going to have to hold them off for awhile. If you have to, say that she's ill. I don't want it to get out that she's missing. Got it?"

Ivy scurried off, and Lee and Thad headed out into the night. They didn't speak a word as they sped toward the downtown address Siddoh had provided, both of them lost in thought over the events of the evening and saddened by the loss of Eamon. The lights of downtown were a blur as they passed through the quaintness of Old Town and headed into the seedier side of Ash Falls. Lee pulled up in the alley behind Dick's Ink tattoo parlor and killed the lights.

Lee looked to the building ahead of him. "This definitely it?"

"Yeah. Contact Team C and have them get down here. Tell them to stay hidden, in case we need backup. Also, call Brayden and have him ready in case anyone else is injured. Tell him to bring backup from the clinic if necessary. I'm going to assume Ty and Siddoh are already inside, so you and I should get up there and clear the room as fast as possible, if they haven't already done so." As he unbuckled his seat belt and cracked open the door, he turned toward Lee for a moment. "And Lee… thanks, man. Seriously."

"You bet. Now…" The older male dashed off a quick text as he jumped from behind the steering wheel. He stopped abruptly beside Thad and stiffened his arms by his sides, focusing his power until a protective shield surrounded both of them. "Try to stay close to me so you don't get your ass blown up, yeah?"

Thad's nostrils burned from the odors left by the displaced and degenerate residents that had passed through the building's dark, dank stairway before them. Old body fluids, drugs, alcohol, and even death assaulted his senses. His jaw clenched. Isabel didn't belong in a place like this.

Thankfully, there was no current activity in the stairwell. The apartments had been condemned, and likely the only residents were out trolling for sex or drugs, or trading sex for drugs, or involved in God knew what other variation on those themes. The stairs groaned and creaked in protest under the immense weight of both himself and Lee as they moved swiftly but cautiously, weapons drawn.

They stopped to listen when they reached the second-floor landing. Nothing. No fighting, no explosions. That could be good or very, very bad. Finally, the sounds of quiet shuffling could be heard, and the two stepped back into the shadows as a door nearby creaked open.

"Oh, good. There you are." Tyra's voice whispered into the hallway. Thank goodness.

Now that Thad knew she was all right, he was gonna kill her.

They entered the apartment and closed the door, locking it behind them. The place was about ten years past being condemned and looked it. The few pieces of furniture, including a small rickety table and a busted-up recliner, looked like they'd been hauled out of a Dumpster.

Tyra materialized in front of him. "Good news. Isabel's fine, I think. She's in the other room, unconscious but definitely alive. There are others—another female who's in real bad shape and a male who's been beaten all to hell. None of them are lucid enough to talk so they can't tell us anything." She gestured across the way to the adjoining bedroom.

Thad growled as he passed her. "You and I are going to have a serious talk later."

"Yeah, yeah." She crossed her arms defiantly as he and Lee passed by.

Thad growled under his breath. She might be his sister, but he was the king, and she needed to start being more respectful.

Thad opened the door to the apartment's only bedroom and took in three dead wizard bodies and three
comatose vampires. For a moment in his head, they
seemed like teams for some messed-up, half-court
basketball game.

Siddoh was kneeling on the floor beside the blonde
female, checking her over while he barked instructions
rapid-fire into the phone that was clamped between his
ear and his shoulder. He nodded in Isabel's general direction. "I think she's all right. I'm calling in transport."

Getting to Isabel's side meant stepping over two
bloody wizard corpses lying side by side. Thad noted
with gratitude that Isabel was most definitely alive—
breathing, heart beating, and all that good stuff.

"Isabel," he said quietly. His hands skimmed over her
body to check for injury. "I'm here, okay? I'm going to
take care of you."

She needed blood, and he refused to waste the time
to get her checked out. His fangs punched through his
gums with record speed and he pierced his wrist, pulling
her chin down to let the blood drip between her lips.

"Come on, Isabel."

Lee remained by the door, one eye on the entrance
in the main room. He turned to Tyra. "Talk to me.
What happened?"

"She went fucking kamikaze in here is what happened," Siddoh said tersely, snapping his phone closed.

Tyra sighed. "I teleported in here and took out these
two." She gestured to the floor. "Sliced that one's throat,
stabbed that one in the back, and that one…" She trailed

off, turning to gesture at another behind her and to the left. "Siddoh broke his neck."

Lee nodded, his eyes remaining on the outside door. "We should assume there could be more."

"I know. Siddoh said another one left earlier." She seemed to sag against the wall.

"How are you doing? Need a break?"

"No, no," she insisted. "I'm fine. Really." Lee didn't try to hide his frown of disapproval.

"It would be good for her to rest," Siddoh muttered from across the room. "She blew her reserves transporting twice while invisible."

Lee scowled, pegging Tyra with a frustrated glare. "It's not a problem if you're tired, Ty. It happens to the best of us, and if you aren't up to par, you're a liability so don't fucking try to be a hero."

Her spine straightened, her facial features becoming hard. Great, she was gonna take that as a challenge. "If I'm out of juice, I'll let you know. Now drop it."

"Fair enough." Lee remained doubtful, but time to argue was in short supply.

Besides, it was important that he be able to trust his fighters, Tyra included. There was a good chance that more wizards were coming, and they needed to be prepared for whatever could happen. If she was strong enough to help out, he couldn't justify sending her packing.

Siddoh's cell phone buzzed. "Pickup's arrived. Let's get these guys out of here."

"Take the other two first," Thad instructed. "Isabel just started drinking."

Lee allowed himself a quick glance over to where

Thad held his wrist steady over Isabel's mouth. He hadn't realized she was coming around, but thank goodness. Lee walked into the next room to look around. "There's a fire escape outside that window. Have the guys come up and grab them that way. Make sure someone keeps a lookout at the bottom."

Siddoh had just begun to heft the blonde female when he paused and straightened. Lee felt an imminent sense of icky as well, and Tyra was right behind them.

"We've got incoming," Lee murmured.

Tyra moved to the other side of the room. "Siddoh, put her down." She bent and curled one long arm around the blonde female's waist and the other around the male, whose mug looked like hamburger.

"Tyra, you can't," Siddoh said softly. "You haven't recharged enough. Your noodle's gonna be cooked."

"Ty..." From his crouched position Thad was at eye level with her. Concern was all over his face.

"Thad," Tyra said urgently, "just shut up, and let me go. We have to get these guys out of here." As if on cue, everyone's heads snapped up when a key started to jiggle in the front door of the piece of shit apartment. "Thad," she said again. "Just take care of your queen. I might not be able to come back right away, but I'll be fine. I promise I'll be careful."

The knob began to turn, and she didn't waste any more time. Tyra hugged both bodies to her sides, and the three of them disappeared.

Lee remained in the doorway, his eyes trained on the turning knob. He pulled his MK23 and quickly affixed the silencer. The gun was in his right hand and a blade in his left. He'd allowed the protective shield to fizzle out but now it roared to life as he placed himself in the doorway to block the rest of the room from attack.

Here we go.

Adrenaline shot through Lee's system as he readied for battle. This was different from what they'd come up against in Orlando. Whatever was about to come through that door was packing a whole lot of power. An odd kind of arousal filled his body. The promise of a good fight always got him hard.

"Hold up, man." Siddoh was cloaked and making a play to squeeze past him. Lee pulled back his shield for a beat, and as the door creaked open, a small noise told him that Siddoh had taken up a position in the other room.

Lee focused on filling the doorway with his shields so that Thad and Isabel would be protected. Faintly, he heard Thad tapping the keys on his phone. Good, he was getting more backup. When the door swung open, Lee was surprised by what he saw on the other side: the dude looked like an ordinary man. No dumb-ass robe, no shaved head, no heart-embossed signet ring. Just an average-looking Joe in jeans and a button-down shirt.

But you couldn't hide the evil just by changing the wardrobe. And this guy? Lee hadn't encountered a wizard so powerful in centuries. The bad mojo was so thick that you could choke on it, and even with his strength and experience Lee felt his extremities go cold as all of his blood recoiled to the center of his body.

"Well, what do we have here?" The man smiled calmly at Lee, throwing some sort of folder down by the door as he kicked it shut behind him. "Company?

And I didn't even set out the tea and cookies," he said in a mocking voice.

Lee remained still.

Staring.

Waiting.

He wanted the wizard to attack first, to show at least one of his powers so they all knew better what they were working with. Lee would draw the dude's attack, and then Siddoh could get him from behind.

"So…" The wizard walked slowly toward Lee, unbuttoning his cuffs and rolling up his sleeves as he went. Like he was getting ready to sit down to a good meal and didn't want to drag his sleeves through the gravy. No apprehension or aggression was apparent in the man's actions. "To what do I owe the pleasure?" A few more steps. "I see you've taken my prisoners. And killed my men. That's not fair, because I don't come to your house to kill and steal things."

The wizard cleared his throat. "Then again, if I knew where you lived, I might. But hey! Water under the bridge, right? What say we call a truce." He approached Lee, hand extended. "Name's Petros." Lee waited. "What? Not interested in being civilized, vampire?" Abruptly a wicked grin appeared on the wizard's face as he sank into an attack stance.

Lee had to suppress his shock as suddenly one man became two. Then there was another, and another. In an unholy instant the room was filled with half a dozen replicas of the wizard, all in the same fighting stance. How the fuck the wizard had done it, Lee had no clue.

It was known that wizards could mutate the powers they acquired into something far more sinister, but without question this was the craziest thing Lee had ever come up against.

He squared his shoulders and braced for impact.

Chapter 30

TYRA MATERIALIZED IN THE ALLEY BEHIND THE BUSTED apartment building, sagging under the deadweight of two less-than-conscious bodies. She pursed her lips and sounded a shrill whistle, the pitch so high that it would only be heard by her own kind or any stray dogs that might be in the neighborhood.

From the shadows emerged two of her fellow soldiers, Zarek and Flay. They each grabbed a body and loaded them as gently as they could into the nearest Land Rover. Tyra sighed gratefully. "Thanks, guys."

"No problem, Tyra." Flay's face was hard and solemn.

"It's a damn shame," said Zarek. He carefully arranged the blonde female on the bench seat, making sure that her hair was out of the way of the door before closing it. "You okay, Tyra?"

"I will be." She straightened and squared her shoulders as best as she could. "Where's everyone else?"

Zarek jammed a thumb in the direction of the building behind them. "Thad sent a text asking for backup."

Tyra nodded. Jesus, she was really tired. "All right, here's what I want you to do. One of you stay and stand guard, and the other needs to haul ass back to the estate and get these two seen by a doctor. Make sure you check for identification. Their families need to be notified." The two nodded. Glancing around, she realized there were only a couple of vehicles nearby. The others had probably come on foot. "Where's Xander? Is he still out of commission?"

Zarek nodded an affirmative. "His wounds are healing but Siddoh's keeping him off active duty for a little longer."

Tyra blew out a sigh. She was probably going to catch hell later for this one, but that didn't much matter at the moment. Besides, being Thad's sister generally granted her a little leeway.

"I want you to get him out here." She held up her hands in response to their dubious expressions. "Not to fight, just to have as backup. He can bring an extra vehicle, and he can stand by just in case. I don't know what they're up against, but that was a whole lot of nasty up there and I'd rather be safe than sorry."

"Yeah. You can feel it even down here," Flay agreed.

"Good." She sighed. "Now, I'm out of here. I've used up most of my juice, and I need to leave before I'm a liability. The shelter's not far so I'm going to chill there in my office till I feel well enough to make it home."

"You sure you don't want an escort?" Zarek looked around the area, brow furrowed with concern. What a sweetie.

"I can handle myself well enough to get where I'm going. I just don't want to drain my reserves." She clapped Zarek on the back, waved to Flay, and headed down the alley toward Broad Street.

Tyra meandered through the winter night. She kept her head down and walked as quickly as she could manage, not wanting to be hit up for money, drugs, or sexual favors. Luckily, there was little activity, given the weather and the holiday. Not many lights were on, and the few Christmas decorations she saw made this part of the city seem even more bleak.

Tyra thought of Thad and said a small prayer that everyone would make it home safely tonight, him and Isabel especially. For all the issues she may have had toward her too-busy father and completely absent mother, she had to admit no small amount of relief at being half human. Thad's responsibility would never fall to her.

He had a long row to hoe, starting with just getting his poor female out of that dilapidated apartment and away from wizard hands. Then he had to convince her to be his mate and his queen, and of course he still had to figure out how to be the kind of leader their father had spent hundreds of years becoming.

No freaking biggie.

God, what a shitty way to spend Christmas. Turning down Broad, she trekked headlong into the blustery, frigid wind, turning her attention to her other big dilemma: the apparently homeless wizard camping out at her shelter of all the crazy messed-up things. Oh yeah, and she *lit him up*, for crying out loud.

But there could be an alternate explanation. He could have found the ring, or he could have been attacked by wizards and grabbed a ring in the scuffle.

When Tyra ascended the steps to the front door of the nondescript shelter building, she had to dig deep in her brain for the security code to get inside. Her brain was so frikkin' fried that she couldn't wait to collapse in her office. Breathing a sigh of relief when the door lock clicked open, she slid through without a sound. The lobby was empty; both resident halls would have been locked down by now. No sound came from the couple of volunteers still on site or the night security guy. Perfect.

She shuffled briskly to her office. Once inside, Tyra closed and locked the door and dropped into the ancient desk chair. She took a few deep breaths to steady herself, and suddenly she was *really* feeling the exhaustion that she'd been fighting since she'd left Thad's side. Her vision started to blur. The urge to simply lay her head down was immense.

She chuckled softly. She was always amazed at how her race could be gifted with such power and strength, but if she overused it, she suddenly could barely push a paperclip. Just thinking about it made her muscles quiver. The wide expanse of her desk beckoned like a bed in a five-star hotel.

Maybe if she just closed her eyes for a little while...

"Do you realize you're still wearing your hairnet?"

"Holy crap!" Tyra shot straight up in her chair and spun toward the low voice behind her. Anton Smith. "How the hell did you get in here?" As the words left her mouth, she swept the previously forgotten hairnet off her head and into the trash can beneath her desk. Why had no one told her?

"I used the door," he said soberly. "I knocked first but you didn't seem to hear me. Are you okay?" He took a small step toward her.

Tyra frowned. "I locked it."

"It wasn't locked." A voice in Tyra's head gently reminded her that she should stop him from getting near her. Whether due to exhaustion or something else, she couldn't quite manage to act on it.

Shit. She held her hand out in front of her. *Yes. Stop in the name of love, because you don't know who you are and I've got more baggage than you can handle, and here I am so wiped out that I forgot to lock my office door. Also, please don't kill me or anything.* Although seriously, if that was the best she could manage in the way of self-defense, she almost deserved to eat it, didn't she?

"It's probably better if you don't come closer. You're right. I'm not feeling well." He seemed genuinely concerned, but she didn't feel up to tangling with the what-ifs in the event that he wasn't. Figuring out his affiliation with the wizards would have to wait until she felt a little less like she'd been run over by a truck. Jesus, she just wanted him to leave.

He sidled to the farthest corner of her desk and perched there, as if afraid to come any closer. From the strained muscles in his neck to the jackrabbit bounce of his left leg, nervous tension radiated from his body, and Tyra didn't need her powers to detect that. Thank God, because she was fading fast. "I wanted to apologize for upsetting you earlier." He swallowed, studied her for a second, and then continued. "It was... inappropriate for me to approach you the way I did. I'm sorry."

Her fingertips lifted lazily from the arm of her chair, dismissing the apology. *Just go... I'm tired.* "You don't have to apologi—"

"Yes, I do. You know, I kept struggling with the feeling that these memories were at the tip of my brain, and you just... felt... familiar in this *really* good way." He breathed out a shaky laugh. "I reasoned at the time that maybe if I spent some time with you, I'd remember

something. But really I just wanted to be near you because it felt good. It was selfish of me to freak you out
like that. I truly am sorry."

Tyra sighed wearily. *God, God. I can't do this now.*

But there he was, staring at her with puppy-dog eyes
and what seemed like real worry for her.

Her vision blurred a bit more. Even weakened as she
was, she was more than a little curious. If he were a
wizard, why hadn't she felt any kind of malicious aura?
Her long-range radar had never been as strong as others of her kind but surely she'd have gotten a read on
something. And if he wasn't one of them, where the hell
did he get that ring?

Tyra cleared her throat and mustered the strength to
meet his gray eyes head-on. Might as well lay it all out
there while she was still semilucid and see what happened. Maybe it was her fatigue talking, but she didn't
believe he would suddenly turn around and kill her.
Maybe, just maybe, it would be enough to overwhelm
him. Make him need some time to go and think while
she finally got some rest.

"I think I know a little something about who you really are." To her own ears, her speech was rather slow.
A little slurred, even? His eyebrows twitched a little, but
she'd expected much more of a reaction. Huh.

His head dropped to his chest for a moment. Eyes
closed, his chest rose and fell with each deep inhalation.
Finally, he nodded. "I know. You don't have to tell me.
I know who I am. What I am," he murmured.

Chapter 31

"OH, MY GOD, WHERE AM I?" ISABEL'S WHISPER WAS laced heavily with anxiety.

"Shh." Thad's body covered most of hers. Heaven forbid that whoever was out there got past Siddoh and Lee; they would still have to get through him.

And they were not going to get through him.

He leaned close to her ear, speaking as softly as he could. "Close your eyes, and try not to move. We're going to get you out of this."

"How?" Well, that was a damn good question, wasn't it?

"Just don't worry. We'll handle it. Now please be quiet," he whispered.

Thad glanced surreptitiously over his shoulder, trying to make sense of the craziness going on behind him. There appeared to be a room full of the same exact wizard freak, and Lee was staring down the lot of them. It wasn't clear which was the real deal until one of them let out a dull "unh" as his head was shoved to the side by an unseen force. Siddoh must have thwacked him a good one.

The replica that was hit turned in the direction of the blow and planted his left foot on the floor, his right leg swinging in an arc to connect with some part of Siddoh's body with a harsh "smack." At once the other replicas turned and descended on Siddoh, kicking and landing blows wherever they could. Thad frowned as Siddoh became visible again so he could focus his energy on fighting back.

The weird got even weirder when another group of copies split off. The new set turned to advance on Lee with what seemed like excruciating slowness. The subtle clenching and unclenching of Lee's fists told Thad all he needed to know. The older male's patient composure in the face of attack had always awed Thad.

Almost unconsciously Thad gave Isabel's hand a reassuring squeeze. He leaned down again, looking her over to ensure that she was well enough. He thought of Eamon, who had passed so abruptly after they'd all thought he would be okay. Thad needed to be certain this time. "Listen, I want you to play dead for a little while longer. Do you think you could move if you had to, though?"

He took the subtle press of her thumb into his palm as an affirmative. They really didn't have much choice. He would throw her over his shoulder and make a break for it, if it came to that.

"Here's the deal: When I signal you, I want you to get up as fast as you can—and I want you to stick to me like glue no matter what. Squeeze my hand again if you understand me."

When Isabel clasped Thad's hand, firmly this time, a heady mix of relief and adrenaline surged through him. He stood carefully and sidled over to Lee, tapping him quickly in the middle of his shoulder blades to signal that he was going to try to get by Lee when the time was right. Lee nodded tightly.

Thad dropped back while Lee drew his gun with the

silencer attached. A rapid "click, click" sounded but the bullets passed right through the six wizards coming at them, embedding in the wall behind them. Lee then quickly aimed at the group attacking Siddoh, firing carefully to avoid hitting their guy. Eventually, one took a hit. There—they had their original for sure this time. Lee shot the wizard's leg two more times.

The really messed-up part was that the dude barely flinched. In fact, the bullets seemed to expel from the wizard's body almost immediately. The phenomenon was fairly common in a strong enough vampire, but not in humans or wizards. Thad had to wonder how much vampire blood this fucker had sucked down.

On second thought, he didn't want to know.

This could be a real problem. Multiple Man kept advancing forward, the wizards' collective faces still and menacing. It reminded Thad a little of the time he'd seen a dusty old Space Invaders game in a pizza parlor. As strange as this all was, he wouldn't have been surprised if the copies had started humming the game's music.

The wizard laughed heartily and jumped back from where Siddoh had curled into a defensive position against the copies still wailing on him. The original wizard's arms crossed over his chest, and Thad wanted to wipe the satisfied smirk right off the bastard's face. The man looked for all the world like he was watching a sporting match rather than participating in a battle.

Thad's skin burned as anger at the wizard's arrogance rose to the surface, along with a burst of fire. He fought to tamp it down. If he let it free now, it would hit Lee's shield and that wouldn't get them anywhere.

Something didn't fit, though: It wasn't like Siddoh to just curl up and take a beating. Thad could only hope that Siddoh was trying to pull a fake-out.

He glanced back at Isabel. The shallow rise and fall of her chest was barely noticeable. If the wizard was aware that she was awake, he wasn't showing it. He was too busy gloating to pay attention.

Lee sounded two high, short whistles to call backup from outside. Just then, Siddoh flipped onto his back, planting his feet into the back of a disgusting old lounge chair in the middle of the room and sending it careening into the corner toward the original wizard. It clipped the dude's leg and slowed him down, if only for a moment. Siddoh planted his hands on the floor behind his head and vaulted to his feet, facing off with the guy, his face red and angry.

Thank. Fuck.

—―∕∾∕―—

It was all just a head trip.

It had to be.

Lee kept one eye on the wizard and Siddoh, and the other on the fucked-up defensive line in front of him. A crash and rumble echoed from outside the apartment, and then another. Backup was tangling with something. His nostrils flared. And an electrical storm was brewing, and… yep… more wizards.

His adrenaline pumped. Soon, Siddoh wouldn't be the only one getting a piece. The waiting sucked ass, but it always paid off.

A crash came from above as the floor boards splintered and gave way. One of his guys fell through the ceiling riding on the back of another wizard like it was a bucking bronco.

And the motherfucker had fangs. Now that was some crazy shit.

Franklin was grappling with the fanged wizard from behind, keeping his arms pinned. That was a wise move. Just like a vampire, a wizard could channel its power through other parts of the body but the hands were the easiest way.

More wizards swung in through the fire-escape window, and as if on cue, a few more of Lee's fighters burst in through the apartment door. The replicas of the first wizard were now strangely inactive, standing before him in attack stance and glowering but otherwise making like a bunch of bumps on a log. Lee was even more confident now in his earlier assessment. There were no replicas, really. The whole thing was a mind-fuck.

He jerked his head back to talk to Thad, who was still standing behind him waiting for an opening. "These guys are an illusion. If we get him to flex another power, they'll either go away or he'll drain his energy. Now, while he's still engaged with Siddoh, would be the best time. Let's get you guys gone first."

Lee looked over to make sure that the two males were still involved in a vicious bout of hand-to-hand across the room.

"All right. On three." Thad took a deep breath and readied for action. "One..." He inched back toward Isabel. "Two..." Lee glanced out of the corner of his eye to see Thad sink into a semi-crouch next to Isabel. He would drop his shield on three.

"Three!"

In the blink of an eye, Thad scooped up Isabel, who was understandably wide-eyed and trembling. "This way," Thad barked into her ear. He moved so that his back was to her front, one hand grasping either wrist to shield her body as best he could while they slid past Lee and along the perimeter of the room.

Lee slammed the door to the room shut behind them and threw his shields up again. Just as Lee was about to fire a dagger at the wizard Siddoh was fighting, a small fiery ball shot across the room like a comet. It missed the wizard but just barely, knocking him off balance and giving Siddoh the chance to gain the upper hand.

Lee smiled slightly with approval. Thad would be off-the-chain awesome with his power as soon as they trained him to control it. Wouldn't help him much cooling his heels at the estate, but one never knew what could happen in the future.

An apparent newbie broke from the pack and went gunning for Thad. Before the wizard had moved even a foot, Lee's arm swept out to clothesline the boy, and one boot landed squarely in the small of the wizard's back. Lee raised a knife and stabbed down swiftly, ending the wizard's life in a far more merciful manner than would have occurred if their positions had been reversed.

At the same time, Fangboy managed to slip a hand free from Franklin. With a flash and a mighty *crack*, the wizard channeled a bolt of lightning from the storm outside… right toward Thad and Isabel. Lee stepped down from the body he had perched upon, ready to move in and deflect.

The ear-piercing shriek that Isabel let out was nothing compared to the massive blast of freeze that shot from her hands as they flew up on either side of Thad in a defensive gesture. With a massive fizz and crackle and a shit-ton of steam, the lightning strike petered out before it had a prayer of nailing Thad. And she'd managed it with her face buried in Thad's shoulder. Well, how about them apples?

Thanks to Isabel, Thad hadn't needed a shield after all.

And now, as the two edged away, a cloud of steam formed between them. Now *that* was a pretty cool trick. Not only did it obscure Thad and Isabel from view, but judging by the heat that radiated from their bodies, this was the kind of steam that could boil a human or make a volcano erupt.

Turned out that even after seven hundred years, Lee could still see new things.

They were almost to the window. "Thad, that one with the fangs. He's the one who brought me here."

"Lee," Thad growled.

No instruction was necessary. Lee nodded. "I'm on it." As soon as he knew for sure that Thad and Isabel were good, he plowed forward... a moment too late. Fanged wizard struggled free and blasted Franklin with a spark to the chest, dropping him like a ton of bricks.

It was clear from one look at Franklin that nobody was home anymore. Fucker was gonna hurt something awful for that one.

Lee paused, noting the evil little glint in the enemy's eye. This shithead was cocky, which would work in Lee's favor. He waited a beat for Fangboy to draw closer, then pulled up his left knee and snapped his leg, catching the guy beneath the chin.

When the dude's head flew back and threw off his

balance, Lee used the opportunity to push forward. He quickly stuck the same foot to the floor and kicked sideways at the center of the wizard's chest. It was enough to send him sprawling backward on the floor just as Thad was helping Isabel down the fire escape.

One of Lee's size-thirteen boots leveraged to flip the fucker onto his belly, and Lee placed that same foot squarely on the guy's neck. With a fast sweep of Lee's other foot, both of the wizard's hands were kicked underneath his own body. Lee hopped up so that the other foot was now resting mid-back. He balanced on the body like a surfer.

Wasn't often he got to be even taller.

The wizard grunted his discomfort. "Yeah, I bet that hurts a little," Lee muttered. He bounced a couple of times for good measure and then pulled his gun again, firing cleanly into the back of another wizard's head as he prepared to strike one of Lee's comrades.

He looked down at Franklin. By Lee's calculations, Franklin's heart had been stopped for a good minute, and as much as Lee wanted to spend time making this son of a bitch pay, he knew there was no time to waste. He had an idea. It was dicey but it might work.

Lee gave a final bounce on top of Fangboy before hopping down to straddle him. Lee's boot took up a new position at the base of the guy's spine as Lee yanked and pinned one of the wizard's arms back with his knee while twisting the other to place an evil palm on Franklin's chest.

The howl of pain over the wizard's wrenched shoulder was music to Lee's ears. Hey, maybe he could torture and make positive progress at the same time.

"Do it," he growled into the wizard's ear.

"You've gotta be fucking kidding." Fangboy's breathing was ragged and heavy. "You're about rip my arm off, and now you want me to shock your friend back to life? I don't fucking think so."

"Do it," Lee growled again. He still had a hand free to pull out a dagger, which he slid in between the wizard's throat and the floor. "Do it, or you're dead, motherfucker." He added a little pressure to the wizard's twisted right arm to sweeten the deal.

A garbled response came from the wizard's mouth. Lee couldn't understand it, but the jerk of Franklin's body told him he'd gotten the desired results. Lee studied Franklin for a few seconds, ensuring that he could see evidence of breathing before his left hand pulled back swiftly and efficiently to cut the wizard's throat.

Guess he'd forgotten to mention to the guy that he was dead either way.

By the time Lee had finished cutting the dead wizard's wrists so the body would bleed and disintegrate, the smoke had all but cleared. About half a dozen wizards lay dead on the floor, but most of Lee's guys were all right with the exception of the standard bangs and scrapes. Except Franklin, of course, who had started to gasp and wheeze while he communed with the blood-slicked floor.

The fight came down to Siddoh and Multiple Man, who was now without his multiples. Lee advanced slowly in case Siddoh needed an assist, but Siddoh had the dude cornered. After a kick to the gut and another to the head, the bad guy was sagging at the juncture of two poor excuses for walls. Sid's FS blade was out and ready to finish the job.

Mid-arc, Siddoh's arm stopped and the knife clattered

to the floor. Siddoh was red-faced and howling with rage like he had probably never howled before.

The wizard was gone. Just… gone.

"*What the fuck?*" Siddoh's arms flew wide. "Come back out here and fight like you've got some balls, you cock-smoking son of a bitch!"

The nauseating nasty vibes were gone. Elvis had left the building. Lee placed a hand on Siddoh's shoulder. "Sid. Stand down. He's gone."

Lee looked around. One wizard was left alive, held on the floor and hog-tied by Lee's team. The man was clearly a newbie. Hell, he was clearly worthless. Wizards grew stronger and more physically fit over time by virtue of the blood they drank. This one was in about the same physical shape as the Pillsbury Doughboy.

He gestured to the two males holding Doughboy. "Bring him."

Siddoh had stepped back at the wall and was still shouting at the shadows. "I know you're still here, motherfucker, and I am *not* fucking done with you yet!" He took a kick at the now-destroyed lounge chair that had come to rest near one corner of the room, sending it flying against the wall one more time.

"Siddoh," Lee gritted through his teeth. He pointed to Franklin. "We need to get the fuck out of here. Franklin needs treatment." He gestured to the group of soldiers awaiting his command. "You guys," he said, cutting an imaginary line with his hand, "grab Franklin and come with us. The rest of you, bleed out the bodies, check to make sure the place is vacated, and then torch the fucker."

He paused again, stretching his senses out. There was definitely a remaining hint of evil in the air, so

Siddoh's assessment that the wizard was still around somewhere was likely accurate. Or there were others. Ordinarily he trusted his team to handle themselves but he couldn't begin to guess what else this dude had in his bag of tricks. "Actually, I'll stay here as well. Siddoh can handle overseeing transport and questioning our detainee back at home."

"No way." Siddoh stopped and jabbed his finger at Lee. "*I* will stay."

Now was not the time for a power play. They needed to handle things back at the estate, redistribute the patrols, make sure everyone got medical treatment, and handle a laundry list of other stuff that did not include having a pissing contest. He jabbed a finger back at Siddoh. "Think you can handle your shit, buddy?"

Siddoh's nostrils were flared, his hands curled into fists, his arms akimbo. "What do you think, *buddy*?"

"Fine. You stay, but keep it cool. This guy's gone so let him stay gone. It's not like we won't have another crack at him." Lee would bet money on it. He didn't know who this jerkwad was, but they definitely would cross paths again.

"Okay. Let's get out of here," Lee said to the team that was already taking Franklin out the window. "I'll see you guys very soon."

Lee waited until the rest of the transport group had gotten safely to the ground before easing out the window himself. He pegged Siddoh with one final don't-you-screw-this-up glare before he jumped down over the rusted fire-escape railing to the alley below.

Chapter 32

ISABEL HAD KNOWN THAD WOULD BE ANGRY, BUT HE hadn't so much as looked at her since they had gotten into the car. Even though she had expected his reaction, it stung like crazy.

She sat rigid against him with her hands folded in her lap, unsure of what to say. Her hands looked the same as they had the day before: pink polish slightly chipped, fingers that she wished were longer, knuckles that she wished were smaller. She glanced at the tiny stork-bite birthmark in the crook of her thumb and forefinger that nobody ever noticed but her.

How could something as innocuous looking as that hand have managed to pull off that parlor trick back there? And what would have happened to Thad if she hadn't accidentally blasted ice at that lightning bolt?

The thought left her trembling.

Thad maintained an iron grip around her shoulders. After he'd barked a few orders to a large male who'd emerged from the shadows in that alley, they'd headed off. While he hadn't done any talking, he also hadn't left more than a millimeter of space between them. Perhaps he thought she might run off again.

She had absolutely no intention of doing that. The decision to go for a walk had been crazy impulsive, and while she also had known it was a little bit stupid, she'd had no idea *how* stupid until far too late. She was cursing herself right and left for the screw-up.

The bad news was that she had begun to care deeply for Thad. That fight back there? She would never have imagined such a thing. She and Thad had shared something special, the way their powers had come together.

Boy, even in her own head that sounded nutty.

Isabel's heart did a little flutter, skipped a beat, and then thunked really hard in her chest. Like it had been running to catch up with something and had tripped a little. Anxiety gripped her tenaciously. Even though she deserved it 100 percent, she wasn't sure she could face Thad being angry with her. And what about the others? There were many from Thad's military in that building. What if they were all angry?

And what had that weirdo vampire-wizard done to her? Isabel was pretty sure the fuzzy memory of her heart having stopped was a real one, but honestly, could she even trust her memory? She was also fairly certain she remembered something about talking to a horse.

If only she could do what she usually did in a crisis: crawl under the covers with a box of Girl Scout thin mints and not emerge until the whole thing had passed. Hell, a box of cookies wouldn't cut it in this situation. She'd need something bigger, like a cheesecake. Or a Krispy Kreme delivery truck.

Oh God, Alexia! Isabel had almost forgotten about her. Sheesh, some kind of friend she was. Would Alexia forgive Isabel for ditching her back at that mansion when she was still healing from an injury? Surely she would. Alexia always seemed to understand, even when maybe she shouldn't.

Isabel consoled herself with the knowledge that had
she wound up biting the big one back there in that disgusting apartment, Alexia definitely would have been
well cared for. And who knew? Maybe that Mr. Tall,
Dark, and Sociopathic Alexia had her eye on would
finally have been willing to throw a little love her way.

Right, that was probably stretching it. That male was
as warm and cuddly as a Frigidaire.

Isabel realized that at some point during her whiny
little self-pity party, Thad had begun speaking. Not to
her, but to the driver, who looked like death warmed over.

The male murmured a sullen "Yes, sir" to Thad, but
for what she wasn't sure.

From the way he was dressed, she had to gather that
he was one of those soldier guys, but his skin was kind
of pasty and his body was hunched, as if he would have
gone fetal had the vehicle's steering wheel not been
in the way. He was missing that confident badass demeanor all the other males she'd seen tonight seemed to
have. Maybe he had been injured earlier?

Isabel shivered a little, thinking about the harm that
might have come to anyone from her failed Houdini attempt. From the looks of things, Thad's men had been
holding their own when she and Thad had escaped
from the melee, but they had all put themselves in
danger to get her back, and she really couldn't forgive
herself for that.

Almost as if she thought she might get reprimanded
for it, Isabel sighed deeply and allowed herself to sag
against Thad's solid warmth. He smelled of sweat
and smoke and leather, and it was the most comforting combination of scents that had ever entered her

nostrils. A shiver—a pleasant one this time—vibrated through her, and she wanted to burrow under his chin and stay there forever.

Oh God, I really do, don't I?

Yes. Yes, she did. But even if her feelings had changed, reality had not. An invisible knife stuck deep into her heart and twisted until a few tears slid quietly down her cheek. Thank goodness it was dark.

~~~

"'Preciate the transport, buddy, but you want to explain to me why you're outside the estate when you were given instructions to stay put until your ass was healed?"

"Tyra sent word. Wanted me available to help with driving. Sir." Only the barest motion indicated that Xander was not just nervous but still in a great deal of pain. The younger male held himself carefully, and the tension of his body gave it away.

Thad cursed at Tyra for managing to create yet another sticky situation. It was maddening, really, although Thad had to concede that in this case her plan had worked. With Xander unable to fight, he was a good choice to play chauffeur. It left one extra man to help Lee and Siddoh shore things up while Thad and Isabel headed home.

Home. It was an interesting choice of word for the mansion since neither he nor Isabel actually lived there just now. Thad had resided in one of the smaller houses at the estate, and until a few days ago, the idea of moving into the main house had seemed... unbearable. Now, he was resolute. It just needed to happen.

As for Isabel, after all was said and done, would

she be willing to consider calling the estate her home as well? Or was she as determined as ever to hitchhike back to Florida?

Thad shifted and tightened his grip around her shoulders. If he were to dwell on how close he had come to losing her tonight, and how damn much that scared him... The last thing he needed was to fall into a puddle in front of Xander. Or Isabel, for that matter. He needed to stay strong for her.

He hadn't anticipated it, but Thad was coming to the conclusion that the hardest part of this leadership gig was not having the luxury of breaking down. Ever. Right now, a great deal of his energy went toward holding up a facade of strength and calm that would shatter in an instant if it was as much as tapped by a toy hammer.

Thad rubbed his forehead. Even his face was hot and tense. This whole fucking thing was crazy. Sure, he'd never been as laid back as Siddoh, who quite frankly seemed to have a few screws lose, but he'd never cared this much about anyone or anything. The whole situation had him questioning his sanity in a major way.

He wanted nothing more than to crush Isabel's body against his, but he didn't want her to feel as if she were stuck in a vice grip. He hadn't managed to look her in the eye since they'd left that derelict apartment building. If he did, he just might lose it. So instead he kept his focus on Xander, not that he knew what to do about that poor bastard's predicament, either.

"So how you healing up, buddy?"

Xander sighed a little. "Doing all right, sir."

Liar, liar... "Xander," Thad said quietly. He tried to

convey with his tone what he didn't want to say aloud. The bandage still adorning Xander's neck made it clear that he was not, in fact, all right. A fully charged and fed vampire could heal rapidly, sometimes in mere minutes or hours. No way in hell should he still be bandaged up a few nights later. There shouldn't be as much as a scab by this time.

The answering sigh was louder this time. "I'm sorry, sir." Xander took a few more deep breaths in and out, likely steadying his nerves. Thad's heart broke for the soldier. He knew the heart-pounding, gut-twisting agony that had nearly brought him to his knees when Isabel turned up missing. But mercifully, it had been short-lived. For Xander, there was no end in sight. No way to soothe the despair except time.

"Listen, man. I know it's been hard since Tam died, and I get why you don't want to feed. I really do. I can't begin to imagine the difficulty of that." Damn, but he did not want to knee Xander in the balls over this. Still, for the sake of everyone, there was no getting around the harsh reality of it.

"But it's dangerous for you and the rest of the team to have you out in the field when you're not operating at full strength."

Xander swallowed hard, then nodded. "I know. Lee and Siddoh both already talked to me."

Well, that would make this a little easier. "Good. So you know we have to take you off active duty until… you get your strength back."

Xander nodded again. Just barely. "I know," he said.

Thad sighed. "You can help out with training if you like, or you can talk to Ivy about some of the in-house security stuff. You choose. But I want you off the front lines until you're back in shape."

"What about the stables?" The question was full of hope. Since the estate fronted as a horse farm, someone from the team was always up there masquerading as the friendly neighborhood farmer, just in case.

Thad shook his head. "Sorry, buddy. I know that post gets no action, but heaven forbid something actually goes down. That's our first line of defense, and whoever is manning it needs to be in top shape."

Xander coughed a little. Could have been that his voice hitched, but Thad chose to assume it was a cough. "Understood, sir."

They were almost back, and Thad was still at a huge loss with Isabel.

Part of him wanted to pull her into a private corner somewhere and hold on to her and tell her how afraid he'd been. How he couldn't breathe at the thought of losing her. Another part of him was so righteously pissed over the whole thing that he wanted to scream until his voice gave out and his ears bled about how fucking stupid she'd been to run off alone into the night in a strange place and nearly get her ass killed.

He thought back to their escape from the grungy apartment where he'd found her and the smokescreen their bodies had created with huge clouds of steam billowing up between them. Right where their bodies met. It had been so perfect.

But... Isabel had remained fairly noncommittal regarding how she felt toward him. No, noncommittal wasn't even accurate. Since they had made love, Isabel had consistently pushed him away. Thad leaned back against the seat, suddenly deflated. What if she really had run away?

He was such a stupid bastard.

While making plans in his head to nurse Isabel back to health and ride off into the proverbial moonlight with her, he had conveniently ignored the fact that she had never given any indication that he meant anything to her aside from really great sex.

Thad looked down at that scar on his forearm, which was still strangely quiet after all this time. After weeks of the thing prodding him for attention, he would have expected a little guidance or something from it.

A shaky sigh from Isabel gave him clarity. His precious bout of anger-driven machismo aside, he really couldn't make her stay against her will. Didn't want to. He only needed to look at what had happened when he tried before. What he felt for her didn't amount to much if she didn't feel the same way. He wasn't into a lifelong commitment with someone who was faking it for the good of their race. Besides, she had made it quite clear that she wanted no part of being queen.

"Listen," he said to her as they pulled up in front of the mansion. "I want you to head back to your room, lie down, and get some rest. I'll go find Brayden or one of the other medical staff. You need to get checked out."

She furrowed her brow. Yeah, he even loved the giant creases in her forehead. "Then what?"

He almost couldn't force his lips to move. As soon as he thought it, his lips pressed into a tight seal of their own volition, and the words clogged his throat so he could barely breathe or swallow.

"If you want to leave, I won't make you stay. All I

ask is that you wait long enough for us to find someplace safe to send you."

Isabel nodded mutely. The frown remained on her face, and her eyes lost focus like she was confused. That was pretty much it, though. If he had expected her to jump into his arms and make a declaration of undying love, he clearly had been fooling himself.

Thad opened the door and helped Isabel out of the car. If he didn't get her inside and out of his sight soon, he was going to start saying things he would regret later.

"I, uh, I think I'd like to stop by and see how Lexi's doing. That would be okay, wouldn't it?" Her tone of voice was strange. There was almost a… meekness to it.

Thad did a little head shake. He'd witnessed a veritable cornucopia of mood swings from Isabel since they first met. She was sexy and cool, confident and assured, hot and cold, aggressive and passive. Crazy as it was, he liked how that kept him on his toes in a good way.

Well, that was just too damn bad, wasn't it?

"Yeah, sure," he said. Holy hell, he was tired enough to drop right where they stood. "She's probably worried about you. I'll send the doctor to check on you there."

He sternly commanded his feet to stay the hell put while she made the short trip down the east hall to Alexia's room. So it was a done deal. Isabel would go back to the human world, and Thad would go on to be most miserable son of a bitch that ever oversaw the vampire society, because no way was he going to find another mate. Not when his goddamn destiny was about to walk out the door.

His insides ached, and his gut was in knots. Big, complicated ones the likes of which Houdini never could have freed himself from. A disturbing sense of vertigo had come over him. If he could have given up every cent he had for the chance to wallow in bed for a few days and cry like a little girl until he died from dehydration, he would have gladly done so.

Instead, he turned to head back out the door. He needed to find the doc, check in on Eamon's pregnant widow, and do who the fuck knew what else. For the second time that night, he nearly managed to plow into Lee in the foyer.

Lee's return was a good sign. He wouldn't have left before the job was done.

"Good news, bad news, as usual," Lee grumbled. He was a mess but kind enough to dust off his boots before he stomped through the main door.

"Good news first. I could use some." Thad sagged against the wall a few feet away. First chance he got, he was gonna sleep for a week straight.

Lee nodded. "Your problem is taken care of. Siddoh just texted me. The building is clear, and they evacuated the tattoo parlor before they torched the place. S'a bad neighborhood so likely no one will think twice about it. Also, he checked out the teeth on that freak—looks like dental work. So now we need to figure out why the hell a wizard is running around with custom caps."

Thad rubbed at the steel cables in the back of his neck. "Maybe they want to blend in, pass as one of us?"

Lee grimaced like he had a bad taste in his mouth. "Yeah, I thought of that too. The question is how well it would work. Most of our kind would know the difference."

"Maybe not till close up, though," Thad speculated.

"Not until too late. Or maybe not one of our kind that hasn't seen a wizard before. Think about it. If we're doing our jobs right, they shouldn't get near the general population."

"True." Lee crossed his arms over his chest. "We gotta figure out how many more of these fuckers are out there and what they're doing. We could be looking at a serious problem if they manage to infiltrate our communities."

"I know." Yeah, this night just kept getting better. Thad straightened, and the ache in his neck crawled up through his jaw to settle in the front right quadrant of his head. "Shit, I don't even want to think about it."

"A little more bad news." Lee's voice dropped to an uncharacteristically hushed tone. "Haven't heard from Tyra. She was last seen in the alley and said she was heading to her office to chill, but it's been a few hours. Siddoh and I have both tried calling, and she's not picking up."

Thad took a deep breath and slowly let it out. "Let's try not to assume the worst yet. She drained herself pretty good tonight so she might just need some extra time." He checked his watch. It was uncomfortably close to dawn. "Probably she'll be crashing back at her place by midday. Keep trying to reach her, though."

"Sure thing." Lee took a few steps toward the hallway. "I need to check in with Xander, talk to him about what's going down."

"Yeah, we chatted a little on the way back. Apparently Tyra had sent him for transport."

Lee shook his head, chuckling slightly. "Wow, she really sucks at toeing the line, huh?"

Thad cracked a slight smile. "It's part of her charm. Hey, listen. Do me a favor. When you can, no rush."

"What's up?" Stopping mid-stride, Lee turned back toward the foyer.

"I want to start clearing out my father's office, like I said. I'd like you to help pack it all up, if you don't mind. I'd ask someone else to do it but I don't know what might be in there that could be sensitive. I know Ty went through everything down there, but I figure better safe than sorry. Never know if she may have missed something." Thad reached for the knob to the front door, ready as he ever would be to head across the way to see Theresa. Eamon's widow. *Shit*.

This was the sort of thing his father would have handled well. With wisdom and compassion. On Thad's best day, he couldn't hope to be half the male his father had been on his worst.

Lee nodded again. "Yeah, no problem. Listen, I'm gonna head to my room and grab a shower, and then I'll add it to my to-do list."

Thad was eternally grateful to have Lee at his back. Even for the small stuff. "I appreciate it, man, truly."

Lee had already turned to start walking again, his bloody leather jacket slung over one shoulder. He threw his hand up in a small wave as he retreated. "No sweat, buddy."

Thad's shoulders slumped. He wasn't sure he had any clue of what was expected of him. Not really. He could spend the next century scared out of his mind and unable to tell anybody. He wanted to believe that he could have told Isabel, but that didn't exactly matter now. Did it?

His hand was suddenly a little unsteady on the brass

door handle. Indecision held him suspended for a moment, while that Viking drum in his chest pounded away. Finally, he spun with a squeak in the marble-tiled foyer and hurried down the hall.

He needed to see Isabel one last time.

Chapter 33

ANTON SMITH, OR JUST PLAIN ANTON—WHATEVER HE wanted to call himself didn't matter. The *only* thing that mattered was explaining himself here and now. That… and whether Tyra believed him or decided to kick him in the balls as he so rightly deserved. Hell, there was a good chance that his balls would be the least of his worries in about two minutes.

Something about that moment when she'd left him standing in the hall, holding that godforsaken ring, had brought the whole thing back. Well… most of it. There were some blank spaces around the part where his father had tried to beat him to death in front of the cadre, and frankly he was good with not remembering the finer details of that particular experience.

He was a selfish jerk for doing this now. Tyra was clearly weak and vulnerable. But the timing had sort of made sense when he'd first entered the room. She couldn't immediately try to take him out without hearing his side of things, and God willing, she would see that he wasn't the monster that the rest of the wizards were. There he went with the God stuff. Maybe he was becoming a believer.

Another headache was coming on, and he rubbed carefully at a sore spot above his eyebrow. For both their sakes, he needed to get this out quickly. He'd be hard pressed to think clearly with a migraine, so it was now or never on the whole coming clean business.

Not to mention that she was staring at him with such a look of stricken disbelief that he might as well have just confessed to killing her mother. For all he knew, someone in his clan had. He exhaled slowly.

God, he hated scaring her like this.

"For… whatever it might be worth," he said carefully, "I have no intention of hurting you. I have never… I have *never* had any intention of hurting you." He made a point of maintaining eye contact with her and enunciating clearly. He didn't want to look like a pansy, and he didn't want anything to be misunderstood. "I won't do you any harm for any reason. I hope you can believe that."

He paused for a moment. Her chocolate-brown eyes were wide, her face otherwise devoid of expression. No response. "I—you know, you pretty much literally flew out of here earlier. After you left me there in the hall, I went to find you in the cafeteria. The doors…" He took a chance and scooted a little closer. There was absolutely no way to get this out that felt right because the whole thing had been so wrong to begin with.

"The doors to the other side of the room were still chained shut. So. See. There should have been no way for you to leave except to come back the way you had gone in, but you weren't there. All of a sudden, it hit me out of nowhere that I knew where you had gone… well, not where," he corrected, "but how."

Tyra's slack mouth closed slightly. A small groove appeared on her forehead, just above her nose. She was trying to figure it all out; he could see the wheels turning. Even in her weakened state, she was still so strong. Anton ached to make this right for her, but that wasn't even remotely possible. The burn of tears behind his eyes was still a shock. It wasn't as if telling her the truth was going make him lose anything he'd ever actually had.

He kept going. If he forged ahead, if he shoved the rest of it out of his mouth hard enough and fast enough, in a moment it would have too much momentum to stop. He rubbed the back of his neck a little.

"My father was… is… the leader of the wizard clan." There. He'd said it. "He commanded me to find you. I was supposed to bring you to him. He knows about your unique ability, that you can acquire multiple powers without…" *The killing*. He swallowed. "I refused, so he killed me. Or at least, he tried to."

Tyra's eyes widened, and almost imperceptibly her fingers tightened around the arm of the chair. Silence stretched out between them, filled with the rush of Anton's blood in his own ears. *Say something. Please.*

Afraid that even the smallest movement might spook her, Anton struggled to hold himself perfectly still. But that became more difficult with each passing second, what with the flock of birds in his chest trying to escape and the fact that he was struggling to breathe in short, painful gasps, as if someone had punched a hole in his lung. If only he could have cut his own heart out and presented it to her, right then. That would have been less painful, less horrific, than divulging his most terrible truth to this woman he loved against all odds—and having her do nothing but stare at him in silence.

The movement of Tyra's desk chair filled the room with a deafening squeak as she shifted to the side, resting her chin on her hand. Still silent, she was studying him as one would a difficult math problem: intensely, with a mix of challenge and frustration… and fatigue. She looked so worn out.

He really was a bastard.

Finally, she opened her mouth to respond. Her inhale seemed to take a lot of effort. Shit, she was weaker than he'd realized. "Your father… your father is…"

"The leader of the wizards. The 'Dark Master,' as he likes to be called. Look, we don't have to do this now. I don't know what happened to you out there tonight but I can see you're not—"

She held up a shaky hand to silence him. "We'll do it now."

Ho-kay. Wow. Even on the verge of collapse she was feisty. He loved that, too.

"Look, Tyra. I swear I was never like him. I never wanted to be. I went along with the charade because it was either that or get myself killed. I don't care what kind of horrifying situation you find yourself living in, your basic drive is still for survival." He paused for a breath. His body trembled just a bit, and he had to press his lips together tightly to keep his teeth from starting to chatter.

"When I saw you, Tyra, I knew I couldn't go through with it. I don't know exactly what he would have done to you, but it would have been death or something far worse. You may never believe me, but I was willing to die to protect you."

Her gaze had drifted to the floor. He moved to crouch in front of her. He needed Tyra to see his eyes for what he was about to say next. Needed her to know he was dead serious.

"I still am, you know. In a heartbeat, I would die to protect you."

Her head listed to the side, slipping off the hand it had been perched upon. Maybe that last bit had been too much. When her body started to crumple, he lunged forward to steady her, pulling her close.

As he breathed in the scent of her skin, his body's subsequent response confirmed that he was the worst kind of asshole. She was ill and exhausted, and had just received the shock of her life. Yet he was aroused— invigorated, even—that finally, after all the wanting and wishing, he was actually holding her.

The cool satin of her cheek against his was better than anything he could have imagined for himself.

"Why?" The question was quiet and breathy, the mumble of her lips so close to his that he could almost taste them.

"I fell in love with you," he said quietly. "You probably don't believe me, but it's really true."

Tyra's eyes squeezed shut and opened again. Her pupils were dilated. Unfocused. Her mouth moved as if she was about to speak, but nothing came out aside from a small quiver of breath. Anton didn't know a lot about these kinds of things, but it looked maybe like shock. It almost seemed as if her body was shutting down.

He thought for only a moment about his healing power before he decided that it should be his last resort. He didn't know how to wield it yet, and he wasn't sure it would work on her. If he tried and failed, he would lose precious moments. Also, quite selfishly, he wasn't ready to show so obviously that he had indeed participated in the ritual. Of course, there was something else he could do for her...

"Tyra," Anton whispered. "You need blood, right? You can feed from me. I won't hurt you, I swear." He didn't know if she was listening or even cared about his reassurances, but he would say it as many times as he needed to.

Anton leaned his head back to expose his throat. Time slowed and then came to a standstill, and he was acutely aware of their hearts beating against each other and the heat of her breath against his skin. He tightened his embrace ever so slightly, feeling the soft, springy curls of her hair with his fingertips as he attempted to guide her head forward. Her skin was cool and smelled delicious. Wintery.

"Please Tyra," he rasped. "Please feed from me."

Fuck, fuck, and triple fuck.

Lee stopped outside the door to his room. The faint smell of gardenias lingered in the hallway, and suddenly it didn't matter how badly he needed a shower. The sweet smell that he had once found pleasant now assaulted his nostrils in an almost nauseating fashion.

Agnessa.

The urge to turn tail and run was considerable, but it wasn't his style to shy away from confrontation. But Jesus, Agnessa? If Lee never saw her again, that would be too soon. The fact that she lived on the other side of the estate ensured that he saw her a little more frequently, unfortunately.

Steeling himself, he pushed open the door and entered

the room slowly. The heavy beat of his heart irritated the hell out of him. He should be well beyond having this kind of... cowardly... *base* reaction to her.

The back of his desk chair was turned toward the door, and a cascade of platinum hair fell over it in waves. Lithe arms were draped over the armrests of the chair, tapering gracefully with delicate-looking hands and ruby-red fingernails at the tips. Said fingernails were tapping softly on the armrest. To Lee, it sounded like a marching band drumming through his head. His lip twitched and curled into a sneer.

Quadruple fuck.

Lee cleared his throat for effect. Not that he needed to get her attention. She'd known he was coming. "Agnessa. Leave. Now." No movement, no response. "Please." He didn't know why he'd bothered to say that. He wasn't trying to be polite, and it sure as hell wasn't going to make her budge faster.

One bejeweled Louboutin stiletto tapped the floor and pushed the chair around in a slow twist to face him. Not that Lee knew jack about shoes, but she had made sure he knew her favorite brands of everything. Like not buying her the right shit had been their biggest problem.

A pair of shapely legs led up to an elegant white skirt, a white barely there tank top, and a diamond-encrusted choker adorning the narrow column of her neck. Then there were the finely chiseled line of her chin and the reddest lips in the known universe. He didn't want to look at her lips, but it was either there or her crimson eyes.

Once upon a time, he had thought she was so beautiful. Being seen with her had been a privilege. But after having been played for a fool a thousand times, all that glitter and flash did nothing for Lee. It was window dressing on an overpriced whore.

Those eyes had been alluring to him. Sexy. Mesmerizing. Now they made his skin crawl. He forced himself to stare dead into those demonic-looking irises without so much as blinking. He wouldn't give her the satisfaction of seeing how much being near her nauseated him, and he didn't have the time or the patience for dealing with her mind games. Not tonight. Not any night.

Those shiny red lips curled up into a catlike smile as the middle three fingers on her right hand splayed provocatively under her chin to prop it up. "Goodness, Leeland. Is that any way to greet a friend?"

Lee's molars clamped down so hard that he could have pressed diamonds between them. "We aren't friends, Agnessa. Now get the fuck out of here before I throw you out."

"Well, now," she murmured. "Look who went and grew a pair."

For fuck's sake, she knew just how to push his buttons.

He dropped his bloody jacket on the bed and proceeded to remove his gun holster, knives, and other weapons, and drop them on the bed as if he couldn't care less that she was in the room. Being ignored would piss her off. The pile of weapons also rendered the bed ineffective for any recreational activities she might possibly have in mind.

He straightened and crossed his arms over his chest, meeting her ruby-colored eyes again. "I'm being serious here, Agnessa. You're not welcome in my room.

I thought I made that clear a long time ago." His voice was low and quiet, but no way could she miss the current of rage flowing through it.

Agnessa stood and started toward him. He barely blinked when the form slinking toward him suddenly morphed into a large albino lioness. The diamond choker remained around her neck. God only knew how she managed that. Or the devil.

He held his ground, even as her now-furry head bumped against his outer thigh, rubbing affectionately. "Come on, Lee," she purred. "Didn't you miss me?" *Christ*.

"No. Now I'm not going to ask you again, Agnessa. Please leave." He was determined not to let her get a rise out of him. But damn, if she continued to slink around and rub her body against his, he was going to throw her out the old-fashioned way.

One error in judgment, and centuries later it was still haunting him.

"Mmm, what's wrong, Leeland?" She sat back on her haunches and licked her paw in a delicate manner. Her head cocked to the side as she studied him, those glowing eyes boring into his skull. "You are so tense. Is it that human you were thinking of before? You know I could take better care of you than her."

He pointed an accusing finger at the lioness in front of him. "Stay out of my head, Agnessa. I don't want you there, and I don't want you here. I am leaving now, and I expect you to be gone when I get back—or I will make goddamned sure you regret it."

He grabbed blindly behind himself, relieved when his hand made contact with the doorknob. Twisting furiously, he pivoted on his still-booted heel and left the room. The door slammed behind him.

Of all the skeletons in his past, this was a particularly shitty one to rear its head, especially tonight. And damn it all to hell, why had he stormed out when his intention had been to kick her to the curb? Too late now. His only concern for the time being was to put distance between himself and the female in his room.

Lee remembered Thad's request to clear out the office. It seemed like a fantastic rationalization for hiding out like a pansy while he waited for Agnessa to clear out. He headed to the basement and strode through the office doors. He paced the room, slowly at first, but it didn't take long for his coordination to fail him.

"Fucking Agnessa," he growled. Why the fuck had that bitch chosen tonight to show up? She had kept to herself on the other side of the estate for a long time now, and he damn well liked it that way. She had mentioned Lexi. Could she have shown up because of the human? He could add that to his list of reasons to stay away from the girl. He shuddered to think what Agnessa could do out of a sense of misguided jealousy.

That she'd sensed his arousal earlier was troubling. Disturbing on a couple of different levels. It indicated to Lee that enough of his blood was within her that she could still feel him, even after all these years of being apart. Moreover, it meant she'd been in tune with his emotions all these years and he'd never known.

Since the time he and Agnessa had split, Lee had gorged himself on the blood of enough other females to effectively purge his knowledge of her. It had given him the illusion that he was free and clear of her when clearly he wasn't. In retrospect that wasn't wise, but decisions made out of anger rarely were.

He needed to take a step back. From Agnessa. From Alexia. The way Siddoh had sauntered out of the girl's room, laughing and—

Jealousy was a luxury he couldn't afford.

He picked up the pace, but walking faster seemed to get him more lathered rather than calming him down. He wound his way past the wingback chairs and spindly Victorian writing desk, then back toward the double doors again.

Alexia… Siddoh… losing Eamon tonight… Tyra being MIA… Finding Agnessa camped out in his room was just craptastic icing on the cake. Mating Agnessa had landed him in Hell for the rest of eternity.

It was all too much.

The thrumming of blood in his ears and the bitter taste of his own self-loathing bore down on him. The impassive cloak of iron will that he so vigilantly maintained was on the brink of total collapse. Even before he'd finally manned up and left Agnessa, he had never been so out of his head.

His body shook until he couldn't hold it all in anymore. As he turned on his heel, Lee let out a bellow that completely drowned out the splintering and cracking sounds of wood beneath his still-clenched fist. That poor froufrou desk never knew what hit it. The thing folded in on itself, and without any real comprehension, he brought his arm and foot down repeatedly until his blood began to splatter over the carpet and the fragments of wood.

He watched with curious detachment while his

bleeding fist landed a final blow on the busted pile of sticks. Even though the poor thing was down for the count, Lee felt the need to start kicking, scattering the pieces around the room until finally his anger had diminished to a low simmer.

It was still there, though. It always would be.

With a groan, Lee dropped into one of the wingback chairs and flexed his hand. Gave it a shake. Ran it over the top of his head. The broken bits of desk now scattered before him, he gave a final halfhearted nudge at one piece with the toe of his boot.

What appeared to have been the bottom of a drawer skittered away from him. Even though he was loathe to do it, Lee knelt on the floor to gather the chunks of desk and pick up the large splinters that had embedded themselves into the carpet. He gathered most of it into a pile and shoveled it into a nearby trash can.

The larger pieces he broke efficiently over his upper thigh before stacking them beside the now full bin. When he prepared to do the same with the drawer, a tiny corner of paper poked out from between two pressed boards.

The envelope that slipped out didn't look terribly old. The cream-colored paper was pristine with no dusty or musty odors. The seal looked and smelled fairly fresh. The ink—Lee's name, written in the former king's smooth script—was dark and bold.

What he saw on the crisp page inside nearly floored him. The letter explained a lot, and it changed everything. He needed to find Tyra and make sure she was okay, ASAP.

It was only a short while until dawn at this point,

but he could move fast enough to make it to her office before the sun came up. He had to talk to her, make sure she was safe. Agnessa, Alexia, and his previous angry outburst would all just have to go get fucked.

He tapped his foot impatiently in the elevator. There was a lot to handle right now. Lee knew he could fix this and leave the bigger stuff to Thad. Bringing his friend into it would be too dangerous anyway. Odds were very good that this was what had gotten Thad's father killed.

He dashed off a quick text on his phone, hitting Send as he stepped off the elevator. Everything would be under control. No problem.

"Shit," Lee muttered. He stopped on the patio outside of the mansion's back door. He had no jacket, no weapons. He'd dropped everything on the bed before running out of his room and away from Agnessa like a damn coward. He shook his head and slipped the note into his back pocket as he did a 180.

Thank all that was good and holy, Agnessa was gone when he got there. Lee grabbed his gear and bloody jacket in record time and sped briskly back out of the mansion. A din of voices floated from the front hall but he was out the door before anyone saw him.

Maybe he wasn't done killing tonight after all.

The bed had been made in her absence. The broken glass in the bathroom had been cleaned up as well, and the towels and robe had been replaced.

Room service moved fast around here.

Isabel was just preparing to lie down on the freshly

made bed when she heard a firm knock. Her blood rushed a little faster. She didn't need to open the door to know Thad was on the other side.

He was braced in the doorway, looking like he'd aged a century or two in the past several minutes. What should she say? That he was in pain was as plain as the nose on his face and evidenced by the dark circles under his eyes and the bone-deep anguish that had welled up within her. Just from the one time he'd fed her, she could feel the exquisite knot of pain in his gut, twisting tighter and tighter.

"May I come in." It was more of a statement than a question, posed flatly and without emotion. She stood back to allow him past her, closing the door behind him. He entered and paced quietly back and forth with his hands on his hips.

"Thad?" She approached slowly. What could she possibly do to assuage what he was feeling? What *she* was now feeling.

His nostrils flared as he stood before her, tracking her with his eyes. Fluttering to the surface from underneath all that agony was something else entirely. He wanted her.

A bright hope flared from deep within Isabel. Maybe it wasn't too late after all. She closed her eyes as his hand slid along her jaw. Every cell in her body practically broke into song in response to the warmth in his fingers. How on earth had she thought she could live without this?

"I came to say good-bye."

Oh. Isabel's head snapped up. Her heart and her spirit had begun to swell and float like helium-filled balloons at the sight of Thad standing in the doorway, but now they popped and fizzled to the floor. "What?"

"I've got a car for you, if you want. If you prefer, Ivy can get you plane tickets." His hand continued to stroke the side of her face in a lazy up-and-down motion. "I don't want to force this," he said softly. "Besides, it's for the best. It's not safe for you. I can't make you a guarantee that what happened tonight wouldn't happen again. Not without making you a prisoner in this house, and I don't want that for you."

It was stunning, the level of disappointment that she felt over losing something she hadn't thought she'd even wanted. The sudden ache in her chest over losing something she had never actually had. Her breathing deepened in an effort to tamp down the rush of tears that welled up.

Bottom line, Isabel had screwed up. She had been right before: he was probably angry at her for leaving the estate. For getting captured. Or maybe she'd handled things badly with that room full of vampires earlier. She'd overstepped her bounds, or perhaps she'd been too harsh with them. She sighed. Maybe it didn't even matter why.

Like he said, it's for the best. The reasons why she'd been hesitant at the outset hadn't changed, after all. "Thad, I—"

Before she knew what had hit her, Thad's mouth and body were on top of hers. Her breath was sucked out of her lungs. Despite the surprise and the fact that he crushed the wind out of her, she reveled in the comfort of his powerful embrace.

Her body melted into Thad's. She clung to him for

dear life as their bodies fell together onto the bed. There
was no heated urgency as before. His kiss was slow and
deep, while his hands wandered beneath the layers of
her clothing and explored in a leisurely fashion.

Wherever his hands wandered, Isabel's skin sizzled.
From the sensitive patch of skin under her navel to her
rib cage to the valley between her breasts. His hand lingered there, and her heart thumped against it. Hard. Like
maybe it was going to miss him just as much as the rest
of her was.

"Everything okay in there?"

No. "Seems to be beating just fine." And that was
really all she could say for certain.

Thad nodded and kissed her again briefly. Fingers
roamed, gently grazing over her nipples and leaving
them hot, tight, and hard.

Aching.

This time, she lay back and drank in the hard body
and warm skin. If this was good-bye, dammit, she was
determined to savor the experience.

Isabel met Thad's gaze as he pulled back long enough
to divest himself of his clothes. His eyes barely left hers
as he reached down to pull down her jeans and then push
her sweatshirt up and over her head. The combination
of despair and lust in his azure gaze nearly broke Isabel
into pieces.

Whatever you do, don't cry... it'll totally kill the mood.
She shivered a little as that now-familiar chill returned to her body, but it was immediately chased away
by the cozy blanket of Thad's body on hers.

Isabel closed her eyes and sighed. Her arms encircled
his back, and her legs wrapped themselves around his.

For a moment, she was home. She allowed herself the foolish notion that they could stay wrapped around each other like this for an eternity.

"Thad," she gasped. He entered her quickly. Their bodies melded together, surging in concert like a cresting wave as he made love to her, slow and deep. And this time, it really was making love. Every sigh and caress was filled with emotion, and for this moment, they both let go completely.

Impossibly, even without the aid of the wine or anything else to heighten their senses, it was better than before. Every nerve in her body and every receptor in her brain seemed wide open and set to receive only pleasure. Thad's pleasure. In moments her skin was slicked with sweat—or maybe steam, thanks to the combination of his inner fire and her inner ice power. It made the slide of his body over hers smooth and effortless.

Thad's blue eyes locked onto her face. His pupils, dilated with desire, were bottomless and mesmerizing. Isabel couldn't have looked away, even if she had wanted to. With each thrust, each heartbeat, she silently projected all the things she couldn't say aloud into those dark pools, like whispering wishes into a well. *I'll miss you. I'm sorry... I wish you would ask me to stay again.*

Her hips undulated, rising to meet his as he pumped into her. She clutched desperately at his back. Powerful muscles rippled and strained beneath her hands with each movement. His quiet grunts and pants in her ear seemed to make promises in a language only her body could understand.

Isabel wrapped her legs around his waist, bringing him deeper still. The change in angle made him strike all of her pleasure points. That delicious pressure coiled inside her so rapidly that she found herself almost angry at the prospect of having an orgasm. If only there was a way to draw it out, to make it last forever.

Isabel curled her head forward to rest on Thad's shoulder. His breath was hot, heavy, and ragged against her ear, and she whispered his name over and over as she steadily approached climax. The thrum of blood resounded in Isabel's ears, and she didn't even try to avoid the temptation. When he threw his head back and shouted his release, she sank her elongated fangs into his exposed throat.

"Yes." After a split second of tension, Thad's hips bucked even harder. Wave after wave of pleasure crashed through her body. Thad's warm blood hit her tongue at the same time her earth-shattering orgasm exploded.

After panting against Thad's shoulder for a few beats, Isabel licked the place where she'd bitten him and quietly rested her head on the mattress. Amazing though it was, the whole thing had been over way too soon.

Thad's blue eyes were again staring intensely into hers when Isabel finally lifted her lids. She blushed suddenly. Drinking from him had been rather presumptuous after he'd made it clear that this was the end of the road for them. "I'm sorry. I guess I should have asked first."

Another kiss silenced her. It was sweet and tender, and when he rose up on his arms to look at her again, his gaze had softened considerably. "You never have to ask."

God, the way he said that made it easy to forget he'd just told her to leave.

Exhaustion moved in swiftly. The previous night's

horrors, the roller coaster of emotions, and the monster orgasm had all left Isabel jittery and exhausted. She didn't want to go to sleep yet, though, not when she might never see him again.

So maybe it was true, what they said about not appreciating what you had until it was gone. A mere twelve hours earlier, she had been chomping at the bit to leave. Now that Thad had set her free she was silently fighting the urge to throw her arms around him and weep copiously until he agreed that she should stay. But neither of them seemed to speak much. Maybe there was nothing left to say.

Be careful what you wish for. Hey, apparently all those well-known sayings really did exist for a reason.

Still… it *was* better for them to go their separate ways. It really was.

"It really was nice getting to know you, Thad. I, uh… I am going to miss you." Holy *cow*, that sounded lame.

Shit, maybe it had been the wrong thing to say. He pulled back from her and retrieved his clothing, pulling it on like he was running late to be somewhere. He buttoned his pants, brow wrinkled and jaw clenched. She was wondering if there was a way for her to backpedal when he finally nodded his head slightly. "Same here."

So that was it, then. Sliding quietly off the bed, Isabel walked over to the bathroom door to retrieve the fresh robe that had been hung there. Thad sat on the edge of the bed, head in his hands.

"Thad?"

"I have to go see Eamon's widow. She's pregnant, and she needs to drain the blood from his body. Before—" His voiced hitched. "Before it goes stagnant."

He pressed his lips into a thin, tight line. "I can't even imagine having to do something like that."

She sighed, fighting back tears and a host of other feelings. Isabel couldn't imagine it, either. Saying goodbye to Thad was hard enough. Having to drink from your mate's dead body... she could only hope never to know what that was like. Invisible icy fingers gripped her heart. Her whole chest tightened so that she could barely breathe. A tremor of panic went through her. Thad's. She couldn't let him do this alone. "I'll come with you."

His eyes widened. "Why would you want to do that?"

Because maybe I want to take care of you, too. While I still can. "Might help to have another female present, you know? Besides, it's too close to morning for travel, so it's not like I'm going anywhere tonight."

He nodded silently, which she read as acquiescence, so she ditched the robe and quickly threw her clothes back on. His hand wasn't quite as warm as it should've been when she threaded her fingers through his.

"Let's go," she said quietly.

Chapter 34

THERESA'S WAILING LAMENT FOR HER DEAD MATE nearly cut Thad down at the knees. Somehow, as soon as the door was closed behind him, he lost command over his entire body. Sweat slicked and trembling despite the recent upgrades to his internal furnace, he slid to the floor in an extremely un-kinglike manner. He couldn't do this.

Literally, he couldn't. His back was glued firmly against the inside of the front door, and his feet and legs refused to work. Even if they did, the floor in front of him blurred and wobbled, making him unsure whether he could make it down the hall before he puked or passed out.

How could he go down there and look Theresa in the eye? Any day now, she was going to be forced to put aside her grief to care for a new life. One that would grow up without a father. And that was entirely Thad's fault.

He tried to think of something—anything—that he could possibly say or do to help her, but he had absolutely nothing. Nothing. His airway seemed to constrict until breathing was nearly impossible, and oh, sweet Jesus, had he gone fetal? He had.

Yes, ladies and gentleman, the king was having a panic attack.

"Thad." Isabel's hand was cool and reassuring against

his skin, which was too hot and too tight for his body. "You have to get up."

He tried to answer. Honestly, he did. But he just couldn't quite command his lips to move. It was taking all his effort just to breathe, slow and deep, through a windpipe that had constricted to the diameter of a drinking straw.

Isabel crouched in front of him, smooth forehead pressed against his. Her hands kneaded his arms, his shoulders, and his neck. Sure fingers made tiny circles at the base of his skull. Her palm rubbed between his shoulder blades. Somehow, he managed to match her protracted inhales and exhales.

"Thad, listen. I know this is hard, but you are the king and you need to hold it together. That female down there needs you to be strong for her."

This time he was able to make eye contact. From down the hall of Eamon and Theresa's house, the screams had quieted to those breathy, hiccuppy noises that indicated someone was all out of tears. Isabel was right. He owed Eamon and Theresa more than cowering in the foyer.

He had to move. "I know. I'm coming."

He braced his feet and struggled to standing. The doctor spoke again in hushed tones, and Thad almost lost it again when he realized that the doctor was preparing Theresa to drink from her mate one final time before the blood was no longer good. His stomach heaved, but he stepped forward anyway.

Damn. Well, he needed to at least show up, even if he didn't know what else to do or what to say. He could do that much. *Would* do that much. There was no other choice. Like Isabel had said, he was king. He brushed an errant tear from the corner of his eye as he lurched down the hall, gripping Isabel's hand.

One foot in front of the other.

Isabel took charge immediately, and for that, Thad was not only grateful but awestruck. She comforted Theresa by rubbing the female's shoulders as she had for him. Murmured assurances and reminders that Theresa had the future of her offspring to think of. That this was what her mate would have wanted for her. Held the pregnant female's hair back while she drank.

When all was said and done and the doctor had removed Eamon's body, Isabel urged Theresa into bed and wiped the tears from her face. And ran those comforting fingers through Theresa's hair until the female's breathing evened out.

Thad stepped forward and touched a hand to Isabel's shoulder. He couldn't leave without saying something first. Taking Isabel's place by the side of the bed, he knelt carefully and grasped one of Theresa's hands. Though he did his best to remain composed, tears pooled in his eyes. He let them go. It was important that Theresa know her mate had been loved by his comrades.

"Theresa." He cleared his throat and struggled to find the right words. "I want you to know how grateful I am for Eamon's service. How sorry I am for his loss. And yours. I hope you'll come to me if there is anything at all that you need."

Theresa nodded slowly. "Thank you, Thad." Her fingers tightened around his, and she drew a shaky breath. "He died doing what he loved. Protecting our kind meant everything to him. I'm grateful, at least, for that." A soft palm touched the side of his face in an almost maternal gesture. "I'm sorry he won't be here to see his child. Or for you to rule. I can tell you're going to be a fine king."

Her words almost completely destroyed him. He could only manage a nod and a murmured "thank you" before he and Isabel slipped out to let Theresa rest.

Isabel smiled and rubbed his arm. "You were great in there."

Thad scoffed. "Me? No." He didn't have the right words to tell her how watching her in there had nearly made his heart explode. How she continued to amaze him. "You were the one who helped her through it."

Isabel scoffed. "I didn't do much." She angled her head back toward the bedroom door. "She probably shouldn't be alone right now."

"Yeah, I'll get someone to stand guard."

"What about Xander? He lost a mate recently too, right? Maybe they could comfort each other."

If it wasn't such a serious moment, Thad would have laughed at his own stupidity. How had he not thought of that? He flipped open his cell and dialed. "Xander. Got a job for you, buddy."

Chapter 35

"BOY, I TELL YOU WHAT. SHIT'S GETTING WEIRDER around here than I've ever seen it, and that's really saying something."

Thad glared at Siddoh through bleary eyes, hands on his hips. His body ached; he was completely wiped mentally and physically; and his irritation at the string of events that had gone down the previous night had him itching to go back to that wall he'd punched earlier and finish redecorating. Worse, his softer side was yearning for a quiet place to wallow in his blasted self-pity. Even worse still, he hungered to go back to Isabel's room and say things he absolutely never should.

Now Siddoh had shown up to give him more bad news, and Thad wasn't sure he was going to be able to stay standing after he heard it. He dropped his arms and sighed deeply. "All right, Sid. Just lay it on me."

Siddoh grimaced at the nickname he hated but continued with his commentary. "Well, I can't reach Ty."

Thad nodded curtly. "Yeah, I talked to Lee earlier. She's probably just resting at her office."

Siddoh stroked his chin thoughtfully and nodded. "Yeah, that's probably true..." He let out a hiss of air as he trailed off. "I don't know though. It just... something doesn't feel right. I hate to bring this up with you, but she and I haven't fed from each other in awhile—"

Thad's stomach lurched and he took a step back. "Dude—"

Siddoh held up his hands in a gesture of surrender. "I know, I know. Just hear me out." He ran his hand through his hair nervously. "Anyway, it's been awhile but... I just get the sense in my gut that something's wrong."

Thad frowned. "You think she's in danger? Injured?"

Shaking his head, Siddoh crossed his arms and began pacing in the foyer. "Not like that. I just... eh, it's hard to explain. I just feel like something's wrong. Like maybe she's sick or whatever."

He paused and then continued pacing, running his hand through his hair some more. "You know, for all of her strength, she drains fast. She taxed herself quite a bit out there tonight. We all like to think of her as invincible, but..."

Thad nodded, staring down at the floor in thought. He wanted to blow off Siddoh's speculation; he needed something to be positive about, for fuck's sake. Still, he had to admit that the idea might have validity. Siddoh still had a connection with his sister, whether Thad liked it or not. Even if it was a tenuous one.

"We have to assume she's safe for now because it's after dawn and there's not much we can do. Hopefully, she'll be feeling better in a few hours and we'll hear from her soon. Keep your feelers out. If you get the sense she's in trouble, let me know immediately."

"We could send Alexia," Siddoh suggested.

"Hell, no." Thad shook his head purposefully. "No way can we do that. She's human, she's got no training, and we would have no backup to send for her if she got into trouble. I can't believe you would even suggest that."

Siddoh nodded slightly, suddenly looking awkward. "I know." His hazel eyes met Thad's. "Look, whatever you may think of me... I just want to know for certain that she's all right."

Thad studied his friend for a moment. This was the wrong time to ask, but his self-control had flown right the hell out the window. "So why didn't you make a commitment to her, huh?"

Siddoh hiked his shoulders. His eyes were full of sadness, and Thad hadn't really been prepared for that. Cocky and defensive was generally more Siddoh's gig. "Honestly, that was pretty mutual. I think I would have if I'd thought she wanted it. I don't wish to talk out of school, but she had some issues. You know, growing up without her mother and all."

Gritting his teeth, Thad nodded once more. He and Tyra had never discussed the matter at length, but it had been a struggle for her. She had been the first born but always felt like second fiddle because she was half human and because her mother had all but dropped her on the mansion's doorstep and left her like an unwanted orphan. Thad thought of his mother fondly. He couldn't imagine growing up without that.

Dropping his hands from his hips, Thad looked up at Siddoh again and crossed his arms over his chest. "So what else is there, eh? I already knew Tyra was MIA so I assume there's something else."

Siddoh's hazel eyes fastened on him again. "Lee's gone."

Jesus. "Gone where? I just talked to him a few hours ago."

"He sent me a somewhat cryptic text a little before

dawn, saying he had to take off and I was in charge of all his shit till he got back." Siddoh held his hands out to his sides, palms up. "No clue where he is."

Thad rubbed his temples. "What would make him go off half-cocked like that?"

"Well, when I came up through the tunnel, I passed by his room. You could smell that gardenia perfume from a mile away."

Thad clenched his jaw tightly. "Christ. Agnessa?" He sighed wearily at Siddoh's obvious implication. "What the hell would she be doing in his room?"

Siddoh shrugged again. "Fucked if I know, but if anything would drive a male to run off into the sunrise, it would be that bitch."

And didn't Thad know it. He hadn't known Agnessa well, and Lee had always been private about the relationship, but Agnessa had done a real job on the poor guy and that was on top of the royal head-fuck Lee had gotten from his father.

The she-bitch had even managed to make Thad an unwitting party to it all at one point. It had always been a wonder that Lee seemed so normal, given the circumstances. It was also a wonder that Lee had never tried to beat the shit out of him.

Thad scrubbed his hand over his face hard, as if that could get the disturbing images and holy-fuck-I-didn't-really-do-that, did-I? out of his head somehow.

"Okay." Thad clunked his head against the wall behind him. "So I assume you've tried calling him?"

Siddoh produced a cell phone from a pocket in his fatigues. "Found this in his room. Guess he forgot it." He flipped it through the air to Thad, who caught it easily despite his bone-weary exhaustion. "I took a quick peek around. Good news is that it looks like a lot of his gear is missing so we can assume he's armed. The bed was a little rumpled but not slept in. Hopefully it doesn't mean that he and Agnessa had a quick tussle for old time's sake." Both males shivered in unison at the thought.

"So," Siddoh continued. "I got the troops all squared away before coming over here. Franklin's hanging in there, just barely. I heard about Eamon. How's Theresa holding up?"

Thad winced and shook his head. "It's not good. I'll tell you that much. Brayden had her drain Eamon's body before the blood was no good anymore." He stared down at the shadows on the floor.

"Shit," Siddoh muttered.

Thad bobbed his head slightly in agreement and continued to stare at the floor. "Can't even imagine what that must have been like. Watching it was…"

"Yeah. At least she's due soon," Siddoh said with a sigh. "Think she'll make it through?"

Thad shook his head. "Hope so." When a vampire female was with child, she needed extra blood to sustain the pregnancy, and only the blood of her mate would do. Losing Eamon was a huge risk for Theresa, as well as her unborn child.

Having to drink from her dead mate had been the only solution, horrible as it was. "Brayden's going to keep a close watch. Worst case, she goes into early labor or needs a C-section so the baby doesn't put her at risk, too. She'll have to be transferred to St. Mary's so the baby can go into the VNICU."

St. Mary's was a private hospital run by vampires

near downtown. It masqueraded as a private church-run clinic, giving them the ability to strictly regulate who received treatment there.

"You know what you need to do? Get a bunch of the other females, the soldiers' wives and whatnot. Have them throw her one of those shower things. The females love that. Might help her feel a little less lonely, ya know?"

Thad weighed the idea for a minute. It was easy to forget that Siddoh was often a lot more insightful than he let on. "You know, I have to acknowledge that's actually a decent suggestion."

"I have 'em sometimes," Siddoh said lightly. "So how's it going with your female?"

Thad grunted. "She's heading out soon."

Siddoh's brows shot up in surprise. "She's leaving? I thought—"

"I don't care what you thought. I said she's leaving," Thad snapped impatiently. The subject was closed. He wasn't ready to have that conversation with anyone. It had been hard enough to say good-bye as it was.

Siddoh nodded. "Sure thing, buddy. I assume the human is leaving, too? I should go say good-bye."

Thad cocked his head to the side. Okay, the bastard was insightful, but he'd bloody well hit on anything that moved. "Why? Getting it on with my sister's not enough for you?"

"Meh," Siddoh said dismissively. As usual, he was not riled in the slightest by Thad's insulting remark. "She's really cool. Friendly. Never been friends with a human."

Rubbing his forehead, Thad deflated. "Sorry, man. I'm being a dick."

"Nah." Siddoh leaned against the opposite wall,

shaking his head slightly. "Gonna be a rough road, my friend. You're entitled to be a dick once in awhile." He headed down the hall, turning to talk back over his shoulder. "Besides, bro, you're the king. You can act however the fuck you want, and we've all gotta bend over and take it, right?"

"Don't remind me," Thad muttered tersely to Siddoh's retreating form.

Holy hell, could he go anyplace in this house where nobody would hear him scream? His sister and his right-hand man were both gone, one of his soldiers was dead, and more were in bad shape. He had a grieving pregnant widow to take care of, and his supposedly destined mate was about to blow town. That, of course, was on top of all the other run-of-the-mill stuff that he was still supposed to get up to speed on.

And mother of God, he was freaking exhausted.

The shakes and sudden inability to breathe slammed Thad all over again, right there in the hall. Sure, it was daytime but anybody in the house could walk by anytime, and he was so, so screwed if word got out that the king had cracked up. He staggered toward the nearest unused room in the house. He could never tell a soul about this.

He had never been more alone.

He didn't want to do any of this without Isabel. The prophecy had said she would be there to help him lead, for fuck's sake. Why would he be destined for somebody who didn't want to be with him?

A tear slipped down his face, and Thad tried to wipe it away casually as he glanced around for signs of life. He was so damn lame that it was embarrassing.

Destiny was a big fucking cheater.

Chapter 36

"SO, ARE YOU PSYCHED ABOUT LIFE GETTING BACK TO normal?" Alexia tossed a pack of Famous Amos cookies into the shopping cart and kept wandering down the snack aisle. No road trip could commence, as far as she was concerned, without first picking up "car food."

After a fitful day's rest, they had made the decision to road-trip it back rather than fly, which was just fine with Isabel. Her mixed emotions churned in her stomach like wet cement and made the prospect of turbulence unbearable.

Isabel folded her hands on the bar of the shopping cart. "I guess so."

Alexia's sympathetic smile gave Isabel the squirmies. "You look miserable, sweetie."

"No, I'm good. Really. It's just all been such a whirlwind. I'm not really sure what to make of my life now, but I don't want to just go back to being a party-girl."

Alexia raised her eyebrows and took an open bag of pretzels from Isabel's hand. "Aren't you hungry? I figured after all you'd been through you'd be starving."

Yeah. Isabel scanned the veritable cornucopia of munchies but couldn't muster enthusiasm for any of them. It was the oddest thing. She'd been starving when they'd arrived, practically ripping bags of chips and boxes of Little Debbie snack cakes off the shelf.

She sighed. "Maybe I'll be hungry later."

Alexia half smiled. "It's okay, sweetie. It's the breakup diet. You wallow in junk for awhile and then you don't wanna eat anything. I guess you hit stage two pretty quickly. Lucky you." Alexia chuckled.

"I dunno." Lucky was not the word Isabel would have used. "I hate to sound like a broken record, but I just feel so confused."

"It'll take time to get perspective and sort it all out. You just need some distance."

"Or a lobotomy," Isabel grumbled.

"Hey now," Alexia brandished a pack of Twizzlers in Isabel's face. "Those things are not all they're cracked up to be. I knew a guy in high school who'd had one, and everybody thought he was drunk all the time. It seriously messes with your coordination."

Against all odds, Isabel managed a weak laugh. "I guess I just shouldn't have let myself get so attached to him. I didn't try hard enough to keep my distance."

"Or maybe you tried too hard. It's human nature to be attached." Alexia lowered her voice to a whisper. "And, uh, you know, the same is true for other species. Think about it. You wouldn't have made it very far past birth if you didn't have the love and care of others, would you?"

Isabel rolled her eyes a little. Damn Alexia for being so smart and reasonable. "I guess that's a good point."

Alexia continued. "They've actually done studies, you know. Babies *need* the touch of another in order to survive. Other species, too, like I said. Monkeys, for example." Monkeys. This prompted Isabel to glare and toss a bag of Baked Lays at her. "K, I'm sorry about the monkey comment, but you see what I'm saying?"

She did. "I'm just not entirely sure how it's supposed to be helpful."

Alexia shrugged. "I guess I'm just trying to say you shouldn't beat yourself up for finally allowing yourself to fall for someone and get attached. Me, I fall in love all the time. I just get right back on the horse when it bites me in the ass. Makes life interesting," she said with a giggle.

"Like that little crush you managed to get on tall dark and whatsisname? Lee?" Isabel fired back with a smirk. Somehow she had shifted into bitch mode without really noticing. But it served Lexi right for her thinly veiled vampire-monkey comparison.

"Touché." Alexia rounded the corner and grabbed a six-pack of Diet Coke. "Like that. See, and I know he's got *zero* interest in me, but I would back over my own grandmother just to get with him. Eventually it'll pass, but until then I just have to ride it out. At least with Thad, you knew that to some extent the feeling was mutual."

Isabel rubbed her head and neck. If she didn't know better, she'd think she was about to come down with that flu thing Lexi got every year. "Yeah, I'm not all that sure."

Damn, she loved Lexi to death and appreciated her concern, but this conversation was more than she could handle.

Alexia frowned with concern. "You feeling okay, hon? You keep rubbing your head."

"Yeah, you know..." Isabel closed her eyes. "I really don't feel well. I thought it was just nerves, but it just keeps getting worse."

"Well, listen," Alexia patted her hand. "Why don't we just stay in town another day? I'm sure Thad would be willing to let us crash for awhile longer if you're not feeling well."

"Hmm." Something was definitely wrong with her stomach. Very wrong.

"Izzy?" Alexia tried to make eye contact, but Isabel suddenly wasn't able to focus.

"I have to go." Abruptly, Isabel slapped her hands on the cart and did a 180, speed-walking out to the parking lot.

She had never thrown up in her life, except the night her parents had died. Fear, disgust over the body she had been forced to leave on the morgue floor, and the dark knowledge that she'd been seconds away from the business end of a Y-incision had turned her stomach inside out almost as soon as she'd gotten off the hospital grounds. As nauseated as she was, she didn't honestly think she was gonna do it this time. She just needed fresh air, right?

Until she found herself heaving like it was her job in a dark corner of the Food Lion parking lot, next to their shiny loaner Land Rover.

"Izzy?"

Isabel's head started to pound. "S'all right, Lex. I think I'm feeling better," Isabel said weakly. Okay, so she was a filthy liar. Really, it was the least of her worries at the moment.

"Hon, no offense but you are far from fine. Should I... try to call—"

"No!" No, she couldn't have Thad riding to her rescue again. Not after the trouble she had already caused him. "I'll be all right... I really am feeling better now. I think maybe whatever it was has pas—"

Okay, so it hadn't.

That Alexia was sitting right there rubbing her back was a huge embarrassment, but she was glad not to be alone.

"Izzy, can I get you anything? Like a damp paper towel or a ginger ale?" The young female proffered a six-pack of Canada Dry.

"No," Isabel said faintly. "Wait, did you pay for those?"

"Kinda threw a twenty at the cashier and booked out. Hey, Izzy?"

Isabel drew her knees to her chest and leaned against the cool metal of the SUV. Slow, deep breathing seemed to be the key. "Mmm?"

"Are you... you know... hungry?"

God, no. Her now-empty stomach gave another lurch. "No offense, Lex, but just thinking about that makes me feel even worse."

Alexia's eyebrow raised in a questioning arch. "I'll try not to take it personally, since you're sick and all."

Good.

"Hey, Izzy, I think it's best if we don't go anywhere tonight."

Isabel couldn't quite muster the energy for a reply, and Alexia didn't wait for one. She allowed her friend to nudge her into the car. Lexi's offer was sweet, but Isabel couldn't even imagine feeding. God, that was weird. When in her life had she ever found the idea of blood distasteful?

But that wasn't entirely true, was it? She remembered making love with Thad that morning, and the sweet taste of his blood on her tongue. Oh, yeah. Just thinking about it made her feel better. It had been like a Chai Tea Latte from Starbucks, all sweet and thick and cardamom-y. If she could just get a shot of *that* with some steamed milk…

Oh. *No*…

She wanted Thad's blood.

Only Thad's blood.

Only… Thad's… blood…

"Shit." When Isabel was young, her mother had once waxed romantic about her father. About their love, their bond… how once they had conceived Isabel, only her father's blood would do. And then Isabel thought about earlier, when Thad's soldier had died and his pregnant mate had needed the blood to carry her until the end of her pregnancy.

Oh, no. *No, no, no, nonononono*.

The earth tilted on its axis as a sudden and unexpected sob burst from her throat.

Chapter 37

ISABEL RESTED PEACEFULLY, HAIR FANNED ACROSS A white pillow, dark lashes against peachy cheeks, and breath even and steady. It seemed a shame to wake her, but if she didn't rouse soon, Thad would have to do just that.

She needed his blood.

His female. His mate. His *queen*. Needed his blood. All the things he had said to her before, about how he didn't want to tie her down or hold her against her will, had gone straight out the window when Siddoh had come to tell him that Alexia was driving them both back to the estate. It was all bigger than just the two of them now, wasn't it?

Thad took back every nasty thing he'd said to Siddoh about making friends with Alexia. That the human had called ahead had allowed Thad time to prepare, to alert Brayden, and to freak out. Not necessarily in that order.

He sat on the edge of the bed. Breath whispered in and out of her parted lips, and he couldn't stop himself from smoothing a hand over her cheek. It was almost a miracle, really. Vampires were only fertile during the full moon. And yet, somehow, Isabel was pregnant. Perhaps it really was destiny, after all.

"Isabel." Thad shook her shoulder gently. When she did nothing but mumble and smack her lips, he shook again. "Isabel, I need you to wake up."

Okay, so on to plan B. Thad made quick work of the buttons on his shirt. It dropped gently to the floor, and he gathered her against him. For a moment he could only hold her robe-clad body tightly, eyes and mouth pressed shut as he worked to bring his emotions under control. He'd had no illusions that being king would be easy, but the preceding days could have given a whole new meaning to the phrase "trial by fire."

But all of it would be easier with Isabel by his side. And now she had a reason to stay. Thad would have time to court her properly. Maybe she could even find it in her heart to love him.

"Isabel." His voice grew in volume and deepened in timbre. This time, he put a little more force into shaking her. Brayden had warned that she might be hard to wake. That her body would shut down to conserve energy for the baby.

Thad's baby.

He went ahead and smacked at her face a little. Gently, but enough that she finally started to stir. He shifted on the bed, leaning back against the headboard so that her body was draped across his, her face in the crook of his neck.

"Thad?" Soft lips brushed his pulse point. Her voice was thick from sleep. "Thad, is that really you?" Despite the gravity of the situation, tiny nuzzles and nips at his throat caused him to harden in his pants. "It smells like you."

"It's me." He kissed the top of her head and jiggled her a little more. She had begun to tremble in his arms, and her skin was too pale and way too cool to the touch. "I need you to wake up so you can feed."

All at once, Isabel was finally alert and definitely hungry. She reared back and struck hard. Tension flowed out of his body along with his blood as she sucked in long, greedy pulls. He'd never been so relieved to be bitten.

Too quickly she began to pull away, but he urged her back with a press of his hand. "No, take more." He wasn't willing to let go until he was sure she'd drunk her fill.

With a deep exhale, Thad closed his eyes and let his head drop with a small thud. He allowed the warmth of Isabel's body and the delicate lapping at his vein to soothe him. Uncertain though his future—their future—may be, this was the way it was supposed to be. Of that, he was sure.

"Thad?"

He forced his eyelids to open. When had she stopped drinking? "Did you get enough?"

"Thad, we need to talk." That, they most certainly did.

"About the baby?"

She blinked. "You knew?"

He frowned. "Of course I knew."

"I don't…" She was silent for a few beats and then shook her head. "I don't remember anything after being at the grocery store."

"Alexia called ahead and gave us the details. You were sick at the store so she brought you back, and on the way you started to mumble that only my blood would do. I managed to piece it together."

"I'm so sorry," she murmured.

"Sorry?" Thad sat up straighter and pulled Isabel against him. Now that she was better, he couldn't help but notice the smooth expanse of thigh revealed by the part in her robe. He smiled down at her. "I'm going to have an heir. That's wonderful." He brushed a stray strand of auburn hair off her forehead. "And I have seven and a half months to convince you to stay with me forever."

Two green eyes, one cloudy and one clear, grew wide. The right eye sparkled like the finest jewel, and he vowed to himself that he would find her the most beautiful emeralds on the planet to compliment her beauty. "You want me to stay?"

"Of course I want you to stay." Grasping Isabel's chin, Thad made her meet his eyes. "I always wanted that. I told you as much, quite adamantly as I recall."

She smiled slightly. "But then you told me to go. After the wizards took me. I thought you were angry. You certainly seemed like you were."

"Of course I was angry. That I nearly lost you. At myself, most of all, for strong-arming you until you felt you had no choice but to run away." He cupped her jaw with both hands. "I decided, for your safety, that I should allow you to leave. But we have a child to think of now, Isabel. If for no other reason than that, I need you to reconsider."

Out of nowhere, she kissed him. When she pulled away, her cheeks were wet with tears. "I wanted to stay, Thad. I had wanted to tell you, but then the wizard attacked me, and then I thought you were angry." She bit her lip and furrowed her brow. "I went out that night because I was overwhelmed by my feelings for you. I made the mistake of wandering off the property because I smelled cinnamon pecans."

"The gas station." He'd nearly forgotten all about that.

Her face stained crimson. "I didn't run away. I got hungry. I was trying to get back when… well, you know the rest. I'm so sorry."

Thad stared, his eyes fixed on Isabel's lips. His heart nearly pummeled its way out of his chest, and he prayed with everything he had that he hadn't misunderstood somehow. If she wasn't in a delicate physical condition, he would have tackled her to the floor and kissed her until they were both out of breath. He tugged her close and kissed her forehead. "I'm just glad you're here. Safe."

He nearly got teary-eyed again when she snuggled her head into the crook of his arm. "I'm glad too. I… I love you, Thad."

His heart did a very unmanly flip-flop. "I love you too, Isabel." As he settled in, a thought sprang to mind, and he turned to face her. "I almost forgot. The moon."

"The moon?"

"We're heading into a new moon, Isabel. There's no way you should have conceived when the moon wasn't full. But you did."

Her eyelids drooped, and even her smile was sleepy. But damn, he loved that smile. He would devote eternity to seeing it light her face just as much as possible. "Maybe it was destiny, after all."

Maybe it was.

"Come on, you need to rest." Gradually, he listed to the side, taking Isabel with him. They curled together much as they had their first evening together. Prophecy, destiny, or just plain coincidence, it didn't matter. Isabel was with him, and he had all that he needed. But his heart clenched the second the thought was finished in his head.

Almost everything.

Chapter 38

THAD LOVED HER. HE WANTED HER TO STAY. THINGS should be good, right? But an inky black tremor of unease slithered through Isabel's veins.

"Thad?"

"Yes?"

"Will you tell me what's worrying you, please?" Isabel wiggled a little and turned onto her back. Blue eyes gazed down at her. "I can feel that you're worried about something. It's not us or the baby, is it?" No, she could sense he was at peace with that.

He opened his mouth but she cut him off. "It must be something else. I mean, if we're going to do this thing, Thad, you know, being together... you have to trust me with what's on your mind. And trust that I'll be able to handle it."

Thad grumbled. "I didn't want to spoil things by bringing this up now, but my sister seems to be missing. She walked out of a fight to recover and we haven't gotten hold of her since. And Lee... he disappeared a few hours later, just before dawn. He left without his phone. Ty's not answering hers. I've got guys out looking, but no word yet."

"Oh God, Thad, I'm so sorry. You came here when you should have been out looking for them—" He held a hand up to silence her, and then leaned in for a kiss.

There was more to say, but he didn't seem to be

letting her. When she stopped trying to talk, he pulled back, his mouth still hovering just above hers. "*Nothing* was more important than coming to see you, Isabel. Nothing." His voice sounded different. Fierce and full of conviction.

Just like it was supposed to be. Like *he* was supposed to be. Pride swelled her chest a little. This was her male.

He exhaled and rolled onto his side with his head on one hand. "I'm not going to lie. I am very concerned. It isn't like either of them to go AWOL and I don't have any idea why they might have. I'm especially worried about Tyra because she had almost entirely drained her powers when I last saw her. I don't know if she could have gotten attacked somewhere and been unable to defend herself, or... But they're both well-trained and smart. I have to trust in that. Deep down, I believe they'll be fine.

"But, yeah. It's number one for me right now, along with making an honest female of you." He pulled her close again, fitting their bodies tightly together. She took a slow, deep breath. How amazing that she could stay in these arms forever when she had never come close to feeling this way for anybody before.

Make an honest female of her. "Wow." I never thought I'd have my own handfasting." She held up her left hand, and rubbed over the top of her wrist where a tattoo would be placed to signify their union. "Or a mating tattoo."

"Shit."

She rose up slightly. "What's wrong?"

He shook his head sadly. "It's nothing you need to worry about, but I'm going to have to find a tattoo artist.

The one that used to work for the family died a few months ago. Wizard attack."

"I'm so sorry," she murmured. "Oh!" She bounced a little and sat up on the bed. "But I may have a solution. I mean I don't know for sure if he'd want to do it, or if you'd want him to, but Lucas, our friend from back home. He does tattoos. He's really good, actually. He did all of mine and some of Lexi's."

"That skinny male with all the hair? From the club?"

She nodded. "Yeah, that would be him. Anyway, he's one of us, you know, so he's got the right ink and equipment and whatnot. He's really good. And he's kind of a drifter, so I doubt he'd mind relocating."

He gave her a warm smile. "We'll talk to him, then."

"So," she whispered. "I don't know if maybe it was your blood, but I've got this sudden little burst of energy. And…" She giggled a little. She sighed deeply and lay down again beside him, tucking herself into the crook of his arm. Comforted. "For someone who thought she never wanted a commitment, or a baby, suddenly I'm sort of excited about all of it." And it felt odd that it didn't feel odd, to whatever degree *that* made sense.

"Good." He smiled down at her. "I'm excited too, Isabel." He kissed her slowly. She sighed her contentment. She wanted to sleep and to wake in the arms of her male. Her king. *Hers*.

He growled happily. "You know, I think I fell in love with you that first time I saw you."

There was that funny, floaty, wonderful swell in her chest again. "Well, I'm sorry I was a little slow to catch up," she said softly, as his lips descended on hers again.

She shivered a little, and he reached down to pull

the covers over them both. Hopefully she could get this power of hers under control or she was going to be freezing all of the time when she wasn't pressed up against Thad. Lovely though that thought was. "I'm just glad you got there."

"Me too," she murmured. That little burst of energy faded just as quickly as it had come, leaving her heavy and sleepy. "Gosh, suddenly I'm tired again." She pressed a little closer, meshing their bodies together. "I'm so glad that you're here, Thad. I don't think I've ever felt better."

"Same here." The tap of Thad's index finger against the top of Isabel's nose caused her eyes to drift shut. "Now, get some rest. We'll talk more later."

Epilogue

ISABEL TOUCHED HER FOREHEAD TO THAD'S. THE DIN of voices around them reminded her of being back at the club, but with less attractive lighting. "Focus on me for a second," she whispered.

His head dipped against hers. "I'm fine."

"I know." She smiled. "I just wanted to be all yours for a second."

The fingers of his left hand threaded through her right. With their palms pressed together, their mating tattoos created perfect mirror images. Dark black ink depicted the symbols that had brought them together: Lucas had recreated the Armenian crosses elegantly and embellished them with swirling arcs and flourishes. The thin swirls interlaced with bold geometric lines to create a truly stunning work of art.

"I'm always all yours." Thad pulled back enough to look her in the eye. The lines around his eyes spelled out how tired he was, but he managed a wicked grin, complete with that little flash of fang that was so, so sexy. "You look so beautiful."

Isabel skimmed a hand self-consciously over the empire-waisted burgundy velvet dress, which was somehow cut perfectly to enhance her newly redesigned pregnancy boobs. The idea, she supposed, was to distract the stuffed shirts on the Elders' Council from the already visible bump of her belly. The one that broadcast, quite clearly, the fact that Thad had knocked her up well before their mating ceremony.

They'd held off for as long as they could, with the hope that Lee and Tyra would come home, but...

Heavy mahogany doors swung open abruptly, increasing the noise level in the hall a thousandfold. "They're ready for you, sir."

When she began to pull away, Thad's grip held her fast. "Thad—"

"They can wait." He took a deep breath. "I need to say something first."

His fingers gripped tighter. "Okay," she murmured.

"You know," he said as he tugged her close. "I don't know what I would do without you right now. It feels like there's so much darkness around us, and you give me the power to go on. You're my strength. My light. You and this little one we're about to have." His cheek pressed against hers. Firm, soft lips brushed against her ear. "I don't think I could have done this without you."

"You could have," she whispered. "I know you could have. But you don't have to."

Siddoh's large body invaded their little intimate circle. "You really should get in there, boss-man. 'S bad manners to keep the Elders' Council waiting."

Thad sighed and backed away enough to link his arm with hers. "Yeah, all right. Let's do this."

Holy mother, the room was bright. It was one of those big amphitheater-type things, chock-full of long tables and chairs at which sat all the members of the local vampire community over the age of one thousand. Some of the nonlocals, as well. There were far more than Isabel had realized. Some hardly looked their age, some did. Huh. She would have to ask Thad about that.

Thad's guards flanked him as they approached a podium at the head of the oval room. A statuesque female with a thick braid of silver hair was ahead of them, grinning broadly. Oh, God, Isabel should really remember her name. Something that sounded naughty but wasn't... "Members of the Elders' Council, it is my pleasure to introduce, in their first official appearance as king and queen, King Thaddeus Yavn Morgan and Queen Isabel Anthony Morgan."

Yikes.

In the midst of the polite applause, Thad winked and squeezed Isabel's hand as he took the podium. Her heart soared. It seemed to do that a lot lately around him.

For all of his self-doubt, it was clear that he belonged there. "Thank you, everyone." His voice was so strong and commanding that she would not have known he was ever unsure of himself. "Thank you, everyone. I want to get right down to business, so let's start with the first item on the agenda, the vote on human-vampire interaction. I want to be clear on this one: the proposed law, as it stands now, will not pass. I cannot—will not—sign off on a law that would make a member of my own family an outcast..."

Murmurs of interest and a few angry yips sounded from the peanut gallery, and Thad stopped to wait for the Council's full attention as the noise level rose again. They were both officially in over their heads, but Thad was feeling his way through beautifully. He would manage. They both would. Together.

And life would go on.

Acknowledgments

Many, many, many thanks to Deb Werksman, Susie Benton, and everyone else at Sourcebooks who made this book happen. To all my friends and family, thanks so much for your support! Special thanks to Mark Hubbard and Catie Brusseau for being brave enough to read the first draft and for helping me see the manuscript through to submission. To Damon Suede, I adore and admire you *so*, so much—this book would not have been nearly as good without you. To Mikki Bruns, thank you for helping to keep my kids in one piece and my house, well, less messy. To Christopher Koehler, thank you for your friendship, your understanding, and for sending me a video of an old codger eating cake when I was up to my ears in edits and in need of a good laugh. Carol Buswell, you are an awesome artist/web designer and an even better friend, and thanks for rocking my socks off all these years. And to Kerri Nelson, your pitch class got the ball on this whole project rolling so thank you, thank you for your help and for cheering me on! MWAH! I love you guys!

About the Author

Elisabeth Staab lives in a menagerie of pets and kids in Northern Virginia with her hero and soul mate, Tom. She has been a telemarketer, a web page editor, a software developer, a reader for the blind, a technical trainer, a coffee shop barista, a teacher, a tutor, a homemaker, a government project manager, a graphic designer, a bookseller, and a professional eBayer. Finally, she's realized that her true passion is writing, which is what her high-school guidance counselor originally suggested anyway.

Elisabeth believes that all kinds of safe, sane, and consensual love should be celebrated—but she loves the fantasy-filled realm of paranormal romance the best.

Hold Me If You Can

by Stephanie Rowe

Without her passions, she has no magic...

It's unfortunate for Natalie that Nigel Aquarian is so compelling. With his inner demons, his unbridled heat, and his "I will conquer you" looks, he calls to her in exactly the way that nearly killed her.

But losing control means losing her life...

That he's an immortal warrior and that her powers rise from intense passions would seem to make them a match made in heaven, but unless they embrace their greatest fears, they'll play out their final match in hell.

With a unique voice that critics say "carves out her very own niche— call it paranormal romance adventure comedy," Stephanie Rowe delivers an irresistible pair of desperadoes dancing on the edge of self-control and pure temptation.

For more Stephanie Rowe books, visit:

www.sourcebooks.com

The Storm that is Sterling

by Lisa Renee Jones

———

He's her best weapon…

Sterling Jeter has remarkable powers as the result of a secret experiment to create a breed of super soldiers. Now he has to use everything he's got to help beautiful, brilliant Rebecca Burns, the only astrobiologist alive who can save humanity from a super-enhanced, deadly street drug.

Sterling and Rebecca's teenage romance was interrupted, and now they're virtually strangers. But the heat and attraction are still there, and even entrapment by an evil enemy can't stop them from picking up their mutual passion right where they left off…

———

Praise for The Legend of Michael*:*

"Jones launches a new series with this thrilling story of love and determination in a society on the brink of war… Readers will be hooked." —*RT Book Reviews*, 4 Stars

"Awesome series…plenty of action and romance to keep you glued to your seat…An auto-buy for me." —*Night Owl Romance*, Reviewer Top Pick

For more Lisa Renee Jones, visit:

www.sourcebooks.com